Airship Shape & Bristol Fashion II

Planes, Trains and Automatons

Airship Shape & Bristol Fashion II

Planes, Trains & Automatons

Edited By
Roz Clarke & Joanne Hall

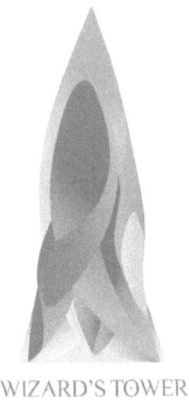

WIZARD'S TOWER

Wizard's Tower Press

Trowbridge, England

Airship Shape & Bristol Fashion II
Planes, Trains and Automatons

First edition, published in the UK October 2019
by Wizard's Tower Press
with the assistance of The BristolCon Foundation

Paperback ISBN: 978-1-908039-91-0

Cover illustration and design by Andy Bigwood
Copy editing by Charlotte Bond
Design by Cheryl Morgan

http://wizardstowerpress.com/
http://www.bristolcon.org/

Contents

I have lived in and around several cities across the length and breadth of this land during my life, and of them all I can honestly say Bristol is the barmiest. I mean this in the nicest possible way imaginable. There is a wilful eccentricity to the place that is endearing and intoxicating (I can't imagine another city that would look at one of its steep roads, a major artery to boot, and decide to close it off while an enormous water slide is built it to allow the citizenry to whoop their way down, soaked and jubilant, for a few hours). Bristol, you see, glories in interesting ways to get from A to B. It was a major seaport, instrumental in the early railway, a workshop and test-bed for the ingenuity of Isambard Kingdom Brunel, and a hub of the aircraft industry for generations. It managed all these wonders in our dull, mundane world. What transports of delight might it have achieved in other worlds where the laws of physics are perhaps more open to interpretation? Don't trouble to reply; that's a rhetorical question because the answer is laid out in the following volume. Grab your thermos and some sandwiches; we're going on a journey.

Jonathan L. Howard

ROZ CLARKE & JOANNE HALL

Introduction

Five long years on from the publication of the first *Airship Shape & Bristol Fashion*, you finally hold in your hands its follow-up volume: *Airship Shape & Bristol Fashion II: Planes, Trains & Automatons*.

Our intention when we published the first *Airship* was to create a series of steampunk anthologies showcasing Bristolian authors and supported by the BristolCon Foundation. We have not abandoned that goal, but life has a tendency to happen, time passes, so it goes. Although we are still closely connected to BristolCon, the city, and the coterie of writers living and working there, we ourselves now live on fifty acres of muddy farmland in Wales. Editing (and our own writing projects) have taken a back seat, as duck-wrangling has come to the fore. That is why this volume has taken such a very, very long time to reach you.

For this anthology we called for stories that built on the themes of the first but widened the geographical scope. Our authors continue to bravely explore topics that challenge the accusation (still oft-levelled) that steampunk is glib, superficial, and re-imagines history without any of the difficult stuff, with the protagonist generally in the role of the wealthy and privileged. Here you will also meet characters struggling against the strictures of a world in which everyone is not equal, technology is not always used for good, and the powers-that-be are not always benevolent. Not every story bears the groaning weight of brick and iron, however: some fly and some frolic, while some slip slyly between one place and another, through portals unseen.

With the shifting position of Great Britain in the world as well as the good and bad in our culture and history so much to the fore in current discourse, this feels a timely contribution to considerations of what it meant to be at the centre of an Empire, and what happens to society when progress and power aren't evenly distributed.

Categorising the pieces into sections wasn't easy as they present a deliciously complex mosaic of themes, moods, and modes of transport, but we have broadly divided them into three parts.

'Iron and Fire' looks at the need to break free of the tracks life has laid down for us, whether we are human, machine, or something in between.

In 'Flying and Falling,' we take to the freedom of the air, by spaceship or dirigible. Maybe it will all come crashing down? How will we know, if we don't spread our wings and dare?

In 'Stranger Ways,' airships make a further appearance, but we also see time travel, interdimensional passages, dark seas, and forms of travel known only in wild imaginings. Wherever they take us, wherever we end up, it's going to be quite a weird trip...

We would like to thank our patient authors, proofreader, Andy Bigwood for the cover art, and our neglected colleagues, ducks, and doggos.

Roz Clarke & Joanne Hall
June 2019

Part I

Iron and Fire

Off the Rails

- Stephen Blake -

I pushed the heavy double doors open and stepped into a fog of smoke. It reminded me of good old London town when I'd step out of my local, unsure if the haze before me was the house whisky or inclement weather, but that had been many years ago, and now I found myself in Bristol. The Clifton Club to be exact. A 'gentleman's club' is how it was described, although many of those outside the hallowed walls strongly debated the veracity of that title.

I fumbled forward through the mists of tobacco. The last time my eyes had watered this much, I'd accidentally insulted a lady who had responded in a highly unladylike manner.

As the air cleared, I saw a group of the members gathered. I approached them as a zookeeper might approach sunbathing walruses. My employer, Sir Reginald Pomfrey, was taking centre stage once more.

"We will hold a series of trials!" declared Sir Reginald. "The very best in the world will be invited to showcase vehicles that will not stop when the rail track halts, will not falter when the waves crash before them, and will not pale when the sky is the only way forward!"

The members of the Clifton Club rose in unison to applaud and cheer. I stood to the side watching their pallid faces turn purple with exertion. As Sir Reginald's secretary, it was my role to observe and record for him all that occurred. I noted his inspiring speech and the nationalistic fervour it created. People cried out that the British were sure to win. I did my best to stifle a yawn.

Many people believe that the all-terrain morphing vehicle was developed by military minds, often the driving force behind invention. Sadly, in this case the innovation was the responsibility of a bunch of overweight pompous 'gentlemen,' who could not be bothered to change their mode of transport from train to boat or airship. This was not some great pursuit of innovation; this was a 'how to help the privileged and lazy travel with minimal effort.' It had all tumbled out of a book discussion. A few had read *Around the World in 80 Days*, and instead of being inspired, they had focused on the amount of walking Phileas Fogg was forced to endure. "Surely one can see the world from the comfort of a single cabin?" one of them had said. They even rankled at the word 'disembarkation,' as though it were a curse word.

Notes were sent far and wide to invite companies, individuals, and enthusiastic amateurs to take part in a series of trials. The prize was a contract to produce the winning vehicle *en masse* for the gentleman traveller.

It was almost a year later that we gathered for the first test at the floating harbour in Bristol. Of the hundreds of invitations sent only a handful had said yes. Of those that had said yes, only four had reached this final stage with their physical prototypes.

It was late spring when we gathered on a Monday morning on Wapping Wharf. The sun shone for once, with only a gentle chill breeze to stir us from our dawn fatigue. Sir Reginald addressed the small crowd of participants and a sprinkling of newsmen. "Gentleman, and ladies if we have any, we are here today to begin a series of trials that will make the two most important 'B's' great again. That is 'Britain' and 'Bristol.' In the past we have played an important role in supplying the New World."

I crossed my fingers that he would not start decrying the end of the slave trade again. He leant on his cane, seemingly considering his next words.

"Times change," he mused, "and perhaps we must change a little with them. There is a large world to discover, nations that we must teach to be civilised, peoples waiting for us to find them, and plenty of places for us to fly our flags." The crowd cheered; everyone likes the idea of a Union Jack flying atop mountains across the world. Of course, we don't talk about the blood spilt to achieve that. That wouldn't be good manners.

"Now," he continued, "is the time of the explorer and traveller. Mind broadening, they tell me. Well, I say let us reach these wonders of the world in comfort, let us not perspire our way to greatness! Let us get there with minimal effort, and back home again without ever having to get our boots dirty."

The club members cheered, their chortling, quaking flesh reminiscent of a jelly dessert being served by a nervous waitress. The journalists simply looked perplexed.

The first exercise was for the participants to simply demonstrate that their vehicles could leave the rail tracks they had arrived upon. Then they were to drive forward on the roadway a short distance, hover in the air, and finally, show that their inventions floated, even if this were only in the event of needing to ditch down.

A single train carriage coasted to the end of the line. Emblazoned across her side was the name *Brizzle Lass*. Her driver was an automaton, whom his inventor had called Maurice. Four large wheels slowly moved down from the sides of the carriage, and bit by bit they lifted the vehicle off the tracks until a loud click confirmed it had reached its correct height. The carriage trundled forward, away from the railway line and made its way to the edge of the water. Again, there was a fair delay as canvas inflated above the roof. Slowly, gradually, it lifted the vehicle off the ground. Impressively, the four wheels now turned on their axles and became propellers to drive the cigar-shaped box forward. Finally, as it hovered above the water, more material was released. This time it came from beneath, and again inflated. The carriage lightly dropped onto the water's surface and bobbed gently up and down. After staying there for roughly five minutes or so, a thrust from the propellers lifted it free from the rippling waves and returned it to land.

We all stood quite awestruck. There should have been clapping and cheering, but it seems the realisation that the proposed mode of transport was actually a reality left all there quite dumbfounded. I shook my mind free and quickly noted that this was Professor Stein's work. I ensured that he would receive one hundred percent of the marks for a wholly successful demonstration.

I walked across to him and shook his hand. "Well done," I said. "That really was fantastic."

"Why thank you, young man," he replied, his bushy grey moustache twitching with restrained pleasure. "May I introduce my daughter Frances?" He gestured toward a demure, dark-haired girl stationed behind him. I nodded her way and immediately I was mesmerised by her intensity. Girl was the wrong word, woman was the right one, and oh, what a woman! Within her emerald eyes burned strength, will, and determination. Never in all my life, at a first meeting with someone, had I felt such strong emotions. Needless to say, I was smitten.

Sir Reginald had recovered from his amazement, and he and the other club members pushed past me to offer their congratulations to the Professor.

"Wonderful stuff," enthused Pomfrey. "Tell me more about your robot."

"Why, yes," replied the Professor as he tugged at his collar. He glanced back at his daughter before continuing. "Maurice is very, uh, unique. Adaptable, truly autonomous, and obviously with him being a crash test automaton, he allows us to carry out these demonstrations without fear of endangering human life." He wiped his brow and quickly pointed across to one of his competitors. "Oh look, the American entry appears ready to go."

The group turned as one and hurried across in an excited bustle to view the latest vehicle to accept the challenge.

They, too, appeared to have adapted a passenger carriage. I am not overly familiar with the various kinds of railway carriages that exist around the world, but this large conveyance had a distinctly American feel to it. This time the demonstration was much quicker. They had not bothered with roadway wheels; instead, they had simply inflated a balloon as the first competitor did and lifted the carriage away from the tracks. Propulsion was provided by large fans pushed out from two large windows on either side. At first, I was unclear how they might come to rest upon the water, and then I noticed the skirt around the bottom of the vehicle, which, as they dipped down into the dark river, I could now see was the hull of a boat. The vehicle did indeed bob up and down as a heavy yacht might. I was not convinced as to how it might cope with stormy waters, but for the purposes of the demonstration, it did what it had to do. The fans thrust it up, out of the water, and landed it beside the *Brizzle Lass*. I saw now that the Americans had named their vehicle also. It was called *Lady Liberty*.

The next two competitors carried out the initial task in exactly the same way, the only differences being the general appearance of the vehicles. A local entry from some Bristolian amateurs had the look of a garden shed on wheels but nonetheless succeeded just as the others had. I say it succeeded but, for the purposes of an accurate record, it is best to state that it pretty much fell apart upon landing back on the dock. The locals swamped their craft and quickly tacked it back together. One turned to me and described the vehicle as a 'jammer.' I have since learned this means 'lucky.'

The fourth entry was fascinating to me and horrifying to Sir Reginald and his cohorts. They had two things going against them. They were French, and they were all women. There had been efforts to have them disqualified upon the evening of their arrival but given the limited number of entries at the time, and the ladies' threat of an impromptu striptease, they had been allowed to compete. It was unfortunate to see the 'gentlemen' sneer throughout the task, expecting and indeed hoping as they did for the ladies to fail.

Fail they did not. Their rather elegant stagecoach had wheels that were equally at home on rail or road. As the others did, they opted for a balloon for flight and, amazingly, their craft was watertight, driven forward by a fair-sized paddle wheel.

I offered my congratulations to Madame Tardi but was quickly pulled away by Sir Reginald who advised that my talking to them reflected badly upon him. It is with regret that I report I did not inform my employer that he was an ass. Instead, I kept my counsel, which I'm annoyed that the coward within me insisted that I do.

I find it fascinating that change blows through our times. My employer was embracing technological advance; you could say that by hosting this event he was even driving it forward. However, a change of the heart and mind towards our fellow humans, male and especially female, seems a development too far for some. There is no doubt we each, as individuals, must contemplate this matter. I must also deal with the dislike of myself for my complicity before I turn my annoyance out towards others.

My inward thoughts were momentarily broken by the chink of china as numerous tea sets were rolled on trolleys across the docks towards us. *Fabulous*, I thought. *A cup of tea is just the ticket*. Unfortunately, they were not for our enjoyment. It seemed the tests for the vehicles had taken an absurd turn.

I hurried across to the vehicles in time to see the last of the tea sets disappear aboard the *Brizzle Lass*. I asked Sir Reginald what was happening but he did not reply and merely chortled. "Wait and see."

So, we watched all four of the entrants do exactly what they had done before. Come up the railway tracks, disembark, then up into the air, down into the water, then rise again before landing on the docks. I could see no difference in what had been previously demonstrated. The only thing this showed was that the first attempts had not been a fluke and that our locals had done a fine job in repairing their shed.

A washing line of sorts was hastily raised before us, with four table cloths draped down.

"What on earth is this all about?" I enquired to any who might know the answer.

Frances came close and quietly said, "Sir Reginald wants to be sure he can fully enjoy his travels without his tea being spilt. I am told this is the single most important test of the day."

She walked past me and gave instructions to Maurice to begin cleaning the cloths once the assessors had examined them.

Three gentlemen gathered before each cloth, engaging in quiet conversation. They reported that no entrant had successfully completed the task. There was spillage from each. It seemed, though, that Professor Stein's *Brizzle Lass* was the most successful. In fact, the crowd remarked on how Maurice quickly sponged away what stain there was until none was visible.

Above the rumble of conversation, a loud gasp was heard. I turned to see Sir Reginald, red in the face. "Who has done this? This is an affront to common decency!" he bellowed. "Was it the French? It had to be those... those *women*."

A timid man mumbled, "No, Sir, it was the entry called *Lady Liberty*. It was..."

Sir Reginald interrupted him, "It was the colonials! I should have known. Disqualify them immediately."

I moved beside him. "Sir, what has happened to have caused you such upset?"

"I can barely speak of it. They did not use tea. They, they... they used coffee!" The look of horror on his face as he spoke the words stifled the wry smile that wanted to come onto mine. "Surely, Sir," I pleaded, "this is no more than a cultural misunderstanding?"

He pulled me close to him, his voice suddenly husky. "Do you not see, lad? This is the slippery slope. First, we let women enter our competition; now, we have coffee instead of tea. What next? The end of the Royal family? A ban on fox hunting? Do you not see? Our very civilisation is at risk if we cannot protect the humble cup of tea."

A small tear rolled across his cheek, and yet again I held my tongue. I did not have the heart or patience to try and persuade him from his entrenched views.

The Americans were summarily disqualified. When they queried it, they found a handwritten rule added to the previous entry requirements forbidding beverages other than tea, sherry, or a good quality whisky.

Sir Reginald drew himself up and straightened his tie. He brushed his hand down his lapels, took a deep breath, and moved to address the waiting participants. "Events today have been unfortunate, but I feel we must not let progress slow because of a few backward barbarians. Onwards, I say, to the next challenge."

He waved his cane towards a marquee I had not previously noticed. From within, three ladies exited onto the wharf. As they got closer, I noticed that all three carried folded fans. Each was taken to the remaining vehicles. As they stepped up into the passenger quarters I noted that, rather unusually, none wore any makeup.

Again, the vehicles took it in turns to adjust from rail to road, to air, to sea, and back again. After a brief pause, each of the women was helped to disembark. Each held up a fan in front of her faces as the small crowd gathered. An unseen announcer called out that should a gentleman explorer have along with him a female companion, most likely a sister, it was only right that they should be able to apply their make up without any difficulty. As each of the women dropped their fans, a horrible flashback came to my mind of a very bad experience with a circus clown as a child.

The women were completely unaware and only became distressed when Maurice, the Stein's robot, approached each of them with a cloth. His mechanical hands flurried before them and within seconds, each was a picture as if painted by an artist. Any hint of the previous Picasso had vanished.

As with the previous challenge, all had failed.

Madame Tardi became very vocal now. "I insist that we do the same test, but with men," she yelled.

"Ridiculous," snorted Sir Reginald. "Do you expect any man here to apply makeup?"

"Very well," she replied. "Then they must shave." Looking directly at Sir Reginald, she added, "As, of course, all true gentlemen do every day."

The discussion went on for nearly half an hour. Finally, a compromise was reached. It was agreed that a close shave may end in the loss of life. However, three men were volunteered to have their impressive moustaches trimmed whilst the now well-rehearsed journey took place.

The three looked like they were walking to the gallows as they headed to their respective vessels. One tried to make a run for it but was grabbed by some nearby dockworkers and roughly pushed on board.

I could not look as the vehicles left the rail. I distracted myself in the company of the lovely Frances. She explained to me that Maurice had been used by her father to test-drive vehicles and crash them for him. However, they had found a way to augment his intelligence with that of their former butlers' brain patterns. It seems the butler had been an extremely capable chap, and as a result, Maurice was even better than that, given that he never tired or even expected to be paid. Looking over my shoulder, she drew my attention to the fact that all the vehicles had now settled on the dock. The local one that looked like a shed had unfortunately finally collapsed. Stumbling from its remains were its driver and the moustached 'volunteer.' I sighed in relief as I realised he was unharmed, then noted his tie and jacket were wildly slashed. The fellow's eyes were open wide, and his mouth was gasping for air. He had the look of a stunned trout.

I looked across at the French entrant. The lady driver seemed pleased enough as she descended with a large grin. The gent who travelled with her was not grinning in the least as he held his trousers together at the waist. It was clear a gap had appeared through his gusset leaving him rather exposed. He, too, was wide-eyed, but instead of appearing in shock, he had the look of a man desperately relieved that something far, far worse had not occurred.

Finally, Maurice made his way off the *Brizzle Lass* with his usual stilted movements. Behind him came the final volunteer. He was also looking shocked, but I quickly realised it was not, in fact, shock but pleasant surprise. As he came closer, I saw that not only was his moustache very well-groomed but also his hair had been styled in a manner I had recently heard those in London now wore. He looked very dapper.

Sir Reginald and his cohorts gathered together and talked for an age in hushed tones. It struck me that this was one of the few times, perhaps the only time, I had ever seen them all in agreement.

I turned away from the gathering. The collective nodding and bobbing heads had become hypnotic. As I looked over my shoulder, I locked eyes with the lovely Frances. She beckoned me to follow her. We boarded the *Brizzle Lass* and I was awestruck to see laid out the finest meal I had ever seen. Maurice clunked and clicked around us as we sat at the small, yet elegant, table. He poured a fabulous-looking sherry and then, to my utter amazement, he spoke. His voice seemed piped in from down in his stomach and had a crackly quality to it, but nonetheless, he clearly said, "Will that be all, my lady?"

Frances thanked him and said it was.

"I am astonished," I said. "I had no idea he could talk."

"Oh yes, I solved that particular problem very early on." Frances smiled.

"You solved that problem?" I enquired.

"Oh, come now, don't disappoint me. I like to think I am fairly shrewd at judging people, and you seem like a thoroughly modern man."

"But you're a..."

Frances held me silent with a stare that could sink a battleship. "Don't you dare go and ruin this meal by being like one of them." She gestured out of the window towards Sir Reginald.

"I apologise." I searched for the right words. "It is not your gender, certainly not. It is just that your father presents himself as the creator. I am merely surprised by the deception."

Frances's gaze softened. She continued to look me in the eye and then eased herself back into her chair. "Father is a wonderful man, far, far ahead of his time. He worries that the rest of the world is not ready for me. He says to wait for them to catch up."

"And what do you say?" I asked.

She leant forward. "I say change is the only constant. Everyone who cannot cope with that will be left behind."

There was a knock at the carriage door. Professor Stein entered, turning his hands over and over. His eyes darted in every direction, never quite settling on us. Finally, he spoke. "My dear Frances, they've made their decision. Unfortunately, no vehicle has done enough to convince them to award the promised contract."

Frances stood. "They are fools. We'll find a way to make it work without them."

The old man looked up at his daughter. "There is another thing, though. They have decided that they do want to go into production on something else. They have even drafted a very generous contract, which is ready to be signed at once."

I could not sit patiently any longer. I rose from my seat. "What has happened?"

Professor Stein replied. "They want Maurice. Or rather, they want a lot of other Maurices." He held his daughter's hands in his own and grinned broadly. "They are very impressed. It seems they think Maurice is what the modern travelling gentleman needs to keep him in tip-top condition, no matter what the circumstances."

Frances stepped back, her lips quivering slightly before she broke into a huge grin. "Can I see the contract?"

It turned out the Professor had told them Maurice was his daughter's invention. Whilst that had caused much consternation, it had been agreed that it would not affect the capabilities of the robots or, more importantly, the sales.

The contract was signed. Madame Tardi and her crew declared it a victory for all women. Eventually, Frances and I found ourselves alone. "Congratulations," I said to her. "You've helped push 'change' on a little further today."

"You have no idea." She smirked.

"Why? What have you done?"

Frances looked over one shoulder and then the next. She leant close to me; her smell was intoxicating. I felt her warm breath on my cheek as she whispered into my ear, "I have a small confession. Maurice's brain patterns are not just based on our butler. I may well be about to send numerous ticking time-bombs out into the world."

I gulped, taking her words very literally. She giggled. "Silly boy, not an explosive bomb. A 'change' bomb."

"I don't understand," I mumbled.

"I used numerous brain patterns. All of them were volunteers, all of them women. And all of them were campaigners for women's rights. It is only a matter of time before part of those personalities comes to the fore."

I struggled for words as I tried to comprehend what Frances had told me. I could not picture what that might mean. I looked across to Maurice, who was cutting and styling various gentlemen's hair. I could not possibly see what could possibly go wrong. Frances and I wandered towards them to admire the results.

The crowd on the other side of us applauded. I stood behind them, my mouth hanging open. Frances, beside me, burst into glorious laughter.

Two letters had been cut into the back of the hair of each of the participants. I could see now that it spelt out: GIVE THE VOTE TO WOMEN.

One of the gents who had had his hair cut turned and smiled at me. It was Sir Reginald.

"Bravo!" I cried. "Bravo! A truly wonderful change!"

He nodded vigorously. "It is good, isn't it?"

He looked confused as Frances called to him, "Keep fighting the good fight!"

A year later and there are variations of Maurice travelling across the globe. They are marketed as the *Gentleman Adventurer's Autonomous Butler*. Frances tells me that they have been a roaring success, climbing mountains, trekking into jungles, and conquering just about every landscape and climate.

That is not to say that there have not been some problems. Frances calls them hiccups. A few of the machines have held up political slogans during photographs of exploring successes. They are usually small and in the background, but enough to cheer many women and irritate many others.

The only serious incident, which has been quickly hushed up, was when a portly gentleman from the Clifton Club was paraded about the town by his mechanical butler in a much too small corset and bloomers. I'm told he resembled a Christmas turkey with the string pulled too tight whilst wearing leg frills.

We enter a new age of equality, and in the halls of the establishment where dusty men resist change, there are a dozen Maurices with a sink plunger, a modern woman's indignation, and not one ounce of restraint to do something about it.

Let a Mountain Be His Gravestone

- Ken Shinn -

History is often made by people too foolish to learn from the past. So, when Sir Colin Stavanger took it into his port-addled skull that it would make a fine spectacle to re-enact the Wild West legend of John Henry in the heart of Bristol, all that was needed to make it so was enough enthusiasm on his part to catch the public imagination, his considerable financial clout, and a blatant disregard of the minor issue that John Henry – who'd apparently prophesied his own fate at the grand old age of three days – was, in the end, very likely nothing more than a legend, not a reproducible fact. Sir Colin regarded fact as a trifling inconvenience.

The public was hungry for spectacle in those days, as the public has always been, doubtless always would be. The novelty of the mighty locomotive, thundering its unstoppable route along the railways expanding their reach over the kingdom, held a firm grip on its imagination, a grip held all the stronger by the brilliant efforts of Brunel and his fellow engineers. The rise of the railway was poised to revolutionise transport, to bring more and better produce, to shrink the distances between friends and families, and to rush His Majesty's troops to where their services were needed. It was poised to open up a brighter, prouder future for the nation.

Hand in hand with that, the previous decade had seen the advent of another great British invention set to secure the crown further mechanical glory. The creation of 'Vapours,' imported slave-workers enhanced cybernetically to make them an even better labour force, had created a land where the idle rich, if they so wished, could become more otiose still. A land where compliant serfs toiled in techno-logical tirelessness to accomplish what mere mortals would have taken weeks, months, *years* more, to achieve. Before, it had merely been the noble savage's place to do the dirty work. Now, he or she could do that work much more swiftly. Which meant those marvellous new railways could spread with greater speed – machine-men pushing forward the gleaming metal paths on which other machines, ones held in far greater esteem by their owners, thundered in glory, proof of the Empire's power.

And one of those machine-men had started to make a name for himself. Tobermory Brown had been brought across the great ocean, first to the Scots highlands, where his erstwhile master had given him his new name and raised him in the ways of righteousness, impressing by word and rod the lessons of enlightenment. It took John Dunlop and two more strong men to administer the rod. Tobermory was a great, dark tree of a man, close to seven feet tall and wide as a castle door, and he didn't much like to be thrashed, but his masters and tutors were nothing if not persistent in their ministrations. Gradually, his resistance vanished, and by the morning of his twenty-fifth birthday, he was as meek yet as mighty a lamb as any man of God could desire. And Dunlop, in his mercy, gave Tobermory the greatest birthday gift that he'd never expected.

He came around from the anaesthetic to discover dull, grey metal sheaths on his arms and legs, partially covering them, fixed by screws and bolts edged with traces of dried blood. There was, he found, surprisingly little pain in mov-ing them, although each movement caused puffs of water vapour to hiss from valves. But for days he moved with the clumsiness of a new-born foal, and he was dismayed to dis-cover that his weight and strength had vastly increased. After several comprehensive beatings and a good deal of self-control, he managed to stop himself from sitting on stools that collapsed under him and from putting his arm accidentally through suddenly flimsy door panels. It never occurred to him to use this power to defend himself. His master, as the Sunday sermons had told him time and again, was a harsh but fair being. He could learn to live with such things.

What he never got used to was the steel cap beaten onto his scalp, extending down to form a mask of metal around his bewildered eyes in the mirror. The cap was stamped with the bold legend: PROPERTY. It was the anonymity he found so unsettling, the feeling of being not only a possession but one so unimportant, so lacking in value, that it didn't even have a specific owner. Hadn't he been a good and loyal servant to his master? What terrible wrong had he done, that Mr Dunlop thought it necessary to turn him into a steam-belching, anonymous monster? He plucked up the nerve to ask the man once, as he stood before him on the immense square of Persian rug in his study. Dunlop's reply had been assured, cheerful – by his standards, anyway. He even smiled slightly, as he went on to volunteer more information.

"You've done nothing wrong, Tobermory. In fact, you're the best worker I have. Which is why I decided to make you even better. As a Vapour, you'll be much more powerful and near tireless – and what man wouldn't be proud to own such a tool? That PROPERTY on your brow is no mark of Cain, it's the highest seal of approval. It shows the world how much I value your services."

Tobermory knew he was no genius, but neither was he a fool. "My services. How much do you value me?" Despite himself, he felt fury swelling inside him. Before he could stop himself, he strode forward. He wanted to grab Dunlop by his immaculate shirt-front, shake him hard – not really hurt him, not damage him, just let the man know what a cold, selfish thing he'd done. He managed one stride, no more, before his own limbs turned traitor. Agony stabbed in his head like a blazing hangover dropped on him. He froze in his tracks, clutching his scalp as his body bowed, dimly aware through the pain of great clouds of steam erupting from his metal joints like screams of dismay. Dunlop waited, his expression complacent, until he recovered.

"And that's another sign of how much I value those services. I've had you fitted with one of the new Staunton Limiters, the 'Clockwork Conscience' as it's popularly known. You'll be a stronger, better, steadier worker than ever – and you won't be able to raise so much as a finger against me, or anybody else, in anger. So, why not relax and enjoy it? You'll be a perfect servant, potent yet mild. A credit to the Lord Himself – not to mention His chosen representatives on Earth!" He chuckled, adding point to that last comment by tucking a manicured hand significantly under one of his own tweed lapels.

Tobermory had learned his lesson. Adjusting to his new condition day by day, he concentrated on his labours on the Dunlop estate, tasks chosen by his master as best-suited to his near-Herculean strength. Day by day, he hefted massive loads of wood, hay, and stone into waiting barns. He lifted wagons from the earth to allow new wheels to be fitted. And, most often, he spent his time hammering in the enormous stakes that Dunlop had purchased to form an imposing, impenetrable boundary around the edges of his formidable holdings.

It was this task that gave him the most pleasure. A pail of water at hand to quench his thirst, he enjoyed the simple, precise cause and effect of the work. Blow by blow, he drove the massive wooden spikes into the resistant, then yielding, soil. An additional joy, which he took pains never to share even with his closest friends, was to picture each stake as John Dunlop himself, his mean, spare frame bound by stout ropes, eyes full of fury and pain, vile oaths reduced to angry mush by the gag in his mouth as Tobermory drove him, hammer stroke by hammer stroke, again and again, into a well-deserved grave. Small wonder, then, his task was achieved with such speed that the construction of Dunlop's fence was soon days ahead of schedule.

It progressed even faster when Tobermory, realising how easy it had become for him to heft and swing one massive sledgehammer, decided to test himself by carrying a second one out into the fields. Time and effort were needed before he managed to co-ordinate the blows properly, but he had enough of both to learn until, a few days later, he'd fully mastered the skill. The sight of the man-mountain wielding one mighty hammer in each hand, smashing in stakes with tireless energy, wreathed in great waves of steam like Vulcan at his forge, soon attracted attention and amazement.

That attention, inevitably, included John Dunlop's. It was a glorious June morning when he strolled up to where Tobermory was labouring, pausing for long moments as he took in the sight of his servant's prodigious work. The two sledges rose and fell, rose and fell, over and over. Thud. Thud. Thud. Thud. Thud. Stake after vast stake was smashed solidly into the ground. Dunlop took a flask from his waistcoat pocket, unscrewed it, and treated himself to a large nip of brandy, refilling the cap to the brim and drinking the second more slowly as he stood in thought. Tobermory, for his part, was so engrossed in his task he failed to notice his master's presence. Ordinarily, Dunlop would have been infuriated, but today he was grateful. An idea was forming, one he was sure a good friend of his in Bristol would appreciate. He owed old Sir Colin a favour in return for the splendid hospitality the man had shown him last Christmas, and he knew about his latest planned spectacle for the general public involving the expanding railways around Bristol. Sir Colin needed a very particular kind of man to make that spectacle real, and, as he watched Tobermory, Dunlop was sure he'd found that man. As he finished his third brandy, he stepped forward, clearing his throat to secure his servant's attention.

"Tobermory – a very good day to you! I've been hearing about your incredible work, so I thought that I'd come and see for myself. I must say I'm very impressed."

"Thank you, Mr Dunlop. I'm just doin' what I was asked to." He seemed bewildered at such positive attention from his master but determined to present a polite face.

"Such astounding industriousness. You're a veritable John Henry, you know that, Tobermory? A veritable John Henry!" Dunlop's chuckle was loud and satisfied as he produced a second capful of brandy and passed it to Tobermory. The latter took it with a pleased but puzzled smile as Dunlop raised his own drink to tap it against his servant's.

Tobermory knew full well he wasn't the sharpest of men, but he knew enough to realise that, when John Dunlop was in an openly good mood, it usually meant bad news for somebody else. In this case, that somebody seemed set to be him. But what did Dunlop have in mind? As his master strolled off, still laughing contentedly, he prepared himself as best he could for whatever was to come. Turning back to his labour, he recommenced bashing in the stakes with a redoubled will, the reassuring rhythm of the work settling his troubled thoughts, at least for the present.

He found out what was being planned only two days later, as he sat – in a first-class carriage! – with Dunlop on a steam train speeding towards Bristol. As he made inroads into an impressively large steak, his master took a long swig from his claret and leaned forward with an air of irritatingly chummy conspiracy.

"Tobermory, we're going to Bristol, at the other end of the country, and we'll be staying there for a few weeks. You remember Sir Colin Stavanger, who I visited last December? Well, I was talking with him on the telephone a night or two ago, and he's had a marvellous idea to advertise the new railway heading through Bristol. He's been looking to find the right man to make it happen. And I'm pretty sure you are that man. I mentioned John Henry to you a couple of days ago. I don't know if you know the story of that man, but he's an American legend who helped in building their railways. And he swung two hammers at a time, just like you can."

"Really? Was he a Vapour like me? What happened to him?" Tobermory drew deeply on his own tankard of stout.

"No, he wasn't a Vapour, according to the story. Just flesh and blood. Which means you'll do even better than he did. He won a race against a steel-driving machine, you see. But that is probably just a story. Imagine how famous you'll be, if you do that for real, in front of a crowd and newspaper reporters!" Dunlop produced his humidor, drew out two massive cigars, and handed one to Tobermory, even applying a match to it before lighting his own.

The Vapour had his suspicions. Dunlop hadn't exactly gone into detail about this John Henry's story, and he felt that certain important points of it hadn't been shared with him. But he did remember Stavanger. From the brief contact he'd had with the man, old Sir Colin had struck him as decent enough – a good deal more jovial and honest than his own master, not that he'd dare say such a thing out loud. As well as that, the idea of attaining possibly national renown from whatever task they had in mind for him had undeniable appeal. And, under that, something further fascinated him. He'd seen – hell, he'd experienced first-hand – the way the average Vapour tended to be treated by the population at large, and maybe, just maybe, what he was going to do could change that for the better. Perhaps even lead to them being treated with something like respect. That appealed to him – again, not that he'd outright say such a thing. Savouring the taste of the expensive cigar's rich smoke, he leaned forward and fixed his eyes on Dunlop's.

"Sounds good to me, master. So, I'll be driving steel as well, will I? Probably a piece harder than just hammerin' in wood..."

"I daresay you're right, Tobermory. But don't worry! Like I said, we'll be there for a few weeks before the big day, and you'll have plenty of time to get used to how much harder it might be. Rest assured," and here he leaned forward further, his face a picture of smiling honesty, "I'm certain you'll do us all proud."

The misgivings remained, but Tobermory clinked glasses in a toast to the plans being made for him, feeling that the positives definitely outweighed any negatives, as far as he could see. Steel, with a little effort, would yield to his blows as surely as wood.

Their arrival in Bristol, and the subsequent days, served to bolster his confidence further. News of the challenger to the mighty steam engine spread fast, presumably encouraged by Sir Colin himself. Wherever he and Dunlop went in the streets, people stared, some applauded. He was mobbed like a celebrity. People even pressed him for autographs, which he signed with a broad grin and a hiss of steam from his wrist valves, under his master's approving gaze. The city seemed to welcome him, with clear blue skies and beaming sun, as Dunlop and, on occasion Stavanger, gave him the Grand Tour, showing him the landmarks, the music halls, the pubs and gentlemen's clubs, and the various works of the great Brunel, including the Temple Meads railway station that he'd designed. Not to mention the final approach to the platforms of the station, two hundred yards of bare stones, track lines clearly marked out and sleepers placed, needing only the great metal guides at each side to be hammered in with massive metal rail spikes. The arena of the combat he had been brought here to fight in.

By the end of the first week, he'd been set to his training. Sir Colin had enough land to provide a practice ground for his lessons, terrain which included patches of soft soil, hard-packed earth, gravel, even solid rock. It proved a sobering revelation. Although his work remained the same, the steel spikes were much heavier than the wooden ones, and the varying types of ground frequently proved much more unyielding than the soil of Dunlop's Scottish estate. The effort was initially back-breaking, even for his enormous, mechanically-enhanced strength, and he was briefly gripped by doubt, verging on fear, that he'd bitten off more than he could chew. But he applied himself with a will, remembering his plan to increase regard for the average Vapour as well as being stubbornly determined to prove his own worth to himself. Day by gruelling day, the labour became easier, and he learned to love the steady clanging of his hammers on the spikes as he smashed them one by one into the ground, each of them another step towards his personal victory. As with his travails in Scotland, he was noticed – and by a lot more people. Something of a local celebrity, he soon found himself cheered on by growing crowds of sensation-seekers, and Sir Colin, ever the shrewd businessman, started to charge them a shilling a head to do so.

Tobermory Brown was being noticed, by a lot of people – a point brought home to Sir Colin as he returned to his walled manor in the city centre on the tenth day after the Vapour commenced his training.

The first thing he saw was John Dunlop being led politely but firmly by two peelers towards a waiting car. He met Stavanger's eyes in silence, looking like a guilty schoolboy, before they directed him into the vehicle and drove off. The second was the duo flanking the front doors, a tall red-headed woman and a short, paunchy bald man, dressed in the grey suits, hats and smoked glass spectacles of the Greyshades, the nation's renowned special security force. Without a word, they gestured through the open doors for him to precede them, following smoothly as they ushered him towards his study door like an errant sheep towards its pen.

All this was bad enough, but it was the sight of the whey-faced, grey-clad man with thinning, combed-over hair, seated at his desk and helping himself to one of his special stock of cigarettes, that caused Sir Colin to feel a twinge of irritation, rapidly swept away by a cold wave of fear. The Greyshades had a public face – not that it was often seen – and this was that face. The figurehead, possibly the very leader, of their number. The man only known as Mr Hyder. The man who, even now, was motioning him to sit down in the seat opposite, before reaching for a decanter of his best brandy and pouring two large snifters – one, somewhat larger, for himself – before passing one to Sir Colin.

"Stavanger." The lack of honorific was telling. "Your friend Dunlop is currently being taken to... assist with enquiries. Do have a drink, old boy, you look like you've seen a ghost." The hint of a grin, reinforced by a large swallow from his tumbler. Sir Colin copied him instinctively, barely tasting the fiery spirit, struggling to understand what was happening. Hyder's next words, delivered in that dry, nasal voice, helped him. "You've seen this evening's paper, I trust." A copy of the journal in question was shoved forward. He picked it up and read the headline, above a photograph of a sweating, beaming Tobermory surrounded by a cheering throng in front of a stubby little steam locomotive. VAPOUR CHAMPION DEFEATS RAIL-LAYING ENGINE declared the legend. As he took that in, he dared return his gaze to Hyder's face. Not even the hint of a smile remained. The half-moon grey-smoked spectacles all but concealed the eyes behind them, making the man impossible to read. The only sure deduction to be made was that he was far from pleased.

"Today, your man Brown succeeded in driving in rail-spikes faster than an actual engine. From eyewitness accounts, it was a struggle for him, but he still managed to beat it by a distance of some ten feet. Let me ask you a simple question, Stavanger. Why shouldn't we just stop this little spectacle of yours from going ahead in two days' time?"

Fear gave way to bluster and badinage. "Well, for the very good reason that it'll be impossible to stop it now. Brown's become quite the talking point in the city. This 'little spectacle,' as you call it, is being discussed as far away as London. It's set to give Bristol's finances a hefty boost. If you cancel it now, there'd be uproar! People want to see the Man against the Machine."

"My question was rhetorical." Hyder's voice gained an edge of coldness. "You are right to say that stopping it would cause... issues. We've been watching this plan of yours with some curiosity, and we were prepared to tolerate it – until the obvious question came to mind. What happens if he wins?"

Sir Colin opened his mouth, but no words emerged as he thought about what the Greyshade had said. Hyder was all too ready to speak for him. "If he wins, there could be even more uproar. Vapours form a sizeable minority of Society at large, and by their very nature they are, at best, servants and, under the worst kind of master, little more than slaves. Your little publicity stunt could well provide them with a figurehead to rally behind. As the paper says, a champion. A champion whose victory could lead to national unrest. Picture a Vapour uprising. Then picture those resentments met by further violence from those who regard them as inferiors. This may not be a harmless piece of spectacle, a nice day out for the family. If Tobermory Brown wins, it could turn this city into a powder keg, and the explosion might reach a good deal further."

This time, Sir Colin managed a nervous chuckle. "Well, maybe – but that's rather the point, isn't it? Today, with a colossal effort on his part, he beat an engine by just ten feet or so. I know that sounds impressive, but on Saturday, he'll be competing against an enormous, vastly more powerful one. One which he hasn't got a snowflake's chance in Hell of beating. I really don't see what you're worrying about..."

Hyder removed his spectacles. His face remained emotionless, his posture unaltered, but something about those clear blue eyes chilled Stavanger as though he'd been thrust into an industrial refrigerator. He suddenly realised exactly why the man was so dreaded. His attempt at jovial defiance was throttled before it could go any further.

"A friend of mine is fond of saying that there are always possibilities, Stavanger. Even a snowflake may have a particularly good day once in a millennium or so. It is essential to our work that we remain aware of all possibilities, however remote they may appear."

Sir Colin bit his tongue, hard. As brandy stung his mouth, he realised his mistake but continued to keep quiet.

"And one such possibility is that – with the aid of his mechanised musculature, a lot of determination, and maybe a dash or two of luck, there is the chance, however small, that he might win. Which leads to one obvious conclusion, Stavanger. Namely, that you ensure that he doesn't. That he be somehow induced to – as the parlance has it – throw the fight." Hyder lifted his glass to his mouth on which the barest flicker of a smile appeared once more. "Appeal to his baser instincts. Offer him a lot of money. Or wine, women, and song. If you feel particularly altruistic, offer him his freedom – I'm sure his master would be co-operative. Just offer him something which will convince him to put up a decent enough struggle that he doesn't disappoint anybody, but which means enough to him that he's prepared to settle for an honourable defeat."

"But what if I can't?" Sir Colin felt a dismaying lurch in his stomach. "He takes a lot of pride in what he's doing. He's dedicated to it. I think that he's rather relishing the opportunity to put on the best show he can."

"If you can't, Stavanger, then the odds are we'll have to deal with you in the same way as Dunlop. Oh, don't look so alarmed. We kill when we must, but we are the King's investigators, even his enforcers – but not his executioners. However, be sure that there are many ways of ruining someone's life without taking it. I'm sure it won't come to that, though. Not if you use a little initiative. We'll leave you to sort that out, but we will be watching this Saturday. Good day to you, Stavanger. Thank you for the drink."

He rose, finished his brandy, and strode out without another word, his two lieutenants flanking him to the gunmetal-grey limousine waiting in the drive.

Sir Colin retired to his study early that evening, a case of indigestion brewing in his guts after a large supper that he'd hoped would inspire him as to how to broach the matter with Tobermory. The more he reflected, the less likely he felt the man would be open to any kind of bribery. And, even if Dunlop would be willing to free him, Sir Colin himself didn't like that idea. It smacked of weakness to him – the sort of weakness that could also lead to imitation. Hyder had backed him into an awkward corner. The Vapour was too prideful, too principled, to be bought so easily, of that he was sure. No, there had to be another way. It was simply a matter of thinking what that may be. As he paced the carpet, swilling brandy and puffing furiously on a succession of cigarettes, he paused before one of his bookshelves, struck by sudden inspiration. He pulled down a heavy volume on the history of horse racing, returned to his wing chair, and began flicking through the pages with purpose.

It took a few minutes of muttering and cursing but finally he found what he'd remembered – an account of hydromel, a mixture of water and honey which some of the more unscrupulous ancient Greeks would give in a bucket to their horses just before they took part in a race. The resultant short burst of energy would give the dosed quadruped an advantage over the competition. And, of course, there was the logical other side of that particular coin – administering something to the opponent's beast that would slow it down, temporarily sicken it. Well, Tobermory was clearly as strong as a carthorse, and that meant that he could be doped like one. If he was debilitated enough, he'd still be able to put up a sterling effort on Saturday, but he would have no chance of victory against the engine. It was just a matter of finding the right drug and administering it to the Vapour without his knowledge at a suitable time before the challenge. Sir Colin slammed the tome shut in triumph. All that he needed to do was visit a pharmacist, or better yet a veterinarian, tomorrow morning with a convincing story and a suitable palm-greaser in reserve, and then arrange a slap-up meal for Brown the same evening. A quick check of his directory and a few phone calls later, he had exactly what he wanted, and an appointment for the morrow. He retired to bed with a huge wedge of Stilton and a decanter of port, feeling a very clever fellow.

The next day went well. Sir Colin picked up the recommended substance – colourless, odourless, and very potent – and invited Tobermory, fresh from another triumphant day of smashing in steel staves, to join him at his favourite restaurant for a lavish pre-contest dinner. The Vapour seemed almost pitifully grateful and, duly scrubbed-up and smartly-dressed, was all too happy to join him. It was the work of a few moments to bribe one of Sir Colin's favourite waiters discreetly, passing him the powder, and asking him to add it liberally to Tobermory's food and separate decanter of drink.

"I want that packet empty by the end of the evening." He smiled, and the waiter laid a knowing finger to the side of his nose, asking no further questions.

Both men ate and drank heartily that evening, and when they finally departed, Sir Colin knew Tobermory had ingested more than enough of the sedative to ensure his loss tomorrow. He worried a little that he'd administered too large a dose, but the Vapour could survive it, he was sure.

The crowd was huge and enthusiastic that sunny Saturday afternoon. The starting pistol barked, the great track-laying engine began its inexorable rumble forwards, and, as the last bets changed hands among the onlookers, Tobermory Brown set himself to defeating the machine.

As the competitors set off, they were side by side. The hammers on the engine thudded down on the spikes with slow but powerful regularity, but Tobermory wielded his enormous sledges, one in each huge hand, like a man possessed. They whirled through the air in a steady pattern, the great steel staves singing as he smashed them home, blow after relentless blow. The Vapour had never felt so joyous, so determined, in his life. Today was the day that he showed everyone the value, the humanity, of the machine-men that so many took for granted. The day when respect would be earned. A snatched glance to his side showed him that the engine-drivers were regarding his labour with open-mouthed amazement before they returned to their travails.

It was as the competitors reached the halfway point on the short but gruelling course that it struck. Tobermory felt a wave of giddiness crash over him, and he staggered in his tracks. Understandable, he thought. He'd expended enormous effort, greater than any he'd made before in such a short time. He could fight his way through it. Shaking his head, he plunged on, his hammers smashing his way closer to the finishing line. He was dimly aware of the engine edging slowly ahead of him, opening up the slightest of leads. Even that couldn't be allowed. Redoubling his work, he drove onward, reducing that taunting gap of a foot or so between them by half, barely registering the rising sound of the onlookers. Both man and engine vented great eruptions of steam, two snorting beasts locked in conflict.

He'd almost caught up when the next spasm shook him. He felt sweat bursting out on his skin, the frenzied pounding of his heart, the sudden silent blast inside his skull. His vision momentarily blacked out. Things were going badly wrong. He faltered in his tracks, letting his hammers fall, clutching at his head. The muttering of the crowd rose to a rumble. The engine, in his blurred vision, began to pull ahead again.

He couldn't stop now.

Lifting his sledges, he leaned forward into the chase, pounding in staves again and again. Clang. Clang. Clang. He had closed the gap once more with desperate effort, drawing level with the engine, when it happened. With only feet left till the end, unable to stand up to his labours, the head of each sledge fractured and flew from its handle. The rumble from the crowd rose to a roar. He slumped to his knees, barely able to see. Was he dying?

Well, if he was, he'd make it count. Lifting his great metal-sheathed fists, he began pounding in the remaining spikes, ignoring the jolting pains, focussing on one thing: beating the machine. His fists were as strong as hammers. He could do this. Inch by agonising inch, he pulled ahead, feeling his heart fluttering crazily. He was about to die. It didn't matter.

One more spike to go. It was almost hammered home when he collapsed, the engine crawling nearer. It was clear what he had to do. Despite everything, there was a smile on his face as he slammed his head forward, smacking that hated PROPERTY into an illegible mess. The spike was in. He crawled forward. Crossed the line. The race was won. The crowd went wild. He gasped. Grinned. And collapsed on his back, gushing steam, unable to rise again. It didn't matter.

From the front of the crowd, a tall Vapour in a neat suit ran forward, yelling to the ambulance men behind him. "I've got medical training, too. Let me by!" He reached Tobermory ahead of them and leaned over him, checking his breathing, his pulse, his caved-in metal skull cap. Making his gestures as clear as he could to the dying man, he shook his head and held him gently.

Standing shocked in the crowd, Sir Colin felt a tap on his shoulder. Turning, he saw a grim face, eyes hidden behind smoked glasses.

"If you'll just come with us, Stavanger."

His companion took his arm, and the two agents led him through the yelling crowd to the waiting car. The opened back passenger door framed Hyder, his face terrifyingly un-readable. Sir Colin's shoulders sagged. He sank down on the rich leather and knew he was finished.

Tobermory looked up into the Vapour's eyes. He had to let him know. "I had to show 'em. Had to make 'em know – we ain't just property. We matter." The other man nodded his understanding as the medics crowded in. Tobermory felt the last of his life slipping away. It didn't worry him anymore. He slumped back with contentment for the final time, knowing he'd won, and that he was bound for a better place.

The Vapour gently closed Tobermory's eyes and let the doctors through to finish their work. Rising to his feet, he lowered his head and removed his hat. Suddenly, a hand seized his arm. Turning, he looked at the flushed face of his master.

"Joshua – come on. There's nothing we can do here. Let's get out before the police get really busy here."

"Very good, Mr Willans." Joshua Sheraton followed in his boss' wake but was unable to stop himself from pausing. From taking one last look back at Tobermory Brown. From remembering his last words. Yes. The Vapours did matter.

So, what was he going to do about it?

He followed in Willans's footsteps, but he was immersed in his own thoughts.

Closets and Chimneys

- Maria Herring -

I feel heavy. Before we left, Nkiru told I that, up in space, everything floated, but my body doesn't feel at all like it wants to float. It feels like it wants to mix with the brass and metal floor beneath I. I try to shuffle around so I can look at Nkiru, my best friend and saviour, to see if she's feeling as heavy as I am. It's a good job I haven't got my arm anymore. That thing weighed a ton. I never would have been able to make even this simple movement with that thing clamped to I. As it is, I can shuffle enough so that I'm looking into her face. I haven't known her face for very long, but it's more familiar to I now than my own brother's. She's blinking rapidly, her dark lashes fluttering over her round eyes, her brow faintly furrowed. She looks like she's trying to remember something she shouldn't have forgotten. I've only ever seen her face look cheerful, so this surprises I. It's like she's not my friend, but I know that's not true. We were friends right from the start.

I remember.

"You're a sweep, are you?" I said, picking the last few bread-crumbs off my lap and eating they. She had to be – her skin was as black as mine. I looked down at her right arm, but it wasn't a brush. "No, you're not."

"No, I am not," she said and smiled. It was a right lovely smile.

I stepped back and knuckled my left hand to my hip. I never seen anyone like she before. She wasn't a kid. I been working with kids all my life and she definitely wasn't one of us. She was too big. But she wasn't big like grown-ups and Masters. More like, her body was big but her face was still a bit young. Not a kid and not a grown-up… What was she?

And then there were her arms. She had both of they. Black as her face and just as smooth. Nothing clockwork to tell me which Masters she belonged to.

"You're a puzzle," I said.

And she laughed. What a sound! Put the bells of St Mary's to shame, it did. I laughed along with she then, because it felt like I could. Not even the coppery taste that laughing brought to my mouth bothered I then.

"My name is Nkiru," she said. "What is yours?"

"M," I said. I was beginning to think she wasn't from Bristol at all. She had a funny accent and her name wasn't like any letter I knew.

"M?" she said. "Like the letter? Or is it short for something?"

I grinned up at she. We were sitting on the roof of the factory, backs against my chimney facing the eastern sun, all warm and comfy. I shifted a bit and pointed up at the giant letter writ into the chimney with white bricks instead of red ones.

"See that?" I said. She nodded. "That's I. M."

"You are named after a chimney?"

"Course. Otherwise, how would the Master Sweeper know which sweep I be?"

"But what name did your mother give to you?" she asked. She must have seen my confusion because she added, "My mother taught me underneath a tree, before the heat of day. She took me on her lap and kissed me, and told me that Nki-

48

ru means 'the best is still to come' in our country. She tells me that, no matter what my life is like at the moment, I will make it better. So, what name did your mother give to you?"

"Here," I said, "you have a mother?"

She chuckled, but it was sad. Not like her first laugh. "You say I am a puzzle, but I think it is you who is the puzzle. But I have to go now. I must pay with hell if they catch me gone before work starts."

"Course." That was obvious.

"But I come back tomorrow with some more food."

I beamed at she. At Nkiru. At my new best friend.

I still can't catch her attention. I wonder if it's the noise. I'm used to noise. This is nothing compared to the uproar the furnaces make when they're all going together. The hundreds of men shovelling coal into the fires, all shouting their conversations over the sounds of their labours and each other. The vats of water they furnaces heat so's to make the steam what powers the cosmic climbing closet of Bristol Temple Meads. But I suppose the noises in here are more... well, they're closer. The crates of freight, even though they be lashed to the floor and each other with ropes, shift and scrape and scuffle. There's iron nails holding they crates together at the seams, and that iron squeals across the metal floor sometimes and makes my teeth jump.

And then the wind be whining in through the slats of this freight carriage. It reminds I of rats or mice getting caught in the traps and the horrible squealing they used to make. Nothing like the soft sound of the wind when it was blowing down my chimney. That sounded like blowing over a beer bottle. A chimney bottle.

I remember.

49

I never liked the dark. At some point during the night, the moon would shine in through the very top of my chimney. It filled the whole hole up. I'd stop work for a few seconds just so's I could look up into that face of light, staring back down at I, its mouth a round O of astonishment, marks of woe, like it was strange to see a kid working so hard in a chimney in the middle of the night. But us kids had to work during the night-time – during the daytime, the furnaces were being used to make fire, to boil the water that made the steam so's the cosmic climbing closet could inch its way up, up to the sky. Couldn't have kids cleaning the chimneys then. We'd be burnt alive.

Anyway, I liked it when the moon shone down and gave I a few minutes rest from the soot black. Because that was the other thing – we couldn't have lamps because of all the soot. Bring a gas-lamp into the chimney with all that soot flying about and there'd be a fire for sure. And then we'd be burnt alive again.

But it wasn't just a break from the dark I got when the moon shone in. Staring up at it, my poor shoulder got a rest from all the sweeping. Those right arms we sweeps had were right heavy, made of brass and filled with clockwork that would send out the right brush for the part of the chimney we were in. Biggest brushes for the bottom, smallest brushes for the top. You could tell another sweep from a mile off, no matter where you came from in Bristol. Not because our skin was stained black with soot – because of our clockwork right arms. I remember after I woke up and saw my flesh arm had been replaced by brass and clockwork, I screamed and screamed. And it wasn't just from the pain. But the Master Sweeper told I it would make my job all kinds of easier. Didn't have to carry no sack of brushes up with I like kids did in the olden days, they were all there with us. My brother

50

though, he told I that Master Sweepers changed our arms so that we couldn't run away. You see a brass arm, you know you be looking at a chimney sweep. Look at the elbow, and you'll see the Master Sweeper's sign scratched into the brass. Anyone in Bristol'd know where to send you back to. There was no escape when you were a sweep. I never liked the dark in that chimney. But at least in the dark, I couldn't see that horrid brass arm.

"Nkiru?"

It takes a few goes until she hears me over the clanking and shrieking, but eventually she opens her eyes and looks at I. She smiles. It's just a little smile.

"How is your arm feeling?"

I look at the stump dangling from my right shoulder all covered in bandages now. "Not as heavy as it was. Still just as ugly."

"You are how God made you. Besides, you will not need those brushes anymore. You are free."

I nod, with difficulty, because I still feel heavy. "It's cold, being free. I'm right shrammed."

I hear Nkiru chuckle, but it only comes from her throat, like she's too tired to open her mouth and let it out properly. "I brought with me some food. Do you remember the first time you saw me? I gave you some bread. I have never seen food eaten so quick! But you know, that wasn't the first time I saw you. A little wraith haunting the chimneys at daybreak. It took me several weeks to convince me you were not a ghost after all! Just a child who needs food."

I listen to her voice, its peculiar but beautiful melody. Much softer now than before we escaped into the climbing closet. But she was wrong; when she gave me the bread wasn't the first time I seen she.

I remember.

Usually, the sweeps slept down in the factory when work was done because it wasn't so easy for the wind and rain to get in there. Me, I liked to sit up on the lip of my chimney in the shadow of the cosmic climbing closet of Bristol Temple Meads, my eyes wandering through each charter'd street. I listened to the bells of St Mary. First, they reminded I of my father, but I always rushed past that memory until I got to my brother. He was dead, but the kids still talked about he, even the Master Sweeper still talked about he. He was the oldest sweep that ever lived, and he was my brother. Now he was a legend. When I thought of he, I thought of my mother – not because I knew she, but my brother did, and he talked of she all the time. I remembered his memories. So I came up here every dawn before the factory opened, when the sweeping was finished, so I could listen to the bells and remember they both.

But this morning was different. It was spring, I reckoned, because the sun was just balancing on the eastern horizon even though I'd finished work. And the chimney stones weren't shiny with ice so winter had finally loosened its grip. I was looking down at that black'ning church with its clattering bells, pretending I could see their mad dance in my mind's eye, when my real eyes caught sight of something. I twisted my head to the left, but I was blinded by the rising sun bouncing off the copper and brass shell of the climbing closet. It was so bright I had to rub my eyes for a moment, which didn't help at all. Alls I did was rub soot into they. I blinked out the water that made, then tried to see if I could see what caught my eye.

There was the brick roof of the factory with its rows and rows of chimneys, like a forest that's had its arms and heads chopped off. Next to that was the nearly-finished grand entrance to the climbing closet, all swooping stonework and glass. I'd heard the Master Sweeper say that when the passenger line was finally built, you wouldn't be able to move in Temple Meads for tourists pouring off the trains to climb to the moon. He said we should be proud that it was our factory's steam what was powering the closet's carriages all the way up to space. Once, I'd asked a kid what space meant, and they said it just meant night-time. So I wasn't sure why I should have felt proud about night-time. It was just dark, that was all. Like my chimney. I had to stay down in night dark while other lucky people got to climb up to the shining face of the moon. That didn't make me feel proud.

Anyway, I couldn't find whatever I thought I saw. It turned out to be my first glimpse of Nkiru. But everything was still again. Up here, at least. The river was still moving, moving all the way down there behind the climbing closet. It was funny – the sunrise sunlight turned the water all coppery, and it looked like the climbing closet was melting. It would take a long time for that to melt, mind. They'd been building it all my life, and even when it was finished, even when the rich people were taking their holidays on the moon, Master Sweeper's steam factory'd still be needed to power it, so he'd always need good sweeps. He always said that with a grin, like we should have been happy about that too. But none of us ever dursn't say anything.

Anyway, the top of my chimney was high enough for I. If you went up to the night-time, that meant you were in the sky, and that's heaven. And that meant you were dead like my brother and mother. I didn't know if I was ready to be dead just then. I wanted to be a legend, like my brother.

"What will you do, M?" says Nkiru. "When we reach the top and we are free?"

I blink, remembering where I am. It's definitely colder here than leaning against my chimney of a sunrise.

"I don't know," I say soon enough. "I never thought about it."

"You never thought about being free?" I feel Nkiru shift suddenly, like she's turned to look at I in astonishment. "How can you not think about it? I dreamt of it every night since they took me from my mother!"

"Kids are sweeps, then we die. Grown-ups are Masters." I shrug. It still surprises I that I can do this with both shoulders now. "I 'spect they die at some point too."

"You speak as though children and adults are different creatures." I hear the smile in her voice.

"They are though, aren't they?"

She chuckles. "Still the puzzle, M. But when I am free up there, I am going to live in a big house on the moon, bigger even than the white house my mother is kept in in Clifton."

I whistle through my teeth. That would be a very big house.

"And I will eat food whenever I want to. Hot food. Big plates of it, steaming and delicious. And there will be no slaves. That is the most important thing. There will be no more slaves."

I only learnt that word, slave, when Nkiru told it to I. Feels like such a long time ago now.

I remember.

"They cut off your arm?"

Nkiru's voice echoed around the empty foyer, and I was scared and shocked. Scared that someone'd catch us down here. Shocked that she was angry at the Master Sweeper.

I came down to see where she worked this time. We were always meeting up on the roof, and I felt like she'd got to know quite a bit about my job. I wanted to know what she did all during the day when I was normally sleeping. She said she'd come up to get I before sunrise so that she could lead I down safely. I might know all the sights above the city, but I didn't know how to get down off the roof to ground level.

And it was grander than I ever could have imagined. Up on my roof, the glass and stone arches looked grand enough. Inside it though. Inside, it was like how I'd imagined the inside of St Mary's. High, and vast, and full of echoes. I saw right then that when the passenger climbing closet was finished, it really would only be for rich folk. It was only the rich that needed to walk in a building all for they and feel like they were gods.

And the floor was that shiny I could actually see myself in it. I looked like a shadow. A human smudge. Except for the slightly paler patch on my cheek where Nkiru had once tried to scrub off the soot with spit on her thumb. Course, it hadn't worked very well; I'd been sweeping for years. The soot *was* my skin now.

"Well, if they don't cut off our arms and replace they with these," I said, holding up my brass appendage with whirrs and clicks, "how would anyone know which Master we belong to?"

"That is the point," she said. "They make you a slave. Look at this." She held out the palm of her left hand to me. It was very pink compared to the rest of her skin, which startled I a little bit. Very pink, except for the picture that took up a lot of space. The edges of that picture were dark and lumpy. It looked painful, actually. Like it could have been burnt right into her skin. But I recognised the picture all right.

"That's the sign for the cosmic climbing closet," I said. "I seen it all over the roofs."

"It is a brand," said Nkiru. "They burnt it into my skin with a fire iron when I was put into this factory. It says which job I do. But this one," she held out her other palm. There was a mark there too, but it was faded and less clear. "This one they burnt into me one day after I left my mother's womb. I cannot remember the pain, but my mother told me later that I screamed for three days without stopping. This tells which man I belong to. It tells people I am a slave. Like my mother. Like my brothers and sisters. We are all owned by one man who lives in a big white house in Clifton. He rents me to this factory for a profit. He sells all of my brothers and sisters for profit."

I didn't really understand all the words she'd used, because us sweeps generally only spoke about food and memories of families, but there was one word that made my heart beat a little faster. "You had brothers? I only had one, but you had more? Tell I all about they!"

The fire that had animated her face with a fierce beauty went out, replaced with a soft sadness. "I do not know where they all are. Maybe some are in Bristol. Maybe some are in the sea-ships or air-ships. Once our mother has nursed us, we are sold. That is the fate of a slave."

"How can you remember your mother?"

"I see my mother once a year every Mothering Sunday. We are Christians now, and it is the God's law that I see my mother on this one day. She whispers my name to me then, just as she did when I was born, so that I never forget who I am. Do you not see your mother?"

"My mother died when I was very young."

"I am sad for you."

I shrugged. It was normal. "Where do you see 'ee to? Isn't she a slave then?"

"Oh yes, she is a slave." Nkiru looked at me then, like she was trying to work out if she should keep talking or not. "She is in Clifton. She is in the Master's house. She... she makes new slaves for the Master."

I had a picture in my mind of a grown-up looking like Nkiru, collecting all the scraps of kids that littered the streets of Bristol, all us sweeps that died of the blood-cough, that the Master left by the side of the road for the corpse cart to carry away. But Nkiru's mother got to us first, took us back to her Master's house in Clifton and stitched us back together again to make new slaves like Nkiru. That's why we had the same colour skin. Slaves were made with the sooty scraps of sweeps. I knew then, with the certainty of death, that I and Nkiru were exactly the same.

"So, the Master is my father," Nkiru continued, "but he is not a real father. Do you have a father?"

I shook my head. "Nah. My father sold me while yet my tongue could scarcely cry 'weep! 'weep! 'weep! Sold me to the Master Sweeper at St Mary's after Sunday service. My brother told I. Because he sold my brother from St Mary's in all. Plenty of Master Sweepers in St Mary's of a Sunday looking for sweeps to buy."

She looked like she was about to say something else, something strong judging by the fire in her eyes, but a distant clanking made us both jump and look around. That was when I noticed that the sunrise was streaming in through this cathedral's glass roof.

"That is the bell for breakfast. I must go," she said. "But I will see you again tomorrow. You can remember the way up to your roof?"

I nodded and scampered away as quick as I could while still being quiet. When I reached the factory wall we'd climbed down earlier, I scrabbled back up, nimble as a spider and just as black.

"I don't know what I'll do when I'm up there," I say when the memory finally recedes. It's definitely colder now. Worser than even the worst winter I remember. I struggle to get my mouth around the words. "Reckon I'm nearly done, anyway. I got to be at least seven. Been five years I been sweeping, and my brother said I wasn't younger than two when I arrived. That makes me about seven. Kids don't last much longer than that when they're sweeps. Except my brother. He was the oldest kid that ever lived. He was ten when he died. He's a legend." My heart fills with warm pride. Pity that heat doesn't reach out as far as my skin.

"But you are not a sweep anymore," says Nkiru. "You may live longer now you are free."

I chuckle, which turns into a cough, and the familiar coppery taste fills my mouth. "No kid's lived longer than ten. Besides, I got the blood-cough. No one survives that. Not even my brother did."

In the dark and the cold I hear Nkiru shuffle and then I'm suddenly warmer. She's wrapped her arms around me in a tight embrace. Even more surprising, I can hear snuffles and sobs. Nkiru's weeping.

I remember.

The day my brother died, the Master Sweeper brought in a new boy. Little Tom Dacre. He cried when his head, with hair that curled like a lamb's back, was shaved. So I said, "Hush, Tom! Never mind it, for when your head's bare, you know that the soot cannot spoil your white hair." The Master Sweeper kept all of our heads bare. Lice was one reason. Fire was the main. Keep letting a kid's hair grow while we're sweeping, and all they years of soot'll make it light up like charcoal. I kept all that to myself, mind. Poor kid was weeping hard enough as it was. And he hadn't even had his arm fitted yet. My brother's old arm.

He did stop crying though, and when he rose in the dark with the rest of us to start sweeping, he told me of his dream about angels who'd rescued us all from black coffins and set us free on green plains, where clouds waited to take us up to play in the sun. That dream of Tom's kept I smiling all through my night's toil because I knew then that that was where my brother was. An angel had finally come down to rescue he, and he was playing on clouds where the rain washed his skin free of soot and the sun made his hair grow like flowers.

But little Tom Dacre didn't even last a year with us. He came to the chimneys in summer. By winter, he'd got the blood-cough. By spring, the Master Sweeper was fitting my brother's arm to another weeping kid.

I held Tom in my arms while he died, as the sun rose on the first day of spring. He was happy and warm.

"I've been a good boy," Tom whispered. "I'll have God for my father and never want for joy."

Those were the last words he spoke on God's green earth.

"I'm sorry, M," Nkiru whispers into my ear. It's warm at first, then I feel it freeze. "I do not think my mother was right."

Even though we've wrapped around each other like blankets, it's too cold now. I manage to push out a few words though. "Not right about what?"

"She said the freight line was safe enough. But I do not think she was right."

She must be talking about the cold. But it was bound to be cold in the closet because it was climbing up into the night. Night was always colder the higher I climbed up my chimney. And what was this closet if not a gert big chimney? Higher you go, colder it gets. It's obvious. I try to say that but my mouth is frozen.

"I'm sorry, M. When my mother told me this was my only chance of freedom, I think I misunderstood. I should not have brought you with me. But I did not understand."

I remember.

Yesterday.

It was Mothering Sunday. I knew that because Nkiru spent the day with her mother while I slept after toiling the night before. When I rose on Sunday evening, it was to Nkiru's face peering over I. Gave I such a fright it felt like slipping down several rungs of my chimney's ladder.

"Here," I said, starting upright. "How did you get in?"

"We must go now," she whispered, like I'd asked a completely different question.

She grabbed I by my brass arm and heaved while she spoke. I hissed back, because it hurt. Even though my skin'd grown back over the rivets, it still hurt when there was too much pressure on it. Wasn't her fault though; she wasn't to know, and also, I sleep curled up on my left side. So my brass arm was the most obvious thing to haul at.

"We must go! Quick!"

Now I was awake, I could hear fear in her voice. "What's going on? Where we be going to?"

"My mother told me yesterday that the Master plans to take me back. She heard him talk to his butler. I will be his new slave maker."

That image flashed in my mind again. The one of slaves stitching together new slaves out of discarded ones.

"I expect you'll be warm and fed, up in that big white house. Dryer in all." Except when she was looking on the streets for slave scraps, but surely that wouldn't be too often. Plenty of scraps to collect in one outing.

"I do not want to go up into that house! I do not want the life my mother has. She does not want me to have the life she has. We have to take our freedom back today."

My hurried footsteps faltered a little then. We were in the alley between the factory and the grand new building. Alley muck oozed between my toes, but I paid it no mind.

"Take our freedom back?" I said. "How we s'posed to do that?"

"The cosmic climbing closet. Already there is a functioning line. It will take us to the base at the top. After that, all we need to do is stow away onto a transport that will take us to the moon. Once we are there, we will have shaken off our mind-forged manacles and finally have our freedom."

I thought about it. I tried to understand it. It was difficult – I just swept chimneys. I knew the steam the Master Sweeper's factory made ran the cosmic climbing closet, but I didn't know anything else. "How do you know all this?"

"My mother told me. Our Master is a shareholder in this company, and she pays attention to what he says when he has guests over. No one ever pays any attention to her, she is invisible in that big white house, so she hears many things. There are people at the top of the freight line, unpacking all the things that the slaves here on Earth have loaded. If they can survive up there, my mother says, so can we."

I didn't know there were already people up there. I didn't even know that the Masters were sending crates up there. But Nkiru always used a lot of words that I didn't understand. In my head, I just thought the climbing closet was built for rich folk to climb to the sky and get to heaven without dying first. It made sense, especially after I went down that first time and seen the grand building on the inside. The climbing closet was for rich folk to go to heaven and be gods.

Rich folk go to heaven and be gods. Poor folk go to heaven and be angels.

And I did like the idea of the moon's face shining on I without a chimney in the way.

"All right," I said. "Let's climb up to our freedom. Tidy step, mind."

"You don't need to say sorry, Nkiru," I say. My mouth hardly moves. I don't think she can hear I now, because she doesn't say anything back. Her arms are cold and heavy around I. I can hear the tinkling sound as the brass floor beneath us turns to ice. I can hear the clenching of the crates as the cold freezes the wood.

"We escaped," I continue. "We got our freedom. And anyway, my brother's come back."

Because there he is. The rain in the clouds has washed he clean. His clothes are white and fresh, his skin is pink and clean. The sun has made his hair grow like yellow flowers. Back on Earth I probably wouldn't have recognised he, but up here I do, because he's come for I.

"Hello, little sister," he says to I, and I weep to hear his voice again. It warms my heart. And this time it does spread out to the rest of my body. My cold, frozen body. "Are you ready to come and play in the sun?"

62

"Yes," I say. And I no longer taste that familiar coppery taste when I speak. "Can my friend come with me?"

"Of course she can," says my brother, beaming. "All are welcome here. All are equal here. And all are free here."

I beam back at he. We did it, Nkiru and I. We found our freedom.

And I climbed the biggest chimney in all the world. That makes I a legend.

Flying Free

- Tanwen Cooper -

Theresa was beginning to feel like the automaton was purposefully trying to annoy her. Once again, she reached over to turn it off, and once again, it twisted away from her. Objectively, she knew it was just a programming fault making the Gripper register her as an obstacle, but still... Refusing to be outsmarted by a machine, she reached forward with her left hand then darted around the back with her right and hit the switch. There was a hiss of steam as the pressure dropped and the machine powered down.

"There we go." Theresa turned to the porter, raising her voice over the hammer and clang of the production line. "All shut down. Take it over to the workshop and I'll have a look at what's wrong. Probably not until the morning, mind."

The man nodded and started to disconnect the machine. It seemed every automaton at the Aerocab Enterprise's Bristol factory needed repairing lately. The robotic workers were just about clanking along, bolting together the aeroplanes that made up the Imperium's fleet. But Theresa felt like she'd walked up and down the mile-long building a thousand times in the last week, being pulled from one glitching automaton to another.

Time to head back to the control room for a nice cup of tea and a biscuit before home time.

The heat from the steam pipes that powered the factory's machines made her sweat more than was ladylike. The air cleared a little when she came to the wide expanse of the assembly floor, so she took a moment to breathe and wipe her brow. One of her black coils of hair, frizzed up by the humidity, made a bid for freedom, so she shoved it under her hat before she got reprimanded for slovenliness.

On the floor, the Assembly team used a Lifter to raise a wing into place so it could be bolted to the side of a fighter plane's fuselage. Her eyes traced the curving plain of the wing, imagining the air flowing over and lifting it fourteen thousand feet upwards to where the air was fresh and cool. She'd only flown once, but she could still recall that moment where the plane levelled out – the world seemed to drop away and, just for a second, she'd floated like an angel. The Air Force pilots had laughed when they found the cook's daughter stowed away in the back of their bomber, but then they let the plane rise and fall so she could feel that soaring feeling over and over. She'd received such a hiding from her mother when she got down to the ground, but twenty years later it was the floating she remembered.

Something jabbed Theresa in the side, pitching her forward into the present. She turned around to confront whoever had hit her, only to realise a Studder automaton had bumped her. "Oh, sorry," she said. It ignored her apology and kept working, pinning sheets of metal onto the skeletal frame of a wing.

Even over the noise of the production line, she could hear something was off in the *thunk* of metal pinning metal. Looking closer, she saw that rather than tracing a neat line of studs into the rib of the wing the machine was drifting. It had already torn several holes in the sheet, so she halted the automaton before it could do any real damage.

Downing her toolbox, she got to tinkering. When she hooked up her oscilloscope to the Babbage Processor, she expected to see a smooth set of sine curves telling her the programming was ticking away. Instead, the trace danced about the screen, as if it was being pulled in two directions at once.

Now, what could be causing that?

She started by rebooting the automaton. That usually worked when she wasn't sure what was wrong. It didn't. She checked the cables between the Babbage Processor and the limb servos. They were fine. Finally, she thumped it with her spanner. All that did was dent the brass.

She touched the dimple she'd made on the machine's mechanical arm, feeling the gentle vibration of the automaton as it idled.

"Tell me your secrets, big man," she whispered to it. "What's ailing you?"

In answer, the machine fired its stud gun into the floor. Well, if it was going to be like that...

"You there! What are you doing? Why is this machine not running?"

Theresa looked up to see the factory manager marching towards her, halting only when she reached a narrowing in the pipework. She managed to push herself, and her skirts, through with some semblance of dignity, though her white skin flushed red in irritation when she saw the oil stain she'd made on her dress.

"Would you care to tell me why this Studder is offline? There's no maintenance scheduled."

"Af'ernoon Miss Jefferson," Theresa said. "I was just walking past and noticed No. 4 is drifting all over the shop." She pointed over the automaton's work station, where the Studder's handiwork had left a geometric pattern of holes through the steel. Though beautiful, it wasn't going to do wonders for the aeroplane's aerodynamics.

Miss Jefferson squinted at it. "So, fix it. What's causing the problem?"

"Don't rightly know," said Theresa. "I think it's the quantum harmoniser. It might be superimposin' a dual program line and–"

"We speak English in this country, girl," said the woman. Her eyes fixed on the tuft of hair that had wormed its way free from Theresa's hat again. Never mind that both she and her mother had been born in St Pauls; all anyone ever saw was the grandfather that the Imperium had stolen from his homeland.

"It's a programming issue, ma'am," said Theresa, well versed in responding to such slights with a civility they did not deserve. "The quantum harmon... the thing that lets the robots talk to each other so fast is broken. It's doing two things at once, and I've not got a clue why. Or how."

"If you know which bit isn't working, why haven't you replaced it?" Miss Jefferson fished out a handkerchief to dab at her temples as she sweltered under layers of petticoats. Her own hair was coming loose from its chignon. "If we miss another deadline, it's not me that is going to pay."

Obviously, thought Theresa. *Because, of course, it wasn't your idea to run the production line at double speed, stressing all the robots to breaking point.* But that's what happened when you promoted a woman beyond her ability just because she had a Clifton address.

"Not that simple ma'am. They're quantum linked." Theresa pointed to where the crystal of the Studder's harmoniser glowed a faint blue. "We have to get the University down to specially calibrate them, and those duffers charge a fortune."

And would then spend half their time playing with the network, if last month's check-up was anything to go by. Aerocab had the largest harmonised network this side of the Greenwich meridian, and the team from the University could never resist toying with it.

"Just get it up and running," said Miss Jefferson. "I have had enough go wrong on me as it is. We are already behind on this month's consignment because some idiot in shipping lost an entire crate of cold air balloons *and* the helium tanks to fill them. If we don't finish off these planes by the end of the week, they'll fine us twice as much as last time. That's if they don't cancel the contract outright and then we are both out of a job. Is that what you desire?"

Theresa looked at the woman in front of her, eyes ringed by dark circles from sleepless nights. She was in over her head, and she knew it.

"I'll see what I can do, ma'am," Theresa said, feeling a wave of pity for the woman.

"Good," said Miss Jefferson. "I'll never understand why we bothered getting the bloody things in the first place. All they can do is the same thing over and over unless one of your lot spends a week and a half telling them to do something else."

"Not for long, ma'am. They're working on that up at the University."

"Pardon?" Miss Jefferson sounded scandalised.

"One of the lab technicians was telling me down at The Aeronaut's Propeller," said Theresa, realising it was too late to pull back from her misstep. "All to do with multi-process networking to make three Babbage Processors do the work of ten. Artificial Intelligence they call it, getting them to think for themselves rather than being told everything."

The woman's top lip curled back as she looked at the Studder.

"Lord, have you ever heard of something so ungodly? Something that can think without a soul." She kicked the Studder so it skittered like an injured animal. "I'd get rid of the lot of them, but workers are only worse. Bloody insubordinates. At least when you give the automatons orders they follow them."

The whistle blew to signal the end of the shift but Miss Jefferson's glare fixed Theresa. "I trust you'll get this finished before you leave." It wasn't a question. Theresa nodded mutely at Miss Jefferson before the woman marched off.

She could walk away now, Theresa realised. March out the door and watch Miss Jefferson flounder without her 'bloody insubordinates' to keep her afloat. But where could Theresa go? Given the colour of her skin, there were few places that would give her the job her qualifications warranted. And here she got to be near the aeroplanes. The company rules forbade her from even sitting in one, much less flying any, but being close by made it easier to dream.

Around her the machines powered down for the evening. She felt a pang of jealousy as they folded into their dormant state. Lord knew how long it would be until she could get back to her own bed. The light through the skylights was dimming as the sun set. She slapped her cheeks to keep herself alert and dug out her lantern from the bottom of her toolbox.

It was nearly full dark by the time she downed spanner, forced to admit that Miss Jefferson wasn't the only one treading waters out of her depth. Theresa was a programmer, not a quantum mechanic. Now, it seemed that lack of expertise would put her in the firing line as Miss Jefferson's next scapegoat. She slumped onto the floor and buried her face in her arms.

When she pulled her head back up, her neck was stiff as a board, and it looked like the sun was beginning to rise. She must have nodded off.

Standing up, she stretched and set off across the assembly floor towards the staff room for a cup of tea. If she was going to be hauled over the coals for not fixing the Studder then she could at least feel human before her shift started.

The fighter was still sitting in the middle of the hangar. She shouldn't. She wasn't allowed. But then again, who was around to know? Before she could bottle it, she ran and climbed into the cockpit.

It hadn't yet had the seat installed, so she had to kneel on the floor. But she was at the helm. The dashboard was missing most of its instruments, but at least the steering rods were installed. She gave them an experimental pull, looking over to watch the wing flaps moving before realising they wouldn't be connected yet. She sighed. The closest she'd come to flying in nearly two decades and the aeroplane couldn't even flap its wings. She closed her eyes and leaned back, trying to remember the feeling of floating on the air. But then she opened her eyes again, and she was back on the ground.

That's when she saw it. A movement in the gloom at the other end of the factory. Had someone else been here all night? Or were thieves about? She squinted, but it was too far away to make out any figures, just the dark shadows of automatons at work.

She should get the police, but she didn't want to look like some panicking girl spooked over machines that hadn't shut down properly. Instead, she clambered out of the plane and grabbed her toolbox, taking out a spanner just in case something more dangerous than a wayward robot needed thumping.

She sneaked through the factory until she was crouched behind the engine assembly line, using the half-assembled mechanisms to shield her from view. The smell of petrol made her head spin, but she blinked back the vertigo and watched.

For a moment, she wondered if the fumes were making her see things. There was a motley collection of automatons against the back wall – Grippers, Studders, Inspectors, even

71

a Lifter. They were all gathered around something on the floor she couldn't see. The glass orb of an Inspector's optical sensor cast its gaze at whatever was on the ground before a Gripper moved itself into position. Its robotic fingers clicked around something metal, then the whir of it lifting, followed by a tinkle as it dropped whatever it was holding. The same sounds came again. And again. And again.

What was it trying to do? Curiosity overtook Theresa's sense, and she moved forward to crouch behind a crate, where she could see without being noticed.

Noticed by what? The thought made her start. There wasn't anyone around operating the automatons, but they weren't just blindly going through their core programming either.

She risked standing up to get a better view. There was a mass of white rubber sheeting on the floor, and she recognised it as one of the cold air balloons Miss Jefferson had lost. It was deflated now, but there was a helium canister nearby should anyone want to fill it. There was something attached to the balloon with a harness – one of the tiny Mobile Inspector units they used to examine hard to reach places. She knew the Imperium used cold air balloons to send spy cameras over enemy lines. Was that what was going on here? Someone had set up this operation, but who, why, and how? Were the automatons running through a program, or were they being controlled remotely?

Or were they controlling themselves?

"Bloody hell, they actually did it!"

The Inspector swivelled round towards the source of the noise, its glass eye glinting in the half-dawn. It stared at her, and Theresa saw intelligence in its gaze. An *artificial* intelligence.

"Can you hear me?" she asked. "Can you understand what I'm saying?"

The eye stayed stationary for a moment, the only sound the clicker-clack of a cogitating Babbage Processor. Then it bobbed up and down twice.

A shriek of delight bubbled up through Theresa. This was amazing! The University researchers must have done something the last time they were down. Run some experiment or tested a new program, and then left a part of it behind. If three machines could do the work of ten, what could a thousand do? Wait until she told them about this. Everyone else in the factory too. They were going to be so excited!

Miss Jefferson's words came back to Theresa, and dread numbed her.

"Lord, have you ever heard of something so ungodly? Something that can think without a soul."

And the manager wouldn't be the only one. What would most people do if they saw this wonder? Kill it. Smash it. Destroy it and melt down the pieces so it could never be built again. Theresa looked at the robots surrounding her. Her eyes fell on the cold air balloon and the Mobile Inspector, its twin optics regarding her like a child filled with wonder at the world, and she realised what the balloon was for.

"You want to fly," she said.

How long had she worked here? Walking past the world's greatest flying machines every day, not even allowed to sit in the cockpit during testing. Wouldn't she send part of herself up into the clouds to look down on the world if she could?

She looked at the balloon. The Gripper was holding the helium hose but had been struggling to connect it, and the Mobile Inspector was still running off the main steam-line. They were intelligent enough to drag themselves over here and set up this operation, but not quite smart enough to see it through and get it off the ground. Not without her help.

"Alright then," she said. "Let's see what we can do. We've not got much time until the morning shift arrives, mind, so we best move sharpish."

She disconnected the Mobile Inspector from the steam line and grabbed a winding key from her toolbox, then swapped them with the Gripper for the helium hose.

"Wind up the clockwork battery as much as you can, and he should run for a good week."

The Inspector moved into position so the Gripper could see what it was doing. The machine took a moment to process what was happening and then began to turn the key twenty times faster than Theresa would ever be able to manage. She grabbed the helium tank and hooked it up before throwing the valve fully open. Soon the balloon began to lift from the floor until only the wires connecting it to the Mobile Inspector held it down. Now they just had to get the skylight open. Time to climb onboard the Lifter.

"Get me up there," she said, bracing herself. The machine surged upwards, and she felt that swooping feeling in her stomach as she raced towards the sky. The Lifter raised her until she could get at the window latches, opening them with a flick of her screwdriver. She tried to lift the glass but the weight was enormous and she could barely move it more than half an inch. The cold wind blowing towards the Bristol Channel sliced through the gap like a knife across her arms, but she braced against it as the Lifter rose again, pushing her and the glass upwards.

Halfway open, the wind caught the huge pane and slammed it back against the roof. Theresa shied away as splinters of glass went flying. The balloon! She looked down and was relieved to see it was still in one piece. Hopefully none of the shards had damaged it.

"Let him go!" she shouted over the wind.

The Gripper released the Mobile Inspector and the balloon with it. They rose up, up, up through the window and out into the night. A gust of wind made Theresa stagger back, blowing the cap off her head and freeing her bounty of curls. It caught the balloon too, pulling it out south towards the city, sending the robot off on his grand adventure.

"Send us a postcard," she yelled after it.

As she stood on that roof, she was a sky-captain on the deck of her zeppelin, hair buffeting about her face as she sailed off to lands uncharted. Her only master was the wind. The voyage was her destination. She could feel that leaping sensation in her chest as the airship moved beneath her, but then she realised it was just the motion of the Lifter bringing her back down to the ground. Back to the shop floor. Back to where she was just plain old Theresa, the technician who fixed the robots that made the aeroplanes she wasn't allowed to fly. The woman who got shouted at for the incompetence of her superiors and had no one to back her up.

A Gripper appeared in front of her, hand outstretched. Theresa wrapped her own around it and the mechanical fingers clamped down before shaking her hand in congratulations of a job well done. Perhaps she did have someone to back her up after all.

"I thought you said you'd fixed No. 4 a week ago," said Miss Jefferson, as they watched the man from Fabrication pull the last of the studs out of the aeroplane wing. They were a scant half-inch from the edge of the sheet, making the metal buckle and warp.

"I have," said Theresa. "That's an alignment issue, ma'am. You'll have to call out Maintenance on that one."

Miss Jefferson was looking less haggard than she had the previous week, though her face was set in a permanent scowl.

The factory had been running more or less to plan, bar one or two minor breakages, and it looked like they would make the next shipment after all.

"Do you have to throw it out? It's only the edge that's ruined," asked Miss Jefferson.

"No can do, ma'am," said the man from Fabrication. "You'd have to cut an inch or two off the top and then it'd be too small. Scrap is the only place for this 'un." He shrugged, before taking the offending sheet away.

Miss Jefferson let out a grunt of annoyance, turning back to Theresa.

"Stop milling about and get this sorted, will you? If it's not your department, then find the person whose department it is and get them to sort it."

Theresa doffed her cap as Miss Jefferson left. As the factory manager passed No. 4, its stud gun fired, nailing the back of her skirt to the ground. When she stepped forward, there was a great rip, and an inch of hemline remained behind. Miss Jefferson looked at the machine in horror, then at Theresa.

"That's dangerous, that," Theresa said, by some miracle managing to keep a smile from her face. "I'll get Maintenance to see to it."

The manager grabbed the torn fabric, then flounced off back to wherever she usually hid herself.

It was nearing the end of the shift, so Theresa made her way over to a quiet corner of the shop floor and sneaked into a storeroom hidden behind a rack of paint cans. The room smelled of burned metal, as a Welder was shoring up the seams on the skin of an aeroplane. The small craft was just big enough to hold one person. Her.

Theresa walked over to where a panel was missing, leaving the ribs of the frame exposed. They were much closer together than the one Studder No. 4 had been skinning. A standard sheet of steel, even one with the top few inches cut off, would be more than enough to cover the gap.

A Painter's nozzle tapped her on the shoulder, then pointed expectantly at the insignia it had drawn onto the side of the aeroplane. At first, it just looked like a series of random lines, until Theresa noticed the curve of the river Avon. It was a view of Bristol from the air, as seen, say, from the bottom of a cold air balloon.

She grinned up at the Painter. It seemed they had their postcard.

Defence of the Realm

- Cheryl Morgan -

Daniel Gooch was filled with trepidation. It was bad enough that it was his first visit to Downing Street. However, it was also the first time for his boss, Isambard Kingdom Brunel. The irascible Chief Engineer of the Great Western Railway had felt slighted for years at the lack of recognition and respect he had received from the civil authorities. Now that it had finally come, Gooch feared that Brunel might let his pent-up frustration out and behave badly.

It was a strange meeting though. On the government's side there were some very big names. The Prime Minister, Lord Palmerston, was flanked by his Home Secretary, Sir George Grey; the Secretary of State for War, Lord Panmure; and the First Lord of the Admiralty, Sir James Graham. With them was a sharp-faced young bureaucrat as well as a balding, bearded fellow whom Gooch suspected might be an academic of some sort.

Palmerston began the meeting.

"Mr Brunel, Mr Gooch, we are very grateful for your presence. The nation has need of your unique talents. We shall explain all shortly, but first I must stress that everything you hear in this room is imparted in the strictest confidence, to be communicated to others only in cases of absolute necessity. Do you agree to this?"

"Of course, Prime Minister," Brunel replied for both of them. Gooch was rather taken aback. What had they got themselves into?

"Good," said Palmerston. "You may find what we have to tell you quite unbelievable. I know I did when I was first briefed. But I have seen sufficient evidence of a real threat to the realm to take the matter very seriously. Mycroft, tell us what our intelligence services have reported."

The sharp-faced young man opened a file of papers in front of him, selected one, and pushed it across the table to Brunel and Gooch. It was one of those photograph things. Brunel had been following the development of the technology keenly because it seemed to have excellent prospects as a means of selling travel. If people could see photographs of beautiful places, he had explained to Gooch, surely they would want to travel there? That meant business for a man who made ships and railways.

The picture showed a clipper ship in a harbour Gooch didn't recognise. Towering above the vessel was an animal. Judging from the head and the mouth full of teeth, it was a giant lizard of some sort.

"Is that a dinosaur?" asked Brunel. "I visited the exhibition at Crystal Palace but I don't recall seeing any models that were bipedal, as this creature appears to be."

"We believe not," said Mycroft, "though who knows what strange creatures will be discovered in the Antipodes. That photograph was taken in Sydney, Australia. The ship is the *Lightning* of Liverpool. It was sunk in a matter of minutes by the creature. Fortunately, one of the dock managers is passionate about photography and managed to take this picture, which he sent back to London on the *Marco Polo*. You may have heard that it broke its own speed record for the journey. As to the nature of the creature, we have invited Mr Darwin here to share his knowledge."

"Thank you," the balding fellow responded. "A dinosaur would have been my first guess too, Mr Brunel, and I am not entirely sure the men who built the Crystal Palace models have understood the skeletons they worked from correctly. However, this creature is one that I know well from my time in the Galapagos Islands. It is a marine iguana, a common species there, but one of prodigious size."

"One wonders what it may feed on to make it grow so large," said Brunel.

"Ah, if only it were a natural process that had produced this giant, but I fear it is not. I fear that this creature has been made, created, by scientific methods."

Brunel sat back and stared at the naturalist, one eyebrow raised. Gooch had seen that gesture before. His boss was getting interested in the subject under discussion.

"For some time," said Darwin, carefully, "I have been working on a scientific theory that explains how animal species are formed. Over the fullness of time, I believe that natural processes guide how some creatures thrive in their environment and others fail. Thus, small changes in the design of creatures are magnified, and new species develop as a result. I call the process Natural Selection because nature selects those individuals best adapted to their environment. I have not made these ideas public before because I fear that the Church will not be happy with them, but this creature may be the proof.

"A young cousin of mine, Francis Galton, had been helping with my work. He became obsessed with finding a mechanism by which changes in species can be encouraged. He thought that if we found such a biological switch we could even change mankind to be faster, stronger, more intelligent, resistant to disease. I paid his ideas very little notice, knowing full well what the bishops would think of such notions. But recently Galton has taken up with a fellow called Richard Moreau, a man given to gruesome experiments in vivisection. I believe that the two of them have created this creature."

"That's astonishing," said Brunel. "Do you have any proof?"

"We have circumstantial evidence," said Palmerston. "A letter was delivered to Downing Street from the two rogues Mr Darwin mentioned. They knew of the attack on Sydney, which we have done our level best to keep out of the newspapers. They claim to be able to control the creature and have demanded a ransom, or they will have it attack Britain."

"Enterprising rogues, then."

"Far too enterprising." Sir James Graham entered the conversation. "Thankfully, we believe the creature cannot swim anywhere near as quickly as the *Marco Polo* sails. We have time, and we are stalling for more. But we must be able to defend our shores. The Navy can keep a lookout, but once in coastal waters, we can't manoeuvre the way an animal can. We need shore defences as well."

"And that," added Lord Panmure, "is where you come in, Brunel. We can station artillery at major ports, but this creature could strike anywhere. Mr Darwin tells us that it is an amphibian and could come ashore anywhere there is a beach. My generals are asking for the ability to deliver artillery to any part of the coast in a matter of hours. And for that..."

"You need trains," said Brunel, a broad smile creeping across his whiskered face.

Oh dear, here we go, thought Gooch to himself. *I do hope he doesn't offend anyone.*

"Before you start, Brunel," said Sir George Grey, "we are not converting the entire national railway network to broad gauge. We want trains that can transport artillery and unload it quickly. You must design versions for both your own railway and for the rest of the country."

"I didn't think that all of my Christmases would come at once, Home Secretary," said Brunel. "Not even Mr Dickens could imagine that. But there is the small matter of legalities. Take the south coast, for example. We need a fast line from London that connects to Portsmouth and Southampton, and then on to my own lines at Exeter. Discussions at the Board of Trade over that line have been going on for years, mainly due to the attempts by the London & South-Western Railway to break the agreement about access to the South West from London that they signed with my GWR in 1845."

Sir George sat back in his chair and sighed.

"Can you build these trains, Brunel?" asked Palmerston.

"Yes, Prime Minister, of course I can."

Gooch was aware that his boss had not so much as glanced at him before committing the company to the project. However, train-borne artillery didn't seem to present much of a problem. There would be recoil to consider. You wouldn't want the gun to throw the carriage off the tracks as it fired, but beyond that it should all be standard work. Or, at least, it would be provided that Brunel didn't have any of his ideas.

"Then I will leave the bickering over details to you and George," said Palmerston. "I want it done. No one blackmails the British Empire!"

Gooch looked at the schematics in front of him with astonishment. Brunel had asked many things of him during his twenty years with the Great Western Railway, but nothing had ever been as ambitious as this. He looked up at his employer and mentor.

"Sir? Are we really going to make these things?"

"Humour me, eh, Gooch? I'm over fifty now. I'm allowed to have a little flight of fancy every now and then. We can make the trains Lord Palmerston wants easily enough, but where's the challenge? These things, on the other hand..."

"These things, sir, look like something out of the sketch-books of Leonardo da Vinci."

"But can you make them, Daniel?"

If he was honest with himself, Gooch didn't know. This was well beyond the realms of normal railway engineering. But these designs of Brunel's were breathtaking. How could he not want to make them work?

"The designs look sound, sir. We'll need the best machinists in the company. It wouldn't do to have one of these things seize up in battle. But yes, I think we can do this."

Brunel smiled. "I knew I could rely on you, Daniel. Let's make history."

Lt Edward Fullerton collapsed into a chair in the mess room. There had been many ways his life could have gone over the past three years. At times he had contemplated suicide, but his sense of duty always brought him back. Not in his wildest fancies, however, had he imagined becoming a train driver.

It was still cavalry, he thought. Anything that didn't involve trudging into battle on the two feet that God gave you counted as being cavalry. And at least this locomotive was armoured, though he supposed that made him heavy cavalry. His mind went back, as it always did, to that terrible day in the Crimea when he and his comrades in the 8th Hussars, along with four other regiments, had charged into the teeth of the Russian guns. Fullerton had been lucky. His horse had been killed under him early on, and he had managed to find his way back to his own lines, bleeding profusely from multiple grapeshot wounds. They'd given him a medal because he was an officer and had lived. Fullerton still felt that he should have been court-martialled for cowardice instead. He should have died with his men.

And now they had him driving trains. Perhaps he had died and was in Hell.

"Penny for them, sir?"

Sergeant Matthew "Taffy" Williams was the young artilleryman Fullerton had been assigned as a crewman. The lad's main job was as a fireman on the locomotive, which he appeared to enjoy. "It's much better shovelling coal into a fire than shovelling it out of a mine like I did as a boy," he'd said. But he also had to be able to operate the cannon mounted on the locomotive. Fullerton would rather have shovelled coal or mined it. He hated cannon.

He stroked his moustache and tried his best to act like an officer.

"I was worrying about the machinery, Taffy. Mr Gooch seems very confident in his designs, and I must say that he has dealt with our various teething troubles admirably, but there are an awful lot of gears in that machine, and it wouldn't do if some thingamabob didn't work just when we needed it."

"Oh, don't you worry about that, sir. Fixing things is my job. A can of oil works wonders most of the time, and if that doesn't work, a sharp tap with a length of pipe generally does the trick. You just have to get us where we are going. I'm glad I don't have to drive that thing. Too many dials to watch and levers to pull."

"Tea, gentlemen?" asked a young woman.

"Don't mind if I do," said Fullerton.

"Thanks, Gwyn, love," said Taffy.

"Do you know the young lady?" Fullerton asked after she had provided them with tea and biscuits.

"Gwyneth, me twin sister. Identical twins at that, though it's not so obvious now we're grown, with her being a girl and all. We've been inseparable since birth. Don't know how she does it half of the time. I told her I'd be doing training on Salisbury Plain, all secret like, so I couldn't tell her about it. Next thing I know, she'd got a job with the caterers here."

"Ah, women," said Fullerton. "Mysterious creatures. Not that I would know much. Eton, Sandhurst, the Army. The only women I know are nurses and cooks."

"Can't imagine that, sir," said Taffy. And then he drank his tea slowly and in silence. Fullerton was grateful not to have to have a conversation. Women were not a subject he was comfortable talking about, especially to subordinates.

Fullerton had to admit that, as deployments went, this one was rather cushy. He'd been promoted to Captain on completing his training. He had his own office in Bristol Temple Meads station. He had to take the *Sir Lancelot* out every so often, just to make sure it was in good working order, and to learn his way around the network. Taffy did most of the work of maintaining the locomotive. It was still classified Top Secret and the Army didn't want any old GWR mechanic poking at it. There really wasn't much to do except wait.

What they were waiting for was another matter. Back on Salisbury Plain, there had been furious debate among the various drivers as to whether the Creature was real, or if in fact the top brass had collectively lost their minds. Cranbourne, who drove the *Sir Bedivere*, was convinced it was all nonsense. Too much opium taken from the Chinese, he reckoned. Government all high as a kite. He was stationed in Liverpool now. Fullerton missed him.

The downside was that it was hard to take time off. No one knew when the Creature might strike. There had been a rumour that it had attacked Cape Town, but the government was continuing to suppress all news of it. The trains had to be ready, day or night, any day of the year. Of course, one had to sleep, so there were reserve crews. Fullerton hated the thought of anyone else driving the *Sir Lancelot*, though. And he hated working with anyone other than Sgt Williams. Still, he had given the lad the weekend off. He should be around by now, though. Ah, wait, there he was.

"Sorry I'm late, sir," said Taffy. "Train from Cardiff was late getting in. Sheep on the line, apparently."

Fullerton knew Sgt Williams very well by now. They had been working together for months. But there was something slightly different about him today.

"Miss Williams? Gwyneth, is that you?"

The girl looked properly shamefaced.

"Yes, sir. Sorry, sir. I told Matthew you wouldn't fall for it. We were always passing ourselves off as each other when we were kids, but it's harder now we're older."

"So where is he, then?"

"At home, sir. He was playing rugby for Rhymney on Saturday. A big prop from Ebbw Vale trod on his arm. Accident it was, but the doctor said it's broken and he can't work for a week. I know how to shovel coal, sir. And fire the cannon."

"I'm sure you do, Miss Williams, but we can't have women in the front lines. It is most irregular. I'll ask for Walters, the reserve fireman, to come in. I'll say you're sick and I have sent you home. But you'll need to sit around the office for a few hours. Walters has only just gone home. He'll be no use to me on two hours sleep."

Just then the telegraph began to chatter. Fullerton reached for his Morse Code book. He'd managed to learn a lot of the code, but he wasn't as fluent as he'd like. Thank goodness they had one of the new-fangled devices that printed out the incoming message rather than expecting you to decode while you listened to it.

"It's Captain Naismith in Plymouth, sir. The *Sir Galahad*. He says that a Navy frigate spotted the Creature off Cornwall. It appears to be headed up the Channel."

"You understand Morse, Miss Williams?"

"Yes, sir. Matthew had to learn when he joined the Army, so I learned with him. We do—"

"Everything together, yes, so he keeps telling me. Does Naismith have any idea where the Creature is headed?"

"No, sir, but it will be Exeter."

"You seem very sure."

"Yes, sir. It was in the papers this morning, sir. The Queen and Prince Albert are going to Exeter to open a new museum. It will be the first train on that new line from Waterloo that Mr Brunel was so pleased about."

"By Jove, I think you're right. We must get underway at once. You do know how to start the *Sir Lancelot*, don't you? Yes, of course you do. Hurry up, then."

"Briers!" Fullerton followed Gwyneth out of his office and yelled down the corridor for his GWR liaison. The portly railwayman came running, out of breath already.

"We are leaving for Exeter at once," said Fullerton. "Have the line cleared for us. Signal Naismith in Plymouth and Fitzwilliam in Southampton. Tell them that I believe that there will be an attack on the city because the Queen is on her way there. I'll meet them at the estuary. Is that clear?"

"Line to Exeter, Naismith and Fitzwilliam, Queen, estuary. Yes, sir."

"Good man." Fullerton saluted Briers. The man might be a civilian, but a little bit of military etiquette always helped get them in the right frame of mind. Then he ran all the way to where the *Sir Lancelot* was waiting. He wasn't sure whether to be pleased or terrified, but at least the waiting was over.

Of course, the waiting wasn't over. Once Fullerton and Gwyneth had got the *Sir Lancelot* up to steam and out of Bristol, it was a long run down to Exeter. The GWR had been as good as their word. A London to Exeter express had left Bristol shortly before the *Sir Lancelot*, but Briers had promised it would be diverted round the Weston-super-Mare loop to allow them to pass. Fullerton hoped that there were not too many dignitaries on-board expecting to see the Queen.

Once he had a good head of steam, Fullerton found that he had little to do but think. He worried that the *Sir Galahad* might get there first, but Naismith had to navigate the twisty route around Dartmoor, whereas the *Sir Lancelot* had a free run through the Somerset levels. He worried about what everyone would say when they found out he had taken a young girl into a battle. But most of all, he worried about whether he would have the courage to face the Creature when it came down to a fight. He listened to the sound of the *Sir Lancelot* steaming furiously down the track beneath him, but all he could hear was the sound of horses pounding down a valley in Balaklava.

Thankfully, Gwyneth needed next to no instruction. Sgt Williams had once told Fullerton that he and his sister had both worked down a mine as children. It was horrifying to hear that a young girl should have been put to such work, but he had heard people complaining about the use of child labour at that new Bryant & May match factory in Bow, and they were nearly all girls. No good would come of it, he was sure. But at least Gwyneth was happy shovelling coal into the *Sir Lancelot*'s furnace. No young woman Fullerton had ever met would have done the same.

The *Sir Lancelot* sped through Taunton and Exeter St David's, finally coming to a halt just south of the city where the railway ran alongside the estuary of the River Exe. There Fullerton found a squad of Royal Marines waiting for him, from the base at Lympstone, across the estuary. A young lieutenant informed him that the Navy had been harrying the Creature through the Channel, but it was hard to engage because it could go a long time underwater and they lost track of it every time it dived. A ship full of Marines had gone out with whaling equipment to try to tackle it, but the lookout at Exmouth reported that the ship had been sunk. The Creature had been seen feeding on the helpless sailors and Marines, and at that grisly thought Fullerton couldn't repress a shudder.

"Captain Naismith should be here with the *Sir Galahad* any minute, sir," said the Lieutenant. "Captain Fitzwilliam is behind the royal train on the line. I'm told that Her Majesty stopped briefly at Salisbury but refused to delay her arrival into Exeter for the *Sir Perceval* to pass so it will be a while before he gets here. Do you need any help deploying your cannon?"

Fullerton smiled. Of course, the Marines had never seen a Knight Class locomotive in action before. Only those people who had been at the secret training ground on the line built out onto Salisbury Plain from Warminster knew what would happen next.

"No, thank you, Lieutenant," he said. "Just have your men stand back out of the way. We'll take it from here. Sgt Williams!"

"Sir!"

"Prepare for deployment!"

Many GWR engineers had remarked on the strange shape of the Knight Class locomotives and the various extra levers in the cabin, but none had come close to discerning the ingenuity of Brunel's design. Fullerton pulled the main lever that triggered the transformation and allowed the mechanism to work its wonders.

Slowly but surely the huge locomotive began to change shape. Legs and arms descended, raising it from the track. The great boiler was raised to stand vertically. Fullerton climbed the ladder to the new control cabin that had opened at the top of the boiler. Gwyneth made her way to the gunnery nest where the cannon now protruded from the *Sir Lancelot*'s chest. The Marines stood slack-jawed and open-mouthed, unable to believe what they were seeing.

The *Sir Lancelot* stood in all its glory, its bodywork of GWR dark green shining in the morning sunshine. From his position in the helmet section, Fullerton could just glimpse the towers of Powderham Castle to the south. *There should be flags waving*, he thought, *and fair maidens cheering as we stride into battle*. Except the only maiden hereabouts was down in the chest section preparing the *Sir Lancelot*'s cannon for action.

"I can see the *Sir Galahad*'s steam in the distance. Naismith will be here soon," Fullerton yelled down. "Tell him I am taking up position to protect the city. With any luck, he'll be able to engage the Creature from the rear."

The Marines were still dumbstruck, so Fullerton had the *Sir Lancelot* execute a sharp salute. As a man they snapped to attention and saluted back. "Yes, sir!" they roared in chorus. Fullerton engaged the leg controls and the giant machine, just like the armoured knight of old after which it was named, strode off along the side of the estuary, ready to do battle.

Using his binoculars, Fullerton ascertained that it was indeed Naismith and the *Sir Galahad* whose steam he had seen in the distance before he turned his attention to the water. Yes, there it was. He could see the head of the Creature breaking the water as it swam slowly up the estuary. Fullerton could make out the spiny crest on its head and the occasional splash far behind from its tail. It left a wake like a passenger liner. God above, the thing was even bigger than he had imagined.

"How are things down there, Miss Williams?" Fullerton spoke into the funnel of the communication tube that connected his control cabin to the gunnery nest.

"All fine down here, sir. What would you like me to load up with?"

"Grapeshot first, please. Mr Darwin says that the best way to get the Creature to engage with us is to make it angry. We need to lure it away from the city and allow the *Sir Galahad* to get a good shot in from behind."

Fullerton was pleased to see his plan working out well. A couple of grapeshot rounds caught the attention of the Creature. At long range both were wide of the mark, but that didn't matter with grapeshot as the stuff flew everywhere. Soon, the amphibious beast was wading into the shallows to approach the *Sir Lancelot*. Naismith in the *Sir Galahad* was moving into position behind it.

Taking a risk, Fullerton moved the *Sir Lancelot* further out into the estuary. He and his fellow drivers had occasionally become stuck in the mud on Salisbury Plain. Mr Gooch had come up with some clever designs to spread the weight of the machine and help the feet dig themselves out, but nothing was perfect. In this case, the risk was necessary. Fullerton wanted to give the *Sir Galahad* a good shot, and he didn't want to be directly in the line of fire behind the Creature if they missed.

Gwyneth let go with another round of grapeshot to keep the Creature distracted, and the *Sir Galahad*'s cannon roared into life. It was a fine shot. Fullerton's instinct was to close his eyes and duck at that terrifying sound, but he managed to keep them open. Then he wished he hadn't. The cannonball smashed into the back of the Creature... and bounced off, splashing into the water beside it.

Emitting a mighty roar, the Creature spun around and headed towards the *Sir Galahad*. The cannon roared again, but this time the Creature was expecting it and, with incredible agility, it dropped to all fours, dodging the shot. Loping up to the *Sir Galahad*, it thrashed its long tail and roared. The Knight Class machines had seemed very agile when they had been training on Salisbury Plain, but Fullerton could see now that they were slow and ponderous compared to a natural animal. The Creature dodged rapidly sideways, its vast, clawed hind feet briefly visible out of the water before it came down from its jump and reared up. Then the tail whipped forward and wrapped around one of the *Sir Galahad*'s legs. Anchoring itself on its muscular hind legs, the Creature pulled its tail back. *Sir Galahad*'s leg came up, the fighting machine overbalanced, and with a mighty splash fell backwards into the shallow water of the estuary.

It all happened too quickly for Gwyneth to get another shot off without risking hitting the *Sir Galahad*. Naismith, his machine flat on its back, opened up with the twin Fafschamps volley guns built into each arm. Brunel had hired a French engineer whose design allowed fifty rifles to fire at once. Some of the shots drew blood but they didn't slow the Creature, which lashed out with its mighty hind legs. Its clawed feet ripped through the metal of the fighting machine. The *Sir Galahad* did not fire again.

"Don't bother firing at its back, Miss Williams!" Fullerton yelled into the speaking tube. "Its hide is too tough. We'll have to hope that the belly is less well-armoured. You'll probably only get one shot, so leave it late and make it count!"

"Got no choice right now, sir," replied Gwyneth calmly. "The mechanism is jammed. Where did Matthew put that oil can?"

Fullerton uttered a brief prayer under his breath and fired one of his volley guns to attract the Creature's attention. He hoped that Naismith and his crewman were still alive. He didn't want them to share the grisly fate of the naval expedition. Then he pushed the lever for forward motion. There was nothing for it. He had to get as close to the enemy as possible. If this meant that he finally got the death he should have had in the Crimea, so be it.

From down the speaker tube there came a stream of language Fullerton recognised as Welsh. Sgt Williams reverted to his native tongue when he wished to use language his senior officers might find indelicate. Fullerton was glad that he didn't understand what the girl was saying. There was a loud clang, of one piece of metal hitting another.

Then the Creature was suddenly on him. He fired the other volley gun, hoping to catch the beast in the eyes, but it kept charging towards him, roaring with that great toothed maw, lashing its heavy tail. Fullerton was about to entrust himself to God when the *Sir Lancelot*'s cannon roared back.

Gwyneth's shot could not have been better aimed. The cannonball flew into the Creature's open mouth, smashed through its palette, and ripped into its brain. The shot was at such short range that it had sufficient power to smash the back of the skull. Though the Creature's head flew apart, its body had no time to react. It was in the middle of a leap when it died and its forward motion could not be arrested. The body of the Creature smashed into the *Sir Lancelot*, driving the fighting machine backwards.

Fullerton leapt clear of the control cabin as the *Sir Lancelot* fell. He landed in the water and surfaced just in time to see the dead body of the Creature slide off the prone *Sir Lancelot* and splash beside it. The water was a few feet deep, not enough to cover either body. Fullerton clambered up onto his stricken locomotive and looked around frantically. Where was the girl? The gunnery nest was buried inside

94

the machine. Was she trapped there? Had she been crushed when the Creature's body slammed into the cannon?

Just then he heard a clanging sound and turned to see Gwyneth clambering onto the *Sir Lancelot* behind him. Water made rivers of the soot that caked her face.

"Thank goodness! Miss Williams, are you alright?"

"A bit damp and bruised, sir, but I'll live. How about you? Did we get it?"

"I'm fine, thank you, and our mission appears to have been successful. I must say that you are a remarkably good shot, Miss Williams. What are you laughing at?"

"Matthew will get a medal for this, won't he, sir?"

"Yes, I suppose he will," Fullerton said sadly. "There would be a terrible to-do if it became known that you took his place here today."

"They'll know in the village though, sir," Gwyneth giggled. "Broken arm or no, he'll be in the pub at lunchtime. There's no way he can pretend he was here too. He'll never live that down. Oh look, is that the *Sir Perceval*?"

Fullerton turned and caught sight of another giant fighting machine on the far side of the estuary. Of course, the *Sir Perceval* ran on standard gauge and would have had to come down the Exmouth branch line to meet them. Far away, the *Sir Perceval* raised an arm in salute to its fallen comrades. Fullerton and Gwyneth saluted back in response.

Just then, the sound of a trumpet blared from behind them. Turning back to the shore, Fullerton saw a small boat being launched.

"Miss Williams, I do believe those the fine fellows from the Royal Marines are coming to rescue us."

"I hope they know how to make a good cup of tea, sir. I'm dying for a cuppa."

It was, thought Fullerton, and admirable sentiment, and one which put his own fears to shame.

"Miss Williams," he said, "obviously we must be careful to keep up your charade for the next few hours, but in future, I would be honoured if you would call me Edward."

Daniel Gooch, Sir Daniel now, he supposed, though that would take some getting used to, looked carefully around the large ballroom in Buckingham Palace where the guests had been taken after the ceremony. It had taken two years for the authorities to reward the heroic engineers, though the Orsini Affair and two changes of government were a major cause of that. Brunel, sadly, had died of a stroke before he could receive any honours. That would not have mattered too much to him though. The Knight Class locomotives had been front-page news in every paper throughout the world. The Japanese, of all people, had been particularly taken by them. Brunel and Gooch had received a great deal of mail in an incomprehensible script which the GWR company lawyers were still dealing with.

It was fair to say that Brunel and Gooch were the most famous engineers in the world. Well, Brunel was. Gooch did his best to stay in the shadow of his egocentric employer. That would be harder now. He imagined Brunel sat in whichever part of Heaven St Peter reserved for engineers, sipping a glass of brandy in the company of Archimedes and Da Vinci and complaining about the incivility of the British government.

Gooch had been promoted to Chief Engineer when Brunel had died which, to be honest, had been his dream job. Unfortunately, it didn't seem like he would have much chance to do it. With Brunel dead, he was the sole surviving genius behind the hottest new property in the global arms trade. Palmerston was already keen to send one or two of the Knight Class locomotives to various parts of the Empire to cow the natives. He wasn't about to be selling the plans to any rival colonial power, especially after German and Russian spies had been apprehended trying to get jobs at the engineering works in Swindon. But there were other countries with money that were more friendly to Britain, and that's why Gooch had been told there was someone he had to meet.

Ah, there was Sidney Herbert, the new Secretary of State for War, and with him a gentleman in a large and improbable wide-brimmed hat that marked him out as being from the United States of America. Gooch extended his hand, which the American shook ferociously.

"Sir Gooch," he said, "I am delighted to meet you. Jefferson Davis, Senator for the Great State of Mississippi."

"I'm honoured, sir," murmured Gooch.

"Now, I don't suppose that the goings-on across the Atlantic make much of a splash here in Britain," Senator Davis ploughed on, "but we are facing some challenges with which I think you could be of great assistance. We are electing a new President this year, and one of the candidates has some very radical ideas. My colleagues and I are very much afraid that, if elected, he could do substantial damage to the economy of both of our countries. There is talk of secession, and even war. Your government has promised diplomatic help, Sir Gooch, but if that fails your steam powered fighting machines could be just the advantage that we need."

Gooch, who had made it his business to keep up with foreign news since it became clear that his creations were in great demand overseas, knew exactly who this radical candidate was and what danger he posed. Abraham Lincoln was an abolitionist. Slavery had been abolished in the Empire more than two decades ago, but the clothing industry, which had proved such a boon for industrial towns such as Manchester, depended on cotton from the Americas. Senator Davis and his colleagues controlled that trade and made much use of slaves in the process. Now it seemed as if the Knight Class locomotives might be sent to America to fight in defence of slavery. Gooch shuddered. This was not going to end well.

Miss Butler and the Last Mail-Rocket

- Julia Hawkes-Reed -

The sky above the port of Bristol was the colour of a theatre safety curtain. I stopped at the concrete of the radiation safety barriers to swap my valise to my other hand, shook my coat straight again, and strode towards the passenger end of the Mail Rocket. I'd seen illustrations of the engine, but I still had to stop and stare at the thing. Close up, it resembled an American frontier loco in the aftermath of a boiler explosion. The snow scoop looked like an exaggerated cow-catcher, behind which was the ring of water injectors where the chimney should have been. Steam pipes radiated from the far side of the red-painted containment vessel while a skein of control lines ran back across the pair of tenders to the driver's cupola above the dynamometer car.

I handed my ticket to the nearest porter. He muttered something that was probably "Slip of a girl travelling to Penzance unaccompanied I've never seen the like" before taking my bag and saying "If you'll follow me, miss" over his shoulder. He knocked on a door labelled '7.'

I stifled a grin when I heard Zoe shout, "Come!" from inside the compartment. She was in mid-bound from her fold-down bed when she realised that three was going to be something of a scrum and managed to slide to a halt in front of the startled porter. I sidled past him, retrieved my bag, and found some remaining space beside Zoe.

"Will that...?" he started.

"Yes!" we chorused. Honestly, it was like being back at school, had school been anything other than a nightmare cavalcade of rules and stupidity. The porter just about had the door closed before we hugged fiercely. It had been two weeks, three days, and seven hours since I'd last seen her. Not that I'd been counting.

I hoofed my bag into a corner, lobbed my coat on top of it, and flung myself down.

"Debrief?"

Zoe nodded. "Debrief. Are we still off Malvern's Christmas card list?"

I rolled my eyes. "Very much so. I get the distinct feeling they wanted to stop us travelling down on this thing, given their boffins supplied the loco, but apparently some other part of the ministry read them the riot act. They gave every impression of being helpful, but they made very sure I couldn't bunk off and poke around the workshops they didn't want me to see."

Zoe shrugged. "It's their own fault. They blotted their copybook by not letting on what the Malvernite was, or where it had come from. Their top brass would still be doing collective laps round the Second XI pitch in penance if the Long Winter hadn't happened. It allowed them to heroically save the day with the results of their frankly disturbing labours. Stopped clocks and all that."

"Stopped clocks do not glow blue in the dark and have the potential to spew radioactive death across the landscape should the fireman trip over his shovel."

She grimaced at the floor and sighed.

"True. Tea?"

"Tea."

Zoe was giving the pot a good stir when there was a noise like someone sitting on the far right end of a pipe organ and fending off the choirmaster with a candlestick. It was loud enough to generate concentric rings in the milk and was accompanied by a dense fog that blotted out the view of the station buildings. I watched the rings in the milk get closer together as the noise rose in pitch.

Zoe was looking at me, wide-eyed. I held her hands across the tablecloth and she squeezed back, shoulders dropping. The pressure in my head was like a sinus headache as the carriage lurched forward, and then a noise like a chimney fire in a brickworks as the train gathered pace. I swallowed to try to clear my head.

"I wish to revise my opinion about the directors of the Strategic Reserve and their horrible rocket engine."

"I concur. D'you think I could have my hands back now?" said Zoe.

I blushed, hid my hands in my lap, and let Zoe pour the tea. She was a little pink, too, but I couldn't drag my gaze from the snowy landscape outside. It glowed under the moon, and incipient thaw or not, there would be another sharp frost tonight. Eighteen months of frost. Five hundred and fifty days of winter.

I was looking at the arclights from the experimental station at Brean Down when I spotted another set of lights that seemed to be floating above it. I forgot that I was absolutely mortified and pointed them out to Zoe.

"What d'you suppose they're at this evening? Anti-dirigible mines?"

Zoe scrubbed the condensation on the window with a napkin and peered towards the coast.

"I can't quite make it out. It doesn't look right, that's... Oh, bloody hell. Under the table, now!"

"Zoe Harker, I am not..."

She gestured wildly and booted her chair backwards. "Small lights on a very much closer airship. Rocket!"

I squeaked as she grabbed two handfuls of my skirts and dragged me bodily under the table. As my bottom met the carpet there was a whoosh, a saucer-rattling bang, and shouts from the other passengers. The brickworks chimney fire coughed twice and then redoubled its efforts. It felt like the train was accelerating.

Zoe and I regarded each other, nose to nose.

"Ow," I said, wriggling to find a less sore spot.

"Not sorry," she said. "Shrapnel, flying glass. I couldn't live with myself." She shrugged and gave me a lopsided grin. "We should go and find some men, so they can explain things to us."

I nodded. "Yes, let's. I'm sure they will provide opinions, if not actual answers."

Zoe rolled her eyes. "Does your sister still ask why you're unmarried?"

"Not since the business in Edinburgh," I said. "Nice young men don't care to speak to girls carrying .410 shotgun walking sticks."

We dusted each other off and went in search of men who knew things.

One or other of father's housekeepers would opine that my bedroom 'looked like a bomb had hit it' should there be stray shoes or a misfiled knitting needle. I was gripped by the desire to find out where she was and demand she come and look at the far end of the dynamometer car, to see the results of an actual bomb. I could also see her saying, "That was a rocket, not a bomb, Olivia." And then beetling off in high dudgeon.

Getting into the car could have been much simpler. In the end, we waited until the people with the waistcoats and cigars had forgotten we existed, and then walked over to inspect the chart recorder positioned halfway down the left-hand side of the carriage. The wind from the missing front corner of the roof was brisk, whipping my hair into my face as my hairpins gave up the struggle.

"This does seem far from ideal," I said.

"Unless a miracle pitches up, we're on a speeding train with no obvious means of stopping, and there's probably an equal chance of the Malvernite cooking off and exploding, or the train derailing and *then* the Malvernite going off," said Zoe. She had a firm grip on the mahogany surround of the chart recorder, and her knuckles were white.

"We could go back to our cabin and set about the brandy."

I was only half-joking. Zoe looked at me, then let out a long breath.

"A tempting but short-term offer." She started going through the cupboards below the windows along the right-hand side of the carriage: rolls of paper, jars of ink, ledgers, and a leather briefcase that made a satisfying crash when she hauled it out. She flipped the briefcase open and lifted out a tray of carefully arranged screwdrivers.

"Aha!"

"You have a plan?" I asked.

She shrugged. "I want to see what's left of the driver's cupola. If we can find the control panel, maybe we can hit it with a spanner until it decides to behave. But that's going to involve going out in that." She pointed up through the hole in the roof. "Help me move one of those chairs so I can get a leg up."

"I'm keeping a firm grip on your ankles if you do," I said.

"Agreed." Zoe smiled.

She was up on the chair and half out of the carriage before I could say anything else. I wrapped my hands round one boot and hung on. It seemed an age later when she slid back down into the chair, looking like she'd participated in a Tesla experiment.

"Well?" I asked.

She raked her hair back and pushed the goggles up to hold it in place. "Most of the cupola's gone, but it looks like the flexible couplings were made of sterner stuff. They're hanging down there–" she waved at the corner of the carriage where there were tall cabinets instead of windows, "with the panel waving in the wind like a brass kite."

"It's not much good out there. How do we get it back in here?" I asked.

"Grappling or boat hook? Something like that."

There was a commotion at the end of the carriage. One of the captains of industry looked like he was going to start poking the chest of a railwayman and using phrases like 'see here' or 'my good man.'

"D'you think an umbrella would do?" I said.

"Maybe. Why?"

"Let me have those goggles, and then be prepared to stop the men from taking fright and stampeding."

I tipped the contents of my shoulder bag onto a chair, fastened all the buttons but those at the top end, and then pulled the buckle tight so the empty bag lay diagonally across my back. Zoe favoured me with a suspicious look and handed me the goggles. I slung them around my neck and trotted up to the captain of industry with the umbrella.

"I beg your pardon, sir..."

He kept nodding as his fellow captain explained the operation of the railways to the railwayman. I tried again. "Pardon me, but..." The chap from the railway glanced at me.

104

Oh, the hell with it.

I twisted the umbrella from his grip and turned back to the windswept end of the carriage. Zoe looked horrified as she worked out what I was going to do. As I strode down the carriage, I swung the point of the umbrella over my right shoulder and slid it into my shoulder bag like a sword into a scabbard.

"I say! Miss!" There were shouts from the men behind me. I took two more strides and bounded onto the chair like a ramp in front of a vaulting horse.

The full force of the wind outside took my breath away. I had just enough time to think that if I'd known it was going to be like this I would never have started, before realising I was hanging out of a runaway train and coming back inside without the control panel would be so desperately awful I would never be able to hold my head up in polite society again. Or rather, that my death would be just messy instead of glowing and spectacular. I wriggled toward the edge of the roofline and peered over. The skein of control hoses hung from a bracket on the side of the carriage. The forward side curved down and back up to a similar bracket on the side of the second tender while the hoses on the far side twisted like an angry snake. I took a firm grip on the jagged edge of the hole, splintered wood digging into my left hand, and swung the umbrella out with my right. The wind nearly took the thing before I fully tightened my grip, but I swung the handle end down and managed to hook it round the hoses. Stretching out as much as I dared, I walked my fingers down the umbrella, then leaned back to haul the thing towards me. It was slow going. The weight of the hoses pulled them through the umbrella handle, making the forward loop larger until the remains of the control panel smashed into my wrist. I yelped into the gale, pulled the panel towards my head, and let myself fall backwards into the carriage.

The control panel bashed me on the head as I hit the floor, although my landing was softer than I expected and huffed, "Jayzus!" I sat up, a coil of control hose wrapped around one arm, to discover I'd been fielded by one of the railwaymen. The panel itself was a tangle of bent brass and steel, spattered liberally with dark red hydraulic oil. I glanced up at Zoe, who was wild-eyed and about to explode, then looked back at the panel.

"Zoe... That's not oil, is it?"

She knelt down beside me. "I'm afraid not."

"Blast. Awfully sorry. Going to have to..." My surroundings faded out as the carpet came up to meet me.

I was sleeping on a terrible bed while someone on the far side of the room went on and on about bees. It was jolly annoying. I tried turning over to block out the droning, but I couldn't move because something was in the way. Honestly, this was all too much. To put the tin lid on everything, someone was driving the bed across a ploughed field.

"Oh, come *on*, Olivia! It's not like it was *your* blood."

What was Zoe doing in my bed? It was an awful uncomfortable bed that smelled of carpet and cigars. I was mildly mortified that we...

... I opened my eyes and stared at the ragged edge of the carriage roof, the blank grey-black sky beyond, and the bundle of control hoses hanging down. Well then. That had happened. I shuffled myself up on my elbows. A semicircle of faces regarded me. I fought the urge to wriggle away from them until I was against something solid and tried to think of something witty to say so the faces would stop looking so concerned.

"What on earth was the business with the bees?" As if the things I dreamed while fainted like someone useless had any basis in fact. Nice work, Olivia.

"Bob in the guard's van, miss," said the railwayman on my left. His hat was missing, his jacket askew. He looked like someone who'd broken the fall of a person leaping from a carriage roof. He pointed towards the other end of the carriage where a lad in an outsized overcoat gesticulated wildly at one of the stewards from the buffet car. "He says one of the beehives has been stolen from the post office van."

I looked at Zoe. She shrugged. "Miscreants in a dirigible loose a rocket which kills the engine driver directly and the rest of us later, then they shin down a rope in the dead of night onto a moving train to pinch a beehive? That actually seems fairly straightforward after that business with your chum from the wrong century."

The railwayman looked as if he longed for an excuse to beetle off and ask people for their tickets. I used the chair to haul myself upright, dusted off the worst of the charred splinters, and started re-filling my shoulder bag. My hands had mostly stopped shaking by the time I was finished. I took a deep breath, straightened my shoulders, and turned back to Zoe and the railwayman. Oh, hang it.

"I'm sorry about the plummeting. I'm Olivia Butler, and this is my, um, friend, Zoe Harker. And you are?"

"Alf Tupper, miss. Fireman."

"Thank you for fielding me, Alf. I think Zoe and I would be interested to find out more about Bob's missing bees, and we'd be jolly grateful to have someone point us in the right direction."

"I'd say go that way and stop when you hear the buzzing, but that would mean putting up with that sod whose brolly you lifted. Follow me," he said.

He led us back through the passenger carriages to the post office van. Most of the caged off sections were filled with mailbags, but opposite the side door was the section for awkward objects, one of which was a beehive. I knelt down beside it and listened. The bees were very quiet. I looked up at Zoe.

"How much should a beehive weigh?"

"No idea." She pushed at it. "But that doesn't feel right."

"Quiet bees made from flatirons? How very odd."

"Bob was right," said Alf. "Look at this." He slid the side door open a couple of feet to let in a blast of night air and a spiral of snowflakes, then slammed it closed. "Someone's broken the lock off."

"Oh, the hell with it." Zoe pulled hard at the lid of the hive. It slid off with a scrape. I flinched, expecting a faceful of angry bees. There was a complete lack of bees and a familiar whiff of light machine oil.

"Well, bloody hell," said Zoe.

I peered into the top of the hive and saw a very new card hopper that looked out of proportion to the machine below it. I couldn't quite make sense of what I was seeing.

"It's a Jaquard-8," Zoe said. "The smaller, faster, and vastly more expensive version of your elephant controller. I think the chaps in the dirigible pinched the wrong beehive. Which implies that once they've handed round the calamine lotion, they'll be back for that one."

Zoe turned to Alf, who was trying to peer into the top of the beehive from a polite distance.

"Is there a parcel manifest of some sort?" she asked.

He dropped back down on his heels and glanced at the small desk between the side door and a Tortoise stove. "Well, miss..."

Zoe glared at him. "I'll take that as a yes, but the source and destination of at least that beehive is to be kept hush-hush?"

Alf nodded and handed Zoe the clipboard hanging from a nail above the desk.

She scanned the list, then handed me the clipboard, with the first page looped over the top.

"Halfway down. The source should be familiar."

"Well, bloody hell."

Alf looked at me, then Zoe, then slumped onto a corner of the desk. "I begs yer pardon, yer 'ighnesses, but would you lay it out for a simple fireman, if I might make so bold... You can tell I've been on the Paddington run and mixed with too many cockneys. Servile bastards."

"That Jaquard," I waved at the thing in the beehive disguise, "is going direct from the factory to the naval research station at Falmouth, which seems to imply some sort of sea-going self-piloted vehicle."

"Jaquard, miss?"

"It's a computation device. Distantly related to the automatic loom, hence Jaquard. Feed it the right numbers, say where it is and where the bad sorts are keeping a gunboat, let it control the steering-gear and when X is close enough to Y, Bob's your explosion and fiery death."

"I'm sure the Canadians would find that delivery awfully strange because our upright and honourable government signed a treaty with them to supply Jaquard-7 units in exchange for food," said Zoe. "I mean, it would probably seem a bit off, given they were keeping a population from starving due to an eighteen-month winter, and in exchange being given the technical equivalent of bean tins and string. Were I in their shoes, I might get rather peeved if I discovered I'd been taken for a nation of mugs. I'd probably consider doing something about it."

109

"Such as lifting some of the good kit and then making sure the scene of the crime remained a glowing crater for at least two decades?" said Alf.

Zoe shrugged and nodded. "I can't say I'd blame them, were I not a passenger on that crime scene and people I care about ditto."

"Does this mean more heroism?" I asked. "Only I'm getting a bit of a bone in my leg, what with all the excitement and striding about."

Alf stood up. "If we're lucky, young Bob will have set about that panel you rescued with pliers, and we'll be able to evacuate the train at Exeter."

We made our way towards the front of the train and came upon Bob rushing through the buffet car, head down and muttering to himself. He bounced off Alf, looking about in surprise and wiping his face on the sleeve that hung over his left wrist.

"Misterdibdensaysyouretocomeatonce!" He rattled it off like going over points at speed.

Alf had him by the shoulders. "Breathe, lad. Now, again."

"Harry says the panel's too damaged."

Alf rolled his eyes. "Does he? Well. You go see if you can secure the door in the goods van, and I'll talk to Harry Dibden."

The men charged off in opposite directions. Zoe and I righted the chairs at the table we'd previously dived underneath and sat down to find out how stewed our tea had become.

Zoe propped her elbows on the table while a fresh pot was brewing. "Thoughts?"

I shrugged. "Several. Primarily 'Stuffed if I'm dying in a fiery explosion for either of their causes.'"

She nodded. "Truth. I wonder if we can bodge something up with handbasin taps and bits of the galley?"

"The fittings would be different. I don't see that Malvern would make anything special, so it's probably the same gauge as the Jaquard-7 interface. Father was dealing with high-pressure steam when he designed the elephants, so he used locomotive bits and... Oh." I trailed off. That would be far too much to hope for.

Zoe leaned forward and grinned. "Oh?"

"We need to go back and look at that Jaquard-8 again. Haul it out and check the bulkhead connectors. If we're really lucky, we'll only have to reverse engineer the controls for an exploding engine built by people who hate us and then hand-stab a complete card stack and get that right first time so we have the train under control by Newton Abbott," I said.

"Or fiery death."

"Or, as you say, fiery death."

The woodwork of the fake beehive slid upwards as a unit after some minor tugging and swearing. I crouched down behind the thing to inspect the connectors on the back. It looked horribly familiar – three rows of threaded ends on a D-shaped panel capped off with brass covers attached by small chains to make them hard to lose.

The Jaquard sat on a small plinth. I took a grip on one corner and made to rock it back and forth to see how firmly it was attached. Zoe, still inspecting the connectors, glanced up to see what I was at, then looked back down as I leaned hard against the weight of the Jaquard.

"Liv!" she shouted. "Don't move!"

I tried not to wobble on one foot.

"What?" I asked.

"Demolition charge."

"Well, blast."

"Hopefully not. Hold on, will you? I'm going to try to avoid fiery death."

Zoe leaned forward and pulled at something. There was a small metallic snap, almost lost against the noise of the train, and she collapsed back against the van wall.

I was all for letting her regain her composure, but my arms were trembling and I felt my fingers slipping against the oily chassis of the Jaquard.

"Um. Zoe? Can I let go now?"

She let out a long breath and pushed herself upright. "Yes. You're safe enough now. That kit's designed to be handled by careless squaddies. Mere women aren't going to trouble it."

I let the Jaquard rest on its explosive plinth and backed away slowly until I had a nice safe section of post van to lean against. After a long while I said, "How much of a bang might one expect from something that size?"

Zoe tilted her head and stared at the base of the Jaquard. "Maybe the axles would survive. There'd be no other remnants bigger than a box of cook's matches."

I nodded. "Good to know."

Zoe commandeered Bob and a sack-truck to shift the Jaquard while I steamed back to our cabin for a box of blank program cards. When I returned to the dynamometer car, Harold and Alf were walking the Jaquard into position against the chart recorder while Zoe had parked the broken control panel on the cabinet alongside, with little regard for the polish on the mahogany. She grinned with manic joy when she saw me and beckoned me round to the far side of the row of equipment.

"You'll want to see this, Olivia," she said.

She was right. The back of the panel was a D-shaped block of connectors, but only half were in use. I tested each threaded collar in turn, and none of them would need a man with a Stilsons wrench to make a mess. I hoofed the panel into position, wedging it steady against a cabinet with one boot. I paused. There was nothing else I could think to do that would allow me to delay the next part anymore. Zoe was already stabbing holes in a fresh card stack. She rolled her eyes when she saw my expression.

"What's the worst that could happen?" she said.

"Hydraulic oil fountain followed by fiery death, probably."

She shrugged and made a face. "I'm sure it will be fine."

The correct way of unplumbing all this would have been to wait until daylight and make sure the system was depressurised. I spun the knurled collar on the first connector with the flat of my hand until the only thing holding the pipe in place was me leaning against the mangled panel, then turned my head and jerked it away. There was a brief spurt of oil followed by a small thud that I felt in both hands as the ball valve in the connector snapped shut. I let out a breath and fitted the hose to the corresponding connector on the back of the Jaquard. I tried to pay attention to the movement of the carriage and the sounds of our progress, but nothing seemed to have changed. Swapping out the rest of the hoses, I propped the mangled panel against the forward wall of the carriage and then peered over Zoe's shoulder at the state of her card stack. It looked very simple. There was an obvious framework for a much more complicated program, but she'd just sketched in some basic instruction to read the state of some of the lines and copy them elsewhere.

I loved watching her work on a problem. It was like watching a street artist pencil up a caricature – you'd see a bunch of scribbles and shading and try to work out what was going on, and at the last moment there'd be a burst of activity and the finished work would emerge from what had previously looked like complete chaos. I just plodded along, putting one instruction after another until something stopped catching fire, but Zoe was an artist, pulling inspiration from the air around her. After another thirty seconds of watching her work and wondering why she put up with such a hopeless idiot, I realised where she was copying the state of the inputs. I hauled the inspection panels off the chart recorder and hooked it up to the remaining connectors on the Jaquard. Now whatever was going on with the engine would be shown on the chart recorder, and the data collected by the dynamometer car would feed into the Jaquard.

Zoe beamed at me. "You're amazing," she said. "I just wanted to use the recorder for debug output, but of course we can set up a sequence of feedback loops and stab in hysteresis and optimal values as the whole thing reaches a steady state."

I blinked. "But your code. It's..."

She flapped a hand. "Oh, I was just fiddling about and hoping you'd come up with something. And you did!"

There was a commotion at the far end of the carriage. I glanced up from the recorder, already composing some cutting remark in my head about men not shutting up when there was important work going on, when there was the sharp crack of a pistol followed by a shout and a clatter of chairs.

I dropped to the floor behind the chart recorder, hoping Zoe had also taken cover and peered round the edge. A tall fellow, dressed for winter in black, waved a pistol at Alf and Bob while Harold knelt over the prone form of one of the captains of industry. He wasn't moving, and a dark stain spread across the carpet.

"You two! Behind the cabinets! Out where I can see you!"

The 'out' gave it away. Canadian. I stood slowly and peered at his face, disappointed he bore no outward sign of angry bees. As he strode towards us, Zoe and I sidled towards the Jaquard, trying to keep him away from it.

"Well, here's a fine how d'ye do. Someone's arranged a demonstration of British ingenuity," He turned on his heel to face the men. "Which one of you gentlemen fixed this up?"

I fumbled for Zoe's hand and squeezed it. Bob started to raise his hand to point in our direction, but Harold burst into a theatrical coughing fit which gave Alf time to move in front of Bob and say, "Me. I did that."

The Canadian nodded, then half-turned and pointed the pistol at my face.

"Excellent. Disconnect it all or I shoot the girl."

Alf moved to the back of the Jaquard and paused. I couldn't turn to see what he was up to with a pistol waving at me, but I saw the Canadian grimace.

"Well? Time's a-wasting."

Zoe stepped away from me. "He can't. He doesn't know how."

"And you do? Really?"

I'd seen that look before. Usually as I was explaining something only slightly complex to some man swirling a brandy snifter and levering himself up and down on his toes.

Zoe turned to Alf. "Thank you, but I'd rather not have Olivia's brains smeared everywhere. I can take it from here."

I heard a rustle of skirts and then a sequence of mechanical noises and sharp ticks as she unscrewed the collars on the hoses and pulled them away from the Jaquard.

The Canadian gestured with his pistol. "You, over there with the rest of them. Hero-boy, get the Jaquard on the sack trolley and follow me." He grabbed Zoe by the upper arm, hard enough that she squeaked. "You're coming with me."

I waited for what felt like an age before peering round the door of the dynamometer car. There was another flat crack of a pistol from the far end of the next carriage, and the door kicked against my side as the bullet hit it. I dropped to the floor with my eyes closed, counted to thirty in octal, then opened one eye to check the coast was clear this time before scurrying back into the dynamometer car. The umbrella was propped against a cabinet where I'd left it. I slung my shoulder bag across my back again, sidled round the body of its owner, and trotted after the Canadian and his hostages.

I found Alf out cold in the post office van, the side door wide open. I leaned out as far as I dared and peered upwards. The dark shape of the Dirigible loomed directly above. I pelted to the far end of the wagon and hauled on the end door. The ladder was on the end of the guard's van as I remembered it, and if I stopped to think now, I would seize up and never move again. I hauled myself up to the level of the van roof and swung round to peer down the length of the train. There were four shapes on the post office van roof. Two black-clad men, the Jaquard in a cargo net, and Zoe, crouched next to it. Above them, the Dirigible struggled to hold stationary as a rope ladder and a grappling hook lashed about in the wind. Leaping for either one would be a swift way off the train, and catching the grapple in the head equally unfortunate. I swung myself onto the roof of the post office van and scuttled forwards as quickly as I dared. While everyone was concentrating on the dirigible, I had the element of surprise.

The van rocked from side to side. I had to time my movements, careful not to rock in the same direction and lose my balance. As I got within umbrella distance of the nearest man, I swung it from its makeshift scabbard and took a firm grip on the pointy end. I hooked the handle round his left ankle and tugged hard when the van rocked left. His arms pinwheeled as he overbalanced and I threw myself forward onto the roof so as not to lose the umbrella. He had time for a single yell as he tumbled sideways into the darkness.

The man with the pistol spun and ducked. He had a steadying grip on the cargo net, and once again, I was staring up at a gun barrel.

"What in the name of God did you just do? Smitty had a family, you heinous bitch. You fucking Brits. If you can't take it at gunpoint, you'll take it by deception and laugh at the victims for being easy marks."

I tried to sink into the roof of the van, to provide a small a target as possible. Zoe had her eyes screwed shut and both hands twisted into the ropes of the cargo net.

The man levered himself upright.

"Fuck this country, and fuck you especially."

The twisting rope ladder wrapped itself round his right arm. He pivoted away from me, trying to free himself without being pulled into the air, and the grapple walloped him square in the face with a wet crunch. He hung in space as the dirigible pulled away, like a rag doll swung from one arm by a toddler.

I scrambled over to Zoe. She tried to twist away without letting go of the cargo net when I touched her shoulder.

"It's me. Olivia," I said.

"Am I still on top of an out-of-control train, in the dark?"

"Yes."

"Bugger."

I slumped down next to her. I was shivering, either because of the cold or because I had started to think about what I'd just done.

Zoe opened one eye. "You look like you've lost a fight with a broom cupboard," she said.

I scowled. You save your best friend from being carried off by airship pirates and...

"Sorry. You're the field agent and I'm the boffin-girl from below stairs. This sort of thing isn't my idea of croquet."

I hugged her to my bosom. Her head was under my chin and I had a faceful of black hair, whipped up by the wind.

"You're frozen," I said.

"So're you. We should get back inside."

"Not without the Jaquard. We have to get the engine back under control before fiery death, and I have no idea how, short of cutting a hole in the roof of the van."

"This is a mail-train, you oaf," she said.

"Yes? And? Oh."

I towed Zoe back along the roof of the van, further destroying our skirts, and vowing that when this was all over, someone in authority would be hearing from my seamstress.

We found Alf mostly awake. I had to push the mailbag netting into position and make a show of returning to the roof before he would consider the idea of lowering the Jaquard over the side of the van, into the net. In the end, Zoe and I lurked by the stove, trying to get warm while making pointed comments about 'fragile womenfolk' having seen off the Bad Sorts whenever any of the big strong men looked like they were slacking.

Zoe followed Bill, Harold, and the sack-truck forward. I hung as far as I dared out of the side door and searched the sky for the dirigible. It was some way behind us but gaining steadily. There was nothing dangling below it, which either meant they weren't going to try to re-board the train but were getting in range for another rocket attack or that they were lining up to drop a full squad of ruffians on us and abandon any pretence of subtlety. I swung the door closed and beetled off after Zoe and the Jaquard.

I caught up with Alf in the buffet car. He was holding a damp tea towel to the back of his head with one hand and had a pint mug of tea in the other. I promised myself that when this was over, I would demand a similarly-sized vessel of tea, and after *that*, people in authority would be hearing from my seamstress.

I sat opposite him and smiled sweetly. He grimaced and drew his tea mug away from me. I rolled my eyes.

"How fast d'you think this train can go?" I asked.

He shrugged and winced. One of the Canadians must have walloped him pretty hard.

"A hundred. Maybe a ton-ten. Why?"

"The Canadians in the dirigible have rescued or abandoned the boarding party and are catching up again. We must outpace them."

The train lurched as I made my way forward. I steadied myself, one hand on each side of the door to the dynamometer car wincing as I realised I'd pulled most of the muscles in my arms. Zoe leaned over the chart recorder, her gaze swapping between the row of inky traces and the loop of programme cards chittering through the Jaquard, like someone watching a vigorous rally in tennis. Harold pointed at one of the traces, brow furrowed. Zoe nodded and circled a finger rapidly, matching the speed of the Jaquard. I moved next to her and contemplated sliding a companionable arm around her

119

waist. Instead, I flexed my fingers and took a breath. There was still an airship gaining on us.

"Is the Jaquard controlling the locomotive?" I asked.

Zoe grinned.

"Yes. You can see from the strain gauges that progress is far smoother."

The traces on the paper furthest away looked like the scribbles one would find in a hard-to-decipher Christmas card, while the most recent ones were either a straight line or a gentle sine wave.

"Can you make it go faster? We're being followed. Alf thinks a hundred and ten is as fast as it will go."

"I think so. Increment the speed on each loop through until there's a proper wobble, then back it off ditto until the wobble goes away?"

I nodded. "That sounds simple enough to be missing something that will cause fiery death. Make it so."

Zoe squatted in front of the Jaquard, staring at something in the middle distance, beyond all the equipment. If I'd not been rootling in my shoulder bag, I'd have done the same. Not looking at the individual holes and not-holes in the cards but at the patterns as they streamed past. I pushed one of my size-0 needles into her left hand. She gave my fingers a brief squeeze, still concentrating on the flow. She stabbed fresh holes in two cards, then sat back on her heels.

I peered over at the chart recorder. Already one trace was starting a gradual climb away from its previous steady state.

I needed to check on our pursuers. I felt around in my bag for the goggles.

"Zoe? Where did I...?"

She raised an eyebrow and pointed at my head. I tugged them down into position, pulling even more hair out, and bounced onto the chair underneath the charred hole in the carriage roof.

The airship was a few dozen yards off to the left of the train, level with the post office van. Although it was sliding backwards at a good clip, they were still far too close. I ducked my head back into the carriage to warn Zoe that more acceleration would be a jolly nice thing when there was a whoosh, a bang, and a pulse of hot air that threw me back down into the chair with a damp huff from the horsehair stuffing and a loud squeak from me as I bruised the rest of my ribs.

I pointed down the length of the carriage and flapped my hand as I tried to get my breath back.

"Guard's van!" was all I could manage.

Harold shot upright. "I sent Bob back there. What–?"

"Rocket!"

We arrived in the post office van to find Bob leaning out of the side door, waving his free hand at the airship. "You useless tossers! You couldn't hit a barn if you were inside with the doors closed!"

Alf grabbed him by the scruff, hauled him backwards, and slid the door to with a clang.

"They, I, railway property, bastards!" jabbered Bob from a heap next to the stove.

"Yes, lad," said Harold. "And what was I supposed to say to your old mum, eh? 'It was all going well enough until your youngest decided to taunt the people with an airship full of rockets. No, mam. I don't know what came over him. No, I don't imagine an open casket would be the thing.'"

I slumped against the wall of the van. I wanted to curl up under something solid and wait until the Canadians were out of range, but until then, they could just take easy potshots at the well-lit and relatively slowly moving target. I slumped further until I was sitting on the floor, legs out in front of me, staring directly at the explosive plinth. I looked towards the guard's van and then back at the demolition charge.

"Alf?"

"Yes, miss?"

"Will the guard's van work as a slip carriage?"

"I don't see why not. You want to try to go faster by shedding excess weight?"

"Not quite..."

"You're a dangerous lunatic. If we get out of this alive, I'm going to have you locked up for the public good. Also, fiery death."

Zoe did not think my idea was a viable concept.

I glared at her, then flinched and swore as another near miss rocket rattled the side door. "If you've got a better idea, then do tell." I could be a right stroppy cow when my life and those of my friends were in danger.

She huffed and glared at the stove chimney to the side of my head. "No. I don't. Your idea is awful, wrong, and expedient." She threw her hands in the air. "*Fine*. Let's make a railway mine."

The demolition charge came with a spool of multistrand wire. Zoe hefted it in one hand. "Who'd like to volunteer to make a big ugly pile of this in the guard's van?"

There was silence. I shook my head and made to take it from her. "Make sure it can't snag unexpectedly, I imagine?"

Zoe didn't release the spool immediately. She held my hand and looked at me, wide-eyed. I couldn't think of anything clever to say, so we stood there awkwardly and silently while the train rattled along and the Canadians loaded another rocket. I shrugged and made a face. What else were we going to do?

I hopped from the post office van into the guard's van. Behind me, Alf and Harold were starting to uncouple the two. At the far end was the vertical iron post of the emergency brake. I looped the long handle of the demolition charge over the handwheel at the top and positioned it so the pin in the trigger mechanism would be pulled straight. Then I hauled out great hanks of wire and spread them as carefully as I could while shuffling backwards towards the rear door. I leaned out into the space between the vans to hand the near-empty spool to Zoe before making a graceless hop past her back into the safer-feeling post van. She found the end of the wire and looped it firmly into the end of the parcel cage at waist height.

Harold braced himself in the doorway. He seemed to have a firm grip on something just off the floor of the van. "Ready?" he shouted.

Before either of us could answer, there was a clang, and the post office van lurched. Harold tugged hard on whatever it was and hauled Alf back into the van by his belt. We scrambled for the narrow section between the end of the parcel cage and the door to the passenger section. I peered round the end to see the wire twitching on the floor as the guard's van retreated in the direction of the airship. Suddenly it went taut and then slack again, followed by a wall of noise and hot air. The van bucked and shuddered as sections of destroyed guard's van buffeted it like wooden hail. There was a second pulse, this one so low I felt it in my stomach more than I heard it, as I was pushed bodily into the wall.

Zoe was gesticulating and looking worried. I shrugged and pointed at my ear. I could hear ringing and muted voices, and that was about it. She rolled her eyes and held out one hand. I allowed her to drag me upright and fell against her. Partly because it was the only way I could hear anything she said, and partly because I wanted her to hold me.

I yawned and leaned back against the sleeper car door. I could hear an old, far off voice in my head telling me I should be more of a lady and cover my mouth, but it was competing with the rest of my body telling me that everything hurt and that some rotter had turned gravity up because I really didn't feel like moving very much.

Zoe slumped beside me and yawned in sympathy, cute and dishevelled. She set me off again, probably looking and smelling like a farmhand by comparison.

"Come on," she said. "Ours is the next door along."

We tottered the few steps, trying to act like grown women, but fell onto the bed on Zoe's side of the compartment like skittles. We lay nose to nose. I felt her breath on my face, and I knew if I closed one eye to be able to focus properly, I would be asleep before I knew it.

"Zoe Harker, can I kiss you?"

"Yes, Olivia, you can."

We kissed. Zoe smoothed my hair back over my left ear while my free hand rested on her hip. After a short while she wriggled closer, and my hand wasn't resting so much as gripping.

A while after that, we came up for air.

"You know, this would be a lot more fun without clothes in the way."

"What would?" I said.

Zoe favoured me with a patient look.

"Oh!" I squeaked. "Yes!"

Zoe and I clattered off the train like excited children. We'd escaped the cable station at Porthcurno after a week of having men repeatedly explain how telegraph repeaters work and how the anomalous signals were the work of Phlogiston deposits in the seabed north of Vigo. In the end, Zoe had suggested they connect one of the signal recorders to a small Ouija board, just to make them annoyed enough to throw us out. No doubt a telegram was already in one of the message canisters that littered Colonel Elliot's desk, complaining of our terrible attitude and impertinent skirt-wearing in the presence of important men of science.

We'd decided to stop for a few days in St Austell and watch the thaw from the warmth and safety of a well-appointed hotel room.

The smoke and steam from the thankfully coal-fired and thus boring engine swirled about the platform. I turned back to peer past Zoe so I could see where the porter had got to with our bags.

"Well, here's a fine how d'ye do."

I stiffened and tried to remember to breathe. Zoe froze, eyes widened. I fought the urge to cower and scuttle back onto the train and instead turned slowly in the direction of that voice.

"You look like you've lost a fight with a grappling hook," I said.

The Canadian agent shrugged, winced, and shifted his weight so he wasn't so obviously leaning on his cane.

"Smitty lived," he said and shrugged again. "Bested by women. Go figure."

I glared at him and half re-considered the idea that had just been delivered by the imp of the perverse. I was not going to be that petty. No.

125

"If you were interested in a short trip, I'd suggest the station at Devonport dockyard."

His brow furrowed and he favoured me with a very odd look but didn't interrupt.

"You mean the depot behind the station?" prompted Zoe, gleefully faster on the uptake.

"I do. It's a remarkable neo-gothic edifice. The transfer bays in the annexe furthest from the station are well worth your attention. I had an uncle who spent several days painting watercolours of various elevations until he was forced to run by a swarm of bees."

"Bees, you say?" The agent grinned lopsidedly and patted a coat pocket. "I believe I have a sketch pad...."

We waved to him as the train huffed out of the station. He did his best to ignore us.

Zoe squeezed my hand. "What did we just do?"

I shrugged. "The right thing, I hope."

"But what about...?"

I picked up my valise and turned to Zoe.

"Fuck the Empire. Let's go to the hotel and abuse their hospitality."

Part II

Flying and Falling

Icarus Unbound

- Piotr Świetlik -

0. Everything's Connected

Tobias Sully moved the slides and pages quickly, his index finger waggling like a puppy's tail in front of a large holo-display. It was all there, the news articles of the *Daedalus* mission, the plague that wiped half of humanity, the forgotten ship's return. As the documents became more recent, they also grew progressively less official. Few mentions in the data streams about the successful return and rescue of the *Daedalus* crew, anything after that was just Sully's compilation of knowledge dug up on darknet or experienced firsthand. The hunt for Benton Hermaszewski by Brunel Corp, resulting in Ezra Stubbings's death. Successful smuggling of the cosmonaut out of the country and the accidental use of the dislocation drive. A progression of actions and consequences in their attempt to understand.

A second holo showed an information map. Recent reports on black op projects, private ventures, sudden changes in corporate allegiance, and unusual financial activity. All was there, yet something was missing. Sully could almost see the connection. Almost. He snapped his fingers, bringing online a third display. There were few places he hadn't dared to explore yet.

1. Pebbles and Stones

"I'm telling you, it ain't gonna work! The amount of possible debris that might end up puncturing the hull and going literally up your arse is humongous. The orbit hasn't been cleaned since 2023!" Crash thrust her finger at the holo. The equations floating in mid-air swayed in reply to the movement.

"And I'm telling you, the system will automatically nullify all exit points that may lead to that outcome!" Benton should have expected this argument. Again.

"Then there's no risk in sending it on an autopilot then is there?" She tilted her head, the first faint signs of triumph forming in her eyes. He wasn't going to back down though, Not this time. Cascades of curls draped over slender shoulders, and chocolate skin showed her mixed heritage. Judging by her temper, she must have had Irish ancestors. Clad in black leather trousers and a thin vest over a loose white blouse, she was just as pretty as when they'd first met nearly a decade ago.

"Autopilot will not replace my experience, and if something goes wrong I'm the only–"

"Oh? Let me quote you, Mister. 'We know that it works and can replicate the effect, but we're not sure why. We're like the cavemen who can start the fire and cook a meal but don't really understand how combustion works.' Sound familiar? Besides, if something does go wrong, you'll be the one needing replacing!" She placed her hands on her hips. "And I can't be dealing with that."

She looked him in the eyes for a brief moment before storming out. The heat of the tropical day spilled into the air conned bowels of the workshop. Crash's ship, a stingray-shaped contraption with double horizontal rotors and an intricate network of copper pipes and cables covering the hull, stood in the centre. It was hooked to an array of holo-displays, diagnostic gear, and power banks. His own corner in the workshop was a strange mixture of technologies with traditional blackboards, a couple of computer screens, and a few large holos. It resembled an alchemist's lair as much as an engineer's playground.

Outside, he could see people rushing about in front of the former Congresso Nacional de Brasil built over a century ago to impress and humble. When they'd first arrived here, Crash said the building looked like a giant 'up yours.'

"Ben!" a deep, thundering voice came from outside, "Are you in there?"

"I'm here!" he shouted back. "What's up, Geni?"

A towering bear of a man, adorned with cropped ginger hair came in, grinned, and pointed at the holodisplay. He preferred a pair of white cargo trousers and a Hawaiian shirt undone at the top.

"Call from home." He looked around. "Where's Crash?" He over-emphasised the 'R's, as always.

"Crash, Sully's ringing," said Benton touching a com behind his right ear. There was no reply. "It might be important," he added then to Jevgienij, "She'll be here in a moment."

"You had a fight again?"

Benton waved his hand.

"I'm here," said Crash, walking in and taking one of the free chairs.

"Hello lovely..." started Geni.

"Save it," she snapped. "I know you're on his side. Just put the call through already."

Obediently, he pressed an ornamented stud on one of the free displays and it came to life, showing the head and torso of Tobias Sully. The self-styled 'information specialist' was sitting in his office in Bristol. Behind him, the view from

133

his windows showed the city at night. The rumpled face of Eddie in his Egyptian incarnation gazed from a faded Iron Maiden t-shirt. Sully's face didn't look happy either.

"This connection should stay secure for a while, but I'll be brief just the same," he said without introduction. "Brunel Corp and, by proxy, the British government just signed a secret cooperation agreement with the Americans and, surprisingly, China's Emperor. One of its points sets out boarding priorities. It doesn't specify what are they boarding or why, but I bet it's nothing good for those that are not on the list. I've seen that list; believe me, it's short."

"Okay. Forgive me if I'm a bit thick today, but what has that got to do with us?" Benton asked.

A humourless smile flashed across Sully's face.

"The instructions attached to the list include launch locations. One of them is Cape Canaveral."

"I see. No more details?"

"None so far. I've contacted a few friends here and there, but they haven't found anything more yet. I'll keep you posted."

"Well, I guess we need to go even more." Jevgeni's bass broke the brief silent spell.

"Right. We'll let you know what we find up there. And thank you, Tobias." Benton suddenly didn't feel like celebrating their nearing spaceship test.

"There's something else. One of my friends across the pond intercepted a brief. There's a Great America's destroyer heading your way. No details on when they've shipped out, but if I were you, I'd hurry." The video stuttered for a moment. "Shit! Someone's trying to hack me. Stay safe."

The connection dropped, leaving the three in worried silence.

"Someone should check on Chuck."

"I can be in Engelsberg in an hour if you'll programme the drive." Crash shot a glance at Benton.

"I will. Get him moved, we can't risk Pentagon getting their hands on him now. Geni, how long before we can launch?"

"Under an hour," Jevgienij scratched his stubble. "We should warn our host." Benton opened his mouth to reply, but a loud rumbling in the distance stopped him. "I have a feeling he already knows. That wasn't thunder."

2. Return to Fairyland

"Nervous?" Jevgienij asked over the com. Benton almost smiled. He had to answer that question every time they were about to take off or do something stupid or risky. Or both. Truth was, this time he actually was nervous. There was so much depending on the success of this test.

"Always." The same reply felt like a calming ritual. "All preflight green."

"All preflight green. Switching to external com."

"Talking about me, were you?" Crash's voice came distorted by the hum of the engines of her ship.

"Of course," Benton replied. Ready to go?"

"Already up. You need to hurry, there are little green men closing in. I'll sort out Chuck and will try to get through to Sully."

"Be careful, my love" As he said that, a crackling followed by static filled his ears and she was safely gone. He checked the screen. About a mile down Eixo Monumental, parts of the jungle were burning. Wisps of smoke also started to rise from a few buildings.

"Let's go," Jevgienij said and started the launch procedures, methodically turning dials, pulling levers, and manipulating holo displays. It was a bizarre combination of para-steam era gadgetry and technology advanced beyond what they were originally trained for. Stylised studs, covered by brass paint, analogue gauges rather than digital displays, all in line with the latest fashion. When he first saw it, he was baffled. It was not his world, it felt cheap and cheaty. But it was the world to which they came back and which they had to make their own. And they did. Especially given that the Victorian era styling, bringing to some minds the veneer of the good old days, was popular only on the British Isles.

"Launch procedures complete. Time to ignition minus thirty–" The controller's voice trailed off, distracted by loud explosions. "Control to shuttle, you have the launch control. I repeat, launch control has been assigned to your panel. Good luck!"

"Control, explain please?" asked Benton, but the response was just static. "Geni, you have the stick?"

"I do. Let's see if we can find out what's happening," replied Jevgienij and connected the main viewer to the outside sensor array. Soldiers in camouflage fatigues were spilling out of the jungle under heavy fire.

Benton looked back at the panel showing the shuttle's connection to various ground systems, fuelling lines, and clamps. Half of the indicators showed green, the rest were slowly changing status as the automated procedures uncoupled the craft from the launchpad.

"What is that?" thundered Geni as the ground shook. Benton glanced at the display. Dozens of birds and butterflies lifted off the trees at the edge of the jungle. Under that rainbow cloud, a steel monstrosity on caterpillar tracks clambered over the fallen trunks.

"C'mon, c'mon!" Benton shouted at the indicators. There was a loud sound as the double cannons of the tank fired upon the nearby building. It collapsed, and the shock-wave made the shuttle sway in its berth. As the final light turned green, Benton moved the remaining couple of dials. "All systems go, clamps ready!"

"Release clamps, we have lift off," confirmed Geni. The shuttle shuddered as the final tethers dropped off. Within seconds, the battle scene below became indistinguishable from the rest of the green canopy. Benton checked the altitude. Just over six kilometres. They were travelling nowhere near escape velocity, but they didn't have to.

"Ready?" Benton asked, placing a hand on the pearl decorated knob, ready to switch the pre-programmed jump sequence.

"Let's do it."

There was a brief delay as the charge from the second generator reached the required level. The crackling sound of the electrical discharges became louder and, without warning, the main display turned the velvet dark of space, studded with diamonds.

"Woohoo!" shouted Benton, clapping a high five with grinning Jevgienij. "Told you it's going to work."

As the shuttle turned back towards the Earth, the ginger Russian's face slowly lost its jolly expression.

"Yeah," he said, pointing at an object that had appeared over the horizon. "But what the fuck is this?"

Whatever the structure was, it was definitely man-made. As they approached, it slowly grew larger on the viewer, with more and more details visible. A spherical shape made of modules and support beams, measuring nearly a kilometre.

Around it, a dozen ships were docked. Most shared the same bulky hull. They all had different national and corporate logos painted on them, but two were definitely Brunel's. Both had the same brass finish as Crash's ship. One was styled after a bottlenose dolphin, complete with fins and all. The other was styled after a diving falcon, with wings tucked closely along the sides and head lowered in search of prey.

"So, this is what Sully was talking about," said Jevgienij.

"Must be," agreed Benton. "But where do they plan to go? The Moon base was never completed, and all that remains of the Mars project is broken and buried under a mile of sand by now."

"There must be something else then."

"Any chatter?"

"No, it's awfully quiet. But I'm detecting faint heat signatures. It's either recently vacated or they have some fancy shielding. I could do an active scan, but..."

"Have they seen us yet?"

"Can't say."

"Better wait then. Perhaps we can get something on passive when we get closer." One of the diagrams spiked.

"I am not sure, but it looks like we are being targeted."

"By what?"

"The station, one of the ships. I'm reading an energy build-up!"

"Loading the reactor. Turn us about, we're not sticking around."

Jevgienij fired up the thrusters and diverted away from the station while Benton adjusted the necessary calculations. The reactor started humming.

"*Job twoju mat!* They've fired missiles. Hurry up!"

"Almost there," Benton took a last glance at the row of equations, trying to intuitively spot any errors. "At least it wasn't lasers," he added, initialising the drive.

They both squinted as the cabin was instantly flooded by the bright light of late afternoon.

"Phew! That was close." Jevgienij smacked Benton across the back.

Benton's lips stopped mid-stretch, leaving his face with a strange grimace as the main screen applied enough filters to show them their surroundings. They were flying somewhere over the North Atlantic Ocean. In front of them, just visible above the horizon, hung a huge cigar shape. An airship. The afternoon sun reflected off the brass coloured hull. As Benton zoomed the image in, he noticed smaller shapes detaching from the Zeppelin. At the same time, the com unit beeped. He considered ignoring the coincidence, but Geni pointed at the active radar screen. There were another half a dozen airships closing in on their location.

"Benton! Geni! Are you okay?" The voice came through on the com.

"Crash? What the hell?"

"You have to surrender. Otherwise they'll shut down your generators."

3. Truth and Other Inconvenient Items

During their short flight to Bristol, Benton and Geni observed the huge machines. They were leviathans, the longest measuring roughly a quarter of a mile. Their bulky hulls appeared to be made from brass, but Benton knew that was just the glitter on top of some modern alloy made to resemble the crafts of old. Each sported a landing strip on the top side, and each had the hull spotted with gun and missile ports. Every one of the ships had a huge Brunel Corp logo right next to the British flag on the fin.

They landed on a strip built on the remains of Avonmouth, near the old docks. The airships accompanied them until touchdown. Two of them gained altitude and took positions overlooking the entire compound.

When they got out of the shuttle, Crash was already waiting for them. She ran up to Benton and gave him a long, hot kiss. Her mop of curly hair, lifted by the wind, gave them temporary privacy.

"Brunel is here and wants to see us," she whispered between kisses, but before he had a chance to ask, someone nearby cleared their throat and Crash turned away.

The man standing in front of them wore a black leather coat brightened up by a yellow vest and purple cravat. The outfit was complemented by a stovepipe hat that made him appear even taller, and neatly trimmed sideburns.

"Good evening, Mr Hermaszewski," said the man stretching out his hand. "You are a hard man to find. My name is Isambard Brunel."

"Please, call me Benton," said Benton, returning the firm handshake. "I trust you don't mean to secretly torture or murder us?"

Brunel snorted.

"Certainly not. All I've wanted all these years is to compare notes and ask you some questions."

"Is that right?" Crash stepped forward. "What about all the people that suffered simply for helping us?"

"Miss Crash, we can argue here all night about whether we had a moral right to act the way we did, but the point is, you are here and, without sounding pompous, the world needs your help."

140

"What are you talking about, and where is Chuck?" grumbled Jevgienij, a vein on the side of his neck pulsing.

"Mr Rogers is safe and will be released to you if you so wish, as soon as I've had a chance to explain what all this trouble is about."

"You can explain on the way to wherever his cryo-capsule is," said Benton.

Brunel looked at him for a few seconds before smiling broadly. "Very well, follow me," he said and led them towards a low building near the landing strip.

Throughout their conversation, a dozen bodyguards stood at various distances from them. Never close enough to overhear their words, but too close for comfort. They looked like the type who could rip a man apart without breaking a sweat.

Inside the train station, Brunel invited them into a tube-like carriage that may have been dreamt up by Brunel's famous ancestor and then decorated by a mad art nouveau designer. The luxurious chairs and couches, and the tables inlaid with mother of pearl and gemstones, seemed to be designed as a statement of status. They sat around one of the tables and, shortly afterwards, the carriage started moving. As it gained speed, the intricately glazed windows increased their opacity, eventually cutting them off from the outside world completely.

Their host poured them drinks before sitting back in one of the chairs.

"So, tell me, what do you remember from your mission?"

Benton sipped the expensive gin and tonic and exchanged a glance with Jevgienij.

"Everything was in the report. I assume you've read it?"

"Yes," Brunel smiled. "It made for very boring reading."

"It was essentially a boring mission. We were the first crew to test long-term flight effects at high velocities. We surveyed one of the TNOs and came back. That's it."

"Ah, but there's so much more. For example, the choice of that particular TNO was not random, and your mission had a hidden agenda. Your vessel was carrying an automated scanning array and probe that was going to determine if the object in question was indeed the source of the transmissions–"

"What transmissions?" Jevgienij cut in.

"The first one was received some fifteen years before your mission launched. The initial analysis confirmed it was of extra-terrestrial origin but no one was able to decipher it. So, eventually, it was decided to send a mission to its origin."

"You're talking about the moonlet?"

Brunel nodded and snapped his fingers. The lights dimmed and a holo projection of the solar system hung above the table. "During your transfer years to Kuiper's Belt, there were a few small successes, but some things were misinterpreted and, sadly, a lot of people died."

"The plague?"

"The plague. There was even talk about abandoning the whole project. And then something interesting happened. The object, thus far travelling a stable orbit, changed course and matched yours for almost six months." As he spoke, the projection displayed the ship, dwarfed by the rock that performed actions reserved for artificial objects. "In normal circumstances, it would have caused a worldwide euphoria or panic or possibly both, but due to the diminished population, only a handful of people even remembered about you."

"So, how come you're one of them?" Crash asked, looking at Brunel with visible hostility.

"My father was a high-ranking officer in ESA and a believer in space exploration. He managed to get access to most of the broadcast, both historical and current, and started working on decryption with whoever was interested."

"What happened to the object?" asked Benton.

"It seemed to have returned to its original trajectory until ten years ago, when you returned, when we realised it was closing in towards Earth on a spiral trajectory."

"So, you were desperate to check what we knew."

"We are, were. It might soon be without meaning. As you've discovered, for the last decade we've been building ark ships in case we couldn't stop the object."

"We have seen them," said Jevgienij, his strong accent conveying even more reproach. "They seem very small."

"So far, we've built a few. There is still time for more. The object won't reach Earth for another fifteen years." The carriage windows lost their opacity, flooding the inside with light. "Ah, we're here. Please, come."

They exited onto what looked to be a small metro station. Lit by crystal chandeliers with walls covered in wood panelling, it exhibited the same extravagant luxury as the carriage that brought them here. Brunel took them through a couple of short corridors filled with people in lab coats until they reached a pair of heavy wooden doors. He opened them wide, revealing a room filled with medical stations, holo terminals, and lab equipment manned by white-clad men and women. The centre of the room was occupied by a cryo-stasis capsule containing Chuck.

"As promised," said Brunel. "Mr Rogers, safe and unharmed. Now, as for the reason I've requested your presence–"

"You want to know how to operate the drive," Benton cut in. "Let the others go and I'll consider helping you."

"Understand, Mr Hermaszewski, this is no longer about me. You would be helping to potentially save the entire world. And think of the possibilities it offers. We could finally colonise the Moon, Mars, perhaps even other systems."

"I'm sure Oppenheimer was presented with something along just these lines."

"I will not argue that there aren't any dangers–" he stopped mid-sentence and went pale. "We've just received a report that the object jumped to a high synchronous orbit above Europe..."

"His eyes," said Crash quietly pointing at Chuck's capsule. The blond American, the third member of their original crew of the *Daedalus*, and the friend for whom they'd risked their fortunes and lives for the good part of a decade, opened his eyes.

4. Icarus Unbound

The following week was divided equally between attempts at communicating with the alien vessel and trying to understand what exactly had happened to Chuck. Theoretically, his catatonic state hadn't changed and yet there were occasional flashes of neural activity all over his brain, and his eyes remained open even though he seemed unaware of any stimuli.

Similarly, the alien ship kept broadcasting on a wide band of frequencies, but it was using a completely different encryption or perhaps even a completely different language than it had been for the last half a century. Brunel kept in close contact with both American and Chinese groups working on decryption protocol, but with no success. They also attempted to send communications to it both in open transmission and encoded with the original encryption. Nothing worked. The ship just hung there, synchronous to Europe's position, invisible to the naked eye, therefore unnoticed by the general public.

"Makes you wonder if they really haven't done anything to him," said Benton to Geni one day.

"The Americans?"

Benton nodded, observing Chuck's empty gaze.

"All the reports we've found said he was like that when they found him. Blaming yourself isn't going to help."

"I know," Benton sighed. "I just wish we could get some answers. Every time we get somewhere, there's just more questions."

Geni smiled.

"Well, my friend, you have just described the essence of life."

"I suppose."

The buzzers of their coms pinged a priority connection. "Something's up."

"Let's find Crash."

They left Chuck with the ever-present team of doctors and went to the Observatory, as Brunel called it. It served as a command centre for his communication attempts. Its round, segmented windows covered most of one of the walls and overlooked Bristol Bay. Brunel and Crash stood by one of the large holo-displays, receiving an update from some excited scientist.

"Hey," said Benton approaching.

"Hey," Crash's gaze softened as she gave him a quick kiss. Her reproachful attitude towards Brunel hadn't faded, but Benton didn't fail to notice a certain amount of respect beginning to form. He'd started to develop it too.

"What's up?"

"Some good news, finally," Brunel said, turning away from the holo-display. He had visibly aged in the last week. "It seems we're now receiving something encoded using our own protocols. We should have it ready any moment."

"Wow, that is news."

A chime told them a file had been received. Brunel moved a couple of wooden sliders and the display came to life.

"This is Earth's science ship *Daedalus*. My name is commander Chuck Rogers. Um... we come in peace and mean you no harm. Can you understand us?" Chuck's face filled in the screen, but Benton and Jevgienij were also visible, smiling in the background. "We are sending you some basic files and hope we can communicate. This is Earth's science ship *Daedalus*. My name is..." The recording played in a loop.

"What the hell?" Benton couldn't remember any of this happening. Another priority connection came in and Brunel brought it up on another display. It was one of the doctors.

"Mr Brunel, the patient just spiked and suffered an MI. We have managed to stabilise him, but I'm not sure he will survive another."

They all looked at each other in confusion. A second connection came in; it was the scientist from the decryption team.

"There was another short burst from the object, sir. It contains a short video and a set of equations. I've sent the file over."

"My name is commander Chuck Rogers. My name is commander Chuck Rogers. My name is..." played over and over again. Brunel beckoned and someone wheeled over another holo display, and when Benton took one look at the equation displayed, things finally started to make a little sense.

"Are you sure this is the right thing to do?" Crash stood next to Benton, observing Chuck's capsule being loaded onto a shuttle. It was a larger vessel than the one they'd used for their test flight. In accordance with current fashion, its brass hull was covered in ornaments, but Benton had seen the technical specifications. It was filled with advanced technologies. Most importantly, its power was generated by half a dozen free energy generators of an entirely unique design that easily fitted in the rear compartment, leaving the cargo hold empty.

"We've been trying to help him for a decade without luck. You've heard the doctors, if he has another attack he won't survive." The capsule was secured and a team of technicians was milling about it, connecting its systems to the shuttle. It would be flown remotely until it reached the sea and then the displacement drive would take it to the coordinates sent by the alien ship. Benton had spent the last twenty-four hours personally checking the drive and making sure everything was entered correctly.

It was almost time. Benton waved at Geni who was talking with Brunel by one of the holo displays showing scans of the alien ship. They paused the video and walked over.

"Almost done?" asked Brunel.

"T minus ten," said Benton. "Learned anything new?"

"*Etoj chuj*," swore Geni. "We cannot even say if what we see is the real shape of that thing. Not to mention learning anything about its interior."

"How big is it?"

"About a mile long, but that's literally all I can tell you."

"Well, let's hope we'll be able to learn more soon."

The chief of the technical crew signalled that the connections were complete and tests came back all green. The shuttle cargo door started to close. When the two halves touched and sealed, Benton half expected to hear a hollow clunk of metal. Instead, all they heard was a long hiss as the seals cut Chuck off from the rest of creation, enclosing him in a private universe, and the shuttle rolled out silently from the hangar.

They followed the craft onto the tarmac. The sky was clear, but the stars were hidden by the lamp's warm yellow light. They stood in a small shielded booth. The large window was holo glass, displaying various items of information at the touch of a finger in blue diagrams that floated in mid-air.

When all that remained was a few seconds, Brunel asked

"Would you like to do the honours?"

"Thank you," confirmed Benton, and he touched the large round hologram of a button with 'Launch' written in Gothic font. With a silent hum, the shuttle lifted off. A pair of zeppelins followed it until the displacement drive's protocol kicked in and the shuttle disappeared.

They were all sitting in Brunel's communication centre, nervously sipping coffee, no one in a mood for conversation, when a buzzer announced an incoming message. Not encrypted this time. Brunel directed it to one of the large holos. It turned out to be audio only.

"Commander Chuck Rogers. Commander Chuck Rogers. Commander Chuck... Hello?"

"Chuck?" Benton moved closer to the display as if that would make any difference.

"Chuck Rogers. Chuck... Yeah, it's me. I think, anyway. Commander Chuck Roge... Damn, this is something else. Commander Chuck... Chuck..." The feed looped again.

"Chuck, mate, it's so good to hear you!"

The reply was a few more loops, then static.

"Is this all we're getting?" Benton turned to Brunel. Crash placed a hand on his knee.

"Give him a moment."

"Chicago... Chicago, is my kind of town..." Sinatra's song came over in Chuck's voice.

"Sir, something is happening to the ship." One of the scientists rolled over a holo frame showing a view of the ship. All along its length it was contracting and expanding in irregular intervals, its elongated shape resembling a delirious earthworm. It lasted for over a minute. And then the ship broke open and unravelled. Parts of it moved and shifted until it finally solidified into a new lozenge shape, tripling its size. Strands of matter began connecting the hollow spaces on the hull. And all that time, Chuck's voice was singing and humming one of his favourite songs.

"I didn't see that coming," murmured Jevgienij.

"Guys? Are you there?" Chuck's voice had a distorted metallic tone to it as if the speaker was broken.

"Chuck! We're here, brother."

"Benny, it's been a while. I... I'm not entirely sure I remember everything, and this is weird. This... this... this... whatever this is. There's so much."

"Are you okay?" asked Geni calmly, but Benton caught sight of a clenching fist from the corner of his eye.

"Geni, it's good to hear you. I... I... I'm... I'm... I am... I am me, we are you... I... I am."

"Can you tell us anything? What happened? Are you in the ship? Is there anyone with you?" Questions came from all of them like an avalanche.

"I can't. Not all... I am here. I am inside. There's so much, so much, so much..."

"Take it slowly," Crash's was the voice of reason. "I'm sure it's not easy. Can you tell us why the ship is here?"

"Hello, hello, hel... We haven't met properly, right? I remember Benny talking about you though though though... It has purpose. We are you. We have purpose. Purpose."

"What is it, Chuck? What is that purpose?"

"Come. Come. Come. Coming. It's coming. It is. Coming."

"What is? Who is? Chuck?"

But the reply was just static. They sat for a moment in silence.

"What do you think your friend was talking about?" asked Brunel.

"I have no idea. I still don't remember anything from our encounter with this thing."

The scientist who'd brought over the holo frame let out a quiet gasp.

"Mr Brunel, we have some readings from the inside of the ship. There's atmosphere forming, and if it continues, it should be breathable."

"That's enough!" Brunel smacked his thigh. "Order the Falcon to get a survey team aboard that vessel as soon as possible."

"Yes, sir."

"You think this is a good idea?" asked Benton.

"Do you have a better one?"

Benton opened his mouth to reply, but at that same moment the main holo frame came back to life. It showed

Chuck's cryo-capsule standing coverless in front of a wall. There were strands of dark matter that seemed to hold it upright. His eyes were closed once again, but the voice that came seemed more coherent this time.

"This is... difficult."

"What is happening, Chuck?"

"I am. I am. I am preparing. I... This... We... are preparing."

"You said it's coming. What is coming?" Brunel stood up. "Do we need to evacuate?"

"Run...Run... Run... Can't... Can't... Cannot run. Help is coming. Here. Is here. We are here."

"You're here to help us? But who is coming? What is the threat?!"

"Old... Cold... Unknown... Unnecessary... Unbelievable. You have to prepare. I, we have to prepare." The holo's receiver started to ping again and again as files were received.

"Chuck, man, are you coming back?" Benton asked, suspecting what the answer would be.

"I, we, us, we will return. Is, are, be prepared."

"We? Wait, what do you mean, we?"

"Look!" shouted Crash pointing at the holo feed from the orbital station. Blue lines, made of electric current, began forming on the surface of the now five mile long ship. Intricate designs pulsated faster and faster.

And then the ship was gone. Without further warning or explanation, it vanished just as suddenly as it has appeared. They sat in a stupor.

It was one of the scientists who finally broke the silence. "Sir, we have received hundreds of files. There are designs and equations."

"Can you decrypt them?" snapped Brunel.

"They are not encrypted."

"What are the designs for?"

"Weapons, propulsion systems, smelting foundries, heavy equipment, medical equip–"

"They want us to prepare for war..." Crash's voice was almost a whisper.

"With who? Why? It doesn't make sense."

"We should make all of that public," said Benton.

"That is not a good idea," replied Brunel,

"I agree," nodded Jevgenij.

"You do?"

"Think about it for a moment. If we tell people about this, we'll have to tell them about the plague's origin too. Can you imagine it? Oh, yeah, there are aliens and they've sent us stuff that almost wiped humanity off the face of the Earth, but it's okay. We can trust them now, let's do what they say. Oh, and they didn't stick around, they've just left a cryptic message and gone. But it's alright. No, really. Do as we say."

"You said yourself, the plague was our fault."

"The public won't see it that way."

"So now what?" asked Benton.

"We do what we've always done. Release ideas and inventions as our own. Get resources and build up a fleet or army or whatever is needed in secret until we have no choice but to tell people..."

Geni placed a hand on Benton's shoulder. "He's right. Now we wait. And prepare."

The Engine at the Heart of the City

- Pete Sutton -

The ornithopters flitted above the town like summer butterflies over a flower garden. Every so often one dipped down and seconds later Madeleine heard the rat-a-tat of its guns and fancied she could catch faint screams. Cally! Her sister was in danger. The dark cloud of the city floated in the distance, its vast jellyfish shape like an evil glyph.

Madeleine was torn. Her feet had rushed her forward, toward her home, her sister, but her head had stopped her at the top of the hill before she could get there. She'd dropped behind some bushes, out of sight. Below, nestled in the bowl between surrounding hills, lay her town.

The raiders from the city plummeted down the proboscis-like ropes trailing from the ornithopters' noses. The town was dead. All that came now was the sound of marching feet, the occasional noise of a kicked-in door, and one or two shots. But what about her sister? They had needed to depend on each other since their parents were killed in the last earthquake.

She snuck closer, keeping to cover.

At some unseen signal, the ornithopters all folded their wings and tumbled out of the sky, and silence fell. Madeleine took another look at the great flying city, the various apparatus – ropes, chains, and other contraptions – that spilled like guts below it, a great dust cloud on the ground beneath, a squadron of ornithopters, the size of gnats at this distance, swarming about it. They were too far away to see her, and the commander of the raiders had not left a spotter in the air.

She checked her gear. She'd been in the bush for a week and had just been returning home when she'd spotted the ornithopters in the distance. She had her rifle with the telescopic sight for hunting. She had her sidearm for personal protection. She had all the means to survive in the wilderness for much longer than she'd already done. She could just leave, if it weren't for Cally.

A new sound froze her to the spot. A long thin wail, a child's plaintive cry. She knelt, a risky move as she could now be seen – if any of the men in long beige coats, leather helmets, and flying goggles had cared to look to the top of the hill where she watched through the rifle sight. They were marching the children of the town into the main square. The children. All of them, or at least what looked like all of them.

A woman in a white coat, buttoned to the neck, dark, thick glasses perched on a sharp nose, inspected them and sorted them into two lines. A man in long black leather, a red bandana tied around his neck, watched impassively with small piggy eyes in a pale bald face, striking his leg every so often with a billy club.

What possible purpose had a flying city for ground-dweller children? She saw Cally at last, her blonde hair whipped in the wind, too far away to see her expression. Thank the stars! She was sorted into the smaller of the two groups.

Madeleine needed to get on one of the ornithopters. She had no way of stopping them taking the children, but maybe she could effect a rescue once they were aboard the city.

She lay back behind the low bushes and shaded her eyes. The behemoth had drifted closer. The sky around it was smudged with pollution, and there was a noticeable hum in the air and the far-off sound of engines. She stared at the multitudinous gas bags – bulging sacs like filthy, taupe-coloured tumours growing from the machinery. The city dwarfed her town. It must hold at least a thousand souls.

She looked back down at the raiders and noted their ruthless efficiency; they had herded the town's children into the largest ornithopters: the troop carriers. The smaller, fighter aircraft were already spiralling into the air, like sycamore seeds returning to the tree.

Shit! She'd better come up with a plan quick. She wormed her way forward looking for an opportunity. The first of the transporters wound up and leapt free of the earth. She risked getting up in a crouch and scooted forward. The second transporter wallowed in the air, a clumsier take-off than the first, but soon rose to join the line of winged shapes heading for the approaching city.

She saw her chance. Each ornithopter, when it lifted off, trailed a landing rope. If she could grab one and hold on for the time it would take to reach the city...

The final transporter, and last of the aircraft, wound itself up and as the wings flapped once, twice, she dashed across the intervening space and grabbed the rope. As the ornithopter rose she was snatched from the ground, still in the process of wrapping the rope about herself and tying herself on. She almost lost hold, then very nearly let go of her rifle, then had to close her eyes as the wind snatched at her as she trailed the flapping machine.

What a damn fool she was. But she'd promised her parents she'd look out for her little sister.

Her stomach attempted to leave via her mouth. Her arms were strained; she'd definitely pulled a muscle. Her eyes streamed, and she couldn't open them to see anything. The sound of the engine above her changed and there was a clank ahead as she suddenly decelerated. Her stomach now tried to drop out of her arse.

She risked opening her eyes and saw that the transporter she was hanging from had just banked and was coming in towards a landing platform. She could see figures below, gesticulating wildly. She watched the transporter immediately in front coming in to land. The one before that was already being pulled out of the way by a small vehicle, using its landing rope.

The same rope on *her* transporter that she was hanging from. She glanced up at the transporter which had folded its wings now and was starting to drop towards the platform. She looked across at the people waving and pointing at her, and she peeked down to see the patchwork broken lands beneath.

A long way beneath.

Like all ground-dwellers, Madeleine had gotten used to the many small tremors and, to some degree, even the large quakes. The floods and droughts were the worst. Despite that though she knew, from bitter experience of trying to farm it, that the land beneath her was hard. And full of rocks. She gulped as her ears popped for what seemed like the tenth time in as many minutes and wondered what her plan was.

That is, the plan she'd had when she'd grabbed the rope. Surely her brain had thought of how she'd get off it at the other end? Nope? Seemed not. Huh.

As the last transporter to land was dragged off by its own little tug vehicle, the one she was hanging from swept its wings open, angled to brake and glided gracefully to the platform. She, however, let go of the rope and hit the platform at what must have been thirty miles per hour and as she was tossed head over heels, cartwheeling and flipping, listening to some bone or other splintering, congratulated herself. What an excellent plan. As she sailed off the platform, she wondered what it'd be like to fall thousands of feet and whether she'd still be awake when she hit the ground.

And then a massive dirty taupe wall slammed into her and she bounced, and it wasn't as bone-jarring or splintering as the previous thing she'd bounced off. And then there was blue sky wheeling, and taupe and then she bounced again. It was her leg; her leg had splintered. And a shoulder. And a rib. Maybe more than one rib. And she bounced again and there was webbing in front of her face and she grabbed for it with both arms which flipped her one hundred and eighty degrees and almost ripped her arms from their sockets. She felt something else snap. She came to a stop. She turned her head, threw up, and passed out.

Madeleine swam in and out of consciousness. Two fat men smelling of diesel and sweat carried her gently. Parts of her screamed, her body telling her that there was something badly wrong in many places; that broken rib stabbed her with every breath she took.

Her eyes drifted closed without her volition.

"And she's off to sleep again. Probably for the best. She'll need a lot of mending..."

Whatever the man went on to say she didn't know; her consciousness was shut off like a door slammed shut.

Next, she woke in a small room, greasy walls, windowless, a soft hum and distant ratchet sounds and a faraway murmur of speech. She had no feeling.

"Now then, don't try and move, you won't be able to. You've been banged up pretty good. We got the doc to shoot you full of no-pain. You'll be numb for a while," one of the fat men, the ones who'd been carrying her, said. She felt ill again but couldn't keep her eyes open and spiralled back into darkness.

When she came to for a third time, the men in overalls had gone and the woman she'd seen in her town, the one in a buttoned-up white coat, appraised her professionally. Without the dark glasses, the woman's eyes were a surprising violet.

Madeleine groaned, she was trying to ask a question. The doctor, for such she seemed to be, straightened and talked across Madeleine to someone on her other side. Madeleine couldn't move to see who it was.

"I can save her. Maybe even the leg," the doctor said.

"Forget the leg, she doesn't need to walk where she's going." The voice was syrupy, high, with an odd catch, as though the speaker was breathing in when speaking.

"The Laboratory?" the doctor asked.

"I think not. This one is not a breeder, I think. Too skinny."

"The machine then?"

"Small hands. Yes, the machine." Apparently the conversation was over as the doctor bent to do something down Madeleine's body, out of sight.

The machine?

When next she woke, she was aware of the deep thrum of the city, of dimly felt movement, and realised that she'd had no awareness of time for a while. How long had she been here? How long had she been out? She could remember an all-encompassing redness, and her throat was sore. She vaguely remembered vomiting up a slippery eel?

"She's awake," the doctor's voice said from somewhere behind her. "I've dialled down the meds, so she should be fully awake by the time you get her to the machine." Madeleine found she could move.

Rough hands grabbed her and she was lifted bodily from the bed, and the room spun as she was swung into a fireman's lift. She came face to butt with a wide overalled back. Her dangling arms were skeletal, wasted. They were also, like the rest of her body, tingling. Sensation returning, like fire ants let loose in her veins.

Her ride took her deeper into the city. Down long staircases, along filthy metal corridors, and as they travelled, the sound of the machine grew.

Giant pistons thrusting, the clank of gears, the hiss of steam. The engine at the heart of the city was monstrous. Few buildings on the ground could match its girth, none could match its height. It was the heart of the city that pumped the gas that kept it afloat. Small hands, small bodies were needed to keep the machine clean, to keep it working. But the machine consumed them – illness and accident constantly thinned the ranks of the children who worked upon it. The city raided a new surface town every few months. All this Madeleine came to know later.

The man who'd carried her through the bowels of the city unceremoniously dumped her in a room full of sleeping children, painted black and anonymous with soot. By that time, Madeleine was in agony. Her guts churned, awakened from their drugged slumber, her leg a rod of fire. She drew her skirt up to stare in horror at her legs.

The right looked fairly normal, scarred and a bit thinner than she was used to; she must have lost weight while bedridden. The left was a real horror show: stick-thin and angry red, criss-crossed with scars and knobbly like the branch of a tree. She couldn't look away.

She tried to move it. It kind of jiggled, a little. She put all her effort into lifting her ankle, sweat beads struck out of her forehead, but it no longer obeyed her. Once the first sob took her, she was lost in a flood of tears.

"Don't worry," a small voice said, "we're the lucky ones. At least they didn't take you to the labs." Through her tears, Madeleine saw a gamine face, black with grease, only the teeth and whites of the eyes shining in the uncertain light. "There are lots of crutches," the child said. "And mostly you have to crawl when you're in the machine."

"They mentioned the labs. What are they?" she asked the girl.

"A bad place, no-one who goes in comes out. They do bad things to you there, fill you full of poison, or disease, or babies, or worse." The child, having delivered this news shuffled back to where she'd been sleeping and rolled over.

A couple of days later, Madeleine watched as that same girl was killed having mistimed her dash between the pistons. The machine was ravenous.

Slowly Madeleine learned the various tasks. The machine was never allowed to rest because without it the city would sink to the ground. An unimaginable amount of gas was generated and pumped, and an army of engineers swarmed over the workings. The children, and a few adults, were required to get inside the machine, small bodies – or thin ones, like Madeleine's, slipped and squirmed inside it, keeping it greased and removing any obstructive materials.

Really, it was more than one machine. The gas was generated by electrolysis driven by batteries but pumped using a great steam engine with two massive cylinders, one under high pressure, with a second, larger, lower pressure one to re-use the steam. Of course, the steam engine needed fuel to run the pumps and charge the batteries, and there was a constant stream of ornithopters that stripped the countryside of anything that would burn. There was a store of coal, but virtually no one mined anymore so it was conserved for emergencies.

Madeleine's exhausting days lasted a nightmare length of time. It was difficult to make any sort of relationship with the army of soot-blackened children. Everyone had to be hyper-vigilant when inside the machinery, any slight misstep could lead to a limb being crushed, a digit being snipped, or a child being horribly mangled or squashed by a moving part. Just more obstructive materials to be removed. And afterwards, everyone was too exhausted to do more than eat the thin gruel they were fed and curl up and sleep.

She'd asked about Cally, of course; she'd even, she thought, spoken to some children from her own town. It seemed likely that the group that Cally had been assigned to was destined for the laboratories. Madeleine found herself, in the rare moments when she could think clearly, pondering escape. She'd become adept at getting around on her crutches. Many who worked the machine had missing limbs.

She'd a worm's eye view of the machine, but from what she'd seen inside it and the times they'd taken her high up on it, she thought she'd be able to work out how to disable it. If she could breach one of the cylinders then the pistons would fall silent and the city would drift. A few vents opened would bring it to ground. Of course, she'd also have to disable the backup system.

Other plans she contemplated involved hijacking an ornithopter or hitching a ride, like she had done to get on board. But first, she'd have to find out where Cally was and rescue her. If she was even still alive. But how to get out of the machine? As she was contemplating this, waiting for her turn to scoot through a tricky bit of the machine, her thoughts were interrupted by a high-pitched screaming. The machine never stopped but workers were often reassigned to clear blockages caused by other workers. This time, the overseer pointed at Madeleine with his whip, and she shuffled towards the screeching child, its arm crushed within a piece of machinery.

The first priority was getting the machine clear and they were not permitted to be delicate, so she yanked the boy as hard as she could. There was a crunching, like a dog chewing a bone, and the boy slid out of the machinery. Well, most of him did. Runners, children who'd a full complement of limbs, chosen for this task, grabbed a stretcher and the boy was manhandled out of the machine. He'd get a few days to recover in the infirmary and then he'd be back. Madeleine had an idea.

She couldn't give herself time to think about it. The leg was useless anyway. She took a deep breath as the piston rose then shoved her leg in place and let the breath out and took another as the piston fell. The leg may have been useless, but it still had feeling. As the piston's vast weight fell upon it, Madeleine braced and squeezed her eyes shut, and wasn't even vaguely prepared for the crunch – felt, heard, experienced full-body. Her agonised scream brought a rescuer who bundled her away from the piston and through the bowels of the machine. She fainted, which was a blessing, but awoke as they roughly shoved her into the stretcher. She caught a brief glimpse of her leg. Of where her leg used to be – the knee a glistening nub of ruined flesh, blood pumping. Someone had tied a belt around her thigh. She fell back with a sob, she begged for no-pain. The children assigned to the task lifted the stretcher and drunken-walked her to the infirmary.

"It was only a matter of time before I saw you again," the doctor said fussing over a flip chart. "The ones that go to the machine always end up here, eventually." The doctor placed the paperwork on the end of the bed and lifted her dark glasses to her forehead and pinched the bridge of her nose. "You'll be here much less time than you were in the hospital, you should be thankful for that." She smiled a glacial smile and squeaked out of the room on rubber boots.

162

Madeleine groaned and lay back against the pile of pillows. The infirmary was darker and less clean than the hospital where she'd recovered from her previous injuries. But it was, she knew, almost next door to the laboratories. The room contained a number of beds, some occupied, some empty. Outside lay an office where the doctor filled in paperwork. If Madeleine could get at that paperwork, she should be able to find out about Cally.

No one could tell her what went on in the lab, just that it was terrible. If Cally had been taken there, she'd have been there for a couple of months; what could they have done to her in that time?

After surgery, they shot Madeleine full of drugs and she swam in seas of darkness for days. Once the meds were withdrawn, despite her still being in great pain, they prepared her for a return to the machine. She only had the briefest window to put in action the second part of her plan.

Deep in the night, she watched as the nurse on duty bustled about her duties. Madeleine had been sleeping during the day and staying awake at night and knew that when the nurse cleaned the instruments she'd have a brief opportunity to get into the office and from the office to the lab.

As the nurse disappeared to run the autoclave, Madeleine slipped out of bed. Taking great care not to knock her stump, she crawled to the orthopaedics cupboard and liberated two crutches. She was adept at using crutches, and she found that losing the leg actually made her more nimble upon them now she wasn't dragging it behind her. It throbbed with phantom limb pain though. As she stood, she noticed that two of the children in the beds were now awake. She raised a finger to her lips. They stared, wide-eyed, but made no sound.

As quietly as she could, she made her way into the office and opened the great ledger she'd seen the doctor writing in. She flicked backwards to a time before she'd entered the city and then forwards again more slowly, looking for Cally's name. And there it was, amidst many other children Madeleine knew that just said 'machine' – her name and vital statistics and 'Laboratory 4.' Madeleine had a destination. She put the ledger back where she found it and scooted back to her bed, after returning the crutches. The next night, she'd be in the Laboratory.

The Laboratory glowed eerily, the only light coming from gas burners and lighted vats full of brownish liquid. Madeleine crouched by a stainless steel table, her crutches hidden beneath it, as the tock of hard shoes against the metal floor came closer.

She'd not been discovered last night and had managed to escape again tonight. The lab had been open, surprisingly, and she'd slipped in. She'd now discovered that the lab was open because there was someone inside. A bank of shiny metal tables filled the centre of the room, and the outside walls were hidden by large vats, some glass, some metal. The room's L shape had saved her from discovery as she'd heard the person moving around before he, or she, could see her. But now she'd become trapped as the nurse had returned to the infirmary. It was only a matter of time before the nurse discovered that the bed Madeleine was supposed to be recuperating in was empty.

Retorts, flasks, and other chemical paraphernalia lay in an apparent pattern on top of the tables and distorted what Madeleine could see of the room. The person walking about, occasionally taking something from a cupboard, sometimes in view, wore dark clothing. Madeleine suspected it wasn't the doctor. She needed to see around the corner. So far, Laboratory 4 didn't seem to contain any children at all.

She shuffled across to the end of the bench and elbow walked across the room until she could see what was going on. Around the L-shaped corner were cages. Cages with children in. Pacing up and down before the cages was the pig-faced man in leather. She couldn't see Cally, or at least none of the children in the cages looked like her sister. She had to get closer.

She crept to the wall and hid behind a vat. Keeping an eye out for trouble, she glanced at the vat and recoiled. Inside, floating free but obviously dead, was a pickled child, and another and then she saw all the glass vats had dead, vivisected children within. She scrambled backwards in horror and slammed into a table, sending glassware scattering to the floor.

The child catcher strode out from where the cages lined the walls and spotted her.

"What are you doing here?" he snarled in his high, syrupy voice.

"What... what is this?" Madeleine asked, not expecting an answer.

"This is science, girl. The study of disease and procreation, of our decline, of fresh blood."

None of that made sense to her. The child catcher stalked forward as he spoke. "How did you get in here, child? You'll not get out." Madeleine hauled herself to her foot and steadied herself on the table. The man's piggy eyes narrowed and he crept closer. Madeleine picked up a flask and threw it at him. He ducked and lunged and knocked her flying; she slid across the floor and crashed into another table. More glassware fell and broke, and a burner rolled across the table and to the floor a few feet away from Madeleine.

The spilled liquid caught immediately. Vivid blue flame sprinted across the entirety of the floor and up the child catcher's legs. He frantically beat at the flames; his trousers scorched and smoked as he staggered backwards. Madeleine threw one last flask of something at him and missed, but it did shatter directly in front of him, adding more flammable material to the blaze that now flickered higher.

The child catcher leapt back and searched for a way out as the fire spread. His back to the cages, he wasn't prepared for the arms of the children reaching out and grabbing his clothes, his hair, and holding on tight. He fought them, but for each arm he batted away, another took its place.

She watched as the flames licked across the floor, through the smashed glass and chemicals. There was a small explosion, and gobbets of flaming liquid sprayed across the wall. This fire was now uncontrollable. A window blew out and the great taupe gasbag bulged outside. Time to leave. "Cally!" she screamed her sister's name and screamed it again and again, but received no answer. She watched as the flames consumed the room, the screams of children joined by the screeching of the child catcher and the explosions as retorts, and then vats, exploded. Whatever was in the vats was also flammable, and the liquid fire gushed ever closer. Luckily, the room slanted downwards towards the vats but with every one that burst open, the lake of burning liquid expanded. Madeleine grabbed her crutches and escaped as rapidly as she could.

She had seen the blonde hair of a corpse as it spilled from a vat and admitted to herself that her sister had perished. Tears stung her too-hot cheeks as they tracked down her face. At least the child catcher was dead.

Madeleine hobbled as fast as her crutches could take her down the corridors, passing the machine, still pumping, to the emergency exit. Already people were waking to the fact that the city was on fire. The great gas bags, lighter than air but deadly flammable, spewed gouts of flame into the night. At the end of the corridor, people were helping each other into parachutes, and some were diving from the platform jutting out into the cold evening air. The entire city lurched

166

to one side as there was a massive explosion; everyone in the corridor was thrown to the floor. People started to panic.

One of the fat engineers Madeleine recognised from when she'd first entered the city helped his twin to stand. Madeleine clambered to her feet and stumped over. "Help me!"

The fat man glanced at her and did a double-take. She wore a tatty hospital gown and had become filthy crawling through the muck of the laboratory when she'd smashed the vats. She'd also been singed when setting the fire.

The engineer looked like he was about to say something when his brother handed him a parachute. He shrugged and grabbed one of Madeleine's arms and shoved it through the parachute strap. Then spun her and put her other arm through the other strap, then twirled her back and clipped it in the centre.

"When you are far enough away from the city, pull this cord. The parachute will open and you'll fall upwards for a bit, but then come down."

"Down," his brother echoed.

Madeleine nodded to show she understood, and the two engineers went to help someone else. Madeleine tore a strip off the gown and tied her crutches together and shoved them through the straps of the parachute and tied them on. She hopped to the edge of the platform and the icy wind took her breath away. They were heading for the river gorge, sheer cliffs below, the old suspension bridge in the distance. Another city-dweller hurried up behind her, and without time to think about it, she leapt into the unknown. How far was far enough?

Her hospital gown was entirely inadequate and flapped uselessly around her frozen body. Another leaper a little below her pulled their cord and was yanked aloft as if by a giant hand. It was time; she pulled the cord and whiplashed upwards.

Madeleine watched as she drifted through the sky along with other parachutists. Ornithopters screamed past, diving towards the river and the village in Cumberland Basin. A tower of fire flicked fingers of flame towards the sky as the city burned.

The city hovered above the gorge, the ancient bridge below it, the town of Leighwood on one side, the ruins of a city on the other, its name lost to history, now just 'the place at the bridge.' Madeleine gently descended, swinging slowly below the silk of the parachute, stunned by what she'd wrought.

The flying city's undercarriage snagged the ancient bridge and ripped the suspension cables away with audible twangs. Another protuberance on the underside of the city wiped away the bridge's east tower like a child smashing a sandcastle. The bridge twisted and ripped apart the hill it was upon as the city continued its fall. The noise was now indescribable; a monumental sound felt more than heard. The town on the side of the gorge was destroyed in seconds.

The towers and skyscrapers of the city fell across it, the city now mostly on its side, its path miraculously towards the east, mostly avoiding the west side of the gorge that Madeleine drifted towards.

Fountains of river water sprayed in all directions as the city gouged a new course and crumpled slowly, majestically, into the island in the middle of the riverbed. An inhabited island, gone; one minute, home to who knew how many families, the next, obliterated.

Madeleine touched down and sought to disentangle herself from the chute. Others dropped like dandelion seeds to the deep grass on top of the hill by the ruined observatory.

She had nothing. Her sister, gone. Her parents, long gone. Her town, obliterated. Her leg, her possessions, her future, lost. And the death and destruction wrought by her hand? How would she live with this? At some point, she would no longer be numb, and the screams of the children, the women, the men of the city would haunt her. All the unknown lives in the town...

The parachute's straps hung from her shocked hand. But she was free. For now.

Ornithopters circled overhead.

Piracy by Any Means

- Gareth Lewis -

The train station was a place of trapped steam, confined by thick stone walls and crowded with the bustle of too many people. They pressed around him, a babble of insects, their skittering fading under the deep breaths of metal beasts of burden resting from their toil.

Captain Peterson stood his ground, awaiting the government inspector. The red epaulettes on his blue jacket identified him as an officer in Her Majesty's Air Division. He wore the full uniform, with the navy padded airman's gloves. The Colonel insisted the display made government types believe they were welcome and respected – possibly to alleviate the inevitable impression of his own personality.

They were usually first from the train – first class carriage, of course. Yet the current inspector – inspector of what, he hadn't enquired – was nowhere to be seen.

Peterson suppressed any hint of irritation. While he had urgent duties, meeting their guest had been a direct order. He'd wait until the train emptied before returning to report the absence, and hope he wasn't sent to find the idiot. Had he got off in Bath rather than Bristol? It was remarkable how many of them had trouble identifying any city outside of London.

The final pair to disembark from the first-class carriage were a man and woman. Their gazes met his, and they advanced in his direction. Hopefully they hadn't mistaken him for a member of staff.

The man couldn't be an inspector. He had nowhere near the officiousness. While dressed as a civil servant, the suit placed him at mid-level, unexceptional. He glanced about too much, as though having heard of all kinds of savagery occurring outside the capital.

In contrast, the woman's eyes fixed on Peterson with unsettling directness. She led the way, taking a sealed missive from her purse as they drew closer.

"Captain," she said, offering him the document.

He accepted it, having no other response to offer. The seal was royal and looked genuine. It wouldn't be impossible to fake, but that was a concern for senior officers. Breaking the seal, he read quickly. It identified the bearer as an agent of Queen Victoria, to be afforded all aid.

Peterson glanced up, his gaze shifting between the two. She had been the bearer, so he should probably defer to her. Her associate certainly did.

While such a situation was hardly usual, Peterson kept his features blank. He had a capacity for not betraying his thoughts. A useful trait for hiding disgust at the stupidity of one's official superiors, allowing someone of relatively meagre origins to rise through the ranks.

He offered a slight bow – uncertain of the lady's station in society. She wore a dark blue and grey dress of fine, though not ostentatious, quality. An everyday garment that would let her pass unnoticed should she wish, were it not for her poise and confidence, which spoke of breeding. Her dark hair, positioned to appear buried under her hat, was actually a shorter cut when he paid attention. It could quickly be altered to give a different appearance.

Was she a spy? Surely not. Though the document gave no clue as to her identity.

"Captain Peterson," he introduced himself, hoping for reciprocation.

She afforded him a brief nod. "You may call me Miss Rawlins."

It seemed that was all he'd get.

Miss Rawlins gestured to her associate. "This is Winston."

The man gave a quick nod. Was he a servant? Maybe a secretary? What kind of spy needed a secretary?

"We weren't expecting you," said Peterson, hoping to elicit a clue as to her purpose here.

"For good reason," she said, "which I shall share with Colonel Turner. The inspector arrives on a later train, but this was considered a necessary subterfuge for me to gain access without drawing attention. The matter is of some urgency."

An obvious hint to get moving. "Of course." Peterson ushered them along. "Is this with regards to the intruder we captured?"

"Possibly," said Miss Rawlins. "Related to, if not entirely regarding."

Suitably vague. He obviously wouldn't get much here. He led them to the steps and up to the roof.

"We're not travelling by boat?" asked Miss Rawlins. Did she sound uneasy?

"It takes too long," said Peterson. "The river can be crowded this time of day." In truth, it was due to Turner wanting to impress the inspectors and make them feel important. Personally, Peterson considered the smoke over the city counterproductive to creating a good impression, but he followed orders.

He led them out onto the metal-reinforced roof, solid underfoot, with freedom above. It was a relief to be out of the station. The steam must feel the same, as it rushed through the vents and vanished into the air.

The entire structure of the station had been rebuilt to support these airship docks. There were berths for six airships, though only the military one was currently present. The layout was in anticipation of more commercially viable air travel, which as yet remained the province of the upper classes. There were no regular flights scheduled. They had to be individually arranged.

Peterson noted that Miss Rawlins regarded the airship with a degree of trepidation as he led them up the steps alongside the mooring dock. While unlikely to be a novice at flight, she may be unfamiliar with military airships and their more apparent armaments, the cannons and pneumatic harpoon guns.

The balloon was longer than the ship, floating just above the complex arrangement of sails. The vents from the steam engine below were controlled by the ship's captain in the cabin on the elevated aft deck, allowing him to guide the ship by expelling the compressed air into the appropriate sails.

The steps deposited them on the foredeck where they'd spend the short trip.

As soon as they were aboard, the ship eased away from the mooring with a gentle swaying motion. Not enough to upset anyone, surely, yet Miss Rawlins avoided the edges, holding fast to the rail separating them from the lower middeck.

They rose above the rooftops, the patchwork below them highlighting wealth and status by the obvious reinforcements to certain roofs, providing protection against sky battle debris. The wealthy districts had more uniformity, as did the clumps of government buildings. Every district had somewhere the locals could go for safety, of course.

At least the smoke was relatively light today. He could make out figures in the streets below.

Peterson stayed near Miss Rawlins, prepared to attend her while seeking any hint as to what this was in regards to, and whether it would affect him. She was visibly uneasy, keeping her eyes fixed on the horizon.

"Have you flown before?" he asked. Maybe small talk would draw something out.

"Yes," she said, her composure a touch forced. "I had no more liking for it on those occasions."

"Is it the motion, or the height?"

"The height. The part of Essex where I grew up had few gradients of note. Ships at sea I can manage, where the horizon is level. It can even fool me this low, provided I don't stare down."

She made such an ill-advised glance, as though taken in by her own words. While not blanching, her cheeks narrowed.

"And you?" she asked, finally looking at him. "Where did you grow up?" It seemed an attempt to distract her attention.

"Yorkshire. A small village – if you haven't lived there, you haven't heard of it."

She fixed him with her unsteady gaze, which nevertheless managed to pierce his skull. "Then I'd imagine you're good at your job, to have risen to this rank from such a background. A degree of competence that would compensate for your superiors while not threatening them."

"I respect the chain of command," he said. Idle gossip was bad at the best of times and certainly shouldn't be shared with someone whose purpose remained a mystery.

Miss Rawlins gave a faint, and faintly uneasy, smile, and risked another glance around. Her gaze caught briefly on the Scar, a strip of collapsed street around the government building where the admiralty offices had been.

"The result of an attack by the Welsh Free Miners Union," said Peterson. "One of their burrowing machines was used to raid the archives. They were driven away, but they undermined the street."

"The Welsh?" she said. "On this side of the Severn?"

"We're not sure how they got their burrower over. Some claim they must have come under the Severn, but most believe it was smuggled above ground."

The burrowers were hideously inelegant, steam-powered contraptions for digging and mining. The Free Miners Union used them to battle what they saw as the occupying forces in their lands. They occasionally struck over the border into what they considered the stolen lands, but seldom this far. They weren't a problem Peterson had needed to deal with personally, so he remained indifferent.

The airship flew just above the rooftops, high enough that only the defensive towers risked catching it. They were small turrets placed at strategic intervals around the city, armed with pneumatic guns firing cabled harpoons. Missed shots would likely land on rooftops, and those living within range knew their roofs needed reinforcing. The harpoons were ultimately less destructive than cannons fired all over. Should they find their targets, they held raiders in place until Her Majesty's Air Division could board and subdue them.

The smoke eased as they cleared the city, flying over the bay to where the Walking Citadel currently sat in residence. The above-water section was a two-level structure modelled on a medieval castle. It was largely octagonal, around a hundred feet in diameter. Battlements and turrets surmounted the top, each turret having harpoon guns similar to those guarding the city. Turrets facing away from the city also had cannons.

The fortress continued down a few levels, with sturdy legs holding it in place above the bay floor. The entire structure was woken after dark and moved to a new position. A security precaution which made little sense, since it remained lit up so passing ships could avoid it.

It had a small dock on the near side for the occasional waterborne vessel, as well as three berths inside the battlements for airships. Two were currently occupied. These were the immediate defence ships, more quickly available from the Division's airfield a few miles downriver.

Welsh burrowers had no way of intruding on this structure. The only submersibles of any size to be a threat were those of the Royal Navy, which held that technology in a firm grasp. That left rogue airships as the main cause for concern, and Peterson doubted sky-pirates would see any profit in fighting their way inside the citadel. There was no immediate treasure within, and what was there was securely guarded.

The airship docked as gently as it had departed, though Miss Rawlins alighted with barely restrained haste. Her associate followed closely, seeming more affected by general nerves than a dislike of flying.

Back on relatively solid footing, Miss Rawlins was once again the model of elegant poise and allowed Peterson to escort her inside.

Windows lit most corridors at regular intervals, gas lights enhancing them where necessary. The inner walls were wood, but the outer ones were metal, and the corridors the narrow kind found on ships. The design wasn't dissimilar, efficiency of space being a concern.

The command room was far more well-appointed and spacious than the rest of the citadel as it played host to the senior officers. It had more of a drawing room feel and was mostly polished wood. A few tables stood bolted to the floor, surrounded by cushioned wooden chairs. There were even a few armchairs in the corner, though a mere captain would have to be invited to sit there.

Colonel Turner was issuing commands to a pair of aides as they entered. He glanced up casually, his words juddering to a halt as he noted the unexpected presence of a woman. He glared at Peterson.

Turner possessed a redness of skin ranging from ruddy when irate – his natural state – to radiant when his fury was fully engorged. Myths spoke of a night battle won by the light of his rage alone. He maintained a stiff posture which seemed to require his chest being inflated for balance.

"This is Miss Rawlins, sir," said Peterson. He wasted no time handing over the unsealed orders and thereby responsibility.

Turner seldom read anything in detail, confident he'd see the truth of the matter once it slapped him in the face. He glanced briefly at the document, dismissed it, and turned his stare on Miss Rawlins.

It took him a few moments to reach a decision. "You're a woman," he said, with the unerring perception Peterson had come to expect.

Miss Rawlins gave him a smile that communicated an absence of amusement. "Colonel Turner, I'm so glad to see your education wasn't a complete waste of your family's money. But I am an agent of the Crown, with urgent matters of a sensitive nature to discuss."

Turner's hue shaded towards scarlet, but exhibiting an unaccustomed degree of control he refrained from an outburst. Because of a lady's presence? He dismissed the aides but said nothing to Peterson, who took this as permission to stay.

Turner's gaze shifted briefly to Winston. "Who's he? Your secretary?"

"You know us women, Colonel," said Miss Rawlins, her syrupy tone conveying none of the femininity it had no intention of feigning. "Flighty, with no head for details. Winston here remembers everything for me."

Grinding his teeth, Turner fixed his gaze on Miss Rawlins now the menials were catalogued. "What is this about?"

"We have acquired reliable information that a Spanish spy has infiltrated your facility and means to rob you of covert documents."

"Preposterous," Turner said in a dismissive tone.

Peterson was less blasé.

"We've caught one infiltrator," said Turner. "Hardly a Spaniard."

"I daresay a decent spy wouldn't appear to be from their country of origin," said Rawlins. Her tone was calm but unbending before Turner's bluster. "It may be that you captured one of their accomplices among the local criminals. They've apparently employed sky-pirates to aid them. It was one of them – one whose loyalty to his country supersedes his loyalty to money – who warned us. Having confirmed some parts of his story, I was dispatched under cover of the arranged inspector to assist you in uncovering the truth."

The *assist* seemed to stick in Turner's craw, but her authority was such that he could hardly dismiss her. Certainly not with the threat of Spanish spies. Turner's head would be full of ideas of them destabilising Britain as they were believed to have done to France – turning it into a mess of robber barons running their own sky-pirate crews, where the authority of the government barely reached beyond the walls of Paris.

"Miss Rawlins?" said Winston, who'd wandered among the tables. He nodded at one.

She strode to his side and ran her gaze across the documents spread over the table. Then she glanced at Turner. "Colonel, are these, by any chance, the plans for the secret project you're working on?"

"Yes," said Turner. He puffed himself up even further – as though he'd played a role in its design. "The Iron Hawk."

"I see," said Rawlins. Her voice offered no clue what she saw, and she paid the plans little apparent attention. "Given the threat, I advise securing them until we've fully assessed the situation."

Turner drew himself up and turned to Peterson, his irritation, if not suppressed, at least vented on an available target. "You heard the lady. Secure them in the safe."

Already moving, Peterson gathered the blueprints and notes together, removing his gloves long enough to roll them up and tie a cord around them. He had a quick glance at them, of course. Curiosity. While they were often lying about, only the Colonel was authorised to inspect them. Paying too close attention could earn one a reprimand.

He took them to the safe in the corner of the room, all the while following the conversation. The plans would usually be stored in the vault at the base of the citadel, but the safe was as secure in the short term. And while Peterson knew the safe combination, only Turner could access the vault, and his attention was occupied.

"An odd design," said Miss Rawlins. "Is the lack of a deck to counter sky-pirates? To avoid them boarding?"

"Merely an added benefit," said Turner. "You're unfamiliar with the project?"

"I know what I need to know. Although now I've seen them, my curiosity will no doubt cause me to dig."

Turner was quiet a moment, but professional pride overcame security concerns. "It's a sealed tube, to allow it to fly higher. Where thin air makes it harder for crews to travel."

"Interesting. I assume it's intended for long distance flights over other countries' airspace. Have they dealt with the fuel efficiency issue? I can't imagine refuelling every couple of hours will be practical."

"Our people are convinced optimal use of winds will allow greater range. Slower without favourable winds, yet still faster than sailing to reach certain countries. The skies are where power over the future will be decided."

It may improve communications and diplomacy, but commerce would be limited. Carrying cargo was still more efficient by sea or land unless that cargo was particularly light. Too much weight and the ship may not reach an optimal height.

Turner was more of a practical man than a scientist, though. He grabbed onto the few ideas he understood and stuck to them.

Miss Rawlins seemed less entranced by the possibilities but disinclined to confront the Colonel's delusions. "An admirable goal, one we should ensure isn't compromised. Will you permit me to see the captive and question him?"

"Her," said Turner, failing to hide his dismissive tone. "I suppose so."

Peterson preceded them from the room and grabbed a couple of men he could rely on to stand guard at the door. Turner nodded his approval at the move, looking awkward at having a woman on the premises. Did he consider it bad luck?

They descended deeper into the facility, down two flights of stairs to the prison section. Seldom used, it held half a dozen cells. It was dirtier than the rest of the facility and more claustrophobic. All the cells had metal walls with little furnishing other than a blanket on the floor and a bucket in the corner. One was larger than the others, to allow room for interrogation.

The prisoner was escorted into the interrogation cell and secured to the harsh chair in the middle of the room by the pair of guards, her wrists tied behind her back.

Not the most professional of guards. Loyal enough, but rough. And the way their gazes went to Miss Rawlins, Peterson wasn't happy having a girl in their custody. Even one of obvious mixed heritage. Especially one such. They'd see her as unimportant.

He should get more reliable men assigned down here. She was a prisoner and should be treated honourably, no matter her actions. Things should be done right. You followed the code and trusted that those giving you orders did likewise. Else the whole structure collapsed.

"This is Dorothy Peel," said Turner, distaste evident in voice and expression. "An associate of the sky-pirate Haversham."

"That's Captain Haversham," said Dorothy, glaring at him. "And I'm Miss Peel to you." She looked Miss Rawlins up and down. "But you can call me Dotty." She smirked.

Peterson frowned but let it go. It was an improper way to address a lady. Particularly for another... female. Yet her entire demeanour was hardly respectable.

Even under duress, her smirk was slow to retreat. And it didn't confine itself to her lips. It was in her eyes. The flare of her nose. Even her ears regarded one with amusement.

While her clothing may narrowly avoid classification as rags, and she appeared undernourished, she otherwise looked in fine health. Her shoulder-length brown hair seemed free of residents, and she retained some of her teeth.

Miss Rawlins moved to stand behind the prisoner before anyone could gainsay her and crouched to check the girl's bound hands.

"Hey!" said Dotty. "I'm not averse to holding hands, but at least tell a girl your name first."

Standing, Miss Rawlins circled to regard the prisoner from the front. "Not the spy. The Spanish have a tattooed pair of thin lines in the groove between their first two fingers. A means of identifying one another."

Peterson wanted to ask how she knew that but held his tongue. It was the prisoner who was to be interrogated.

"In what role do you serve Captain Haversham?" Miss Rawlins asked the girl.

"I'm the captain's cabin boy." Dotty grinned in an entirely inappropriate manner.

"Boy?" scoffed Turner.

"Yes," said Dotty, pretending offense. "I should not be barred from any profession simply because of my gender."

"Dear God," said Turner. "She's also part of some women's movement!"

Dotty gasped. "Sir, a woman's movements are her own concern, and none of yours."

Turner's shading increased with the strain of holding his temper in check.

"Colonel," said Miss Rawlins, "I seem to recall that this Haversham has never been seen. Is this true?"

"It is," said Turner, audibly struggling to control his fury.

"Then how can we know this is not Haversham?"

Dotty's eyes widened in mock surprise.

"Balderdash," said Turner. "The men would never follow a woman."

Miss Rawlins raised an eyebrow at him. "The Queen is a woman."

"The Queen is not a woman. She is the Queen. And such men as would take to a life of piracy would never follow a woman. Certainly not a girl. And an idiot at that."

"Who's sitting right here," said Dotty, sounding mildly affronted.

"Do you deny the assertion?" asked Miss Rawlins.

Dotty opened her mouth to do so, then thought better of it and shrugged. "My uncle always said I had nowt twixt brain and mouth. Which I never really understood. Because there's bone, teeth, tongue, all kind of stuff between them. I think he may've been a bit touched. What was the question?"

Miss Rawlins stared at her a moment longer before turning to Turner. "Maybe she isn't Haversham."

"Even if she is part of some scheme," said Turner, "they have no means of getting in here from sky or ground."

"Ground?" said Dotty, in disgust. "You wouldn't catch us underground. Well, you wouldn't catch us anywhere."

"Yet you were caught somewhere," said Miss Rawlins.

Dotty began to respond but closed her mouth with a frown.

"The Welsh are less of a problem anyway," said Turner. "They stay out of sight. It's the sky-pirates who demand attention. The skies are not the province of the common man."

"Because we have to know our place," said Dotty.

"You have the freedom of the land, child."

"Freedom? You mean of the rails? Travelling along set paths, like those your kind set for our lives? You can lay no tracks in the skies. That's true freedom."

"The freedom to prey upon law-abiding citizens," Turner growled, his ire rising. "Raid villages for what you want, or simply ignore the debris rained down upon them as you battle each other in the skies. Simple people, who only want to get on with their lives, now regard the skies with fear."

"We never raid the people."

"Your *kind* do." Turner loomed over her now, fists balled.

"Colonel?" said Peterson.

Turner glared at him but relented a step. "They're scum, one and all. Hating civilisation for no reason."

"No reason?" There was a hint of steel in Dotty's voice. "I was six when I watched your soldiers murder my father in the streets. A peaceful protest, it was, until your *kind* decided to change that. So, I had reason to hate. And I did hate. Until I met the captain. Told me there are two kinds of people in the world. Those who define themselves by what they love, and those who define themselves by what they hate. You're a hater." She turned from him with a dismissive twitch, staring instead at Miss Rawlins. "I therefore chose to love my freedom, sailing the skies, and my captain."

"All of which may be denied you should you not cooperate," said Miss Rawlins. "Tell me, what else does your captain say?"

"*Stop that, Dotty*, is a favourite."

"I can imagine," said Miss Rawlins. "Anything regarding your mission here?"

"Or the spy's identity?" said Turner.

"I doubt she'd know it," said Miss Rawlins. "Or that Haversham would. More likely they were contacted by an intermediary, so as not to compromise a cover. They're hardly reliable allies. No, I'm more interested in what they gain by allowing her to be captured."

"Allowing it?" Turner scoffed.

"Colonel, she is not the Spanish spy. If the Spanish are intent on something within these walls, they'd hardly rely on a native thief acquiring it and handing it over. Even if she were capable of penetrating your formidable security further than she did. No, it's more likely she's a distraction, or part of a distraction, to allow the real spy to achieve their ends."

Peterson grew more alert with every word, as the danger became apparent. A glance at Turner showed a slower acceptance, but even he could only deny common sense for so long.

"Colonel," said Miss Rawlins, "I'd suggest increasing security around the plans until we've got to the bottom of this."

Before Turner could respond, the alarm clamoured above them, echoing down the citadel's corridors.

"Damnation!" cried Turner and strode out. Expressing little shock at his cursing, Miss Rawlins followed, Winston close behind.

Peterson turned to the soldiers. "Shut the prisoner in her cell, then join the defence." He followed the others out and up the stairs, hurrying towards the battlements.

On reaching open air, the cause of the alarm became apparent. Three airships were headed their way, pirate colours displayed in broad daylight.

A cannon fired, the shot flying wide of the mark. The ships altered their courses to be more irregular, making themselves harder targets until they got closer.

The sirens echoed across the water from Bristol itself, first one and then more of the hand-cranked mechanisms and their loudspeakers, though the citizenry was unlikely to be in danger. The citadel was the target of this attack.

Colonel Turner bellowed commands, calling troops up to repel boarders, and ordering the docks sealed. He'd soon command that the citadel be made mobile, though hopefully he'd hold off on that a while. He didn't get the chance to issue the command, anyway.

"Another distraction," said Miss Rawlins.

Turner spun to face her, his expression dumbfounded.

"They can't believe they'll fight their way to the plans," said Miss Rawlins. "You should increase security on them immediately."

While he bristled at what was almost a command, from a woman – not the Queen – Turner wasn't a complete imbecile. He turned to Peterson. "Increase the guard, and check the plans remain secure."

Nodding, Peterson led a couple of men below, slowing occasionally to squeeze past troops rushing up.

In the corridor outside the command room, the pair he'd assigned to stand guard were still present. He ordered the men to secure the corridor while he checked the plans.

Opening the safe, he didn't waste time unrolling the documents, instead shoving them under his shirt. He sealed the safe again and headed for the door.

"They're secure," he said. "I want two of you by the safe, the other two hold position here. None but myself or the Colonel are to be permitted access."

They saluted and took up positions. He ran off along the corridors, towards the dock. Opening it from the inside would be simple once he'd dispatched the guards to aid the defence.

That woman could still spoil it. Coming in knowing too much. But she was simply doing her duty, as was he. Neither of them had decided any of this.

She was too late, anyway. The Spanish submersible would be waiting near the dock for his signal. Not as advanced as the British ones, maybe, but it had got this far undetected.

From the sounds above, the distraction was still underway, though there was no telling how long the payment would hold the pirates in the fray. They'd stay out of range of the harpoons, but the cannons would be a threat.

He rounded the corner to the dock doors and stumbled to a halt. There were more than the two guards he'd expected, and Colonel Turner and Miss Rawlins stood with them.

Turner glared at him, incandescent at the betrayal. "Surrender yourself and hand them over." He spat the words in suppressed rage.

A glance back the way he'd come showed more guards. No way out. And little point in a futile resistance. He'd done his duty.

He met Miss Rawlins's even gaze as he took out the purloined plans. "How?"

"Balance of probabilities," she said. "You claim to be from some remote village no one would have heard of – which I'm sure exists; you always keep those gloves on, hiding the tattoo, and you're one of the few senior enough to know the safe combination. You could hardly rely on the plans having been left out when the diversions started."

He stared at her, with nothing left to say. Then he was escorted away.

Miss Rawlins politely ignored the curse that escaped Colonel Turner as they stood on the battlements and the awkward look he sent her on realising he'd sworn in her presence. She'd heard worse, and aimed at her.

"The prisoner is missing," he said. "The girl."

Miss Rawlins nodded. "Maybe Peterson passed her the key or the means of effecting her escape. To provide an additional distraction. I don't imagine she'd hang around."

"She could've swum for it in the chaos." Turner expressed little interest in searching for her. She was hardly worth his attention.

"It matters little," said Miss Rawlins. "The plans are secure, a foreign spy captured. You've performed your duty admirably, Colonel."

"With your aid." He stood awkwardly, as if unsure whether to salute or bow.

She nodded to him, and he gratefully returned the gesture.

Then she turned and led Winston onto the waiting airship, with no hint of her earlier unease. Another officer escorted them to the train station, as decorum required, and offered a polite bow as they took their leave and approached the train.

She recognised the delayed inspector alighting and passed the flustered man without his noticing.

They boarded the train then disembarked down the far side and headed for the back way out of the station. Her stride became less formal as they went, though she'd feel more comfortable in trousers.

Miss Rawlins didn't react as a soldier fell in alongside her, though Winston started.

"You seem to have missed your train, ma'am," said Dotty, wearing a ridiculous grin and an oversized uniform.

"Stop that, Dotty," said Rawlins.

"Yes, Captain. Still say I could've gotten the plans. Even if the memory man there can now build it on his own."

"Push off," said Winston, undoing his top buttons and finally breathing easy. "I can only remember what I see. Having the pictures in my head don't make me no shipwright."

"Leaving the plans let us reveal the Spaniard," said Rawlins. Or Haversham. Or whichever name she chose to use at that moment. "I may not like our government's rule, but I'll hardly accept the interference of another state. This way, they remain oblivious to the theft, and the Spanish to our duplicity."

"Could just've told them where to go," said Winston.

"And not take their coins before betraying them?" said Dotty. "That'd be stupid." Grinning widely, she skipped on ahead as they departed the train station.

They remained free, with a pocketful of Spanish coin, and a headful of secret plans. It had been a good day's piracy.

Dead from Above

- Ben Wright -

"I'm sorry, Miss Iles," Inspector Massey said, "I'd like to help, but I just don't have the men available."

Ordinarily, Mrs Margaret Iles would not have let the 'Miss' go by lightly, but she was asking the inspector for help, so she was prepared to be lenient with him. He had the earnest look of a man who was trying to do a great deal with nowhere near enough.

"I appreciate that this is a serious matter, but every pair of hands I have is busy keeping order at the dirigible stations."

He waved an arm at the window behind him. The three major airship mooring stations were clearly visible against the grey sky, but they were not alone. Every moderately tall building was at risk of having a docking pylon forced onto its roof; sometimes without the assent of the building's owners.

"I'm afraid it's hard enough to retain the men we have. Rigid thinkers at the Home Office are not convinced of the need for Airway Police."

He gave her a sad smile. "I agree that a fall from an airship is the likeliest explanation but probably an accident. That's all too possible with the sheer number of the blasted – pardon my language – things in the air these days. No evidence of foul play. There's really not much more that can be done."

"Hmph," Mrs Iles said.

It was a cunning syllable. It conveyed reluctant acquiescence with the promise that the matter would be reopened at a later date.

"I shall write a report," Massey added.

"I daresay someone might even read it," Mrs Iles said, dryly.

It had long been a principle of hers that, when a task was ignored by the people she felt were responsible for it, she would complete it for them; and do a good job of it besides in order to show them up. She had resolved, even before the inspector had politely but firmly shown her the door, to settle matters herself.

She followed the walkway back to solid ground.

She was unsure what to say to the fishing boat's captain. He was a tough man, used to working a dangerous job in a dying industry and not the sort of person to shock easily. Yet he had been very badly shaken by what he had seen. At least she could tell him that the body was going to be removed.

The body in question had fallen out of black skies onto the foredeck of the boat and nearly caused it to founder. The crew had nursed their vessel back to port and gone in search of help. They'd found Margaret Iles, member of the Women's Police Service in good standing. As a volunteer, she had none of the legal powers genuine police constables had, but the uniform and her insistent manner made it easy for people to forget that. The captain was not callous in being primarily concerned about who would pay for the repairs; if he had to cover it himself, it would be taking food off his family's table.

Margaret pursed her lips. She looked out over the river.

The Airway Police Station was the abandoned gondola of a dirigible that had met its end in the mud of the Avon. The gas bag had long since been reclaimed, perhaps even by its original owner, by the time Massey had sought permission to base his nascent special police company in the remains. In the river beyond, a dredger was working its way upstream, fighting the losing battle to keep the waterway navigable. Only small vessels could make it to the city now. Sooner or later, the port authorities would accept the inevitable and Bristol would never see a boat again.

The man couldn't have fallen from a dirigible from one of the big companies, Mrs Iles thought. *They have passenger manifests and so forth. Railings, too. So, it must be one of the small, independent operators. Easy to cover up an accident. Hard to definitively place anyone aboard.*

This will require subterfuge.

It wasn't that being out of uniform troubled Mrs Iles. Hers was a part-time volunteer position, after all, and she had lived a full and interesting life before the idea of volunteer women police had been dreamt of. No, it was having to dress in the manner of a working class woman that left her unsettled. With neither the police uniform nor the attire that befitted her social status she felt exposed and vulnerable. There were limited measures she could take to protect herself. One of them was rolled up in the waistband of her apron.

Discreet enquiries were placed in a handful of likely places over the next few days. It was nearly a week before there was any answer.

She met her contact, June, in a small pub a short walk from the city's largest airship depot.

"You don't want to get involved with them cloudrunners," June said. She'd ordered gin since Margaret was buying.

"Why not?"

"You can't trust 'em. Crooks. Liars. You think: 'I wants to get out of the country while I still can.' You know how things is collapsin'. So, you pay what they ask and you get nothing. Nothing."

"What did you pay them for?"

"I learn slow. Paid 'em *twice*. I should have known, right? But with no word of my Dafydd I tried to get to America myself. Took me nearly two years to save up what they asked, and once I'd handed it over I never saw them again."

She swore. Margaret did her best not to flinch.

"What happened the first time?"

"The plan was for Dafydd to go to America ahead of me, get set up, and then he'd arrange passage for me. But I never got no letter. I sent letters to the police in New York, never heard a word back. So, I needed to see for myself."

Not everyone who set out for America arrived safely. With the conditions of the Atlantic what they were, as many as one in five passengers who travelled by ship perished in the attempt. Airships were more reliable now but still inherently risky. Mrs Iles tried to steer the conversation toward the information she wanted.

"Who were the companies you engaged?" she asked. 'Engaged' was the wrong word for her persona, she realised, but June didn't appear to notice. "Any of the big three?"

"Not at the prices they were askin'. I never got the names of the second lot, the thieves, but Dafydd made a deal with someone called 'Amelia.'"

"Do you know where Amelia might be now?"

"She still does business out of an upstairs room on Polygon Lane. I tried to have it out with her, but she said she dropped him off and heard nothin' else. Had her bully boys chase me out."

She fixed Margaret with a fierce stare.

"Do you think he met someone else? Dafydd, I mean. Me mam says he must have taken up with someone else but I don't believe that. He's ill or stuck somewheres."

"I think we will both have a better idea what happened to him after I talk to Amelia."

194

It didn't take long to find the garret where Amelia conducted her business. Mrs Iles went straight there from her meeting with June, just in case word got back to the airship coxswain that someone was looking for her. Margaret had only a little time to rehearse an appropriate tale of desperation that she hoped would be convincing enough. She needn't have gone to the trouble.

"To America? I only do America. Just for you? Have you got the money on you?" Amelia fired off a barrage of questions while Mrs Iles was in the process of introducing herself.

"I... I wouldn't carry that amount of money around with me."

"Pity." Amelia looked at her calculatingly. "I'm afraid I'm very busy at the moment. Very busy. Want to make a down payment now so I hold your seats?"

"I said I didn't have any money right now. I might be able to bring some tomorrow–"

"No good. Unless... you might catch me on Brandon Hill before I have to leave this afternoon. Else it'll be two weeks before I can see you."

The old tower on Brandon Hill was sibling to two un-official airship mooring towers, despite the complaints of nearby residents. Living near a mooring tower meant living with the non-trivial chance of a dirigible falling through your roof.

"I'll see if I can do that. Thank you."

Amelia hurried Mrs Iles back out onto the landing.

A short interview but an interesting one. The emphasis on money was not exactly unexpected – venal ambitions drove all commerce and industry, after all – but the complete lack of any paperwork was. *Caveat emptor* applied to travellers as much as anyone, but it was unusual for a businesswoman to care so little about her own records. Unless, of course, Amelia was up to no good and wanted to make sure there were no papers to give her away.

Margaret sought out a public convenience and changed back into her uniform. Her experiment in plain clothes investigation had proved partially successful.

She emerged to see two large men leaving the vicinity, making a dreadful attempt at nonchalance. They struck her as bruisers, up to no good and many different kinds of bad. She had been followed, and it was fortuitous that she had changed her clothes. The uniform was apparently enough to scare them away. If they had indeed recognised her rather than simply panicking at the sight of a volunteer police officer, there was the risk they would alert Amelia. The coxswain might leave the city for good. She had transport, after all.

Margaret wasted no time in returning to the Airway Police Station. She laid out all she had learned for the benefit of Inspector Massey.

"That's fine work there, Mrs Iles," he said. Perhaps it was a mark of renewed respect that he remembered to use the correct honorific. "I'll round up some constables right away. We'll be at the hill within the hour, depend on it."

"Will that be soon enough?" Mrs Iles asked in a tone that made it abundantly clear she thought it would not.

The inspector drummed his fingers on his desk for a few seconds.

"You are right, by God!" he exclaimed. "This is a chance to show that the Airway Police Service is a force to be reckoned with. We've been sent these new whistles, we might as well get some use out of them."

The two of them ran out of the station and across the boardwalk. Inspector Massey went red from blowing his whistle.

They had not gathered any other policemen by the time they reached the hill, but they could be certain that some were on their way. Mrs Iles was rather unused to such a level of physical exertion, and it was only because Massey was quite a portly man that she kept up with him.

The hill had once been a peaceful area of grass, picnics, and birdwatching. Now it was a mess of crowds, cargo, and unofficial construction areas for new dirigibles. The decline of shipbuilding had forced the workers of Bristol into a new trade, and happily for them, the skills needed to build watertight hulls transferred well to the construction of airtight rigid gas bags. The old docks themselves were ill-suited to this new industry, and any open space large enough to build an airship in was at risk of being co-opted by an entrepreneur. Brandon Hill, as a public common, had become infested.

"There!" Margaret caught sight of Amelia in the crowd and pointed the woman out to the inspector.

"She's boarding one of the airships!"

The vessel in question was a small one.

It was not easy to fight through the crowd towards the mooring tower. England's prosperity was in decline, her rivers choking one by one. The engines of industry had grown ever hungrier until their effluvia had blocked the ways by which their food came to them. There was a greater demand than ever for passage to the New World and the fresh start it promised. Once the exodus had begun, it had attained its own, terrifying momentum. Nowhere was that more visible than at an unsanctioned airship station.

They reached the top of the mooring tower just as the last lines were being cast off. The gangplank was long gone, but in her haste to leave, Amelia had left one of the cargo hatches open.

Mrs Iles made the jump easily. Inspector Massey, on the other hand, thought better of making the attempt. Constables clustered around him on the narrow platform as he looked up at her with concern.

"We'll commandeer another one!" he shouted across to her. "Hold on tight!"

The airship rose with greater speed than she was expecting. The narrow hold was not designed for passengers and she wound a rope around her forearm to make sure she wasn't shaken loose.

"I say there!"

Mrs Iles looked around in alarm. On closer inspection, one of the walls dividing the compartments had a crack in it large enough to see through. The adjacent compartment held a family of three who were looking very alarmed indeed.

"Is there a problem?" the father asked. "All we were told was that we were leaving early."

"There are some irregularities," Margaret said, exercising her talent for understatement. "How many crew members are aboard?"

"Just Miss Amelia."

"I see. Please sit quietly until help arrives."

She looked around the hold. Some small boxes were secured by ropes but there was rather a lot of empty space. Two things Amelia had said came to Mrs Iles's mind: 'I only do America' and 'it'll be two weeks before I can see you.' A fortnight was grossly insufficient for a return trip to the

Americas, and it was clear that the airship wasn't carrying nearly enough supplies for such a long journey.

Mrs Iles ground her teeth. The full, heinous truth was becoming apparent to her. Amelia was not just in the business of exploiting the desperation of those wanting to leave the country.

The poor man who had caused the fishing boat crew so much consternation might even have still been alive until he landed on the boat. Dafydd had probably met a similar fate long before June grew concerned that he hadn't contacted her.

Margaret crouched down and felt along the wall. Sure enough, there was a stout iron bolt leading to an unseen hasp somewhere in the passenger compartment. One firm pull and the helpless victims would plunge to their deaths.

Through the open cargo hatch she could see a second dirigible gaining height. If it was under the control of Massey then pursuit would begin shortly. That made the situation all the more precarious. Amelia was likely to try disposing of any incriminating evidence before she was caught. That evidence happened to include three innocent people.

Mrs Iles had never thought of herself as a physical person, let alone one of violence. The weight of fear and righteous indignation was behind her knuckles when she threw the punch, not to mention a goodly quantity of heavy brass. Amelia had just reached the bottom of the stairs into the hold and didn't even see the blow coming.

She was propelled out of the open cargo hatch and into the empty sky.

Mrs Iles's friends and family would have been scandalised if they had learned she'd been carrying brass knuckles around for the entire day, but sometimes proper ladylike behaviour had to yield to practical considerations of personal safety. She rubbed her sore hand and sighed.

This was as good a time as any to learn how to steer an airship.

The Final Voyage of Vulcan's Breath

- SJ Higbee -

"**Y**ou porridge-brained morons!" Betha's voice rang around the crowded cargo deck of *Vulcan's Breath*. "That there is Gaius Tragus Ision of Abona you're swinging around like some ballast. You bust him up, you'll be answering to his paterfamilias."

"Shh, Betha!" Johannes laid his hand on her arm, wishing once more that they were travelling on a passenger vaponimbus, but Master Ision's steam suit was highly visible. No regular luxury airliner would consider him as a passenger, given he was a convicted felon. True, he was a very important felon and therefore treated reasonably well. Unless he was being winched aboard a coal cargo airship...

Ision was dumped on his back in the middle of the deck and released from the harness by a hulking slave with shovel-sized hands.

Betha rushed to him. "Get your filthy paws off him, you great ox!"

"And you open your mouth once more, on *my* ship, slave bitch – I'll rip your tongue outta your head and make you eat it."

Betha's chin jerked up, her red hair flaring around her face as she swung around to face the Capis who was stalking across the deck towards her. What she should have done was bow her head and mutter an apology.

Johannes felt a twist of fear as, instead, she narrowed her green eyes in scorn. Johannes hadn't told Betha of his visions of her wearing huge dresses glittering with jewels, but the haughty look she loosed at the captain reminded him of those images.

Meanwhile, Capis Casio's expression was as black as the coal-smeared deck as he glared at Betha, standing over the Master. Johannes hurried to help, but the metal casing skidded along the deck as they tried pulling Ision to his feet. Hot steam jetted from his lumpy knee joints, forcing Johannes and Betha to jump clear while Master Ision crashed onto the floor again. His predicament caused raucous laughter from the crew taking their cue from their capis, who leaned against the battered guide rail, openly sniggering.

Master Ision, red-faced and furious, bawled. "If you don't get me upright right now, then I swear by Jupiter's bollocks there'll be a new capis on this stinking tub within the week!"

Capis Casio looked across to Specular Robertus Ridolfus, raising his eyebrows. Specular Ridolfus's answering nod sent a trickle of fear snaking up Johannes's back. So, the Vulgate agent was in league with this surly cargo capis. Johannes recalled it was Ridolfus who'd suggested *Vulcan's Breath* might accommodate them when Ision was unable to find any passenger vessels to take them to Syracuse.

As three brawny sky-sailors hauled Master Ision upright, the sense of wrongness grew in Johannes's gut. He leant close to Ision, muttering urgently, "I sense dark forces ranging against us on this craft–"

"With *respect*, Equites..." the capis' tone conveyed nothing of the sort, "...me and my men need to load the *rest* of the cargo. Therefore, I'd be obliged if you'd move along to your quarters."

Johannes's mouth dried. His precognition twanged painfully, and it was an effort not to run back down the passenger ladder and onto solid ground. "Sir. Please. There is danger here. We need to find a safer vessel."

But Master Ision snapped, "Gods alive, Johannes! After nagging me to get to Syracuse with all speed, now I've finally managed to secure a passage you're clamouring to leave!"

A dull-eyed girl with a bruised face approached, cringing. "Pl-please, honoured sirs, I'll show you to your quarters."

Ision hated seeing slaves abused. Surely he wouldn't spend three days on this vessel, under the command of such a man?

But though Ision sighed, he merely said, "Lead on, little one."

They filed along narrow walkways, skirting the coal-crammed cargo holds. Johannes steadied Betha, who was holding Guillelmus's hand as the boy muttered, blank-eyed, "By the pricking of my thumbs, something wicked this way comes..."

The boy often babbled when he was under emotional stress, but Johannes's scrying with his obsidian mirror showed he was crucial to this undertaking, and when Johannes had finally tracked him down herding sheep, half-starved and frozen, his astounded owner was delighted to accept Ision's generous payment. Not that Ision had any cause to regret his purchase. The boy soaked up learning like a sponge and now his beautiful, flowing handwriting rivalled Betha's own script.

Vulcan's Breath bobbed in the breeze on its mooring, causing Johannes to lurch against the flimsy guide rope. Master Ision's suit hissed as he swayed unsteadily – and this time it was the Vulgate agent who prevented him from slowly toppling over.

"Let us hope this new invention of yours is worth all the discomfort, Johannes," Ridolfus commented, glaring at him.

Johannes swallowed, wondering dully what it must be like to live without fear.

The owner's quarters that Master Ision secured for the journey weren't as bad as Johannes had feared, although the narrow bunk beds meant he wouldn't be sleeping with Betha on this journey.

A wind had sprung up, causing the deck beneath their feet to yaw like a sailing ship, creating constant balance problems for Ision, trapped within his unwieldy metal casing. If this was a seagoing vessel, he'd have been automatically freed from his steam suit – a consideration that had Master Ision determined to travel to Sicily by sea. Until Johannes, finally, divined the date for the vital conjunction necessary to their venture, and Ision realised they'd never make their destination in time unless they journeyed via an airship.

Johannes was still in disgrace over that wrinkle, although he'd repeatedly warned Ision that while his calculations and the mirror's visions were ultimately always accurate, there was an interim period when the readings could be misconstrued. Ision often sulked when things didn't go his way. It was a tendency that masters could indulge and slaves couldn't, even when they were co-conspirators...

Johannes supervised the luggage being delivered to their quarters while Ision lay on his bed, rolling within the steam suit as Betha fussed around him. Johannes gritted his teeth, wondering if the Master's faint-voiced protestations that he was fine were designed to appeal to Betha. She certainly responded – ordering the household slaves to provide him with cooling drinks and warmed oils while she tended to every little chafe and blister once the steam suit came off each night. As if he were a sick child instead of a spoilt man who'd indulged in a senseless act of rebellion against Rome, narrowly escaping a terrible death, along with his whole household. Crucifixion. Johannes shivered as he ordered which trunks were to go where. Bad enough to endure it himself – but the thought of Betha and young Guillelmus sharing such a fate made him nauseous. Yet men, women, and children were routinely nailed onto trees and wooden crosses throughout the Empire.

It was only Ision's reputation as the inventor of the infamous fire-jet, instrumental in bringing down the Aztec Empire of Montezuma, that had saved his life. During his trial, when he'd wept in the Senate, guilt-racked over the thousands of Aztecs cremated in the firestorms caused by his terrible weapon, his counsel had passionately argued that the senators should show mercy. The oratory had been favourably compared to that of the great Cicero of the Golden Era. Johannes smiled, proud of Guillelmus and his uncanny ability with words, as the boy had composed Ision's defence for his counsel to deliver. A secret known only within the household. Fortunately, Ision's household was good at keeping secrets. They had to be. Their lives depended on it.

Though the Senate were persuaded that Ision's reason and loyalty had temporarily deserted him under the pressure of his crushing guilt, not everyone in high places was placated, and Master Ision was sentenced to be imprisoned inside the steam suit between the hours of sunrise and sunset for five years. Specular Ridolfus was also assigned to Ision's household, apparently in charge of security – not that he hid his true identity. Ridolfus was far too proud of being a Vulgate agent, part of Rome's feared Secret Service, to bother to act the part of a mere security officer.

His presence was another reason Johannes had been late in divining vital information, for Ridolfus frequently shuffled through his paperwork, disrupting his calculations. It was only his facility with Welsh – shared by Betha – that allowed him to finally get to work, explaining to Ridolfus it was a mathematical language that facilitated his logicwork necessary to design this new terror weapon for Rome. Which didn't stop some of his papers disappearing, but Johannes had assumed that they would, so he'd invented a code using Welsh words as the key, taking more valuable time away from the main task. For which he was also blamed by an increasingly ill-tempered Master Ision.

The battered slave girl cowered in the doorway. "Would Master St-steam-Suit and his retinue come to the bridgedeck to see the ship's disembark-k-ation?" She clearly expected a beating for the disrespectful message she was forced to deliver.

The disgust Johannes saw in his master's eyes helped dissipate his simmering fury. In a handful of days, this child would no longer suffer. They'd come this far against all the odds. Surely, no vile-tempered cargo capis or suspicious spy could stop them now.

"Tell the capis we will be along shortly," said Betha.

It took four of them to lever Master Ision onto his feet as the vaponimbus strained at the mooring ropes, constantly unbalancing him. "Wouldn't put it past the Hades-cursed cur to be purposely revving the engines," he groaned, lurching drunkenly.

"Methinks he is in league with Specular Ridolfus," Johannes muttered, while one of their burly luggage bearers grasped the Master round the middle in order to steady him.

"We may be in some peril during this voyage," Ision announced. "Take care how you conduct yourselves."

Johannes kept his face blank as everyone in the cramped cabin nodded and murmured they would, indeed, take care. Freedom. Johannes rolled the word around his mind, wondering how it felt.

Ision promised that he'd filed all the necessary release papers to free him and Betha at the end of this adventure. Johannes wanted to believe him, but a stubborn nugget of suspicion remained to gnaw at him. Master Ision had been furious when Betha had asked permission to get married to

Johannes. She wasn't beautiful in the conventional sense – he'd told himself so when wrestling with his passion for her... Too thin, too pale, too sharp-featured. But she vibrated with energy and passion. Her facility with languages was little short of amazing and she shared his love of word games and puzzles. Johannes knew Ision had also fallen under her spell but was too proud to press his suit. More fool him. Johannes loved her more than life itself. He would have abased himself by wriggling through mud like a worm to win her affection. Fortunately for him, she'd responded instead when he wooed her with puzzles and word games for her entertainment, while Ision pompously dictated wordy family histories, under the illusion he was impressing her with his lineage and importance. But she was protectively devoted to him, nonetheless. And ferociously loyal to the Cause they were all working towards.

Johannes had a nasty feeling Ision couldn't bear to let Betha go – while more than happy to see him elsewhere, once he was no longer a vital part of this plot. He was uneasily aware that a slave with his abilities would fetch a high price, and that several of Ision's gambling companions had made offers for him. It wasn't a concern he'd shared with Betha.

The bridgedeck was on the lowest level of the gondola, with a reinforced glass plate set in a curving sweep around the bows. It guaranteed an impressive view once they were in the sky.

"Thank you for honouring us with your presence, gentle visitors," Capis Casio's words were respectful, though his insolent tone and the sniggers of the bridge crew spoilt the effect. "To keep us all safe, my commands are law on this deck. You must accept this condition to stay here."

Johannes tensed. The man was watching Master Ision intently, while *Vulcan's Breath* slowly started rising.

Ision had wedged himself in a corner with Betha standing protectively by his side. As if her slight form would keep him upright! He knew why she watched over Ision so carefully, but a jealous pang stabbed him anyway, mixed with a strong presentiment of danger. He approached, hoping Ision would sense his unease, make his excuses and leave. But the Master's gaze was fixed on the view as the ground fell away beneath them.

"Master, do I have your agreement that you accept my authority on this deck?" prodded Casio.

"Hmm?" Ision reluctantly tore his attention from the window and waved his hand, the steam suit hissing at the elbow joint. "Of course, Capis. This is, after all, your livelihood."

"How fearful and dizzy 'tis to cast one's eyes so low. The crows and choughs that wing the midway air show scarce so gross as beetles..." mumbled Guillelmus, his eyes locked onto Johannes, wide and scared.

Johannes shook as swirling smoke surrounded them, coating the back of his throat with a sharp acrid taste. He coughed, eyes watering. And in the time it took him to gasp for cleaner air, they had passed through the layer of sooty smoke and were looking down on it... through it. Onto the gridded city that was Abona, where steam chariots puffed up and down orderly ranks of roads, all lined by villas, shops, apartment blocks, amphitheatres, colonnaded temples, where sprawling factory complexes spewed out soot and ash that smothered trees and bushes, turning them into stunted, leafless corpses. The ribbonlike rivers cutting through the landscape shone in the sunlight, no longer the scummy, stinking waterways he knew them to be. However, from up here, he could see only too clearly the damage the illegal broadsheets were increasingly describing. Despite the new laws forbidding such discussions, store holders worried aloud about falling crop yields and street beggars who used to work the land; they warned of poisoned water and sickening animals.

Johannes swallowed. The pollution below *Vulcan's Breath* was even worse than he'd feared, particularly when he compared the yellow haze in front of him with the visions that regularly sparkled out of his mirror. Of landscapes covered in green fields and forests, dotted with occasional towns of attractive half-timbered buildings meandering along winding tracks that led to solid stone square-towered temples –

The vaponimbus lurched. Bracing himself, Johannes saw the sky-sailors grinning as Master Ision tottered and fell. By the sound of the engines, it was unmistakably deliberate – confirmed by the malicious grin on the captain's face and the sneering folded-arm stance of Specular Ridolfus.

"Master!" Betha knelt beside Ision.

Precognition flickered redly at the edge of Johannes's vision, prompting him to call out, "Elisabetha!" A warning to keep silent. If only Ision would reassure her that he was unhurt, she'd calm down.

But his face scrunched in pain and he whimpered.

Betha rose, as Johannes moved to intercept her, only to find the Specular gripping his arm.

"You better hope the Master is unhurt," she snapped, her face flushed and beautiful. "Or you'll be–"

She was swung off her feet by three sky-sailors in a clearly orchestrated move.

The Capis growled. "I'll not have any insubordination, slave-bitch. I warned you. And my word on this deck is law."

At his nod, a trapdoor swung open in the floor and the men moved towards it. Johannes froze in horror. Waiting for them to drop her onto the decking, maybe with a kick or a punch. For the doors to be closed. For the Capis to gloatingly tell them all that they could go back to their cabin, now he'd played out his little power farce.

Please...

Her beautiful green eyes locked onto his as she held herself still. No screaming. No struggling. "I love you, Johannes," she said. "Make this count–"

They let her go the same instant Ridolfus released him. He flung himself onto the floor, leaning over the edge of the opening, and caught sight of her robes fluttering down, down, through the clouds. A meaty arm obscured his view as he was hauled back to his feet.

"That's what happens to slave scum that disrespect me on my own airship. Hope that's clear to you all." Capis Casio's voice was thick with satisfaction.

Johannes watched the hole where Betha had disappeared. There was a keening, whistling noise. The wind. Which abruptly ceased when the doors swung shut with a heavy thud. *Or is that Betha hitting the ground?*

Master Ision was back on his feet, his supposed agony gone as he spluttered, "What've you done, you imbecile? Sh-she is part of the team. Irreplaceable!"

"I'm sure you can find someone more satisfactory to warm your bed, Sire." The Capis grinned. "She wasn't pretty. Or that young."

The numbness invading Johannes began to thaw. "She was my *wife*."

My world... my reason for getting involved in this madness...

"The thane of Fife had a wife. Where is she now?" moaned Guillelmus, white-faced.

"She spoke and wrote nine languages. Nine!" squeaked Ision, jabbing a shaking finger at Ridolfus. "You better hope your superiors have deep pockets."

210

She was my wife! Blazing with grief and fury, Johannes couldn't recall reaching for the obsidian mirror, but there it was. In his hands. Something fundamental had shifted now Betha was no longer in this timestream. She was important – he'd always sensed it. But the *difference* buzzed in the air. Rasped in the sound of his breathing. In the way the mirror heated and shimmered...

The conjunction had been pulled closer. He'd worked with the calculations for so long they were embedded in his being, so he could taste the changes now pulsing through the mirror.

Vulcan's Breath suddenly bucked and the engines stuttered. Johannes felt the glittering torrent of unused potential in this timestream pour out of the mirror. Could almost measure it, down to the last scrupulum. Hauling *Vulcan's Breath* sideways through the air, which sparkled and flared in whirling rainbow shades as the mirror's stored charge split the very light itself.

"You dog's *mentula*! What're you doing to my ship?" the Capis roared, signalling one of his brutes. He lunged at Johannes who flicked the mirror at the Capis. The man's face bubbled and twisted. Arms and legs bent into impossible shapes. His ribs burst through his uniform. As he stretched his face to scream, his lips folded in half lengthways as teeth splintered and his tongue burst free of the bloody hole that used to be his mouth, still wriggling. Blood and viscera hung in the air, shivering to an eye-blurring whine before seeming to pop into nothingness.

One of the sky-sailors who'd thrown Betha to her death howled and charged him. Johannes's hair lifted from his skin with the energy permeating his marrow as he aimed the mirror at the man's torso. Snaking entrails spilled out from the scarlet gash gouging his belly. The man's face registered wide-eyed surprise as he grabbed at his innards before the

211

deadly stream continued twisting him into unrecognisable chunks of meat that were swallowed up and gone.

Like Betha...

"Anyone else want to end up the same way?"

The rest of the crew clumped together, muttering their surrender and sinking to their knees.

Johannes let out a sobbing sigh, savagely disappointed they'd surrendered so tamely... And realised that he had to push away his grief at Betha's going. Because if he lost control of this, now, the world... its past, present, and future, along with all potential timestreams, could be annihilated. *Do I care?*

"To be or not to be – that is the question," Guillelmus's treble voice rose above the roar of tortured air. He recalled the hours Betha spent teaching Guillelmus, and her love for him.

In the instant Johannes acknowledged that, for him, life had turned into something worthless without her vivid presence at his side, he also knew that Betha felt differently.

Make it count. That's what she said... She didn't mean flicking the whole world into this spinning vortex, he was sure.

"Johannes! What are you doing? You can't... Surely... this isn't the right time," bleated Master Ision, cutting across the muttered prayers, curses, and whimpering from the terrified crew.

"Betha's death changed it all. I told you she mattered." He continued focusing on the calculations rolling through him.

"I demand in the Name of Rome you make it stop, or we'll drop out of the sky like a stone!" shouted Ridolfus.

"Like Betha?" Johannes snapped, breaking his concentration. He felt the stream falter with his surge of fury, causing the gondola to drop, knocking Ision off balance. He crashed down onto the deck, face-first. Johannes hoped he'd at least sustained a broken nose.

"This is it? Your weapon? You'll kill us all!" Ridolfus screamed.

"Jupiter and Jesu – shut your shit-eating gob! I can't think!" Johannes roared, as the potential strained to break free.

And – apart from a few whispered prayers to various gods – the bridgedeck fell silent. Johannes managed to regain sufficient control to check their fall, realising that the air canopy was now a useless bundle of material and the steam engine was damaged beyond repair. It was only the energy pulsating from the fast-approaching conjunction and streaming through the mirror that was keeping them in the sky.

"Begging your pardon, sire," said a hesitant voice. "Could you not turn poor ol' *Vulcan* so we're slicing the air bow first? At this rate, reckon she'll be setting to bust apart."

Johannes momentarily shut his eyes to realign the energy flowing around *Vulcan's Breath*, allowing the gondola to swing round ninety degrees. She spun sickeningly and sped up. Every seam was groaning as the ground below passed in a blur, and an ominous drumming thrummed through the lightweight construction.

The sky-sailor who'd spoken scrambled to his feet and fumbled at the controls. "Need to release the canopy. It's shredded to buggery an' back again, anyhow. An' it's tearin' us apart."

"You do that, acting-Capis," instructed Johannes.

As the man wrenched on a lever, the shuddering ceased while the gondola sped up. Most of the crew lay on the deck, moaning with fear. An acrid stench prickled Johannes's nose as someone pissed himself.

"Knowledge is the wing wherewith we fly to heaven," said Guillelmus.

Specular Ridolfus knelt beside Master Ision. "This weapon – how is it powered? Is your slave some demonic spellcaster?"

Ision was thrashing around in the steam suit, which was whistling. "Ahh. I'm a-fire!"

"Hold still, Master. Here..." The Specular fished around in his pocket and with a couple of quick twists, had the steam suit cracked open and hauled Ision free of it. Just like that.

If he'd done that earlier, Betha would still be here... That thought had *Vulcan's Breath* bucking like an unbroken horse. Johannes had to battle to regain control. Once the gondola was again zipping through the air, faster than a firework, Johannes found he was able to relax. A bit. With the canopy gone, the gondola sliced smoothly through the sky.

"This weapon, Master Ision..." the Specular prompted.

"It's a series of arcane calculations invented by Archimedes of Syracuse," babbled Ision.

"I thought he was the famous inventor of the very first steam engine. And gunpowder and cannons," Ridolfus commented.

"Yes. Archimedes is the key to Rome's continued greatness, that's right enough," Ision burbled. "Do you know that if Archimedes had not made his discoveries, the whole of history would've been different? There's a chance the great library of Alexandria would have been destroyed before all the scrolls housed there had been copied and scattered across all the noted academies of the Roman Empire."

Johannes willed the pompous fool to stop prattling their secrets. Ridolfus was a lot of things, but stupid wasn't one of them.

Ridolfus ventured, "So... you're headed for Syracuse to see if you can discover more about this terror weapon of yours? Render it more controllable, perhaps?"

Johannes nodded. His fingers gripping the obsidian mirror were blistering, but he didn't dare shift his grasp.

"What I can't understand is how the slave-woman was involved."

Johannes's control slipped. Joints groaned as the gondola twitched.

"Shut yer mouth," yelled the acting-Capis. "Don't matter how we got here. We're goin' faster than a sodding cannonball an' it won't take much to bust us apart."

Sweat dripped into Johannes's eyes as he managed to straighten out *Vulcan's Breath*.

"You're speaking to a Vulgate agent," snapped Ridolfus. "You're the one who needs to shut your mouth."

"Marcus," bawled the acting-Capis, "that there Vulgate agent opens his trapdoor mouth again, you stuff your boot in his gob."

"Aye, Capis," grunted one of the brutes who'd dumped Betha overboard.

Vulcan's Breath started twitching again.

"Age cannot wither her, nor custom stale her infinite variety." Johannes was drowning in Guillelmus's haunted brown eyes. "Other women cloy the appetites they feed, but she makes hungry where most she satisfies."

Johannes nodded, the pain around his heart easing to something bearable. *He knew her... he understands.*

Vulcan's Breath started slowing.

"What's wrong?" Ision sounded panicked.

"We're over Syracuse. We've arrived," Johannes announced, shaking with sudden exhaustion.

"How do we get from up here to down there in one piece, Master?" asked the acting-Capis.

Guillelmus tiptoed across the deck, avoiding the pool of piss, and stood next to Johannes. He put his hand on the mirror – in the middle of the energy stream.

Johannes flinched, expecting blood, bone, and flying fingers. Instead, a breath of Betha's incisive logic fanned his face.

And *Vulcan's Breath* was on the ground. True, the viewing panes were all crazed and daylight streamed through most of the seams, but no one seemed to mind as they cheered, grinning with relief.

Except for Johannes, who wanted to throw his head back and howl his loss till his voice cracked.

A vaponimbus suddenly appearing in the middle of Syracuse's busiest thoroughfare caused something of a sensation. Steam chariots hissed as they tailed back in a long line, and interested crowds gathered. It would be only a matter of time before unwelcome official attention would start poking its long Roman nose into their business. But there was no doubt in Johannes's mind that they were in exactly the right spot. The energy flaring from his obsidian mirror had now slowed to a tame trickle of sparkling light motes, allowing him to flex his burnt fingers.

The crew clustered together like lost sheep.

Specular Ridolfus clapped his hand on Master Ision's shoulder as if he were his newest best friend. "What now?"

"We change into the soldiers' uniforms we brought with us, in the style of ancient Rome." Master Ision avoided Johannes glare. "If we want Archimedes to trust us, we must blend in."

Ridolfus's grin showed too many teeth. "Of course. Meantime, I must step out to our local HQ and ensure this craft is left undisturbed."

"You'll probably need to report back to Londinium." Johannes hoped to get the deed done in his absence.

"Don't think that will work, Johannes," Master Ision said. "While our voyage may have been swift, the conjunction has been brought closer. Surely?"

"Difficult to tell," muttered Johannes. If Ision had the brain of a frog, Betha would still be alive. It didn't help that he was completely untouched by her... going.

Johannes swallowed, hoping the lump lodged in his throat would shift. But grief for Betha consumed him, as he knew it always would, while still grappling with the notion that they were actually *here*. On the verge of executing the plan that they'd spent weeks... months... years... working towards.

And just half an hour later, they were walking along *Vulcan's Breath*'s narrow corridors towards the conjunction, disguised as Roman soldiers with their slave boy. Not that Guillelmus needed much in the way of disguise – small slaves from 1,788 years ago didn't look so different from modern slave boys.

The fly in the milk was that Specular Ridolfus insisted on coming. And Ision – may the gods curse him to Hades – thought it a good idea! Even had the gall to say that without Betha, their calculations would be out if he didn't accompany them. As if Ridolfus was an acceptable replacement...

Johannes tightened his grip on the mirror, which was now pulling him onward.

"To-morrow, and to-morrow, and to-morrow creeps in this petty pace from day to day,
to the last syllable of recorded time..." Guillelmus stumbled alongside Johannes.

"What's with the idiot boy?" asked Ridolfus.

"A gifted scribe and bright as they come." Ision was too comfortable chattering with the cursed agent. "Just occasionally comes out with these sayings."

"You certainly find some odd creatures to serve your purpose," Ridolfus remarked with a patronising laugh.

Ision joined in the laughter. Johannes clutched the obsidian mirror tighter, finding solace in the agony flaring through his fingers as the constant tug jagged his blisters, towing their small party to the entrance of the engine room, warm from the fires still glowing in their furnace boxes. He felt a rush of satisfaction when the sight of the twisted crankshaft and broken linkages had Ridolfus swearing under his breath.

He gritted his teeth. It was getting difficult to hold... on... Until the mirror twitched like a divining rod and flared with rainbow colours as the energy nexus sited over the timestream conjunction continued splitting light right in the middle of the engine room, hard by the furnaces. "It's here."

"You sure?" Ision frowned.

"Of course!" Johannes struggled to maintain the balance as the energies shifted and coalesced. "Master," he added belatedly.

"Out, out, brief candle! Life's but a walking shadow..." said Guillemus. And with an ear-sucking pop, the portal snapped into being. In the centre of the cobalt and indigo flickering, another Syracuse could be clearly seen. A Syracuse bathed in bright sunshine, with shouts and screams coming from the streets.

The crew, who'd followed them, started murmuring.

"Fellow travellers, you are witnessing the Britannic conjuror create a magical gateway to the great Archimedes!" Ridolfus cried, his face alight with excitement.

As the Specular ordered the crew to the farthest corner, away from the site of the timestream portal, Ision sidled close to Johannes. "I may have given the impression that we're here to retrieve Archimedes," he murmured.

Johannes blinked. "He'll be furious when he realises the truth."

Ision's jaw tightened. "It won't be my problem. I'll be the one to do it."

"But..." Johannes was consoling himself with the prospect of soon joining Betha, convinced that Ision wouldn't risk his patrician skin.

"Least I can do, after having lost Elisabetha." Ision's voice broke.

"A poor player that struts and frets his hour upon the stage, and then is heard no more." Guillelmus was holding onto the side of the portal. Johannes could see his knuckles whiten under the pressure. "A brave new world. Go. Now."

Ision jumped through. Heart hammering, Johannes stepped in after him.

It was a different time. He immediately sensed it. So did the mirror, which gleamed silver and felt light in his hand, looking like any other reflecting glass. The sun beat harshly off the cobbles, blinding Johannes after the dimness of the engine room. They were standing in a street amongst fleeing, panicking civilians and other soldiers.

But Ision wasn't paying attention as he gripped Johannes shoulder. "Look – out there. How clear it is! And look how the land stretches out into the sea... It's true what the sooth-sayers have been saying – the waters have risen!"

Johannes nodded, although he'd never been to Syracuse before, unlike Ision. However, he did notice there was no taint of coal fumes. No smudge of steam smoke hanging on the horizon. This ancient world was *clean*. He raised the mirror, trying to get his bearings just as an officer jogged past them on the pavement.

219

"You two!" The soldier's Latin was oddly accented and difficult to understand. "Get going before Apelles catches you looting. You know what a sodding prig he is."

Johannes quickly tucked the mirror inside his leather breastplate as Ision saluted. They were standing in front of a familiar building. Johannes had seen its depiction many times in various historical accounts. Ision swung into the villa entrance with a set look on his face, his sword drawn.

A tearing sound behind them heralded Ridolfus's entrance. "Wait for me!"

Johannes plunged into the anteroom on Ision's heels. The villa was furnished in the old style he recognised from ancient books, the walls decorated with frescoes depicting the classic Pantheon. Ision didn't hesitate as he jogged into the study where a frowning bearded man was sitting amongst a mess of parchment with a single cannonball on the desk in front of him.

"Archimedes of Syracuse?" Ision held his sword in front of him.

The man didn't even raise his eyes but announced in ancient, heavily accented Latin, "Go away. All morning I have been distracted by the noise of the Roman barbarians rampaging through our fair city. Give me just a bit more time and I'll have a ball to blow them back to their own sty."

"You've run out of time, sire," Ision replied. "My pardon, for this." And he thrust his sword through the defenceless man.

Johannes dimly heard Ridolfus's roar of rage behind him as the study and the dying man flickered and faded.

A high-pitched whine grew to a scream as the tortured air ignited in a maelstrom of glittering lights while timestreams jumped into nothingness and others reshaped the world into a new pattern. Johannes had known that this would happen. Calculated and planned for it. Knew he needed to recite

Guillelmus's magical words. Betha had realised this was the
boy's role, and she had written down these particular lines to
channel the world into the correct pattern so it was a better
place, with no more Roman Empire.

"To be or not to be, that is the question..." Johannes
howled over the tumult "...for in that sleep of death, what
dreams may come, when we have shuffled off this mortal
coil–"

Syracuse was no longer...

Betha! Here she was...

His heart sang with a joy that was only half-remembered
as he found himself bowing his head in respect to Betha...

Elizabeth...

Gloriana...

"Your Majesty," his mouth said. "I fear I am slightly over-
come. The heat..."

The familiar face, now heavily painted, turned imperi-
ously. "A stool for poor John Dee. Quickly."

He slumped onto the small stool, panting. Under the
heavy perfumes and tang of unwashed bodies was a sweet
freshness to the air. No steam. No taste of coal. And... no
dead-eyed, collared servitors ringing the room.

We did it! No poisoned air. No slavery...

The wash of relieved triumph faded as he became aware
that he was the only person seated in front of his Queen. He
caught sight of Ridolfus...

No... Ridolfi – it was Roberto Ridolfi – glaring malevolent-
ly at him.

Johan– John felt the obsidian mirror press against the
inner pocket of his heavy tunic. Pulling it out, he blinked. *If
I may presume upon your Majesty's precious time, I have discovered
some fascinating scrolls...* the words unrolled upon the mirror,

flaring insistently until he started to recite them, when they faded, to be replaced by other words.

Words from a different timestream. For their brave new world.

Part III

Stranger Ways

Until the Ice Breaks

- Scott Lewis -

You never truly know your friends from your enemies until the ice breaks. – Inuit Proverb

24 October 1842

My dearest Lucy,

God forbid you ever read this, but if you do then you have to know that it's all over. It's cold, Lucy, so very, very cold, and the moment of my death draws ever closer. My pistol looks most inviting, laying on the table before me, but before I pull the trigger I have to tell you why. Why I'm not coming back to you like I promised. I know you hate me, curse me for leaving like I did, but I need you to know that I did it for you. I did everything for you.

More importantly, the world needs to know the truth, needs to know what we've found. It needs to be *warned*.

The first time I laid eyes on her was at Fisherman's Wharf in Boston. I fell in love with her the minute I saw her. She was older than I'd thought she'd be, squat, a little bulbous, and no great care had been put into her appearance. Her paint was peeling and tattered, with long rust streaks from her anchor hawsers, deck fittings and anything else that could oxidise. Yet she was sound and sturdy, and beautiful, in her own way.

I remember how Mister Carrigan slapped me on the back as we looked at her. "She's not much to look at, Fairway, but she'll get us where we need to go. *You* will get us where we need to go."

I simply nodded, taking in every line, every curve, eyeing her up like a brothel madam reviews a new girl. The *Port Hunter* wasn't a pretty ship by any means, but she was mine and I loved her already.

I wish I'd known then that she was as cursed as she has proven to be – her and that bastard Carrigan. But that's the thing about curses. You only find out about them when it's too damned late.

Carrigan was an oaf, but a rich one and frankly any fool who offered me the big bucks he had to take him into the North was a good man in my book. He'd found the crew himself, called them his 'hand-picked bonny bunch' as if he was some freebooter fresh from the Caribbean with a keg of rum and a hold full of doubloons. He was about as nautical as a cabbage, and his constant interruptions and critiques of my proposed navigation tracks were more than a trifle irritating. Also, he was far too fat to be any use at sea, and his grey muttonchop sideburns and gleaming bald crown made him look like a caricature from one of those cartoons in *Punch*. He was also the boss, and that was the worst thing about the man.

When he'd come up to me in the taproom of Perkins' House a week prior and told me what he was after, I'd laughed in his face. Most folk within earshot, including Tom the landlord, had a good chuckle when they heard the Englishman's proposal.

"You want me to take you, with a strange crew and a ship I ain't even seen, up the coast and round the top of Canada?" I gestured with my tankard. "Look here, Mister Carrigan. The Northwest Passage is a rumour, and no more. You might be thinking it's there, but it isn't. The ice is too thick, and it always will be. So no, I'm not interested in taking you up there."

"Then allow me to change your mind." Carrigan smirked, which made his jowls wobble slightly. "The company I represent are offering forty thousand dollars to the captain of the vessel that finds the passage. I'll even provide the ship. All you have to do is help me chart and survey a clear route through to Anchorage."

Forty thousand dollars. Five grand in advance. A decade's salary for a year's work. And all I had to do to get it was take a thirty-year-old ship and a cobbled-together crew on a sea voyage around the top of the world. I was a captain without a vessel, and here it was – a golden opportunity to really make my mark, to make my fortune. If anyone could do it, Lucy, I could. I was overconfident, and more than a little drunk on the ale, the money and my own ego. I signed up on the spot. I admit now that there was more than a hint of arrogance behind my decision to take up his offer, but also I wanted to do right by you. To fulfil that wish you'd expressed, that desire to be acquainted with people who had achieved things. To pay off the debts, and to give you the home you always wanted.

The North-West Passage, Lucy... Can you imagine what would have happened if we'd found it? People have been looking for it since the turn of the century, but no-one has ever made it through the ice. Even airship crossings haven't been possible because of the atmospherics. A mythical golden trade route, over the top of the Americas to Russia and the Orient. The money it would make would have been phenomenal, and I knew why Carrigan and his company were so desperate to be the first to chart the way.

And now here I am, alone in the *Port Hunter*'s stern cabin, with a revolver in one hand and a pen in the other, and all I can think of is how I've failed you. I mistook your desire for self-improvement for a stinging rebuke, a slight on my manhood, and look where I have ended up.

We sailed from Boston on the fourteenth of June, 1842, carrying eighteen months' provisions for what I reckoned would be a year-long voyage, if we had to winter over *en route*. There were thirty of us on board, myself as captain and Carrigan as master. The others were a mix of sailors, engineers, deckhands, stokers, scientists, and a squad of soldiers, decked out in the uniform of one of the British Aether Extraction Company's private Marine regiments.

Anna was there too. You remember her? We sailed together on the *Temperance* back in 1838; you met her at that luncheon Captain Hamblin threw for the crew. She was just the best first mate I could have asked for. She was the only other member of the crew I knew personally, and the one pick Carrigan conceded to me – largely because I said I wouldn't sail if she didn't.

Our route took us north, keeping just in sight of the New England coastline. We stopped at Halifax and St. John's to resupply and take leave – the last we'd get before we reached the edge of the Arctic circle. In Nova Scotia a new member joined the crew, an Esquimaux by the name of Divok. Carrigan insisted on hiring him, claiming that he knew the area we were aiming to push through as well as any other man alive. Idly I wondered why, if that were the case, he and his Inuit fellows hadn't pushed a way through the Passage. But then, the Inuit are hardly one of the great seafaring powers, are they?

The *Port Hunter* was proving to be just the dream I'd hoped she would be. Carrigan's company had fitted her out well, and she scrubbed up nicely. Her hull had been repainted, her fittings replaced. Fresh sails billowed from her twin masts, leaving the newly-installed steam engine to conserve fuel. We had enough aether-enriched coal on board to last us through the year, and if need be the boiler could run on plain fuel further down the line. As we left Halifax behind us the morale amongst my crew was high. I remember standing on the *Hunter*'s quarterdeck as the men and women played quoits, or did exercise, or simply went about the everyday business of the sea. We were happy in our own way, despite the ever-deepening chill in the Arctic air.

The middle of July saw us arriving in Baffin Bay, and we made our final stop in vaguely civilised territory at the Hudson Bay Company's outpost at Cape Dyer. Carrigan took Divok to talk to some of the local Esquimaux, whilst I went with Anna, our ship's doctor and two of the scientists to see a seal colony further up the coast. One of the lads, a husky Bostonite named Frank Ireland, shot a caribou – a large Canadian deer that required a team of eight to bring back to the ship – so we set a fire on the shore and butchered it, joined by some of the locals and the Hudson traders.

We rounded the northernmost part of the Canadian mainland two weeks later, heading west, and it wasn't long before we saw the first vestiges of pack ice. There was something surreal and majestic about those large floes meandering past, a premonition of what could befall the unwary.

I was stood at the rail, watching another of the floes glide slowly down the port side, when Carrigan came to join me. He had lost weight since we'd left Boston, and his clothes hung poorly.

"They're beautiful, aren't they?"

I simply nodded. He may have been my employer, but I still didn't like the man.

"Doctor Cornwallis says that some of the ice is hundreds, maybe thousands of years old."

Another vacant nod.

"We are going to make it through, aren't we, Fairway?"

I laughed.

"Bit late to be having doubts now, Sir. There isn't any turning back from here. Once we get into the ice field, it's Anchorage or bust."

Carrigan stared at the ice floe, then shook his head. "We'll be fine, Fairway. I know it."

As we reached the Westernmost part of the bay, the ice grew thicker. We rounded the northern tip of Baffin Island just before sunrise on the fifteenth of August, and there ahead of us lay the waters of Lancaster Sound… completely unhindered by ice and freely navigable. We celebrated with dinner in Carrigan's cabin – roast beef and potatoes and a couple of carafes of wine. Carrigan hosted all the officers that day – myself, Anna, Doctor Cornwallis, Ginny the chief engineer, Misters Swale, Withers and Harding (my Bosun, Mate and Coxswain, respectively) Lieutenant Timbridge of the Marines, Doctor Nixon, the surgeon. The lads and ladies were all given another half-pint of small beer, and a tot of rum to help fortify against the cold. It was a merry evening, Lucy, and through it all I found myself wishing that you were there with me. Outside on the deck one of the hands was playing a skirl on the fiddle, and there was the sound of dancing and merrymaking. The *Port Hunter* was a happy ship that night.

Three days later we hit Beechey Island, and it was here things began to go awry. The ice was already beginning to close in, and some of the crew thought we should take early shelter in one of the bays along the coast, set up for the winter, and strike for Anchorage as soon as the pack began to thaw in the spring. Carrigan was incensed, and demanded we press on through the Sound and head south for the natural harbour on the uninhabited Prince William Island, where he claimed we would be much safer. He had a point – it would be easier to lay the ship up there for the winter than in the pack itself, but other than that there was little reason why he should insist upon it so vehemently.

It is here I must confess to my first failing of command. I sided with the man who held the purse strings rather than my crew. There were blazing arguments throughout the night as I tried to convince Anna, Swale, Ginny, and Harding to see my view. Withers had the watch on deck but I am sure he would have sided with me, for he was eager to return home. My stalwart employer, rather than backing me up, retired to his cabin and left it to me to face down the others. Eventually, I was forced to raise my voice.

I glared around the room, passionately entreating them to trust in my judgement – flawed as I now know it to have been – and reminding them of the handsome fee that we would receive upon completion.

I looked at them all, one by one. Ginny nodded slowly, Swale turned and stormed out, and Harding followed. Ginny took her leave minutes later, leaving me alone with Anna. I sat down at my desk, pulled out a bottle of bourbon, and poured two glasses.

"Tell me I'm doing the right thing?" I asked her. Even then, I was unsure that I had made the right decision.

"You're doing the right thing."

She was lying. I know that now. We both knew that if the pack came in, we would be in trouble. The *Hunter* wasn't robust enough to handle an ice crush.

I tossed back the sour mash, wincing as it burned my throat. I still hate bourbon, Lucy. Never could drink the stuff. I needed the Dutch courage though – I had another admission to make.

Carrigan had threatened to halve everyone's pay if we didn't make Prince William. Whether it was concern for the ship or his own safety, or for some other reason, I couldn't tell. Anna had her own theory to put forward: that Carrigan was as mad as a basket of frogs.

I poured another, and she and I proceeded to get drunk. In the black night outside, a cold wind began to blow.

The *Port Hunter* sailed further east, and each day the pack grew thicker. I watched it encroaching upon my ship like a cat stalking an unsuspecting mouse, and each mile seemed to bring with it even more certainty that we would be caught like a rat in a trap, devoured under the huge, crushing icy jaws that slowly encircled us. Lucy, I wish I had listened to my crew, my instincts, everything I knew about seafaring. Twenty years a sailor, man and boy, and for the prospect of one single, fleeting moment of glory and a huge payment I forgot everything I had learned. I saw the signs, and I ignored them. Even when I saw the other wreck, I refused to turn back.

It was the glint of sunlight on metal that first drew my attention. I took out my telescope and trained it on the spit of rock passing down our starboard side, a good three miles away. In the lens I made out a warped, twisted metal skeleton, tattered strips of cloth billowing from spars bent out of any recognisable shape. It took me a good few seconds to realise that I was looking at the remains of an airship, one which had obviously tried and failed to make the same voyage by air that I was attempting by sea. It sent a shiver down my spine, Lucy, and I still swear that it was simply another omen that I failed to heed. I could even make out and identify the gondola's livery, as it was the same as that of the *Port Hunter* and my employers – the green of the British Aether Extraction Corporation.

I wish I had asked myself a hundred questions back then that I know the answers to now, and each would have made me turn the *Hunter* around and head straight back to Nova Scotia. I pressed on regardless, and on the morning of August 25th, a mere six miles from the relative safety of the natural harbour at Prince William Island, the jaws snapped shut.

It happened in the dead of night. The sound of giant claws rending sheet metal heralded the moment we first struck the pack. The *Hunter*'s strengthened bows managed to smash aside the young ice at the edge of the sheet, driving her deeper into the cold embrace of countless tonnes of solid frozen water. She ploughed deep, until a full third of her length was wedged hard into the vice-like grip of the floe. The *Port Hunter* ground to a halt, and within seconds the alarms were raised.

Most of the crew rushed straight up to the deck, whilst the engineers made their way for'ard to check the hull for damage. Leaning over the rail, all we could see was the solid pack ice glittering in the moonlight. We were well and truly stuck, and even firing up the boiler and giving her full steam astern couldn't wrest her free of that frozen grasp. Slowly, a hush fell across the deck. The only sounds we could hear were the arctic wind whistling through the sails, and the protesting creak of the *Hunter*'s timbers as they strained under the pressure of the pack's crushing caress.

Ginny's head appeared from the hatchway. "She's sound, Cap'n," she beamed, then her lips twisted into a half-frown. "Well, for now. Reckon she'll hold up, provided the ice doesn't get much thicker."

I called Cornwallis over. The old scientist was the closest thing we had to an expert on the ice floes on board. "What do you think, Doctor? Is that ice going to get any worse?"

The Doctor pondered, then shook his head in resignation. "It's not looking good. Daniel, it's not even September yet. When winter hits properly and this freezes over we can expect a lot more ice than this. That means more pressure on the hull. A *lot* more pressure on the hull." The Company scientist looked at Ginny, who had gone pale. "If my guess is correct, and the Engineer's face suggests I may be, the *Port Hunter* will be crushed to splinters before the winter is over."

The first party sent over the side and down to the ice confirmed what the doctor and engineer had said. The ice was already expanding against the hull, buckling the steel-strengthened bow and causing splintering where it ground inexorably against the *Port Hunter*'s timbers. Initial estimates put the ice surrounding us at several feet thick, making digging ourselves out impossible. I called the officers in to the main cabin for a conference.

I had to finally be entirely honest with them. We were stuck in the ice, with at least at least eight months of winter ahead of us before the pack thawed. We had provisions and supplies to tough it out, but one thing was certain.

I looked around at the faces surrounding the table, all anxious, each hanging on my every word, each given a gaunt cadaverous cast by the flickering oil lamp suspended from the deckhead.

"The *Port Hunter* isn't going anywhere. Not for a while."

The temperature outside had already plummeted by the time we began making the ship into our home for the winter. The crew set to windproofing the inside of the hull as much as possible, and we abandoned the ship's watch routine in favour of something more domestic. It would be important for all to conserve energy during the months ahead. Food and alcohol was rationed even tighter, though Divok would prove invaluable in the weeks following as he showed us how to fish through the ice. For two months we sat waiting, eking out an existence onboard the *Hunter*. On the 19th October, everything changed.

We had just opened our second-to-last case of pemmican rations when Carrigan came storming into my cabin. "Fairway, what the deuce is going on? When will this wretched ice bugger off and let us continue on our way?"

I eyed him from my table, where I was busy filling in the day's log entry. "The ice will release us when it deems fit, Mr.

Carrigan." All pretence of caring that he was our employer had long since passed the crew – and myself – by. Even his marines didn't care a jot for him any more. I pointed out – for the tenth time that week – that we would not be going anywhere before Spring.

He huffed, jamming his hands in his coat pockets as he paced up and down the cabin. "Well, I don't like it. This inactivity isn't what I'm paying you and your crew for, Fairway. My company will be most distressed at the misuse of funds."

"Mister Carrigan, there is no 'misuse of funds'. The crew are working day and night to keep the *Port Hunter* in a reasonable condition so that the minute the pack starts to thaw, we can attempt to resume our journey."

"That being as it may, there is another task I believe requires our undertaking." Carrigan looked at me, his eyes bright. "The airship we saw before we encountered this wretched ice. It was a British Aether Extraction Company craft, was it not?"

It took me several moments to realise what he was referring to.

"The crash site? That was a good fifteen miles back across the pack ice. But yes, it was... why?"

"There may be supplies and records in the wreckage. As we're not going anywhere for some time, and as the closest Company asset, it is our solemn duty to discover the fate of the crew of that craft."

I stared at him, dumbfounded. The man was truly mad. Trekking fifteen miles across the pack, when we didn't have the supplies, instruments, or manpower to spare to go off on a happy little jaunt?

"I wasn't asking your opinion, Mister Fairway." Carrigan's tone was icy, his eyes cold and hard. "The Company is financing this expedition, and while I am happy enough to take your lead in matters nautical, the employment of the personnel whilst we are icebound is my prerogative. Pick four of your sailors to accompany myself, Divok, Corporal Benton, Private Cowes and Private Samwell. We leave at first light tomorrow."

I wish I had never elected to join Carrigan on his little trip, for then I would have been spared any foreknowledge of what awaited the crew of the *Port Hunter*. I left the ship in Anna's charge, with instructions to sail for Nova Scotia should we fail to return, and took with me Doctor Nixon, Ginny and a stocky young deckhand called Nesbit. We loaded up a sled with tents, equipment and provisions before setting out across the pack ice.

It took us the best part of thirty-six hours to cover the distance back to the downed airship, which I had greatly underestimated. Thankfully, Benton proved to be an accomplished land navigator and was able to guide us back to the crash site with almost unerring accuracy. Yet when we got there, what we found was not the site of some catastrophic airship accident. The envelope may have been torn to shreds and the skeleton damaged by the elements, but the gondola itself was sound.

There had been no crash, but a controlled landing. We walked around the gondola, taking stock of what we had found. In golden lettering on the bow was written the vessel's name – the *Arctic Destiny*. The structure was intact, except for severe weathering. The main deck hatch was wide open, allowing snow and ice into the saloon. As we stepped inside, we found the first of the bodies.

The corpse had obviously been there some time, as the flesh that remained on the bones had turned black with necrosis. The cold climate must have preserved it as there was little sign of decay – however, this allowed us to see that the corpse had been savaged. Ragged strips of flesh hung from an empty arm socket, the partially-gnawed limb lying a metre or two from its unfortunate owner. Parts of the face and

238

chest had been gnawed away, and several large chunks were taken from its legs.

Three of us were violently sick, myself included. Even grizzled Benton went pale, and clutched his rifle tightly.

"Polar bear?" Nesbit gave voice to the thought which we all shared. I nodded, as did Doctor Nixon. The only dissenter was the Esquimaux, Divok, who stared at the corpse muttering something in his own tongue.

"Aninialurk, sapummivaa katingajuut qiluuva wendigo.."

We found six more bodies, all equally ravaged, and one in the wheelhouse with a self-inflicted gunshot wound to the temple. Eight in total. Ginny confirmed that the engines were fuelled and in working order – the *Arctic Destiny* had certainly been set down purposefully. But why here? What did the Corporation want with Prince William Island? These questions *must* be answered, Lucy, and that's why I pray these words reach your ears.

We performed a simple burial service for the unfortunate airship crew, loaded the sled with what little supplies we could find still on board, and made ready to start our trip back to the *Port Hunter*. As we were preparing to leave Carrigan disappeared back into the gondola. He emerged some fifteen minutes later, carrying a large leather satchel bearing the Corporation's insignia. "Charts and navigational data," he muttered when questioned about the contents. "Things the Corporation will want to know when we get back."

"If we ever make it back..." Nesbit muttered, just loud enough for me to hear him. Something about the finality in his tone sent a shiver down my spine.

That night, the blizzard came.

We were about ten miles from the *Port Hunter* when the last vestiges of the sun disappeared over the horizon. We'd pitched our tents just prior to sunset, Ginny and I sharing one and the rest of the party split among the remaining four.

I assure you, Lucy, my bunking with Ginny was simply a matter of necessity and that all propriety was observed. The wind rose as the final rays of sunlight vanished, leaving us in the dark of the polar night. It howled through the thick canvas of the tent, chilling us to the marrow despite the thick sealskin sleeping bags and blankets we had swathed ourselves in. Through it all, I swear I could make out noises, like someone stalking around the camp, footsteps crunching on freshly-fallen snow.

Neither of us slept as the bitter cold assailed our little shelter, and it wasn't until the first glimpse of morning rose in the east that the wind stopped as quickly as it had begun. We emerged from the reassuring cocoon of our tent, and took stock of our situation. The sleds had been destroyed, their supplies and equipment scattered across the ice as if by the hand of a spiteful giant. Cowes had contracted a nasty case of frostbite in his cheek, and Carrigan was looking decidedly unwell also.

This may have been because he had been the first to put his head into Nesbit and Samwell's tent. I apologise for this graphic description, Lucy, but it needs must be told, for you to appreciate the reality of what we were facing. The two junior members of the expedition had been ripped to shreds, completely dismembered and torn limb from limb. Huge lumps of flesh had been gouged out of arms, legs and torsos as if by some kind of giant carnivorous beast.

Even stranger was the fact that they were mottled a vile purple and black by necrosis, much like the bodies found aboard the airship. Divok collapsed to his knees, sobbing and spouting yet more gibberish in that Esquimaux tongue of his. Ginny went white as Cowes screamed at the top of his lungs and disappeared into the safety of his tent, whilst Benton and Doctor Nixon examined the bodies.

"This... this isn't possible" exclaimed the doctor in a shaky voice, all colour drained from his face. "Even if they'd died a week ago, the flesh shouldn't be this far gone. I... I have no explanation for this, Captain."

"Let's get back to the *Port Hunter*. We don't tell anybody of this. If anyone asks, Nesbit and Samwell died of exposure. Do I make myself abundantly clear?"

"What... what about the sleds?" Ginny piped up timidly.

"They fell. Through a hole in the ice. Questions?" I looked around at the assembled band, then looked back at the tent.

"Burn it."

Benton took a flagon of lamp oil, dousing the tent in it before taking a match to the canvas. We stood back as the flames took hold, and Benson crossed himself as he watched the flames.

"Ain't bloody natural, that. Nothin' whatsoever natural about it," the big marine muttered to himself, shuddering slightly. I pulled my snow goggles down to hide the fear in my eyes, and started off back in the direction of my own shelter.

"Let's get camp struck, and make a move back to the ship. The sooner we're back, the sooner we can put this whole episode behind us."

The squat green hull of the *Port Hunter* coming in to view over a snow drift was a welcome relief after the harrowing trek back from the airship. As expected, we were faced with a barrage of questions about Nesbit and Samwell, and the supplies that were conspicuously absent. If anyone suspected our deceit it wasn't clear, but several people mentioned how our Esquimaux guide appeared shaken and unlike his usual self. I called him in to my cabin later that evening, and offered him a brandy, which he gratefully accepted.

"Divok, something about what happened out there has troubled you. What is it? Do you know what killed Nesbit and Samwell?"

He looked at me, his deep brown eyes drilling into me from his flat-nosed, weathered face. The flickering light from the lantern cast dark shadows over his nut-brown features. He looked down at the floor, shuffled uncomfortably in his seat and grasped his mug tighter. "My people have old story. Sometimes, when snows come hard at night, the other ones walk the ice."

"Other ones?"

"Those not of this world, but of the other world, the old world on the other side. Sometimes, they come to walk our world. There are many, but worst, worst of all we call *wendigo*."

"*Wendigo?*"

The old Esquimaux shuddered, and his eyes bored into mine. His voice dropped to a whisper.

"*Wendigo* is tall, hungry spirit. He stalks the ice, bringing blizzard, bringing snow. When he finds his prey, he feasts on flesh and life. Sometimes one *wendigo*, sometimes many. Whole tribes have been taken by *wendigo*. *Wendigo* came, took our friends. If *wendigo* hungry, *wendigo* come for us."

I held his gaze, fascinated by the tale my Inuit was telling me.

"How do they get here?"

"Sometimes, just come. But in place where old world and our world are close, they can be brought across by words or deeds."

"What are you saying, Divok?"

The lamplight flickered, and for a second his eyes lit up with a flame born of utmost fear.

"The *wendigo* has been brought upon us as punishment. Your sky ship... they brought it here. They set it free."

I lay in my bunk that night, staring up at the wooden deckhead a few feet above. The carriage clock mounted on my writing table glinted in the light of the candle that provided scant warmth and illumination to the otherwise chill cabin. I shivered, pulling the blankets around me as a sudden gust of icy wind whistled through the ventilation shaft. I put it down to fancy, but I thought I heard a sound as I huddled there. A screeching, keening sound, like nails on a writing slate.

Seconds later, the screaming started.

By the time I'd thrown on a sealskin and grabbed my Paterson revolver from my desk drawer, shots were already ringing out up top. I dashed up the ladder to the deck above, hauling myself into the clear, dark night. Lieutenant Timbridge lay on the wooden floor, his sword fallen from his lifeless fingers as a dark stain spread over the woodwork above him. Streaks of blood evidenced the movement of bodies across the deck, and over the side. Sergeant Murphy, the big Irish Marine, stomped over to me.

"Captain, Sir. We've got four men of the watch missing. One of the topsmen is over here, an' he's hurt bad. The Lieutenant must've been taking a stroll..." He looked regretfully down at the corpse of the young man. Wordlessly he turned, leading me to where the wretch who had been injured lay propped against a barrel of pitch. Doctor Nixon was trying to staunch the flow of blood from a gaping wound in his stomach. The man looked at me, gurgling something through a throat rapidly filling with blood.

"Easy, Gibbons." I knelt beside the stricken man, who spat a stream of claret onto the deck and looked at me.

"Cold. Eyes like ice. So cold. Eyes like ice..."

He squeezed my hand, and his head lolled forward.

"I think he's gone." I removed his hand and made to stand up when Gibbons began to thrash and convulse. His mouth foamed with blood-flecked spittle, and his eyes opened wide. It was like he stared right into the depths of my soul, Lucy.

"More are coming!" He spasmed once more, then lay silent.

We doubled the watch for the rest of the night, arming every man and woman on the deck. Carrigan came up shortly after Gibbons expired, demanding to know what had happened. I filled him in, and the cretin's jowly face drained as pale as Gibbons had. As I was contemplating voicing my utter disdain for the Company man, I heard a cough from behind me.

"Captain Fairway."

I turned to find Doctor Nixon stood with his arms folded. Though he was maintaining his composure, the look in his eyes was of a man frantic and on the verge of panic. I must admit to no small admiration for his bravery and self-control now I know what it was he had seen. He led me to the barrel of pitch, where he had covered the unfortunate Gibbons' body with a swathe of sailcloth.

"I was examining the body post-mortem, to try to conclude what implement had been used to kill him." He lifted the cloth so that only I could see what lay beneath. Gibbons lay topless, his body rapidly cooling in the biting Arctic wind. Around the gaping rend in his stomach the flesh had already begun to blacken and mottle, taking on a similar cast to Nesbit and Samwell's. Nixon lowered the sailcloth back then stood, gesturing towards where Timsbridge lay similarly covered.

"Would you like to see the Lieutenant as well? It's..." he gulped before continuing. "Much the same."

I had no desire to see the young Marine officer's corpse in any greater detail than I already had.

The dawn brought an audible relief, and an immediate disturbance among the crew. Anna threw my cabin door open as I was shaving, causing me to nick myself with the razor.

"Daniel, you have to get up here. Withers is about to kill Carrigan!"

Once again throwing on my sealskin jacket, I headed up on deck. The Mate was arguing loudly with Murphy, who was shoving him back from the hatch down into Carrigan's quarters. Benton stood behind his Sergeant, finger resting in the trigger-guard of his rifle. Behind him, two of the other Marines flanked the hatch. Withers and six of the crew were facing off against them, carrying everything from a whaling harpoon to the cook's meat cleaver.

"Get out of the way, Greencoat," Withers snarled. "We're getting the hell out of here, and your bloody boss is going to give us what he owes us."

"I've told yer once, Withers. Get back to your cabin, before this gets ugly." The Sergeant's eyes were level, but I could see his big, meaty fists clenching.

"There's a dozen of us, and only a handful of you. 'Less you want to end up like that Rupert of yours last night, get out of my blinkin' way."

"Withers, stand down." I stepped forward, trying to keep my voice as commanding as I could. I was aware of some of the other officers behind me, or up in the stern. "What's going on?"

"Thing is, Captain..." Withers looked at me with a sneer, teeth rotten from years of tobacco, rum and tea. "Thing is, we didn't sign on for this, bein' butchered in our sleep by God-knows-what. So we're takin' our pay, takin' the food, and we're heading back. Overland, if need be. You're welcome ter come with us, Cap. You've been a good boss. But we're leavin' that bastard Carrigan here. Him, and that Esquimaux witch-doctor, and his Greencoat gorillas."

I looked him square in the face, then turned what I hoped was a steely gaze upon each of his would-be mutineers.

"We're miles from civilisation. We split up now, we're as good as condemning every man and woman here to death. You'll stay on board, and you'll like it." I raised my voice so all could hear.

"The events of last night are a tragedy, but it's a one-of a kind thing. An animal attack. We'll batten down from here on in. A curfew, come nightfall. Nobody on the upper deck. But let me get this straight. Nobody is leaving this ship."

"See, Cap'n, that's a crying shame, because we are." Withers lunged for me, swinging at me with a large belaying pin. A shot rang out, and the bullet from Benton's carbine made the Mate dance like a broken marionette, crashing to the ground beside me. After a second of baffled silence, all hell broke loose. Howling, the crew threw themselves at Murphy and his men. Two of them bore Corporal Bowbright to the floor, setting about him with lead bars. Murphy laid out one of the stokers with a single blow, whilst Benton used his carbine like a club to knock the wind from another. Ginny and Anna struggled to restrain one of the deckhands, whilst a knot of men struggled over the hatch. I saw Cowes go down, the shaft of the harpoon protruding from his chest.

The sound of Cowes' body hitting the deck seemed to be the turning point in the fight, because the Marines ceased trying to avoid damaging the mutineers at that moment. Murphy threw one man clear over the side of the ship, and little Marine Chapel somehow managed to drive his knife between Frank Ireland's ribs. By now the initial shock had worn off and I waded in along with Nixon, Swale and Harding to separate the combatants. Eventually we managed to restore order, Murphy, Benton and the two remaining Marines securing the mutineers in one of the fish lockers below decks, where they sat miserably looking up through the bars and calling for forgiveness.

Of the thirty-one men who had entered Baffin Bay, only nineteen of us remained. Of those, three were detained, and

Corporal Bowbright was suffering from multiple broken bones and internal injury. Doctor Nixon feared he wouldn't last the night, a fact I now note with some irony. Gods, Lucy, I've never seen men turn on each other with such ferocity. It was like they were creatures possessed. From the ship's crew only the steward LeFevre and a topsman named Cabot weren't dead or detained.

We spent the rest of the day burying the dead. It wasn't until halfway through the day that I noticed Divok, our stalwart Esquimaux friend, had refused to leave the *Port Hunter*. I found an excuse to talk to him that afternoon, and he turned to me as I approached.

"The *wendigo* will come tonight. I heard them on the wind in the dark, calling to their brothers. Many more will be here, and they will come for feast. We must flee, flee now. Take little boat and escape. More will come, more, more, till all are dead." His eyes were practically brimming with tears, and his voice sounded like it would break at any second. He clasped my hand, pressing something into it. It was an ivory disc, with something carved into it in crude scrimshaw. The ink looked fresh – Divok must have been working on this recently. A face, malevolent and wicked. Divok stared into my eyes.

"I give to all crew. We die as flesh, but our spirit not become *wendigo*."

That night I did exactly as I said I would. I locked all the upper deck hatches myself, and released the three mutineers to Murphy's custody. We sat in the galley, listening to the creaking of the *Hunter*'s trapped timbers and the howling of the blizzard outside. There was little conversation, but two bottles of rum and a carafe of brandy were doing the rounds. I noticed most people had one of Divok's tokens, either stencilled onto an ivory disk or onto wooden chips he had made from a broken spar. Some held them, others had them on thongs around their necks. Carrigan clutched that ledger tight as death, his flabby face drawn and pale with fear. At the stroke of midnight the noise began again, that spine-crawling nail-on-slate screech. This time it seemed to come from all around, and the temperature in the galley began to drop. We looked at each other, and the fear was tangible. We could hear them prowling, clawing, scratching at the hatches, at the deck above.

Ginny broke first. With a wail, she collapsed to her knees and began sobbing. "I'm so cold... they're coming. We're all going to die here, Daniel!" She stared wide-eyed and grabbed my arm. Old Cornwallis moved to put his arm around her, startling her, and she leapt to her feet. Backing towards the door she reached behind her for the key. "We have to run. We can escape if we run!" Her expression was wild. In the corner I saw Murphy's hand go to his rifle.

"Ginny, don't open that door..."

"Can't you hear them calling, Daniel? They want us, they won't leave until they have us!" She sobbed uncontrollably, and her fingers fumbled with the lock. It clicked, and then she turned to pull the door open.

"We have to go now!"

Murphy's carbine barked, and Ginny whimpered. She dropped the key and put her hand to her side, where a crimson stain was spreading across her shirt. She stumbled through the door, collapsing on the steps leading up to the hatch.

"Nobody leaves, right, Cap'n?" Murphy's face was stone. Benton had stepped back from his Sergeant, bringing his own weapon to bear.

"What the fuck, Murph?" he growled. "Have you gone mad?"

"Nobody goes out there, Tom. Boss's orders."

I turned to Carrigan.

"Orders? I give the orders on this ship, Carrigan."

"No... the Sergeant is right. If we stay put we're safe. That's what Divok said. Right, Divok?"

The Esquimaux sat in the shadows, looking thoroughly miserable.

"We are not safe. They have come, and they are hungry. We called them, and they wish to feast."

As if in response to the melancholy Inuit, the scratching began to get even more frantic.

"How did we call them, Divok?"

I shook him by the shoulders, and he looked at Carrigan. I followed his gaze towards the satchel Carrigan cradled protectively.

"What is that?"

Carrigan turned away. "I told you, charts."

"You're lying."

Carrigan gulped, and I advanced on him.

"Open it."

"Daniel..." Anna placed her hand on my shoulder.

"Carrigan knows something. What is it?"

The fat man gulped. "Sergeant Murphy! If this man lays a hand on me, you shoot him!"

"That won't be happening, Mr. Carrigan, Sir." Benton's voice was flat. He kept his weapon pointed at his Sergeant. "Give the Captain the satchel."

The room fell silent. I stared at Carrigan, Murphy stared down the barrel of Benton's carbine, and the rest of the crew fell quiet. Suddenly Carrigan swept his arm, flinging the bottle of brandy at me. I ducked, and he stood up and ran for the door. Murphy lunged at Benton, and the two men fell struggling to the floor. Regaining my feet, I chased after

Carrigan. He had shot back the bolt on the upper deck hatch, and threw it open to the howling wind and snow.

"Carrigan, no!"

I stood at the bottom of the stairwell as Carrigan turned to run. Suddenly, it was there, towering over him. Nine feet tall, the creature was gaunt to the point of emaciation, desiccated, mottled blue-grey skin pulled taut over its bones. The creature's eyes were sunk deep into its sockets, and tattered lips peeled back to reveal fangs the like of which you've never seen. It let out an eerie cackle, and thrust forward with wicked, icicle-like fingers which tore into Carrigan's chest. He squealed like a pig and dropped the satchel. I grabbed it, and dashed headlong down the passageway to my cabin.

Here comes the most shameful part of my tale. I barricaded the door. Pushed my chest against it, locked it, the works. I could hear the creatures stalking through the galley. I heard Anna scream as she was devoured. I heard Benton and Murphy putting up a resistance, I heard Divok chanting.

I did nothing.

Eventually I saw the sun come up through the porthole. The ship was silent, so I cautiously moved the trunk and unlocked the door. The stench of death and decay hit me as I walked to the galley. They were all dead, Lucy. All of them. Anna. Divok. Cornwallis. Nixon. Swale and Harding. Benton and Murphy and the marines and the sailors. I was the only one left alive, captain of a ghost ship.

So I've come back to my cabin, and I've penned this missive to you. The papers enclosed in the satchel come from the crew of the *Arctic Destiny*, and they tell of an expedition to find a new source of aether in the Northern Territories. That's the Company's real interest here, and it explains the presence of scientists like Cornwallis. The *Destiny*'s crew dug to find a source that they could tap – a ley line, anything – and something they did somehow disturbed or summoned the *wendigo*. The Company brought them through from their world to ours, Lucy. They caused this, and they have to be warned of the consequences of their actions.

Alas, I won't be there to do it in person. Night is falling, and with the dark they will come again. But they will find nothing alive here. The pistol is staring me in the face, a lump of cold metal my final comfort. I'm sorry, Lucy. I did this for you. It was all for you.

May the Lord have mercy on my soul.

Daniel P. Fairway

Captain, SS Port Hunter

Lieutenant James Walter Fairholme, Royal Navy, tucked the letter back into its envelope and gave the shrivelled corpse in front of him a salute.

"I'll see this gets where it needs to go, old boy." The young officer couldn't help but swallow back his emotion. "The least I can do." He picked up the satchel, and made his way out onto the deck of the creaking hulk.

"Fairholme, hurry up! The Old Man wants us back aboard the *Erebus* sharp-like!" Commander James FitzJames stood impatiently on the ice below. A few hundred yards away Her Majesty's Ships *Erebus* and *Terror* sat at anchor. Fairholme knew that in his cabin on board the Old Man – the renowned explorer Captain Sir John Franklin – would want to know what he had found. As he and his party left the battered green hulk behind, he heard the men talking in whispered tones.

"Never seen bodies like that before..."

"...at least two of 'em 'ad been shot..."

"Reckon they ended up starvin' and eatin' each other."

As they rowed the short distance back to the *Erebus*, Fairholme turned to look at the doomed ship once more, and shivered involuntarily as a chill crossed his spine. He couldn't shake the feeling that someone was watching him. He shivered again, felt the frigid air begin to stir. The wind was picking up. He couldn't help but curse. An Arctic blizzard would be here soon.

The Martyr

- Ian Millsted -

It was the second night of the new moon as I stood in Bristol harbour awaiting the arrival of the *McKinley* on her maiden voyage from New York when the hitherto dark night was illuminated by the full flare of an explosion. Throwing their arms up to protect their faces, the crowd started shouting and barging past each other.

Wilkins, the news reporter and my colleague from the *News Chronicle*, shoved his way through the crowd to reach the best vantage point. He yelled to Joseph, our photographer, to follow him. Neither of them gave me a second thought but I followed anyway. We'd been sent down from London to interview notable passengers voyaging on the *McKinley*. It was three years after the Tunguska explosion and my exclusive interview with Professor Gorsky about the full implications of the substance that had rapidly been named aether. Yet it was the male reporter, Wilkins, who was to interview former U.S. President Theodore Roosevelt about his plans to mediate between Britain and Germany over the Heligoland issue, while I was to write a piece on Roosevelt's niece Eleanor, who was travelling with him. This was expected to be a standard women's page feature about a woman whose uncle and husband were both politicians, but I was less irritated than usual by the condescending assignment. From what I'd read, Eleanor Roosevelt might prove to be something of a surprise to the editor. If she was still alive.

While most of the crowd was retreating, fearing some kind of danger or attack, the three of us found some space at the very edge of the harbour wall. An emergency aether beam shone down from the suspension bridge directly onto the spot where the *McKinley* tilted precariously. Smoke billowed out from so many exit points that they merged into one. There was an orange glow behind the smoke, and I could just make out people in the water and some smaller boats, possibly lifeboats from the ship, towards the edge of the area made visible by the beam of light. Joseph took a photograph of the rapidly sinking vessel, the flashbulb dazzling us all, and then she was gone. The *McKinley* had sunk below the surface more quickly than I would have imagined possible. There were shocked cries and sobs from all around us. I stood stock-still. Wilkins was shouting something about the 'damned Heligolanders' while Joseph hugged his camera close to his chest, knowing he had what was probably the last picture of the *McKinley*.

The harbour guards and a throng of volunteers were bringing in survivors and bodies from the water for the rest of the night. By dawn it was just corpses, the last living passengers and crew having long since been taken to the Bristol Royal Infirmary. Early editions of the local newspapers carried the announcement that the *McKinley* had indeed been the victim of a bomb exploding in the engine. Wilkins had sent a similar article to London before midnight. None of us had slept. Joseph and I bought breakfast at one of the harbourside cafes while Wilkins telegraphed more copy to London, and then we all walked to the hospital to await news of the survivors. By nine o'clock in the morning, a large crowd of journalists and well-wishers had gathered in the visitors' reception. Wilkins was mingling with his colleagues and competitors from the other London newspapers, so I took the opportunity to wander around and see what else I could find out.

It was in the Ladies' Cloakroom that the first interesting communications of the day occurred, not for the first time in my journalistic career. While washing my hands I heard a voice behind me.

"Excuse me." The accent was American. "Do you know where I might be able to purchase some hairpins? I'm afraid I look in something of a state. Someone has been kind enough to lend me some clothes, as my own are all soaked, but my hair is not co-operating."

"I have half a dozen or so with me, if that will be enough," I replied.

"I'll make it enough and consider myself in your debt." I reached into my handbag for the pins.

"Thank you, Miss..."

"Isobel," I said. "Isobel Wintringham." I offered my hand which she shook firmly. "And are you Mrs Roosevelt?"

Eleanor Roosevelt raised her eyebrow but acknowledged that she was. I explained that we had been scheduled to do an interview that morning, but I understood that events would likely mean that would not now happen.

"Nonsense," she replied. "One of Uncle Teddy's secretaries is being treated for burns and we need to make sure he is alright before we travel further, so I have time for the interview. The hospital has arranged for us to have a private lounge. Would that be a suitable place to proceed?"

She knew it was, and she didn't wait for an answer. We left the cloakroom and walked away from the public area of the hospital to a small, comfortable room. Usually a waiting room for one of the consultants, the newly painted 'private' sign indicated its conversion into a lounge for the Roosevelt party had been both recent and hasty. The former President was not there, but present were two men dressed in suits which in neither case quite fitted them right. More borrowed clothes, I presumed. Mrs Roosevelt sent one of them to find a pot of coffee while we sat down and I took out my shorthand notebook.

I barely had to ask a question. Eleanor Roosevelt described the events of the previous evening as she had experienced them, and I frantically tried to keep up with her narrative, aware that I was getting a scoop which Wilkins and the others might stop short of murder to get. Maybe. Just.

The *McKinley*'s voyage had been trouble-free until the approach to Bristol. There had been some discussion between the ship's captain and the port authorities about times and tides in the final approach to Bristol harbour and regarding who should make decisions, but they had been resolved after various people had come aboard to explain the difficulties. The rest was much as it had looked from the harbourside. The passengers had mostly been on deck, watching for the city and admiring the suspension bridge as they passed underneath when an oilskin-wrapped bundle landed on the deck right in front of Mr Roosevelt. Despite one of the stewards advising it be thrown overboard, the former President proceeded to open it. Inside was a single sheet of writing card bearing a short, typed note advising that there was a bomb planted on the *McKinley* and that everyone should leave the ship as soon as possible. As soon as it was shown to the Captain, he ordered the lifeboats readied. When the explosion came, the passengers and many of the crew had time to climb or jump into the water and were rapidly picked up by the lifeboats. Those of the crew engaged in trying to find the bomb were less fortunate.

"Did the note say who it was from?" It was the obvious question but I had already guessed what the answer would be.

"Nothing apart from a monogram. A letter M in front of a cross."

On my notebook I sketched an image I'd seen in recent news stories. "Did it look like this?"

"How could you know?" Eleanor Roosevelt adopted a more patrician tone of voice. "Can you explain this?"

"It's the sign of the Martyr." My host looked somewhat quizzical at this information. "It's been appearing in London the last few years at the site of various crimes. Sometimes it's on a calling card, other times it is drawn on the walls or in the sand or similar. Scotland Yard has tried to downplay it, but the newspapers have found out enough to run stories anyway. Some claim that he's a criminal; some say he works for the police. There's also a theory that the Martyr is an organisation."

"And what," Mrs Roosevelt asked, "do you think?"

Before I had time to reply, another woman entered the room.

"Miss Wintringham," said Roosevelt, "do you know Martha Wilson?"

I did. Thanks to inherited wealth, she owned and ran a small fashion house in west London. She was also something of a regular in my society column in the *News Chronicle*. She offered me her gloved hand, and with a perfect poker face, I took it.

"It was Martha who gifted me these clothes." Mrs Roosevelt asked one of her uncle's aides to bring a third cup so that she could pour some coffee for Martha Wilson.

"I'm afraid I must decline," Miss Wilson said. "I'm due elsewhere. Perhaps we might meet again in London?"

After thanking Mrs Roosevelt for her time, I also departed. I found a telegraph office and sent through the essentials of the interview and the inside account of the attack on the *McKinley*. I didn't tell Wilkins, and he didn't deign to ask me what I had been doing.

The receptionist at the Grand Hotel on Broad Street sent me straight up to Miss Wilson's rooms, saying I was expected. The door was opened by a masked face. The figure behind the mask gestured for me to enter. She was dressed in a fencing outfit and holding a foil in one hand. Inside the lounge area of what was obviously a suite of rooms I saw Martha Wilson, also dressed for fencing but with her mask off and a warm smile.

"Isobel, welcome. Do you mind waiting just a couple of minutes while we finish off?"

I watched as Miss Wilson and her fencing tutor ebbed back and forth, probing with the swords. They were of similar stature but the tutor was quicker and more agile. Miss Wilson managed to score some hits but the tutor, oddly silent and communicating only by gestures, was the overall victor.

"What did you make of Mrs Roosevelt?" Martha Wilson asked as her fencing partner left the room.

"Intelligent," I replied. "Sharp enough to ask the questions you don't want people asking."

"With your articles all identifying the Martyr as a man? I don't think we need worry."

"What are you doing here anyway?" I asked. "We agreed that you would let me know whenever the Martyr was to appear."

"I was in Bristol on other matters when we heard that another survivor of the Tunguskan gateway was in the area. Marthe believed this one to be of the faction seeking to remake this world like their own; provoking a war between Britain and Germany is their goal."

At this point, Marthe, now in a silk robe to replace the fencing outfit, re-entered the room. Even after knowing them both for three years, the sight of the two physically identical women, Martha and Marthe, amazed me.

"Hello Isobel," Marthe said. "I'm sorry we did not get the information in time to stop the bomb exploding."

"And, of course, the assassin remains at large," added Martha. "We must remain vigilant."

"I'm travelling on the same train as the Presidential party," I said. "I will keep my eyes open."

Wilkins was furious that I had sent in a news story without telling him first. I smiled and said I'd just done the interview with Eleanor Roosevelt as planned. Joseph looked amused. He usually sided with Wilkins, seeing that as the way to get his photographs on the front page, but they were colleagues rather than friends. However, to give Wilkins his due, he was the one who had made the arrangements for the three of us to be on the same train as Roosevelt party. They had the whole of first class booked exclusively for them, but there was always the chance that further news items might cross our paths.

Inside Temple Meads, it became clear that the rest of the London press had the same idea. The ticket area was packed with journalists trying to get tickets, local press getting the last pictures of Theodore Roosevelt, and members of the public intrigued by the whole thing. For the first time I noticed an increase in police presence. Had they received information that further attacks might be planned?

A carriage pulled up just outside the entrance and I saw, through the crowd of people, the Roosevelt party step through. The police pushed the crowd to either side as they processed towards the platform gates. My thoughts were interrupted by a loud crack, audible even above the general hubbub.

There were screams and I heard people shouting about gunfire. A crowd had already formed around the Roosevelts.

I saw Joseph holding his camera high in the hopes of getting a picture. I shuddered to think of what. There seemed little point in trying to fight my way through; I'd leave that to Wilkins. Turning around, I saw Martha Wilson running in the opposite direction and bursting through a door marked STAFF ONLY. I followed.

The door led to a dingy staircase which went upward only in a series of short twisting sections. I could hear footsteps above but could see nothing. I kept going but slowed as I neared the top. I became aware of my own breathing and realised that I could no longer hear Martha's steps ahead of me. The sudden silence from above contrasted eerily with the continuing screams and shouts from below. At the top of the staircase was a solid door. I pushed tentatively, but once it was open a few inches I forced it wide. Beyond was a small room with another door on the far side and a coal-smoke stained window that might afford a view down onto the platforms. Martha was standing just inside the door looking down at the only other person in the room. At first, I thought the figure, a man, was dead but then I could see he was merely unconscious. He was lying face down on the floor with his arms bound behind his back and his ankles similarly tied. There was a rifle about a foot away, on which rested the Martyr's calling card.

"Perhaps we should draw the attention of some of those policemen down on the station floor so they can take this fellow in for questioning once he wakes up."

We did just that. The man was pushed into a secure office behind the ticket desk, while Miss Wilson explained how she, or rather we, had come across him. The senior policeman asked us several times over if we had seen the Martyr. I answered that I hadn't. Miss Wilson gave the same response. In turn the police informed us that the assassin had failed to shoot Mr Roosevelt but only by a whisker.

The train had been held to double-check there were no further bombs or threats present. Miss Wilson and I were escorted to our respective carriages. She was to travel with the Roosevelts. "I'll try and come back for you and see if I can get you in as well, once we get going, what with you and Eleanor knowing each other," she promised. I wasn't hopeful; she seemed to make more of our brief acquaintance that it merited.

My own carriage was shared with Wilkins, Joseph, and three other gentlemen of the press. As I took my seat, they were already deeply engaged in conflicting theories about who was trying to stop Theodore Roosevelt arriving at the Heligoland conference. Wilkins maintained his assertion that it was the *Frei Heligoland* group. It was true that they had claimed responsibility for certain acts in the past, but I wasn't convinced. The few comments Roosevelt had made about the situation before travelling to Europe suggested he was at least partly sympathetic to the idea that the people of Heligoland should be able to decide their own destiny. Opposite Wilkins was a well-groomed man who dismissed my colleague's views with an air of omniscience. "Of course," he said, "the Kaiser is trying to stir up trouble as usual. Just like Zanzibar all over again. He's got his agents all over the place. This'll be his work; take my word on it."

A bespectacled man in the rear-facing window seat spoke up for the first time. "It's all about the aether," he said. "Since the Tunguska event Britain, Germany, France – America too, probably – have all been collecting as much of the stuff as they can, investigating and testing like mad to see what they can get it to do. I've friends up at Oxford who tell me things I'd prefer not to imagine were possible. They've been developing weapons; weapons that can do terrible things, and some of our great leaders are itching for a chance to use them." I was the furthest person away from the man, unable to ask him more as our colleagues between us returned to their arguments about what would happen at the conference.

I wondered at the idea of aether weapons. No one quite knew what aether was. The name itself was appropriately plucked from common parlance to name this new substance. A decade into the twentieth century and we were still using classical terms for anything new. What was public knowledge was that the explosion in Siberia in the year '08' had brought something new into the atmosphere. University departments had isolated enough to start examining its properties but had failed to find a place for it in the periodic table. Some groups had arisen claiming that aether represented a return to the days of magic. Others said the whole thing was a fake, propagated by those in power to keep everyone else in their place for fear of it. It could be used to amplify electric lights and to render so efficient the use of helium or hydrogen that airships could now be built at half the size but with twice the passenger capacity.

Unlike the men in the carriage, I had the benefit of knowing Marthe. I knew that the Tunguska explosion had been powerful enough to open the gateway between dimensions. I grasped, too, that a substance so powerful must surely have a host of possible uses. That some of those uses could be dangerous or malicious alarmed but did not surprise me. Put into the hands of man – men like Kaiser Wilhelm – God only knew what might happen.

Through the carriage windows I watched the Wiltshire countryside rolling past. I might have nodded off to sleep, following the deprivation of the night before, had not Martha Wilson knocked on the door and asked me if I wanted to accompany her. Knowing the reaction this would provoke among the men, I accepted the offer immediately. We walked through the dining area to the first-class lounge. Inside, I saw Eleanor Roosevelt who introduced me to her uncle, who was sitting nursing a glass. He broke off from a conversation with one of his aides and another man long enough to greet me warmly and invite me to order whatever the steward could supply. As he resumed his conversation, I could hear enough to discern that the man I hadn't seen before was a British politician, sent by someone other than the government, I suspected, to make representations to Roosevelt before he spoke to others.

I accepted the offer of tea and followed Martha to take a seat with Eleanor Roosevelt. I asked them if they had any theories as to who was trying to attack Mr Roosevelt. The target's niece shrugged nonchalantly and declared that she didn't know enough about the local situation to make a judgement. Martha, however, was more forthcoming.

"Surely it is a matter of asking the right questions? What motives would anyone have to gain from stopping Mr Roosevelt attending a conference intended to find a peaceful answer to the rising tensions over a small island in the North Sea?"

"Who would stand to gain, you mean?" I offered.

"Or, who would have the most to fear from a successful conference?"

From across the lounge, I heard the British voice exclaim something about "Heligoland is British – we can't be seen to be giving in to these terrorist demands. Look what they've already tried to do to you and your niece."

I stayed a little longer and shared with my companions some of the theories of the gentlemen of the press. Mrs Roosevelt laughed at most of the ideas, while Miss Wilson listened particularly attentively. As we approached London, I made my way back to my own carriage. I glimpsed Marthe at the far end of the passage, heading away from me.

On the slow approach to Paddington, the train started to run parallel to other lines seeking the same destination. The journalist with the spectacles was peering out of the window when he suddenly exclaimed. "What was that? Did you see? There was a reflection in the window of the other train. It looked like someone on the roof above us."

I shouted for everyone to get away from the window.

Before anyone could reply, I heard the too-familiar sound of an explosion. This was nearer than the one I'd heard across the water the day before. I leapt up to look out of the window and saw a burning coal engine on a service line. This time I didn't give way to the others but leaned across to ask the reporter by the window what he thought he had seen reflected in the other train.

"It looked like someone riding on top of the train. Black clothes covering most of him. I thought they were waving to someone in the other train, but now I wonder if they were throwing something."

"A bomb, you mean?"

He said nothing further, merely nodding.

At Paddington, the station guards ordered all external train doors remain closed until the Roosevelts had been escorted out of the station. Given all that had happened I couldn't blame them. However, as soon as we were free to leave, the entire cadre of journalists hailed cabs to take them to the airship port at Greenwich. With three attempts so far to kill or halt the agreed mediator before he could reach Heligoland, which journalist would risk the ire of their editors by missing out on what might happen next? We, and to my shame I included myself, were like a pack of hyenas.

The airship waiting to take both the Roosevelts and the British foreign secretary to Heligoland was moored on the hill just above the Observatory. While Wilkins pushed himself to the front of the watching journalists and Joseph sought the best spot for a panoramic photograph, I waited at the rear, watching for events on the fringes. I didn't yet know what would happen, but I was beginning to believe I knew

264

who it might involve. Apart from the crowd watching the political figures climb the steps to the cabin, there were crew members all around, ensuring the airship was ready. I walked towards the rear of the airship and was surprised to pass unimpeded to the far side. There were police at all points of the compass but few physical barriers of any kind. There was no one on the tarmac engaged in anything that looked out of place.

I looked up at the grand airship, large enough to dwarf the Observatory itself. And there they were.

At the very top of one of the anchor cables there were two people fighting. Both were dressed in black. Marthe, the Martyr, was fighting another of her kind. I shouted at the nearby police and one ran over to stand next to me. I implored him to go to the aid of the woman who was risking her own life. No one seemed to know what to do. I called out Marthe's name but by then a crowd had gathered, all shouting and screaming, and nobody heard my indiscretion. The Martyr's opponent had a gun. He gained enough space, while the other was hanging for life from the cable, to raise the rifle to his shoulder and fire down at the police, who scattered in response. After that, the gunman climbed from the cable onto the surface of the airship itself. In pursuit, the Martyr was once again secure on the cable and trying to reach the airship. The gunman swung the gun and aimed at the Martyr. My heart pounded as I heard the crack of the rifle and felt sure the other must have been shot, but what looked at first like a fall turned out to be an evasive manoeuvre, allowing them to jump from the cable to the netting that enveloped the skin of the airship. My hands covered my mouth. *Marthe!*

Reacting to events at last, the police were evacuating all persons from the airship. I saw the Roosevelts ushered away to a cab. Another shot from the top of the airship rattled ineffectively on the tarmac. The gunman threw down his gun as if he was going to give himself up.

But even from this distance, I could see him reach inside a pocket and withdraw a small object. A light shone from it.

"An aether beam," said a voice next to me. I realised it was Martha Wilson.

He fired the beam down towards the Roosevelts cab. It illuminated the cab, and where the beam centred on the roof, an orange glow appeared. There were screams. The passengers scrambled out and dropped to the floor, running in all directions with several falling to the floor in the chaos. The beam followed them, slicing a path of red heat into the ground. What that might do to human skin was not something I wanted to see.

Atop the airship, the Martyr was now upright again. She made a grab for the source of the heat ray. The assassin knocked her back only to see her get up yet again. Then they locked together in combat and it was difficult to see quite what was going on. After a few moments, the assassin stood alone again and raised his device to once again strike at his intended victims. The beam hit the ground, flicking this way and that as if the wielder was mad with the power of it. For the first time I could see his face. It was the politician from the train who'd tried to persuade Roosevelt of the terrorist nature of the Heligolanders. I saw the Martyr stand once more and reach for the assassin from behind. She succeeded in reaching around him to the aether device. The beam swung round so that, instead of pointing at the ground, it was now directing right into the chest of the assassin, and through them to the figure behind. And beyond them to the skin of the airship.

"No!" Martha and I shouted together.

It was too late. Even as the two climbers fell to the ground, their bodies were consumed by the explosion of the airship.

I felt a force, like the kick to the chest from a wild horse, knock me to the ground.

I next became aware of myself in a finely decorated parlour.

"How long?" I asked.

"A few hours," Martha answered. "The police and hospitals had enough on their hands so, once I knew you hadn't suffered any burns, I had you brought here to recover."

"Marthe?"

"No."

Martha had tears in her eyes. "She was me. The best part of me. Braver than I could ever be."

I raised myself to a sitting position.

"Stronger than me. She liked you. She was the one who first said we should trust you, and she trusted few. She fought so hard to stop this world becoming like hers. She tried so many times to tell me what that world was like. I'm not sure I really comprehended. All irrelevant now, I suppose."

"Unless we have to face more arrivals without her," I whispered.

"God forbid."

Martha put her hands to her head and groaned in pain. "No, not now."

"This is what happened before, right after Tunguska. But she's dead. How can this happen again?"

She screamed.

It seemed like she'd never stop screaming. Then, suddenly, she broke off, pointing to the rug in front of the hearth. A shape was coalescing out of thin air. A human form. We both watched as the figure solidified. It was Martha. Another

Martha, this one dressed in little more than rags. What world could this be?

The new Martha looked at us both and around the room. She clutched her hands around herself in a protective manner.

"Don't send me back," she said. "Don't ever send me back."

The Ends of the Empire

- Felicia Barker -

Transcription from a series of dated and time-stamped wax cylinders presented to Alworth Alderson, attorney to Mr Clarence Meredith Farthing, by Mr Farthing himself and containing an apparent oral reckoning of Mr Farthing's late activities:

Cylinder One – 17th June, Year of Our Lord Eighteen-Hundred and Forty-Six, Five of the Clock (Afternoon)

Rule Britannia! Britannia rules the plane!

Cylinder One Continued – Five of the Clock and Seven Minutes (Afternoon)

Well, aha, not– Not technically, of course. Britannia rules a sphere, which, as one will be aware, resembles the plane only locally. And, indeed, that is rather– rather the point! For we– I– we... The Empire itself! Stands upon the cusp of a revolution which will make the whole spherical expanse of the planet local to every one of us! But you must forgive my uncharacteristic attempt at witticism, however imprecise, for it is this very revolution which has me so animated! Soon, every Briton shall have the liberty of all the globe! For I now possess the properly certificated and recognised papers of appointment from the Imperial Science Board to produce for Queen and country an apparatus for the very *translocation of matter itself!*

Yes, from the beginning, then! Seven years ago, my studies into the aetheric and magnetic fields of the planet led me to believe that if one could draw together those fields, as one might bunch a sheet in one's fist, one would create a commensurate distortion in the opposing hemisphere of the field, and that these 'singularities' would, at the point of infinite compaction, thus connect in the manner of... Oh, how can I describe it? Of an apple core! Two opposing dimples – fundaments – at either end of a sphere which join together to form... Although an apple core is not hollow. Hmm. A cored apple, then! *[Ed: Here I have eliminated several minutes digression on the nature of apples.]* Perhaps it is, ah, not so much like an apple.

I conjectured that propelling matter through these aetheric fundaments (dimples) would instantaneously stretch the matter between the two points, ejecting it on the far side of the planet from whence it came. The very ends of the Empire should be within every man's reach!

One could only imagine– That is to say, one only did. The immense potential in the theory. Revolutionary potential! But at this time, George... Ahh... This was that period when my friend, my dear friend, first became stricken with that mysterious sickness that has plagued his recent years. We were each of us bachelors and both lived alone, but in a few weeks, it was increasingly plain that such a life no longer suited George. He was not– not yet an invalid, nor has he ever given in to incapability, but I saw that it could benefit him – both of us – to take rooms together. Despite the ill-omened catalyst for this proposal, it was an idea that filled me with warmth. Months later, George would confide that he shared the emotion.

Ah, but, all the same, there were necessary concessions to the arrangement. I could no longer maintain my private laboratory and was forced to seek out greater academic patronage. But, of course, I could hardly disregard my work! No, indeed! Here, I knew, was something that would change the lives of all it touched, could it but be refined. I am a modest man (how paradoxical to say!), yet I could not deny the terrific potential of my research. And so, for the uttermost part of seven years, I have put before all else the pursuit of funding for a practical test of my theories.

Progress has been slow. I have been compelled to spend a maddening amount of time in teaching or other trivial projects so as to maintain the financial security of our lives. All the while I have built the necessary credence and reputation required to put my papers before the eyes of those who matter. I daresay George would have succeeded in half the time but I am not a forceful personality nor given to self-aggrandisement. Until today, I have found myself a place in the background milieu of the world. It is still half a dream to me to find myself stepping onto the... the apron of the Imperial stage!

How, then, has my name progressed from the sundry nameless players to the *dramatis personae* of this narrative? Oho! Because, eight days ago, I performed the actual translocation of a white mouse through the aetheric magneto-sphere! (It is, of course, unfortunate but unavoidable that I could not be present to observe the trail-blazing *mus musculus* at the termination of its journey. If my calculations are correct, it will have arrived some nautical miles off the coast of New South Wales.)

Ah. I fear George has been beckoning me to our meal for the last several minutes and has progressed to the ejaculation of certain utterances that I hope this cylinder has not the fidelity to record. I shall resume my tale on the morrow.

Cylinder Two – 18th June, Year of Our Lord Eighteen-Hundred and Forty-Six, One of the Clock and Twenty-Three Minutes (Afternoon)

I confess that a pernicious doubt had settled at the base of my mind in recent days. Indeed, during the darker nights of my conscious, I came parlous close to despair. If I am...

Hnfff... If I am quite truthful, George's condition has worsened greatly in recent months, and though I present to him a stoic face, I know that he needs the attentions of a specialist physiker in the immediate future. I knew that my research, if vindicated, would secure such resources and reputation as would permit me to acquire for my friend the attentions he deserves, and so it was for more than personal triumph that I toiled. Yet my position at the Merchant Venturers School – hard-won a year ago – was soon to end, and with it would go access to the moneys and facilities upon which my progress depended. Secretly... Ah-hm... Secretly, I did not believe dear George would survive however many more interminable years of lecturing and trivialities it would require for me to receive another bursary.

Thus, the dark seed was planted in the night soil of my hidden thoughts. A doubt, a lack of faith, in the very system of our Empire. I shall blame, aha, a daemon of my conscience, which whispered to me during sleepless nights and long evenings in the laboratory. How, it asked me, was it right that wealth existed in such amounts throughout the Empire, and yet such a virtuous and good fellow as George languished for lack of skilled ministry. There is, surely, within the great people of Britain, the knowledge and the skill to heal him, and just as surely there is the coin to acquire it. Yet here I was, with a contribution of my own to make, to exchange the one for the other for the next, and the opportunity for universal betterment which I was surely privy to was imminently to elude me. I wondered if God had chosen to punish my friend and I for, hrm, for transgressions the nature of which I could not speak to. But if that were not the case, then was it the very workings of the Empire that had failed me?

Hmph, yes, a most pernicious doubt. And, I am glad to say, wholly misplaced. Industry, learning, and Christian virtue are, surely, the united elements that make our Empire greatest under God and is commerce not the crucible? It is the driver of industry, the fuel of the enlightenment. It elevates the great men of society and provides the mechanism by which alms and philanthropy may descend upon those less fortunate. Faced with a limit, a deadline upon which my vital work would be forced to cease, I questioned this wisdom. How foolish! For it was that very limit upon my time that gave me the necessary impetus to finally realise my work!

I am, ah, a cautious man. Yes. I have mentioned already that had I George's more forthright nature I would surely have acquired sponsorship more readily. The Merchant Venturers' School had realised the potential of my work and allowed me a year of almost free reign to utilise their facilities, and I am ever indebted to them for it. Now that year was almost spent, and looking back upon my work I saw that the great expanse of my labour had yet progressed so little because it was so consumed in minutiae and fastidiousness. Such attentions are a virtue, assuredly; however, the lesson of my research is that one must also show daring and drive! With the end of my tenure approaching and George's health upon my mind, I was driven to make a leap into the unknown. I withdrew all the moneys available to me, no longer mindful of the risk or the great terror of debt. I sealed myself in the laboratory for days at a time (though it pained me to leave my friend unattended). I had made sufficient projections and estimations to create a theoretical model of the magneto-aetheric bridge and now, without further hesitation, I set about constructing it in the real!

Ah, I am no storyteller, it is true, for you will note I have already dispelled the tension in this moment of climax. You know already that the white mouse I held in my palm that June morning would be successfully displaced from those rooms on Coldharbour Lane to a point some four thousand leagues or more away (as the mouse runs) – two-thou-and-half leagues diametrically – on the other side of the world! As I secured the electrical terminals of my device to the School's Voltaic conduction grid, I, however, had no such presentiment about the success of my work. My mind was filled with the threat of financial ruin, with the bristling of conscience at my misappropriation of School resources, and, of course, with fear for my dear, dear friend to whom all my work was now dedicated.

Ho, but when the Chancellor and two clerks arrived at my workspace some seventeen minutes later, they found me in very different sorts! Still chortling with a fervour bordering hysteria, rolling about like a child in paroxysms of laughter and joy. No! I should say in *transports* of laughter! *[Farthing laughs.]*

Oho, it took me some while to explain the circumstances that had led to the failure of the School's entire Voltaic grid, the explosive discharge of the many Leiden Jars, and no small number of small fires in the laboratories. Once the true scale and moment of my accomplishment were properly conveyed, however, events gathered a pace that has, in the last seven days, seen more radical change than in the whole seven years prior! Word passed around the Venturers within the day about the capability I had demonstrated. I am not acquainted with precisely who belongs to which circles nor who may have communicated what to whom, but what I can say is that by the Friday of yester-week, my work had gained the attention of men positioned in the highest ministries of the land. Men who – finally! – realised the great value my work could bring to the Empire. Today, I shall meet with a representative from the Imperial Board of the Sciences and we shall set forth a compact by which I shall produce for the Empire a full realisation of the magneto-aetheric bridge! Let doubt never shadow my thoughts again, for fortune is truly with myself and with the Empire!

Cylinder Three – 19th June, Year of Our Lord Eighteen-Hundred and Forty-Six, Eight of the Clock (Eventide)

Mercy me, but I am glad I am not a bureaucrat! I may be accused of verbosity, aha, but I am veritably succinct in comparison to the documents being produced by my liaison from the Board, by name one Charles Caruthers who has in tow a whole legion of clerks! Two days on and not yet done! I have contracted an attorney under advisement from colleagues at the Venturers' School. I was, hm... perhaps naive in my assumption that a simple signature was all that the Imperial organ should require before I be left to my, aha, 'own devices.' The nature of the work, it seems, is to be of a more collaborative nature. I shall co-ordinate weekly with the Board. Ah well! I am sure there will be a share of frustrations in negotiating the bureaucracy and demands of functionaries whose expectations are not married with a true understanding of the science, but we have all been there before. For the realisation of my life's work, I shall merrily defer to the will of HRH the Empress of Britain and her Colonies, as manifest in her representatives. That shall be no cost at all. And if the stipend agreed me is not quite the figure I may have o'er-eagerly fancied, still it is surely enough to tend the exigencies of George's wellbeing and to maintain a satisfactory existence besides. I have passed along my diagrams and calculations as regards materials and expenses – a tedious business but necessary – and now await a final decision on the specifications of the contract. Then the great work can begin!

Cylinder Four – 24th June, Year of Our Lord Eighteen-Hundred and Forty-Six, Two of the Clock and Thirty Minutes (Afternoon)

A most innovative contribution from the Science Board! (I confess I am mildly surprised.) I have been quiet for some days as progress moves maddening slow against the inertia of government. But today there is veritable and exciting news! The first 'transportation engine' (so the device has been re-christened) is to be constructed aboard a seagoing vessel! (This I believe is already under construction by the notable firm of Hill & Sons.) Thus, not merely two points of the planet's surface shall be bridged, but all the great breadth of the ocean shall become a station of arrival and departure. (A second mobile platform shall be needed to host the counterpart device, of course, so as to prevent returning travellers from having to traverse considerable distances from their arrival point to make their return.)

Cylinder Five – 25th June, Year of Our Lord Eighteen-Hundred and Forty-Six, Three of the Clock and Forty-Nine Minutes (Afternoon)

There is to be no return apparatus. I am most confused.

Cylinder Six – 30th June, Year of Our Lord Eighteen-Hundred and Forty-Six, Two of the Clock and Thirty Minutes (Afternoon)

Today I was released from a misapprehension. Certain assumptions I had made were... misplaced. I have seen now the full design to which the first– No... The *only* transportation engine shall be turned. It has been a perturbing illumination. I had thought myself in yoke to the Office of Vessels and Transport (through the intermediation of the Scientific Board). The truth of the situation, as clarified to me today by Caruthers, is quite different. The Imperial ministries have evaluated those costs and designs as I provided them. They have ascertained that the expense per passenger exceeds that of Brunel's great network of movement – the steamships and atmospheric rail – by an amount that (in their, hmph... wisdom...) is not balanced by the revolutionary trait of instantaneous movement.

   [A second of silence.]

They are wrong. And there it is. But that is by the by, and cannot, my attorney Alderson insists, be changed. However... It seems that the clerks of the exchequer reasoned that, if one were to dispense with the need to translocate passengers in both directions, one could omit the commission of one of the two necessary devices... And pursuing this reasoning, they stumbled upon an expense for which the transportation engine suited their purposes, for it would alleviate the costs of provisioning and maintenance that in private transport would be leveraged from the passenger but in this situation fell upon the state. And so, the clarification of my position: I do not serve the Office of Transport, but rather I serve the Office of Justice, in the realisation of a more efficacious means of penal transportation.

Cylinder Six Continued – Four of the Clock and Thirty-One Minutes (Afternoon)

The contract between myself and the Office of Justice is as such: I shall produce for the Empire the designs necessary to construct a single transportation engine of considerable scale to be installed upon the prison ship *Dolores*. This ship shall make anchor in the Bay of Biscay (for better or worse, Brunel's advances in shipbuilding make those waters no longer the hazard of the past). At that point, the antipodal fundament of the bridge so instantiated shall be the southernmost tip of New Zealand – that island colony recently separated from New South Wales. Thence shall be conveyed upon the six-month all prisoners sentenced to transportation by the courts of Britain, that mechanism to be accelerated and extended to a wider field of convictions, and so seeing a reduction in those criminals sentenced to the gallows and a commensurate expansion in the labour force of the colonies. There is, hrm... A strange hollowness in my heart when I consider this. But this is justice, and I know not why I am troubled.

Cylinder Six Continued – Eight of the Clock and Seventeen Minutes (Eventide)

I have just told George of the contract. His reaction seemed to speak to that emptiness that has developed in my soul this day. He was... He was enraged. I cannot put it otherwise. If some hidden part of me drew back at confronting that reality which is the business of transportation, it was in George by no means concealed. He has always been forthright regarding certain practises of the Empire. Though I have not always understood or agreed, I recognise the moral virtue in these expressions: he wills only for us all to be our better selves. It is one of those characteristics of my friend that is the root of my, ah, loving respect for his nature. Hahh... He has expressed in no uncertain terms his revulsion with the practise of transportation, and... And indeed... And, indeed, with me.

Cylinder Seven – 18th July, Year of Our Lord Eighteen-Hundred and Forty-Six, Eight of the Clock (Eventide)

I have not spoken in some while. A silent, fraught tension seems to envelop my days like a pall now. I continue to work to the contract struck with the Imperial Office of Justice. I continue to care for George, though our interactions are a sadness and a pain to me. I have never shied from his suffering, but it is all I can do to face his unspoken disappointment in me. I feel I have in some way failed. Was I correct, when one month ago I believed I had incurred God's displeasure? Do I do so now? I work for the Empire which I have always known to be a Christian nation under the Lord... And yet, somehow it is... Wrong.

The only blessing in these days has been my engagement of a doctor from Stratford for George. Doctor Farrow is a man of immense learning, a fellow of the Royal Society, and undoubtedly the person best equipped to care for my friend. Already, George has rallied under the potent tinctures Doctor Farrow has given to him. Ah, I have awaited such a turn for so many years. Always I anticipated how we would celebrate. But now the day has come, and our rooms remain silent and funereal but for those times when they are ruptured by my friend's rage.

Had it not been George whose condemnation fell upon me, I would not have credited the truth of it. The scale of my friend's disgust at our great nation's practise of justice seemed irreconcilable. But for the trust and faith I place in the man – that very good and virtuous man – I felt I must apprehend the truth full-facedly. I have spent some time in recent weeks undertaking a better understanding of the practise that I am now, hmph, complicit in.

I knew, of course, that controversy surrounded transportation in those quarters most outspoken against the Empire. But these were fringe elements and radicals, given to fanaticism and hyperbole. I was certain the truth must fall short of their outrageous claims. But now – in service both to my work and to my curiosity – I have visited the convict vessels. I put questions to the men who crew them and hearing their accounts, I begin to fear that, whatever is published in the handbills of rabble-rousers, the reality is yet far worse.

Cylinder Eight – 9th August, Year of Our Lord Eighteen-Hundred and Forty-Six, Seven of the Clock and Fifteen Minutes (Eventide)

You will have noted the gulf of time since last I recorded my thoughts. I no longer feel a compulsion to speak about my work. It is an embarrassment to me. But still, events progress, and speak of it or not, I am a part of them. So, I shall record further testimony, though it has become an act of penitence, a confession with no absolution in sight.

Today I completed the work. The final refinements of the designs were set to parchment and delivered to Caruthers.

They shall be implemented forthwith. The fabrication of the necessary components has been underway now for some days already. The transportation engine shall be complete within the month.

As regards my knowledge of transportation, I am compelled to seek all the wisdom I can. It has become a queer form of self-flagellation, for each mote of knowledge gained is more terrible than the last, and I suffer for the knowing of it. Four days ago, I travelled to Bristol New Gaol and met with Mary Hansham, a convict there. Hers is a case which among those objectors (who once I termed rabble-rousers) has been most proclaimed as a travesty. Some imp of guilt drove me to speak with her.

Mrs Hansham is a mother and was wife to a husband of some nine years. This man was not, I believe, a good man. Though any man may fall prey to indulgence, this man was unrepentant in enslavement to liquor. The spirit incurred in him a temper, and he was like to vent this dark mood against his wife by way of his fists. This to an extent exceeding any notion of spousal discipline, but categorically a wroth unbecoming and untenable in any virtuous person. The story as Mrs Hansham conveyed to me, and which I take to be true, is that upon returning home in his cups one inauspicious evening, Mr Hansham began to hold forth in fury upon some trivial manner in the way to which Mrs Hansham was by now accustomed. On this occasion, however, the child (of some two years just celebrated) awoke to the commotion and began to clamour. Hrm. My bile rises to say that Mr Hansham then approached the infant as though to inflict upon him the same 'admonishments' to which his wife was subject. Out of all care for the child and spurred by the extreme emotion of the situation, Mrs Hansham threw herself upon her husband, and at this it seems the man fell backward, and his head was thrown against the protruding stone lintel of the window. His skull was thus cracked, and though Mrs Hansh-

am is recorded to have run into the street and raised great
hue and cry, the man could not be saved.

This story brought before the courts, the child is now in
the care of an aunt, and Mrs Hansham in Gaol, convicted of
murder and sentenced to transportation to the colonies. She
has told me she does not expect to survive. Many convicts
suffer for dysentery and typhoid – this I saw for myself.
There is no undertaking to give them aid nor to protect
the healthy from becoming so afflicted. Aboard the *Dolores*,
they shall be held in close quarters, shackled in human filth
as if they were chattel (I have seen the spaces they shall be
held... I have seen the shackles also). I am not a student of
medicine, but even to my knowledge it is clear that disease is
like to spread akin to fire. At least the transportation engine
shall relieve them of the lengthy sea voyage, scarcely provisioned or watered, but that does not absolve my part in
this. In the colony, it is likely Mary shall be subject to hard
labour, for the court has judged her to be the worst class of
hardened criminal (a nonsense!). These convicts are chained
and lashed to undertake the work of slaves. No doubt many
will be already in diminished health and many more shall
become so, and the privations of these conditions will only
hasten their wasting. If she is... hm... 'Lucky'... Mary may be
made to work in servitude for one of the settler families. She
is well advised, she says, to seek marriage quickly if this is
so – though, of course, the circumstance of her conviction
all but eradicates such hope. Domestic service may seem a
more hopeful fate than I imply, but stories reach me... Those
in service who offend again in the colonies are committed to
the chain gangs. Employers may make... unworthy demands
of the convict... With the threat of being labelled a recidivist
held over them, they are compelled to submit.

At the end of our meeting, I explained to Mrs Hansham my place and purpose there. When she comprehended
what I had done, she thanked me; for at least, she said, I had

spared her the terrible sea crossing. Her words only sickened me.

Cylinder Nine – 17th August, Year of Our Lord Eighteen-Hundred and Forty-Six, Six of the Clock (Eventide)

I tried to talk to George of Mrs Hansham the other night. He would not listen. His revulsion is absolute. He says now he shall no longer accept the care of Doctor Farrow. I am at a loss.

Cylinder Ten – 20th August, Year of Our Lord Eighteen-Hundred and Forty-Six, Ten of the Clock and Forty Minutes (Night)

It can be endured no longer.

Cylinder Eleven – 21st August, Year of Our Lord Eighteen-Hundred and Forty-Six, Seven of the Clock (Eventide)

Well... And so... I have conceived a plan to introduce, by iterated modifications, a most subtle flaw in the transportation engine that will cause it to fail completely and terribly, though without easy diagnosis, such that the Empire will be forced to abandon it in perpetuity lest they throw good money after bad. I believed I had, in my very words, afforded the Empire 'the liberty of all the globe.' Hah. A sour irony. I have facilitated the infliction of a travesty of justice upon our people. In the last months, I have come to understand what the Empire truly values. And so, hah, I shall put forward in stages the alterations of my design under the guise of savings in efficiency which will put more coin in the pocket of the treasury. This, I am certain, they shall take interest in.

When the device fails, it is likely the *Dolores* shall be destroyed. It will claim lives. In many cases, I shall be restoring a death sentence to convicts who escaped it. But it shall be done once and no more, and that will be an end. And, yes...

I recall something Mary Hansham told me – that even a god-fearing woman like herself had, in the darkest moments, thought of self-murder when confronted with the future afforded her.

Cylinder Twelve – 11th September, Year of Our Lord Eighteen-Hundred and Forty-Six, Six of the Clock and Twenty Minutes (Eventide)

My designs proceed as I anticipated... Yes. And now I stand near ready to complete the project of dismantling all that I have built with my ill-starred life. Only... Ah... Only George... George has worsened. He is more troubled now than he was even before the arrival of Farrow. I do not... I do not know how long remains for him. And I cannot leave him. I have convinced Caruthers I must be present to oversee the final implementation of the 'perfection' of my design. Hmph... The implication for my own future is as it seems. However... I cannot go. I cannot enact the final stage of this dreadful undertaking and desert George. I have told him as much. Whatever he thinks of me, I will not let him die alone.

Cylinder Twelve Continued – 12th September, Year of Our Lord Eighteen-Hundred and Forty-Six, Four Minutes Past Mid-Night

As I recorded the last entry, George swallowed Farrow's laudanum. He is dead.

This concludes the transcription of the cylinders produced by Mr Farthing. Appended to the collection was this hand-written note, handed to Mr Alderson upon his final meeting with Mr Farthing at Bristol New Gaol, on the first day of October, Eighteen-Hundred and Forty-Six:

*My name is Clarence Meredith Farthing. Mine is the respon-
sibility for the creation of the so-called 'transportation engine'
which has seen, in the latter part of this year, the great increase
in the policy of transportation of convicts to the colonies of New
Zealand and New South Wales. How this came about I have
documented in a series of wax cylinders now commended to the
hand of my attorney, Mr Alworth Anderson.*

*What remains to say is very little. I have come to understand the
evil of this policy and to find my own part in it an ineradicable
stain upon my nature. I have sought in recent days to orchestrate
the destruction of the machine. Subsequent to the death of the
one man dearest to me in the world, I put this intent into motion.
In my haste or in my nervous disposition, my object was given
away before I could act upon it. I was arrested aboard the ship*
Dolores *on the Seventeenth of September of this year.*

*Through a truly exceptional commitment to his office, Mr Alder-
son has saved me from a sentence of treason. This commutation
came at the requirement of a statement from me in which I apol-
ogised unreservedly for what was deemed a grief-stricken act
of brief insanity. This letter I intend shall be released sometime
after I am gone from the gaol. I have written it to make known
that my apology was nought but a sham. Though I deeply regret
that my undertaking threatened the loss of many lives and (for
what it matters) a vessel of the Empire, still I cannot truly apologise. Not, at least, for the aim of eradicating the accursed engine
I created. No – my apology is that I ever created the engine in
the first. My apology is that I continued to work for its realisation even once aware of the purpose it would serve. My apology
is to every man and woman now living out their sentence in the
colonies or who has already perished under such a sentence.*

*I await my own sentencing still, but my attorney, Mr Alderson,
has told me what to expect. It is fitting. I know I shall not survive it. If the gaol and the journey do not claim me, I will surely
claim myself, for I am weak. But I would rather be condemned*

284

to serve one score-thousand days as a transportee than for one more day to serve the ends of the Empire.

Bath Time

- Andy Bigwood -

The Pump Rooms, Bath Spa

The circular pool of water glowed blue-white, as if the static electricity generated by the doctor's marvellous medicinal machine and discharged into it was frozen at the moment of maximum intensity. A minute later, a decapitated head flopped onto the 2000-year-old stone floor, and the smallest of the Roman Baths returned to a semblance of normality. Of the gentleman and his party, nothing remained, not even a ripple.

Mr Charles Wisdom, towel attendant, took one look and ran for the stairs. His cries of "Mr Grimsdale! Mr Baverstock!" echoed through Bath's world-famous spa.

Three months later

Tom glanced again at the scribbled note in his hand, the smear of a bloody fingerprint giving immediacy and urgency to the message.

Meet me in the coal cellar of The Crown *on Westgate. As your life depends upon it, tell no-one.*

- Emms

Of course, he had ridden out post-haste. Emms (Emmaline) was his eldest brother's fiancée and an inveterate trouble magnet. They had first met during what the *Evening Post* had called the 'Lanterns of Death Affair.' He'd been an air-boy aboard the naval airship *Great Southern* and had received a midshipman's commission as a reward for his part in it. He suspected she'd also had something to do with 'The Hotwells Horror' and of course the infamous 'Leigh Woods Lycanthrope' incident (although she'd denied the first and claimed the latter had just been an Irish Johnny down on his luck).

A clatter of boots on the wooden steps of the cellar signalled the girl's arrival. Emms eschewed skirts, favouring the scandal of riding boots and dockworkers' denims.

"Thomas? What on earth are you doing here?" she asked, a two-shot derringer appearing in her hand.

Tom handed her the note, ignoring the gun.

Lowering the pistol, Emms scanned it and then handed it back along with a crumpled paper, clearly of the same provenance. "It seems we are both at the pleasure of some third party."

Emms's note read: *Spring-heeled Jane, it is to your advantage to investigate the oddity of Westgate Street at* The Crown.

Tom raised an eyebrow. 'Spring-heeled Jane' was a notorious masked adventuress and suffragist, her exploits in the cause of female liberation serialised in broadsheet cartoons. Upon reflection, it made entirely too much sense that Emms and Jane might be one and the same.

"Okay, let's skip forward past the conversation where Emmaline says she's not Jane and Midshipman Bishop denies he's secretly still crushing on her." The young-sounding voice came from the back of the cellar. "You don't have time, you really don't."

Raising his lamp, Tom turned it upon the shadowed corner to reveal a boy of about his own age dressed in a dark grey riding coat over an army-red shirt that appeared to have a hood instead of a collar. The boy crouched next to the decapitated head of some giant reptile, its jaws wider than

288

the boy's torso, shark-like teeth decorated with strings of rotten flesh from its last meal.

"It's a Megalosaurus bucklandii, a juvenile. Obviously, not meant to be here." The boy poked the head with some sort of telescopic metal pointing stick. "Don't give credence to moving picture presentations that claim a Meg can't see you if you stand very still; that's what they have nostrils for! Sorry, rambling a bit there. You needed to see it. My credentials, as it were."

"You have our attention, Mister...?"

"Student. I'm just a student. I'm not allowed a name, copyright reasons apparently." The boy shrugged, pulling back his hood to reveal short red hair and piercing green eyes.

Tom noted the cleanness of the cut that had severed the beast's head, sliced straighter than a Frenchy's steam-guillotine. A feeling of dread crept up his spine. He'd seen a cut like that before. "This is about the hot tub incident at the Roman Baths, isn't it?"

"Yep." The student nodded once and flicked a glance at Emms. "As you are both aware, electrical energies are currently being touted as a cure for everything from madness and the common cold to... er-hmm... *ladies' problems*. Three months ago, a true genius in the field came up with the idea of combining the benefits of hot spa water with electricity for double the benefit in a single bath."

"I know about this," Emms said. "The maniac had just fried three ladies of questionable morals, along with Lord Hungerford, when the staff intervened. After the *Evening Post* put it about that Hungerford had died of a heart attack, I investigated. I've found that an aristocratic heart attack so rarely involves the participation of an actual heart these days."

"Even that's only the official story," Tom added. "I was put in charge of the team the Navy sent to clean up the gore. All they found was a young lady's head, sliced clean through the neck. The admiralty thought the quack might have discovered some new sort of death ray, very exciting. The next day, one of our marines shot a chap for being where he shouldn't. The scoundrel was very angry, armed with a short sword and dressed like a Roman. My air-boys were sent back to the ship after that, sworn to secrecy."

The Student glanced at a small pocket watch strapped to his wrist. "It was a gladius, not a short sword. So, moving on.... The sacred waters of the Tuatha Sulis, what you know as the 'Roman Baths,' contain trace amounts of Praseodymium Flerovide. Which, when hit with a static electrical charge, reverses polarity to become an unstable time crystal. Lord Hungerford and his questionable associates have been Schrödinger-ed. Lost in time, theoretically neither dead nor alive until someone observes them. Obviously, I need you two to go in after them and save the world as you know it."

Emms raised her pistol, aiming squarely between the Student's eyes. "I must congratulate you, mister Student. Your flim-flam is top-notch. One question though: why us? If you are telling the truth, we must inevitably conclude that you are yourself are an experienced time traveller. Surely such a person has a greater chance of success than a midshipman and... a rapscallion?"

The Student grinned. "You'd be right. My interference is strictly forbidden. I'm a student, I'm not qualified to lord it over the timelines. Even this conversation is going to be hard to explain if it gets back to The Preceptor. That said, we're doing it anyway, and it's traditional to have companions on this sort of caper. You know, to do the heavy lifting, make the tea, that sort of thing."

Tom was somewhat surprised the last comment hadn't evoked a bullet from Emm's piece. She was that sort of a girl.

Abbey Green was quiet, despite its proximity to the nearby tourist attraction, the notorious bakery where Sally 'Sweeny' Lunn, the bloody baker of Bath, had sold her sausage and two veg pasties. Presumably the heavy military presence was deterring most of the usual lollygaggers.

Tom ducked back out of sight. "They've tightened security around the Roman Baths since I was last here. We have a brace of Scots Greys riding Mark IV automata patrolling the courtyard. There's at least one redcoat on the perimeter wall and a murphy-be-darned Harrier class airship moored directly over the main lido."

The Student seemed unperturbed, checking the watch tied to his wrist.

"Relax, Tom," said Emms. "The clues are there if you care to think on it. You will observe that The Student frequently checks his pocket watch therefore time is of the essence. I will warrant that, like a boy playing toy soldiers, he's arranged all of the playing pieces just so. This hour will doubtless be the most opportune time for this enterprise."

"Spot on, Spring-heel," replied the time traveller. "The airship is why we are doing this today and not three months ago. The government's scientific adviser has by now figured out that all three of the Roman bathing pools can act as time-portals. The Navy is about to send that Harrier through the larger lido pool on a recon mission. As for 'why now?' In about five minutes, the Duke of York will be arriving to 'take the waters,' unaware that the Navy has commandeered the facility. Old Yorky is most particular about things going as he orders them."

"Denying his royal stuffed shirted-ness access to his hot-tub?" Emms grinned. "That won't go down well at all."

The Student handed Tom a cardboard folder punched through with a green treasury tag and stamped 'top secret' in red ink. "This will get you past the guard post in the novelty rock emporium."

"That isn't going to work," said Emms. "Whilst it's plausible that Midshipman Bishop might accomplish such a feat, any guards worth their salt will not allow an oddly dressed civilian boy to accompany him, much less a girl."

"Technically, I'm already inside, being arrested for my fashion sense, but that's not important right now. Sorry Emmaline, but you'll have to use your legendary Spring-heels to get in. You get to draw all the attention from the armoured cavalry until the last second."

"My capacity for leaping tall buildings in a single bound is entirely a product of the gutter press," whispered Emms angrily. "The springs allow a single jump of five feet, not fifteen. The perimeter wall is quite beyond me."

Instead of answering, the Student opened one of the ash cans next to the wall of the chip shop and extracted a pair of ski-boot adaptors that ended in futuristic-looking re-curved blades.

"I borrowed these from an Olympian. You'll do fine," said the Student, glancing at his watch again. "It's time."

In the distance, someone shouted "*Hodie, ego nova pisces vendere, captus est hodie!*" A moment later the same voice yelled, "Today, I sell fresh fish, caught today!"

Glancing in the direction of the street market, Tom noted several of the shoppers appeared to be dressed in the Roman fashion. He blinked, only to see the same shoppers now dressed more appropriately for an English gentleman.

"Did you see…?"

"Never mind that! Look!" interrupted Emms.

Dwarfing the Abbey stood a bronze statue of a Roman emperor, its hand level with the tip of the spire. On the pedestal were six words that turned Tom's stomach to ice.

PRIMUS IMPERATOR AUGUSTUS REX
CHARLYS HUNGERFORDUS

"Seriously? 'Primary imperial emperor-king?' Compen-sating much?" muttered the Student. "Tom, Emms, you need to go now. We are officially out of time!"

Tom tried to remain calm as he walked toward the check-point, still doubting that he had even the slightest chance of success. His doubts ended when he saw who was in charge of the checkpoint; his brother Matt.

"Tom? What on Earth are you doing here, little chum?"

For a second, Matt's uniform included a crested helmet before reverting.

"Hello, Matt," Tom replied, annoyed at the 'little chum' epithet. He stood nearly eye to eye with Matt these days. "I'm delivering documents from Lady Emmaline. You know, the same sort of thing as *last time*."

Matt's eyes widened. 'Last time' had involved Emmaline and Tom in the affairs of a notorious Zulu freedom fighter. Quickly, he mouthed the words 'Be careful!' and raised the red and white striped pole-barrier.

The interior of the aristocracy's favourite resort had re-ceived something of a naval themed make-over since Tom's last visit, with new steam pipes and rubber-coated cables of indeterminate purpose. The journey through the Pump Rooms to the great Roman Lido was uneventful, the furi-ous shouts emanating from the front entrance appeared to occupy the attentions of redcoats and white-coated scientists alike. The situation only went south as he stepped out into the Lido itself. A few paces away, next to a tightly wound steel Chambers-coil, he found a pair of guardsmen. Their Gatling-pistols were aimed at a surrendered Student, his hands raised above his head.

"Student?" Tom blurted out, causing the nearest guardsman to swing his six-barrel in Tom's direction.

The guardsman was about to speak when the air was rent by the terrifying steam whistle of a Mark IV armoured cavalry automata, followed by the pop-pop-pop of its two-pounder Puckle gun. The entire group turned to see one of the twenty-foot tall behemoths stagger backward, hitting the outer wall of the lido.

Dislodged from his control-saddle, the rider tumbled head-first into the redcoat who'd been patrolling the wall, sending both flying.

At the last instant, Spring-heeled Jane leapt clear of the stricken automata. Somersaulting, she landed on the lowest of Bath Abbey's roofs, immediately leaping to the higher roof of the nave as the second Scots Grey engaged. A line of white circles punched its way along the soot-darkened ecclesiastic stone as the automata-rider let loose with a burst of two-pounder hardshot. There followed the roar of its shoulder-mounted six-pounder and the clatter of ejected shell casings against the cobbles.

For a moment, all four of them stared up in awe at the mayhem caused and the neat round hole punched through the ancient spire. Military manuals all said battle-mechanisms were unsuited to urban combat. The Mark IV's rider was giving a textbook demonstration of why that was so.

Regaining his wits, Tom gambled on deception. "You men, I'll deal with the prisoner. Report to the duty officer at the front entrance. The Duke of York's life may be in danger!"

Once the two had rushed away, he turned to the Student, who still had his hands raised.

"What next?" he asked.

"You... *know* me?"

"Yes, I jolly well know you, you time travelling jackanape!"

"Okay, sorry. This is obviously going to be even worse than I thought if I'm cheating like that," said the Student, lowering his hands. "I'm an earlier 'me,' you see. The version of me that you appear to have met knows how this bit goes and has arranged for you to help me out. It's cheating of the worst sort, and I will definitely be having words with myself later. But enough of that, what was my plan?"

Tom sighed. "He... you.. didn't say much past getting into the airship they were going to send through the Roman bath time portal."

"I really annoy myself sometimes. Future-me only does the absolute minimum when he cheats," said the Student, marching toward the Chambers-coil and pushing the forked lever into the 'on' position. "He says it's good for our mental discipline not to be spoon-fed every single time I nearly die."

"Oh, that's encouraging," muttered Tom, following behind. "What do you mean, cheat?"

"Well, obviously this is a do-over, a second or third run-through as it were. I tried to stop this whatever-it-is and got caught by those guards. So, Future-me added you to the scenario and also the young lady who's frankly rocking those running blades!"

A rope ladder dropped in front of them. Glancing up, Tom could see Emms – Spring-heeled Jane – waving from the Harrier's gondola. Beyond the wall, the second Mark IV was stalking around, the rider clearly having lost sight of his target.

Tom had just put his foot on the bottom rung when the world went white.

Lacking time to move it along, the light of the universe stayed exactly where it was, overloading eyes that relied on photons that didn't waste time hanging around.

Eventually, Tom was able to make out the grey canvas hull of the Harrier, dimly lit by an electrostatic bulb. The wide glass windows of the airship's observation blisters were dark, reflecting only the yellow bulb-light and nothing of what lay beyond.

"Oh good, you're up. Do you know how to drive this thing?" asked the Student.

Tom scrambled to his feet and jumped to the ship's wheel, pushing the young time traveller out of the way and strapping himself into the coxswain-seat before doing a swift check of the most critical dials and pressure gauges. "Airships have pilots, not drivers. If you're not qualified, then touch nothing!"

The Student stepped away from the wall of brass valves and levers he'd been nearly brushing against, almost comical in his care.

"Give me a report. What's our status?" snapped Tom, eight years of naval discipline coming to the fore.

"Our lady-friend is still recovering from the polarity reversal of the time crystals. We're still over Bath, obviously." The Student licked a finger and held it aloft as if testing the wind direction. "It's about 6am, in an early January, not sure which one though. Oh, and we're not currently crashing."

The time traveller paused for a second, before adding, "From the lack of city lights, I'd guess we're relatively far into your past. Either fire-use is rare, or we're in pre-pre-history."

"What in Nelson's telescopic eye is pre-pre-history?"

"History is when people write shit down; Pre-history is when people don't do writing yet and tell each other stories instead; Pre-Pre-History is when there aren't any people to tell stories." The Student used his extendable metal stick to prod the compass binnacle. "It's a new word I made up. Do you think it will catch on?"

"No. It won't!" replied Emms disapprovingly from the deck. "I, for one, think it's somewhat irresponsible for a student to history to go around inserting new words. Also, the casual swearing in front of a lady... It smacks of carelessness and disrespect. I'm sure Tom would agree that it's a sad reflection on the moral state of the youth of tomorrow."

Tom winced. He'd heard Emms use that tone on her fiancée, his oldest brother. "Don't drag me into it, Emms! And don't pretend that 'Spring-heeled Jane' hasn't heard coarse language at every turn. I warrant you know some choice phrases that'd make your fiancée blush!"

"That's as maybe, Tom," grumbled Emms. "But one would hope that politeness and self-discipline still had their place in years hence."

The Student glanced away, looking embarrassed. "I suspect my future-self had more than one agenda when he selected you. Sorry, Miss... Emm-Jane...?"

"You may call me Spring-heeled Jane, as you've not given your true name."

"Jane, then. You're right to call me out. We time travellers tend towards arrogance. It's a bit like the Empire's attitude to Africa. It's easy to see a people with less advanced technology and make the assumption that it's the people who are lesser rather than their tech. As a student, I'm given this world in the same way a preschooler is given a sand-box. They say it's a toy, just one world and a single aeon to play about with until you're older. But it's also a trap and a test. An unwise student does the obvious and treats you all like lead soldiers and dress-up dolls, playing out childish scenarios and watching it all burn because boys like fires. The test is to have a world that still functions when you're called home, and most especially not to get any sand on anyone's carpets either before, during, or after."

"I have changed my mind, Mister Student," Emms replied. "You may call me Emms, or Emmaline if we are in polite company. Now, to business. At your behest we've stolen a very experimental scout ship, crushed a 2000-year-old national treasure, and shot holes in the Bishop of Bath and Wells' favourite church. What is our next step?"

Tom glanced over his shoulder at the pair. He'd been thinking on their state of affairs whilst the others bantered. While the Harrier was a fine ship, state of the art for a scouting airship, the one thing it most definitely was not was a time machine.

"I was wondering that myself," he said. "Our ship looks like it was well provisioned, but I'm not seeing any obvious time engine for getting us back."

"The correct term is time-rotor," the Student huffed. "Not that we'd be allowed access to one anyway. No, I expect we'll be improvising. The Bath time pools are always present here, so all we need to do is give the big pool a quick zap of electricity and away we go. Because of quantum entanglement, we don't even need to worry about 'when' Lord Hungerford might pop up, we'll always be materialising close by."

"I don't understand."

"I'll explain later. The important bit is that Lord Hungerford's party always arrives at the pool and can only get as far as they can manage on foot. I'd expect them to stay close by at first, given they won't know what the fu– what on earth... has happened. Due to timey stuff, there's a thirty percent chance he's somewhere below. If he's not there, we'll charge up the ol' flux capacitor and roll the dice again."

Tom noted how thoroughly complacent the time-travelling boy looked. It was infuriating, particularly as the clever so-and-so had missed something important. "We don't have electrics. The Harrier relies on a steam turbine for power with a state-of-the-art mechanical difference engine control system. An air-cruiser might have room for electric lights, but a lean fighting vessel like the Harrier doesn't."

Much to Tom's annoyance, the Student seemed unbothered by the revelation.

"Well, I'm sure my future-self wouldn't have made such a schoolboy error. There has to be something around here or he would have given you a power core to bring aboard."

"All we were given was a 'top secret' folder full of chopped up *Evening Post* pages and the footwear of some Greek god for Emms," replied Tom, turning the wheel so that the Harrier's course avoided the bulk of Beechen Cliff looming out of the dark.

The student lurched across the cabin as the airship heeled over, dropping to his knees next to Emms. "Emms, have a feel around the top of your new heels. I expect you'll find a secret compartment."

"There!" Emms held out six small cylinders, each with a copper coloured end and the logo of a tastelessly cheerful rabbit. "I infer that these were powering the new spring-heels and that the heels are now inert?"

"Nah, you're still good to go. A spring is still a spring. These were just giving someone a slight competitive edge in performance." He twisted around to give Tom an insufferably cheery grin "It seems 'other *me*' has supplied us with six shots at this rescue."

Tom poked the roaring fire, sending up a flurry of sparks and then turned the improvised spit with its cargo of a wild 'thing' that smelled reassuringly like roast chicken. They were in their third time-zone now, and the novelty had worn off somewhat. They'd spent two days overflying the dense forests of the first time-zone and another day overflying a second. The only difference was the preponderance of pine trees and the whatever-it-was in this one, rather than the oaks, beaches, and chestnuts of the other two.

It was evident that Lord Hungerford wasn't present in the primordial forest, but they all needed a rest. The next time-jump might drop them atop the errant lord and they needed to be ready.

Emerging from the forest, Emms crossed the clearing in two easy spring-strides, having seen to 'the essentials' away from her companions. She'd taken to always wearing the spring-heels when outside, even when they might otherwise have been inconvenient.

"It smells good, Tom. I'd say he's nearly done."

"Well, your guess is as good as mine. I'm fairly sure Mrs Beaton's book had very little to say about preparing a pig-sized reptilian rhinoceros covered in peacock feathers," replied Tom. "By the way, I set aside some of the display feathers from its head-frill for you. Should you ever go to Cheltenham races, you'll have the only hat with a Triceratopsid feather."

"You won't catch me wearing anything so impractical near a horse," Emms said, cocking her head to one side, clearly considering something before glancing away toward the tree-line. "What do you make of the Student?"

Tom gave the animal another turn. "God-like powers, might actually own our world, out of his depth. He relies far too much on that future-self of his to bail him out. He has all the flaws of an aristocrat, but at least he knows they're flaws. If you're wondering if we're patsies in some criminal enter-prise... I'd say no. I think he's just like us, a teenager trying to clean up after a house party before the Lord of Time comes home and asks where the elephant came from."

Taking out his air-navy combat knife, Tom sliced into the flank, testing that the juices ran clear. He paused, mid-cut. "Oh shit!"

"Language!"

"Sorry. It just occurred to me what the principal difference is between the current Student and the one we first met."

"Which is?"

"The one we are with right now doesn't have a Meg's head yet! Want to bet those puppies are native to this era right here?"

"Oh shit!"

The Student of time looked increasingly ill at ease as Tom explained about his Megalosaurus bucklandii.

"I am definitely going to give myself a good talking to about this. Bottom line, you're right. This is exactly the place you'd expect to run into three tonnes of near-sighted carnivorous rage monster." The Student paced back and forth, clearly in deep thought. "You say the head was sliced clean off? Not shot or stabbed?"

"Cleanest cut I've ever seen," said Tom. "Not only that, it was a single stroke. We'd need a battle mechanism wielding a ridiculously large broadsword for such a feat."

"It wouldn't be a broadsword. Only novelists call weapons broadswords. The correct term is an 'arming sword.' But that's not important right now. I know how we can do it. You really won't like it though."

Tom strapped himself into the gunner's chair in the Harrier's nose turret, steam hissing as he twitched the turret left, right, up, down. The tight confines, the canvas fabric of the seat, all of it had the comforting familiarity of good honest navy tech.

He had severe reservations about leaving the Student in charge of the Harrier's wheel. But there was no choice. If a navy ship was to fire its guns, then, by God, it would be a navy-boy who fired them. Next, he checked the weapon itself, a two-inch rifled twelve chamber Puckle gun. On his right hand, a ready-rack held ten magazines, five marked blue for solid shot, three yellow for incendiary, one white for star shells, and the final magazine coded red for explosive. In practice, he only had sixty rounds; the special ammo was unsuited to the task at hand.

Much to his surprise, Emms hadn't had a problem with her role in the affair. He could only assume that 'Spring-heeled Jane' led a far more dangerous life than had been officially recorded, inuring her to the risks of her part in it.

In the distance, something exploded, followed by a ridiculous high pitched 'Cheep!'

Tom felt slightly embarrassed for the poor brute. Any good author would have had it go 'Roarrh!' rather than 'Cheep!' He resolved that should they survive, his diary would definitely say 'Roarrh' and liken it to the call of one of the wild African carnivores.

Seconds later, Emms bounded into the clearing, her sleeve ripped by a pair of parallel slashes.

"Cheeeep!" exclaimed the enraged Megalosaurus bucklandii, snapping conifer branches like toothpicks as it lunged after its spring-heeled prey.

"No, you bloody don't!" he snapped, training the Puckle at the centre of mass and firing.

Boom! Click... click... click... Boom! Click...click...click.

302

Intellectually, Tom knew the gun was the fastest firing weapon in the Royal Navy's arsenal, but at that moment it seemed the firing chamber took an age to release, rotate, and lock the next chamber in place.

Emms dodged, her left spring-heel sliding dangerously on the riverside mud. The creature's jaws opened to an impossible extent, like a cobra's but with many more teeth. It lunged, Emms rolling to the side at the last instant.

Tom repeatedly pressed the button that would turn the turret, desperate to get the Puckle back on target. He expected the Meg to twist around, devouring his brother's fiancée in two swift gulps, the first ripping her in half, the second tossing the remnants into the air to be gulped down completely un-chewed.

Somewhat to his surprise, nine-foot tall feathered monsters with implausibly long teeth had exactly the same resistance to 'five rounds rapid' as a Johnny Foreigner did.

Instead of devouring Emms, the head hit the ground, making a small trench in the mud, whilst further away the body slumped awkwardly into the ferns.

A 'thump' and the rocking motion of the gondola informed him that Emms had leapt aboard. A second later, the Student dropped the electrical cable into the steaming time-pool, sending the airship and the Megalosaurus head hurtling through time.

Once the purple spots had faded and Tom could actually see, he noted that they'd finally found civilisation. Below was a small settlement; in Tom's time, it would hardly have counted as a village, consisting of a single impressive brick building, four streets worth of timber and thatch roundhouses, and a six-foot-high stone wall that might keep a foreign Johnny out for all of about three minutes. At every street corner, white and purple banners in the Roman style displayed Lord Hungerford's profile be-decked in laurels, clearly signalled that their quarry was at bay.

"*Aspice! Caput autem belua!*" (Look! A monster's head!) cried a voice below.

He glanced over his shoulder at the Student. "I assume you have deployed some sort of translation mechanism?"

"It's a state-of-the-art i-Colloquialiser 6; you can rely on a completely accurate translation," replied the time traveller cheerfully. "Although it does still have trouble with Zulu rhyming slang and the word 'apple.'"

"They are going to notice us at any moment," called Emms from the landing skid she was perched on. "Our presence will doubtless cause consternation."

"It's okay, I have a plan!"

Tom glared at the Student, trying to shift his fingers out of the ropes binding his hands behind his back.

"Take me to your leader? Seriously? That was the plan?"

"Trust me, works every time."

"Flying is easy, it's the landings that'll kill you," muttered Tom darkly.

"Oh hush, both of you," said Emms, adding in a whisper, "Now, follow my lead."

Having already freed her hands, Emms pushed past the startled legionaries, striking what could only be called a hero pose. The Romans had not thought to remove her heels and she stood a foot taller than everyone in the room.

One of the courtiers whispered "Atalanta," which Tom understood to refer to the female Argonaut of legend. Suddenly he had a sneaking suspicion that a sailing trip off Gallipoli might lie ahead.

"Lord Hungerford, I presume?" said Emms, voice dripping with contempt.

The contempt was easy to understand. Charlie Hungerford had definitely gone native. The Member of Parliament for Jersey lounged on purple cushions and was being fed grapes by scantily clad maidens (who looked a bit cold given the ambient temperature of southwest England in May), a wreath of laurels on his brow.

"The Devil! Spring-heeled Jane?"

"You've been a naughty boy, Charles, and it's time for you to go home."

"In a pig's eye! Why would I wish to give up all this?" Hungerford waved a hand at the court he'd assembled. "Besides, as an Englishman, I know a damned sight more about running a proper empire than some spaghetti farming Johnny from Latium ever will."

Ignoring him, Spring-heeled Jane cast her eyes around the court. "If this pile of barbarian lard were gone," she asked the court at large, "which of you would rule in Rome's name?"

Several of the toga-wearing courtiers suddenly started paying a lot more attention. Predators sensing wounded prey, one and all.

"Now, see here!" protested Hungerford.

Without warning, an amphora shattered against Hungerford's head, wielded by one of his maidens. A cricketer of another era might've called that swing a yorker.

"That one's for poor Alice, rest 'er soul. Besides, Charlie-boy only paid for one night. And I likes me modern comforts, I does," said the maiden. "Come on Millicent, let's get 'is Augusty-ness 'ome to Blighty."

"No argument here, my lubber," replied the other courtesan. "But I'll want to take Sextus Magnus Gallus with me."

The handsome young guard she'd just batted her eyelashes at stepped forward to cut through Tom's bonds with a single stroke.

"Excellent, that's that sorted then," said Emms. She pointed to a particularly corpulent Roman who rivalled Hungerford in the over-fed stakes. "You... you can play at being in charge, whilst we take this scoundrel to meet his fates."

The piggy little eyes narrowing, the designated consul licked his lips and signalled one of the slave boys to pick up Hungerford's fallen laurels.

"Is it me, or was that entirely too easy?" asked Tom as they pushed the groaning aristocrat through the gondola's hatch.

"It's you," replied Emms, the Student, and the two 'ladies of Lansdown' in a creditable chorus.

"Ironically, Time doesn't like change," explained the Student, pouring a vial of liquid into the steaming sacred pond that would one day be Bath Spa. "Think of it like a river, sometimes a dam will cause a course change, but mostly the river flows back into the existing channel because it's easier."

"What was that stuff?" Tom asked, his suspicion rising.

"Flesh-eating bacteria," explained Student cheerfully. "We'll have far fewer time travel accidents if the waters' healing properties involve your nose dropping off."

Emms and Tom exchanged a worried glance.

"Just kidding," replied the Student. "Now, let's see, a quick pop backwards to establish Emms as the legendary female argonaut 'Atalanta,' then pop in at a local post office so that you two get your mysterious summonses to *The Crown* on Westgate, and then back home for tea. Job's a good 'un!"

Tom sighed, knowing the Student's optimism was entirely unfounded. Vaulting into the pilot's chair, he slammed his hand down on the big red button they'd improvised for discharging the electrical battery into the hot bath. Time Travel, he concluded, was entirely over-rated!

(Note to readers: electricity and water really don't mix well. Please don't try this at home! *Spring-heeled Jane is inspired by genuine 19th century 'man-of-mystery' Spring-heeled Jack.)

The Pilgrim

- Amanda McLachlan -

Absorbed in flossing the bones of a corset, Sarah was as startled as the shop bell when the door flew open.

She slipped through the dividing curtain and found the widow Empire Brown on the threshold, holding a handkerchief to her nose while her maid, Nes, deflated her skirts.

"Oh, Mrs Brown – this is an unexpected pleasure."

"I trust I don't need an appointment to visit my own corsets, Miss Fisher?" The widow's eyes crinkled with humour.

"Of course not. Please, come in." Sarah could feel the warmth from her shop rushing out past her and down Christmas Steps. She pulled her shawl high up around her neck.

Nes worked quickly and soon Mrs Brown was flattened enough to be able to pass through the door and be seated.

"They took three hours to inflate this morning," said Mrs Brown. "I was unable to call on Mrs Dando. I do wonder if, perhaps, you were correct in thinking that inflatable skirts were more of an encumbrance than my crinolines. But I cannot seem to prevent myself from embracing new ideas."

"I can show you some of my new designs if you wish."

"I have a fascination with the process, Miss Fisher. The mechanics of it. Bonamy taught me a good deal about the business of building ships and he often took me to the yard to watch, but since he died, I've been left in no doubt that the docks are no place for an unaccompanied woman. I have been turned away from college lectures. I am too old for school. I fear my mind is becoming decrepit. I would be very interested to see how you work – you have always had such a neat hand."

"You would like me to sit and sew at your home? I don't–"

"No – I can sit in your workshop and watch. I will cause you no nuisance."

"Well... my workshop is... is..." Sarah thought quickly. "I'm sure you understand the private nature of my work. The mannequins are named and wearing their garments."

"Oh, dear me, no. I shall sit here then, and you shall show me your makings. Agnes will bring us some tea."

Sarah hustled Nes through the curtain into a dark narrow room.

A sleepy oil lamp limned a trestle table set up with pins, thread, lacings and facings, a hole punch, and an iron. An assortment of mannequins crowded around the table like mourners at a wake.

Sarah hurried to the fireplace where she kicked aside her mattress then pulled a tray with cups and a teapot on it from a shelf.

"Sorry, it's a bit cramped in here, I couldn't let her..."

"It's all right," said Nes. "I know."

Nes was a washed out watercolour of a girl with large country hands which she had learned to keep quiet. She set up the tea things and put the kettle to boil on sullen coals as Sarah gathered up an armful of baleen and her pattern book.

"Nes – there's a slice of seed cake under that cloth. You're welcome to it."

Sarah got back to the shop in time to see a gang of Steps boys run away from the window, leaving their sharp nose prints behind.

"Ah, this must be the whalebone you use. Do you know, I've never seen it in person until now?"

The widow took a piece of baleen, the colour of an old tooth, and flexed it.

"Have you ever seen a whale, Miss Fisher?"

"No, Mrs Brown, but my cousin who lives in Hull has heard tales about them. They sing to each other, apparently."

"Tea is ready, madam." Nes had slipped through the curtain without seeming to open it.

She had a crumb in the corner of her mouth.

After pouring the tea she stood silently at the window, the bellows for inflating the skirts at her feet, her hands resting in front of her.

"My cousin says that every lady in England must have a whale's worth of bone in her wardrobe by now."

"Sing, you say? The whales?"

"Beg pardon, Mrs Brown?"

"Sing?"

"Yes. That's what the sailors tell at the port. Are you all right, Mrs Brown? Mrs Brown?"

Sarah caught the widow as she slumped forward, pearls of sweat on her brow.

"Nes – get a bucket."

Sarah and Nes fanned Mrs Brown as she vomited and dabbed at her mouth when she finally sat up.

Her eyes stormed. "They sing? Do you mean to tell me that I have been entertaining angels in my wardrobe unaware? That my wardrobe teems with dismembered angels?"

The widow Empire Brown startled the shop bell once more as she rushed out of the door, and Nes had to run to keep up with her as she strode up the steps to her carriage. Mrs Brown had not even waited to have her skirts inflated for the walk.

That night, Sarah woke to a loud crash. Wrapping her shawl about her, she hurried through the curtain to see a pile of glass on the shop floor and a brick in the middle of it.

Looking out through the hole where her window had been, she saw a woman bundled down with her baby in the shop door opposite.

"It weren't me," said the woman. "I seen a Gennelman do it."

Sarah spent the rest of the night shovelling broken glass as the city's early morning breath blew through her shop.

At first light, she went to her cash box. She was wondering how those few shillings were going to pay for boards to be put up and new glass to be put in never mind food and rent and suppliers' bills, when a great commotion roared up Christmas Steps, a stampede of hobnail boots, shrieks and shouts and hoots and whistles.

It can only be Gullock Tyning, she thought.

She stepped outside to greet him. He was striding up the cobbles balancing planks on his hands, and upon those planks, two on each end, sat near full-grown Steps boys.

"Off," he said when he reached the shop.

"I hear you had some trouble last night," said Gullock, resting a plank against the window frame.

"It wasn't the Steps boys. It was a Gentleman that did it."

Gullock barely raised his eyebrows. Nothing surprised him.

The gathered crowd had hushed, waiting, and got their reward when Gullock banged nails directly into the planks with the flat of his hand.

Sarah helped him pick up the pennies thrown at his feet and brought him inside for a breakfast of bread and dripping.

She lay awake that night, listening to her money worries trampling through her head but heard nothing else, so she was taken aback the next morning to find, when she opened shop, a quotation painted on the boarded-up window:

"Within these premises are the trappings and the suits of woe."

The Gentleman came back the next night, disappearing into the river fog after leaving another message:

"Repent: for the kingdom of heaven is at hand."

The Steps boys gathered to watch Sarah's reaction and they attracted clusters of sightseers at their edges.

"This is what happens when you invite a man such as Gullock Tyning into the back of your shop. This is where it leads," sniffed an apple seller, tugging her shawl tightly around her.

On the following night, Sarah lay in wait. A moment after St John's had struck three, she heard the scuffle of a step. Gripping the fire poker in one hand she flung open the door, alarming its bell, and caught him, the Gentleman, with his pot of paint, accompanied by a shame-faced maid.

The Gentleman was quite unabashed. He issued Sarah with a bold stare and said, "One thing I know, that whereas I was blind, now I see."

His lips poised to say more, and in that gesture, Sarah recognised him.

"Mrs Brown?" she said.

The widow was wearing her husband's clothes – Sarah knew the cut of them – and she had clearly given up on corsets for Sarah could see the outline of her breasts tucked into the trouser waistband.

"I am come to make you an offer, Miss Fisher. I intend to remake the Whale."

"She is preaching all over," said Gullock wiping his mouth. Sarah had cooked him a pork chop. "The crowds are bigger than mine on a Saturday afternoon. The Queen Square boys throw stones at her from the trees – it doesn't deter her."

"When she has a passion, nothing will stop her. For years I have seen her progress to excess through the size of her crinolines."

Seeing her expression, he said, "You admire her."

"I do. She could be sat at home taking callers, but instead she is building something never before built. Making work for people. Making something beautiful. It amazes me, what she has achieved by sheer force of her will. She is magnificent."

Gullock smiled. "And wealthy."

"For now. But at least if she bankrupts herself she can have a place in your troupe."

A jolly fire crackled in the grate. The whole room radiated with the glow of a series of lamps which brightened the dark corners and garnered a metallic gleam on the table: a new sewing machine. The mannequins had been stripped and pushed into a corner from where they watched over the proceedings like a host of stout angels.

Sarah had a whale in her workshop.

She had unpicked reams of black mourning silk, baleen, and inflation tubes from Empire Brown's entire wardrobe and reassembled it into the skin and skeleton of a whale.

Galantine de Poulet, a French naturalist, had been brought over from Paris by Mrs Brown. He could not speak English, and Sarah had no French, but somehow between them they had managed to draft a pattern while Mrs Brown looked on, tap tap tapping her stovepipe hat with her cane.

"Ready then?" said Gullock, scraping back his chair.

He put his fingers in his mouth and signalled a whistle. A Steps boy put his head around the curtain.

Gullock lifted the fabric body of the whale and fed it through the curtain and onto the raised arms of the Steps boys. Sarah watched it slide out of her workshop and out on to the street. Gullock stood under the head end and the boys lined up in pairs behind him, and the street roared when Gullock whistled and the whale began to walk in slow procession down Christmas Steps.

Sarah followed, feeling the whoops and cheers rain down on her from open windows, wincing whenever the silks got too close to a wall or a sticky child reached out to smooth them.

The crowds grew and jostled behind her as the whale body flowed across town like a black sail, and as word spread, the whole of Bristol turned out of factories, shops, leaning timbered houses, taverns and alleys, courts and yards, and passages. They followed it, cheering, alongside the clotted stinking River Frome. Down the Anchor Road it poured and past Canon's Marsh where a horse shied and broke off at a gallop, stirrups flapping against its sides. Through Hotwells went the whale, beneath the terrace-clustered hillside, and out spilled the ale drinkers, the card sharpers, the pickpockets, and drunken undertakers. The Steps boys never broke stride, not one nipped away to cut a purse or steal a pie; they followed Gullock Tyning beneath the whale, two abreast, streaming across the bridge and down the Cumberland Road where the Wapping Road girls came down to hiss at them, and the whale floated on to Albion Dockyard where it was met by Charles Hill, shipwright, and the look of grave dismay upon his face.

The widow Empire Brown stood next to him, entranced, her eyes filled with divine light.

"He will not put his name to it," confided Mrs Brown, as the shipwright strode away and closed his office door behind him. "Be mindful of your skirts, this ladder is treacherous."

As Gullock distributed shillings to the Steps boys, the widow and Sarah climbed down an iron ladder set into the wall of the dry dock to where the flat-bottomed hull of Mrs Brown's darling waited.

A rectangle of aggrieved faces stared down at them.

"They do not agree with my proposal to do away with secondary sails. Surely the screw propeller negates the need for such things? Besides, a mast would spoil the aesthetics. It must be beautiful."

"You want to sail it? In the harbour?"

"Of course I want to sail it! The Whale must be returned to its natural element."

Sarah looked around at the gear wheels, gear chains, cylinders and saltwater boilers, the engine that would drive it all.

"How far will you go with it?"

But Mrs Brown did not reply; she had marched away to issue a stream of orders to a row of sober-faced engineers.

Sarah felt a tweak at her sleeve.

"Nes – what happened to you?"

The girl looked paler than usual. A thin red crescent curved around her left eyebrow.

316

"I caught a stone. Sarah – you don't need anyone, do you? You must be so busy. I could help. I want to leave her, but I don't want her name on my character."

"Oh, Nes... I daren't take anyone on. I've had to turn away my customers lately and I don't know if I'll ever get them back. This Whale has been a godsend, but one piece of luck doesn't necessarily lead to another."

The engineers were beginning to form up inside the hull, each holding a pair of bellows.

"I'd better go." Nes rubbed away a tear with her wrist and went in to join them.

A great shadow fell over the dry dock. Sarah looked up and saw the whale skin she had stitched being lowered on to the hull.

For a moment, the silks draped over the engineers' heads and the whole effect was that of a withered runner bean pod, but then Mrs Brown gave a shout, and the bellows were applied to the inflation tubes; the skin inflated with a lurch, and with thunderous creaks began to grow out of its sags and wrinkles. The great Whale took shape, groaning and panting as though it was birthing itself, and its silken flanks shimmered in a sudden breeze as though it was already swimming.

Mrs Brown ran up the iron steps and stood on the dock looking down on her creation.

"Behold the Whale!" she cried. "'A King of shreds and patches.'"

Below her, all hands worked on the Whale, attaching the skin to the hull, as Sarah walked carefully around the outside, pins pressed between her lips, dressmaker's chalk in her hand, noting where she needed to put in a dart or ease a hem to ensure a perfect fit.

Any remaining goodwill felt at the shipyard for its previous employer Bonamy Brown, deceased, had been used up by his widow on her project.

She had responded to the air of disapproval and distaste by doubling wages, but reluctance lingered and the yard was not a happy one. Each new phase of building moved like an ungreased cog against the next.

Sarah was the exception to the rule. She embraced every instruction with gusto. Poverty had been bred into her bones, so she felt almost giddy, almost guilty, when she collected her wage slips at the end of each week. She took to pinning them to her walls so that when her earnings inevitably became patchy again, she would never forget that she had once felt almost rich.

As soon as the whale skin had been fitted sleekly to the hull, Sarah was tasked with caulking the seams, which she did up a rope ladder slung from the Whale's sides, with a piping bag and a palette knife to make the job as delicate as possible and without ruining the silks. The phenolic pungency of the pine tar made her nearly as giddy as her wage slips did.

Beneath her, under the skin, worked the carpenters laying out the insides: cabins, berths, stalls, saloons, a dining salon, and a chapel at the head end. Engineers worked in the boiler room.

The Whale sang a new song every day: its notes were made by hammers and saws, chisels and planes, pins and split pins, nuts and bolts, valve gear, connecting rods, bearings, dials, and gauges. Its lyrics were a chorus of curses.

And then came the glassmaker: Mr Alfred J. Nott, of Stapleton Road. He turned up one morning with two yellow eyes, black pupils the size of dinner plates.

There had been some confusion over what a whale's eyes actually looked like. Galantine de Poulet had not responded to any of Mrs Brown's letters on the subject.

Under the press of time, Mr Nott had taken the matter into his own hands and visited a fishmonger where he'd sketched out the eye of a John Dory.

Mrs Brown took the morning off from her preaching to make a ceremony of it.

Sarah climbed down her rope ladder, pot of pine tar in hand, and stood in amongst the small crowd that had gathered. Mrs Brown signalled for hush while Mr Nott and a joiner fitted the eyes into the Whale's head, to make windows in the chapel.

"The eye is the lamp of the body," she said when the glass had been slotted in and fixed. She led a stuttering round of applause, then shinned up to the hatch, disappeared inside the body, and reappeared behind the stained glass bearing lit candles, one for each window.

Quoted Mrs Brown: "His eyes were like a flame of fire!"

No one heard, for at the moment the Whale's eyes flared with light, it seemed to become truly alive, and the spirit of the yard soared like a ship on a wave, and by the time Mrs Brown's head had breached the hatch door, she had a glisk in her eye and two spots of high colour in her cheeks, warmed by the heartfelt cheering of the crowd – "Glory! Glory!"

For this Whale would be something to make the city proud. Where was Hull, where was Liverpool, where was the Port of London, in the manufacture of such a creature? Only Bristol had the vision, the engineers, the shipwrights, who could remake a whale.

The ship workers cheered so loud and so long that Mr Hill was forced from his office to set them all back to work.

Glory! Glory!

From then on, the crowds that had flocked to mock Mrs Brown's preachings came to listen to them instead, and the first boy to throw a stone was dragged from his tree and his ears treated to a cuffing.

Bolder ladies began to leave their corsets idle and walked around the city in pairs wearing their husbands' clothes.

Corsets became unfashionable. Stay-makers' businesses were on the brink of collapse until one had the enterprising idea of making miniature whales out of the discarded corsetry for children to sail on ponds. A wave of imitators followed, and soon the Frome was a graveyard of silk and cotton whales run aground in its sludge.

Letters were sent to the *Chronicle* by Disgusted of Clifton who asked 'Where will it all end?' But it was becoming increasingly unBristolian to question Mrs Brown and her ideas. Leave that to the Fuddy-Duddies!

(Although, in the quieter corners of Gentlemen's Clubs, the issue was raised: if it is difficult to lightly beat your wife because she is wearing your trousers, is it permissible instead to strike her across the face? Could you still call yourself a Gentleman?)

The *Mercury* printed an illustration of Britannia wearing a morning suit; the potteries reproduced it on plate sets and teapots and sold them in their thousands.

The Whale's eyes were kept lit at all times and a legend was born: if ever the light in the Whale's eyes went out, sorrow would fall upon the port of Bristol.

One evening, Sarah stayed late to finish the last of the caulking. Her eyes were raw with fatigue. A full moon lit the dry dock. Water lapped behind the wall. The city's bustle was hushed and far away; only a distant shout from a Hotwells inn carried across the water.

As Sarah applied her brush, a silver shimmer rippled across the surface of the silk. She looked up, but the moon only stared back, flat-faced and still. Dizzy, she steadied herself on the Whale's silken flank. It flinched.

Footsteps clipped across the cobbles.

Mrs Brown's silvered face appeared at the foot of the ladder. "Miss Fisher – is that you?"

"Yes, Mrs Brown."

"I thought no one was here." Mrs Brown laid her hand against the Whale's side, and Sarah felt a thrill run across its skin.

"Miss Fisher, I am glad to see you, as I have another instruction. You see, I have given this Whale a body, and now I wish to give him a voice. Red Maids School has agreed to lend me thirty of their sweetest girls for a choir. I shall provide you with a bolt of fine red cotton – I would like you to make each Maid a set of robes."

Word spread. Gentlefolk travelled far to have a tour of the Whale, while commoners were left to push and shove to get a glimpse of it.

By contrast, Gullock Tyning's troupe was attracting far smaller gatherings and his takings were down.

"I am being pressed to ever greater feats just to break even," he said. "She came up to the Downs twice last week and I lost my crowd, all except for a drunkard who challenged me to an arm wrestle." He put his head to one shoulder then the next. "I feel I'm getting old, Sarah."

"She's a novelty, that's all. Are you coming to the Christening?"

"Why not? There is a rumour Prince Albert will attend."

On the day of the Christening, Prince Albert's train had been delayed, or cancelled, or maybe he never set foot on it.

Gullock whispered in Sarah's ear, "Perhaps the Prince is concerned that his Queen will take on the Bristol fashion while he is gone, and he'll return to find her wearing knicker-bockers and wielding a golf club."

Sarah stifled a snort with her shawl.

The Christening went ahead without the Prince, but first the Whale had to be put in water.

Local dignitaries packed the dock; husbands and wives wore matching frock coats and brightly coloured cravats to indicate the holiday of the occasion. A throng of pie sellers, hurdy-gurdy men, jugglers, and conjurers accosted the hordes of men, women, and children who piled out to watch. A conductor gathered his band around him. Newspapermen pushed to the front.

The band struck up, the dogshores were struck away, and the Whale began its progress down the slipway which had been coated with a foul-smelling mixture of soft soap, tallow, and whale oil to ease its movement. Sarah and Gullock grasped each other's hands as the Whale rushed down the slipway, and the crowd roared when a crash of water signalled its entry into its natural element.

Men lashed the Whale to its moorings.

Mrs Brown cleared her throat and fixed the crowd with her charisma. The band fell silent.

"One morning," she said. "I awoke to the song of a choir in my closet. The song of a whale. I saw my vision clearly–"

"Glory! Glory!" broke in the engineers.

Mrs Brown got her dander up. "I saw my vision clearly. And behold – thou art made whole! I name this Whale, *The Pilgrim*."

She swung a bottle at the bow. It spiralled through the air and landed in the water, unbroken.

The first rumbles of discontent came from the sailors.

Nes relayed the conversation to Sarah over a meat pie. She had been stood, as usual, at the back of the room, hands quietly in front, when Mrs Brown was taken to task by Mr Hill and a roomful of reluctant ship's crew.

"He said he had built the Whale in good faith, never believing it was meant for the open seas. He had indulged her. Mrs Brown had asked for a whale, and a whale is what she got. And a whale is not a ship."

"And how did she reply?"

"Her whiskers quivered. She said that any man knew that a whale could swim, even in the roughest seas. If they had, indeed, as they declared, given her a whale, then it would be perfectly at home in the Arctic waters. They went to and fro for a while, but it boiled down to this – the sailors feel that the Whale is unlucky."

"Why?"

"First, the bottle did not break. Second, she has changed its name from the Whale to *The Pilgrim*. And third, she insists that it's a He, not a She. And everyone knows ships are She."

"But they said themselves it's a whale not a ship."

Nes shrugged. "The crew will not work for her. She will have to advertise."

Sarah's work at the yard was coming to an end. She had been on hand to stitch minor tears where the silks had snagged, but as the fitting out was completed, there was less and less to do. She lent a hand wherever she could. No orders waited for her at her workshop. The Red Maids' robes had been fitted and finished. She had placed an advertisement, offering the sewing machine for sale.

The Pilgrim floated in the harbour, tugging at his moorings, his eyes lit with flame.

One day, in the thin light of dawn, as the river mist rose around him, he began to sing hymns.

The wharf came to a standstill. Men laid down their tools and listened.

The Pilgrim sang with thirty voices, each the voice of a child. Water lapped at his sides. A piano played along inside his head.

Sarah heard it from Cumberland Road as she walked to work. By the time she got there, the singing had stopped, and Mrs Brown was leading a procession of Red Maids, children of the deserving poor, to a well-deserved breakfast. The tiny girls wore their identical red robes and they flowed across the ground in pairs, holding each other's hands.

Pin Shifter and his crew turned up a fortnight later.

Sarah learned about it from Mr Hill. He rushed into her one day as he left his office, head down.

Without apologising he said, "You must use any influence you hold over this woman to persuade her that her ideas are reckless."

"Mr Hill," she replied, "the lady has spent her life untroubled by the inconvenience of self-doubt. She will not let me or anyone else put a dent in her."

"She must not put upon the sea, not with that crew." He tipped his head towards a trio of men who leant against a wall smoking tobacco. "They are canal men come from the Midlands. Canal men!"

The men nodded a greeting.

Pin Shifter, a man thin as his pipe stem, wore a Captain's hat. His face was the colour and texture of pumice, his eyes like chips of coal. His crew was more substantial – Badger Faced Jem kept a full black beard streaked with white, while The Pie Man wore a butcher's apron and had pale lips like strips of pork fat.

"Mr Hill..."

"Yes?"

"Do you believe... have you ever heard sailors say a ship can have a soul? Have you noticed anything strange about the Whale?"

"Everything is strange about this Whale. Go and get some rest, Miss Fisher. And think on how to call that woman's sense back from where she left it."

Gullock stood in the shop doorway, running his hat through his hands.

Sarah held open the curtain, her workshop dark behind her, the faint outline of redundant mannequins just visible in the corner.

"You ready, Gull? I made us a picnic."

Gullock's eyes stayed on his hat. "Signor Gomez arrived in Clifton yesterday. The Modern Samson. He has twenty years on me, Sarah, at least... I'm finished here." He glanced up then looked away. "Our juggler knows the manager of a music hall in Liverpool. They always need a strong man on the door. It would be a steady wage. I– I plan to earn my passage to America... there's a parcel of land for every man and pure, clean air. I'm packing up my leopard skin," he said, with a shallow laugh. He looked up. "You understand?"

Sarah answered immediately. "Yes. Of course. A parcel of land... Well. Good luck."

They walked out into the crowds.

The Pilgrim was to sail North, to the Arctic.

Gullock kept his hand on Sarah's shoulder as they pushed through the crush of people making their way down to the harbour.

"There must be fifty thousand, at least," said Gullock. "I wish I still had my copper pipes to bend for them."

A fine drizzle drifted down to meet the rising morning mist, weighing down flags and bunting. Men, women, and children crowded windows, perched on rooftops all the way up the hillsides; steam packets and pilot boats, wherries and fishing craft thronged the harbour. A group of Steps boys exchanged catapults and stolen cigarettes.

Gullock cut a path through the masses, all the way to *The Pilgrim*'s wharf where they were guests of honour, next to a dancing bear muzzled and in chains.

Mrs Brown, standing on a crate, wearing her husband's best suit, cleared her throat.

Nes slipped away from her side.

"Goodbye, Sarah."

There were lilac rims around her eyes.

"Oh, Nes. Good luck."

"I'll need it."

"I wish you could stay here. I wish I could give you a job, but I'm having to take in piece work now. Couldn't you try somewhere else? You don't have to go. Please."

Empire Brown's voice rose. "And I shall fight against this harvest of flesh, this silencing of sacred song—"

"I'll visit you when I get back," said Nes. "Maybe things will be brighter."

"... and this Whale shall be returned to his pod!"

"Glory! Glory!" cheered the crowd, and Nes slipped away.

A mighty bellowing broke out over the cheers, and Sarah's gaze turned upwards to a cow, swinging through the air on leather straps, being lowered through the hatch.

Then the crowd hushed and parted as the Red Maids flowed hand-in-hand, each of them carrying a pair of bellows, dark rain splashes on their red robes, their faces solemn, into the hatch and out of sight.

A plume of white steam poured from *The Pilgrim*'s funnel. Mrs Brown gave a final wave and followed the Red Maids, closing the hatch over her head.

A tug boat pulled at *The Pilgrim* and towed it away to the locks.

Mr Hill stood watching from his office door. He caught Sarah's eye, nodded, and came over. Beneath the shouts of "Glory! Glory!" he said, "I have sent word to all ports. They are to do their utmost to persuade her to cancel the voyage. It is out of my hands now."

With one last look at *The Pilgrim*, he walked away.

"Come on," said Gullock. "I have got us a place on a carrier's cart. He will take us as far as Avonmouth – we can watch her put to sea."

The cart caught up with *The Pilgrim* at the second lock where a commotion had broken out. *The Pilgrim* was butting nose first into the lock-gates, while the lock-keeper tried desperately to open them.

"What is all that about?" asked Gullock. "What is the crew thinking? Surely canal men know how to go through a lock?"

Sarah hesitated. "Maybe the Whale is impatient to be at sea."

The locks opened, and *The Pilgrim* sailed through on to the Avon. The rain stopped and streams of sunbeams fanned out across the sky.

Through the Gorge he sailed. People ran alongside the river or hitched rides on carts; a stampede of feet and hooves kicked up limestone dust. Flags and hats and shawls streamed in the air.

"Look at that," said Gullock, pointing high up to the rope slung from the Leigh Woods abutment to the Clifton side of the Gorge. A lady had hired the wicker basket that rode along the rope to get a better view of the spectacle, but halfway across her courage had failed and all that could be seen as she sank into a faint was the whitened grip of her knuckles. Her little dog was stouter of heart: he yapped and barked on the edge of the basket, tail threshing, his fierce orange eyebrows bright against the pure cool blue of the sky.

The carter's horse clipped along the road, scattering people left and right.

The Red Maids sang 'Abide With Me' and the cow bellowed. *The Pilgrim*'s eyes burned fierce as he pushed downriver, past Sea Mills, past Shirehampton, and people ran from their farms and cottages, left their looms and ploughs and babies in cots, to bear witness.

"Glory! Glory!" they cried, running and jostling each other.

An old newspaper seller was knocked off his crutches by a gang of boys whipping up a pony and milk cart. Hansom cabs cantered past, out of control, their passengers clinging to the roofs.

Two men, long past their youth, carried an ancient woman between them who cursed at them for not being quick enough.

Sarah watched it all, her hands bundled inside her shawl. She felt Gullock glance at her often to read her face, but she looked straight at *The Pilgrim*, her eyes fixed. He reached out for her hand; she pretended not to notice.

At Avonmouth the carter dropped them off. They stood, looking at each other, each waiting for the other to speak as the crowds streamed past them.

Gullock reached out as though to take Sarah's hand, but instead took off his hat. He placed it over his heart.

"Sarah..." His knuckles trembled.

Sarah covered his hand with hers. "What say you, Gull... do you think they might need corset makers in America?"

Gullock was about to reply when a shout went up.

"What's he doing?"

A strange cry ran through the crowd. People rushed to the railings. Sarah and Gullock followed their pointing fingers.

The Pilgrim had turned abruptly and was racing with unnatural speed into the waves, smacking over the water, black smoke pouring from his funnel.

"Did you know it could travel so fast?" asked Gullock.

Sarah shook her head. She squinted into the sun. *The Pilgrim*'s skin glistened with droplets of water. It shivered as though with excitement.

The Red Maids sang on, but now their voices were catching on the words of the hymn until all that could be heard was a series of clicks and chirps.

The cow cried a long low moan.

Sarah sensed the Whale gathering, gathering speed, gathering power, until with a roar, it leapt high in the air, its propeller spinning. It flew in a wide arc, a curious smile upon its face, and then it dived, dived deep into the sea, deep deep down as the crowd watched in utter silence.

The Pilgrim did not resurface.

There are tales... tales of broken baleen washed ashore at Portishead, wrapped in shreds of red cotton and black mourning silk. Children are sent to scavenge them to sell them on to the Bristol corset makers.

And yet there are other tales too, tales that cannot be discounted, for they are told by the salt-faced fishermen of Reykjavik and Aberdeen: tales of a mysterious Arctic whale who sings Psalms and whose eyes burn like fire.

Sixty-Four of These Things Are Not Like the Others

- Deborah Walker -

"What's that device you're tinkering with?" Sergeant Ives asked Private Wiggins.

Wiggins smiled proudly. "It's an automated abacus, sir. And much improved on the ordinary abacus. At least it will be, when I've finessed the design."

"Bring it here."

Wiggins placed the device on the Sergeant's desk. Ives examined the frame which was twelve inches in height. Instead of an abacus' rods and beads, the device had thirteen steel tubes running horizontally and intersecting at intervals with verticals tunnels.

"You're an abacist, Wiggins."

"No, Sarge. I have the honour and the privilege of being a member of the Bristoll Dissenters Church, man and boy."

"Very funny, Private. And this small steam engine powers the device, does it?" asked Ives, examining the fist-shaped engine attached to the frame.

"Yes, Sarge. The steam moves the counters within the tubes according to the formula input. And you can see that the counter moves not only on the horizontal but here, at the intersections, they can move and down, according to the difficulty of the calculation. I'm calling it up and..."

"Up and down?" asked Ives, tasking a wild guess.

"No, Sarge. Up and Nancy. The downward direction being named in honour of my fiancée."

"Perhaps Nancy would prefer to be named after the upward axis. The direction of up is generally considered more positive than its lower sister."

"Sarge, I think you're right." Wiggins shook his head in agreement. "The possibilities will be: left and right, Nancy and down. Thank you, Sarge. I reckon you've saved my bacon there, with your superior knowledge of the mysteries of the female persuasions."

"Glad to have been of service, Wiggins." Ives turned the object over in his hands. Although it was a prototype, it had been made with care and skill. Private Wiggins was a talented metalsmith. Yet Ives detected a couple of minor flaws within its design. "There appears to be no way of linking any formula to the steam input, Wiggins."

"Yes, Sarge. I haven't perfected that aspect yet."

"Nor any way of reading the results."

"That's next on my list, Sarge. I've got it all worked out in theory. I know what it will do when I make it do it."

An explosion of noise interrupted their conversation. The faint scent of superheated propellant permeated the office even through the closed window. Neither man commented on this occurrence, which was a regular event, unsurprising as their premises bordered the munitions field.

Wiggins sighed. "But I've been having problems approaching infinity, Sarge."

"That's a bit out of my line, Wiggins. You better see the chaplain about that."

"No, Sarge, as you well know, I was referring to mathematics. Pacifically, the iterations of the device, the exponents, as I've worked them out in here," Wiggins tapped his ginger head. "They can get very fast very quick."

"Yes?"

"And the mistakes they do creep in, Sarge. Like rats they are, ferreting about in the arithmetic sewers. And there's something else, Sarge. Sometimes I get two answers for the same question." Wiggin paused to look significantly at Ives. "Or even more, Sarge. And all the answers are correct. That can't be right."

"It sounds unlikely, Wiggins."

Wiggins flashed his superior a wounded look. "Unlikely or not, it's true. Anyways, I would like to see my Nabacus get built. No doubt the Engineer Corp can iron out the quirks."

"Possibly," said Ives, although he wasn't sure the engineers would like to bother with a device that gave more than one true answer to a question. It wasn't very military.

Ives took a moment to stare at the window, wondering if he should voice his thoughts. He liked Wiggins. And there was no denying the lad was a phenomenon, with extraordinary talents in the applied sciences. It was a pity the boy was so uneducated. If Wiggins had been born in another part of the city, he'd have been astounding his professors at university. He didn't want to discourage the lad too much, but Ives decided a few words to temper his ambition might be in order. "An abacus is a good tool, Wiggins, used for thousands of years. Why try to complicate it?"

"To bring glory to Bristoll, Sarge!"

"Yes. Fair enough. Well, it's certainly inventive. But these accounts won't reconcile themselves, you know." Ives gestured at the pile of invoices and procurement tallies. "And there's the tobacco tax records to organise and the pensions to pay." He sighed. "And I've got to work on this trade report. The General was quite displeased with the trade deficit between Barth and Bristoll last quarter."

"Even though we've been allies these last five years, Sarge?"

"Even so. It doesn't do to be indebted to any other city, even to your ally. We've got a lot of work to do, Private Wiggins. And it won't get done if we spend our days inventing devices."

"I just thought..."

"What did you think, Wiggins?"

"Well. The Quiet War has been going on an awful long time. And the war is very complicated, so maybe it needs complex tools to sort it out."

Ives shook his head in afformation. "I doubt that maths or any calculating device, no matter how complex, can change the world. What is needed is... Well, if I knew that, I wouldn't be a sergeant in the Office of Accounts. Let the mucky-mucks sort out the war, Wiggins. Work on your abacus—"

"Nabacus."

"—your nabacus on your own time, Private."

"Yes, Sarge."

Sergeant Ives turned back to his report. It seemed to him that all of life, and all of war, was laid out upon his desk. The numbers and accounts told a story. The flow of money, into Bristoll and out again in commerce; money was on a journey. The money he was tallying might move from Bristoll to Barth and then perhaps to Londorn (enemy of Bristoll, but ally to Barth). From there it might move to any part of the Empire. Ives had never left England.

Wiggins toiled at his figures, but he was not a soldier engaged for long by the demands of the numerical. "Sergeant...?"

"Yes?"

"I'm in the wrong job here. I know it, and you know it."

"Where do you think you should be?"

"I think I should be in the engineers."

"Maybe you'd be good in the engineers," said Ives. "But consider that a lot of our trade is in weapons. Perhaps the General's office thought your mechanical aptitude would come in handy when tallying the trade figures and writing the munitions reports."

"I want to move."

"You'll have to wait. The gears of war grind slow, but they grind exceeding small. If you're in the wrong place they'll figure it out and move you."

"But maybe I'll get good at this." It was incredible that Wiggins didn't know already that he was good at this. That he could build an abacus – sorry, a nabacus – in his mind was an astonishing performance. If Wiggins had been born in a different class, he'd have been heading to a professorship at Oxingham or Cambcastle. "You are good at your job, Wiggins, but you'd be better at it if you'd stop lollygagging."

Wiggins looked crestfallen. "If I'm too good, I'll be stuck here. What should I do, Sergeant?"

"I can't tell you what to do."

"You're my commanding officer," said Wiggins.

Ives smiled. "Yes, but I've never been very comfortable with giving orders."

"I'm not like you," said Wiggins with a sigh. "I'm not happy here."

"Being good at a thing doesn't mean you like it."

"Sarge?"

"Think about the journeys a man can take, Wiggins. For me, they'll all end in Bristoll. Bristoll is in my blood and in my bones, and I will be ever faithful, but there are many possible journeys. Approaching infinity, you might say."

"Only Nancy had her dream again."

"The one about you on the battlefield? The one of you carrying your comrades on your shoulders, rescuing them?

Time after time going back into the fray? With no regard to your own life? With you, in other words, on your first engagement with the enemy, proving to be the biggest hero Bristoll has ever known?"

Wiggins blushed. "That's the one, Sarge. My Nancy made me promise I'd mention it to you, again."

"Do you believe she has the sight?"

"I find it sensible to believe in her powers, yes, Sarge."

"Ah, a pragmatic man. Well, I consider myself told." Ives looked through the column of numbers. "You can, if you will, tell Nancy about a dream I've been having lately. Perhaps she'll find it interesting."

"I didn't know you had the sight, Sarge."

"I doubt that I do, but all men dream."

"What was your dream, Sarge?"

"I saw Tample Meads. All was quiet. I saw the turning device they have there, the great wheel with rail tracks spoking off from every part of that wheel. A train drove onto the middle of that wheel and waited until an unseen man turned an engine. Then a cloud of steam obscured the view. When the steam cleared, I saw the engine turning slowly on that circle, and as it turned by degrees, it matched with other tracks. It could set off on a different direction, but it did not, it kept turning."

Wiggins shook his head. "That certainly sounds like a seeing dream. That's called a railways wheelhouse, that device you saw."

"Is that right?"

"So, what is the dream saying, Sarge? That a man can move a train, if he has the proper device? That a man can do *anything* if he has the right tools?"

"No expert, me," said Ives. "But I thought it said that a man can be set on any number of tracks in his life. What would you say about me, Wiggins? Would you say that I will be an accountant in the Bristoll Army forever?"

"I would say that, Sarge, I have never known a man with such a facility for numbers."

"I like the mathematics and the work here fair enough," said Ives. "Yet a man can be captain of his fate, young Wiggins. And even in war, it is for a man and a soldier to decide what track his life will be."

"But always for Bristoll, Sarge."

"Yes, Wiggins. Always for Bristoll."

The talk with Wiggins had set Ives's mind in a certain direction. He completed the trade report, and then, as night drew in, he said goodnight to Wiggins and sought out the General.

"I'm ready for a new assignment, sir. I want to do right for Bristoll," he said as General Baxter inspected the new vapour rifles in the twilight. They were Londorn made, sleek with cold lights along their flanks, making them suitable for firing during evening and night. Whatever else they were, the Londorners were good mechanics. For the last two years, Ives had been the Londorn liaison, buying their machines of war through covert means. He had an aptitude for understanding Londorn science and negotiating favourable deals. But it was not all he wanted to do. Ives had a great longing to leave Barracks Town and see more of the world. In this way, he felt, he could best serve Bristoll.

"You're not ready," said General Baxter.

"General, you always say that an efficient leader uses all the tools at his disposal." For five years, Ives had trained in active duty procedures. But his career had been sidetracked into account and trade. If he didn't secure an active assignment soon, Ives knew he'd be trapped in an office forever. "I'm an under-utilised tool."

Baxter smiled. Ives didn't like that smile. He didn't want to amuse the General.

"I have no active assignments that suit your talents," said Baxter. The vapour canons exploded in a coordinated precision blast. The straw men targets exploded into fragments.

"I have a well-sourced lead," said Ives. "I know about a group of dwellers living on the Western edges of Lamplight Marsh. My intel tells me that they're sometime tobacco smugglers."

"Then let the Queen's guards deal with them," said Baxter.

"My intel leads me to believe they're not only traders and smugglers. I believe they are part of a Londorn conspiracy to undermine our alliance with Barth."

"How so?"

"The detail is unclear, but I believe it involves a scheme to besmirch two great families of Barth and Bristoll, and set them against each other. The potential allegations are unclear, but something to do with trade irregularities, I am led to believe. I have a contact. I want to meet with them, posing as a trader, and find out more."

"So, their plan is to set Barth and Bristoll against each other? Divide and conquer?"

"It would be a good strategy for Londorn to see us fighting against each other," said Ives. "Bristoll is strong. They want to weaken our influence."

"The Londorners are good strategists. They play the game of war like chess. And you and I cannot see the board, Ives. Only the city council knows everything. But I hear things, and I haven't heard anything about this. Are you sure of your sources?"

Ives shook his head. "Yes, sir. This is what my intel indicates."

"And how did you acquire this lead?"

With many jugs of ale, spent in the Ghetto taverns, where Londorn refugees congregated. But Baxter would not sanction an assignment based on drunken gossip. So, Ives felt it was appropriate to enhance the truth. "My cousin's mother's lives near the city. She attended a séance a few weeks ago." Ives knew Baxter was a devout spiritualist. "She was contacted by her departed brother who was lost in the marshes. He warned her about these Londorn agents."

Baxter sighed. "You do good work here, Ives, buying these weapons, for instance. But you don't have the temperament to make a good undercover operative. You can be reckless. An undercover operative cannot afford such a trait."

Ives bit back a response and stared respectfully to the horizon. It was not good policy to disagree with the General.

"The Lamplight Marshes are full of Dwellers and noncon ghosts."

"I will take all precautions, sir."

"Hmm," said Baxter. "It may be true that you're an under-utilised tool. You deserve a chance. If you wish, you may investigate this on your own, infiltrate this smugglers' gang and find out what they are doing."

"Thank you, General Baxter. You won't be disappointed."

Ives set off that very next day, leaving the General no chance to change his mind. During his preparations, he found time to call into his office and leave a very disgruntled Wiggins in charge.

"When you talked about a man having more than one journey to make, I thought you was referring to me, Sarge."

"I'm sorry, Private. I'm sure your time will come," said Ives with a wink.

Late afternoon found him confidently traversing Lamplight Marsh, the great marshland of the Avon floodplain. Evening found a less confident Ives, lost and waving his neckcloth through the cloud of steam. It had been a bad time to lose his map. It was an even worse time for the marsh glider to blow a gasket. He opened the hood and poked the broken gasket, forgetting the metal would be burning hot. With a curse, he waved his burnt finger in the air. The engine would need a few hours to cool down before he could replace the seal.

The sun hovered, red-gold above the sepia horizon. It would be night soon. A few hours ago, he'd seen an Empire dirigible gliding about the marsh. *That* was a civilized way to travel, without marsh mud plastering the glider's screen, covering his hair and clothes, clogging the engine filters.

But Ives was posing as a son of the Castle family, the Bristoll trading house. He was supposed to be a minor relative down on his luck who couldn't afford civilized airship travel.

He glared at the marsh glider.

What do you expect? It seemed to say. Couldn't you see my rust? Weren't you suspicious of the 'good' price you paid for me? I'm old and was bound to break down sooner or later.

Ives kicked the marsh glider's tyre.

He was on his way to meet dangerous men and women: Londorners, non-Bristollians. Breaking down along the way wasn't an auspicious start.

But this was his first active assignment in the Quiet War of the Cities. A war fought only occasionally by public skirmish. It was a war of covert assassinations, kidnappings of key workers. City against city as they vied for trade and fought over the grievances that war brings. Industrialisation had bought much wealth to the Empire, but the price was internal strife as the cities jealously held their inventions.

This was Ives's chance. Very probably his only chance. There was honour in serving Bristoll in any capacity. But Ives had always felt his talents lay in espionage, seeking out Bristoll's enemies, using his intelligence as well as his fighting skills. But how could he do that if the stinking marsh glider had collapsed?

It's not my fault, the marsh glider seemed to say. You should have been more careful.

The glider was right. But Ives had been so eager to leave Barracks Town and start the mission. It had been careless to buy the first glider he'd seen in the market. An operative couldn't afford to make these minor mistakes. And no matter how Ives tried to reframe his actions as eagerness or passion, the marsh glider knew the truth. But the possibility that his talents didn't match his ambition wasn't something he liked to dwell upon.

He was stranded on Lamplighter Marsh, lost, with the sun about to set. Ives didn't relish spending the night in the glider. It wasn't robust enough to withstand the claws of any passing marsh dogs. He needed alternative shelter.

He used his periscope and scanned the horizon, not expecting much, but from the sun's dying shadows a shape appeared, angular, an unexpected dwelling in the marsh.

The Lamplighter Marsh Sea was Dweller territory, tent-living marsh vagrants. The Dwellers constructed elaborate cities of baked mud bricks, where they gathered every seven years for their great festival. And although it was not a festival year, there would be a caretaker tribe.

Dwellers lived outside, scorning City and Empire laws. Their religion and practices were not those of decent urban citizens. For many years, the council had talked about ridding the marsh of the Dwellers, but the Quiet War was always a more pressing need. One day, these marshes would be cleared and bought under the auspices of Bristoll. But for now, there was an uneasy truce between the Dwellers and the city folk.

Ives reached for the carpet bag on the passenger seat. He gave the glider another undeserved kick and set off, striding quickly across the marsh in the dwindling light. Perhaps he would find something of interest in the Dweller city. Granny Tonkins, who'd raised Ives after the deaths of his soldier mother and father, claimed Dweller kinship. Admittedly, Granny never told a truth if a lie was more interesting. But most Dwellers were hospitable people. In the mudbrick city, Ives would find company, a hot meal, perhaps chicken baked in a root pot, and strong reed wine. And maybe there would be something of more interest. Ives would gather intelligence. Perhaps these Dwellers knew about the tobacco smugglers, or perhaps they harboured city noncons. He quickened his pace, already planning auxiliary missions based on imagined misdeeds. Ives's ambition was large, perhaps as large as his carelessness.

When he arrived at the city, the sun had disappeared and the face of the moon lit the gaunt buildings. And the moon was mocking because this was no Dweller festival city.

Ives stood at the edge of a ghost town, a deserted noncon city. The long-gone noncons, so forgotten that Ives had not even considered that this could be one of their near-fabled cities.

The skeleton of a marsh gurney stood outside the broken city walls. Painted above the main gate was the motto 'Union Through Industry' and a tattered three-colour flag, red and white and black. This was once a noncon city, expelled from Bristoll at the start of the century. These noncons had been skilled, and above all, they'd been wealthy. They'd built gleaming factory cities in the marsh. They'd taken men and women to work in the factories. They'd produced marvellous goods, invented spectacular devices. But they'd withered and died because all the cities had refused to trade with them. No English city could countenance such independence, because if the Bristol noncons thrived, what was to stop the non-conformists of their own cities leaving their protection? No city could afford to let the Bristol noncons prosper. And the noncon marsh cities had failed.

Yet this ghost town remained. It was a place of coldness, and Ives did not like it.

But still, there might be something within the white, worn walls that could prove useful. And Ives did need a place to sleep. Within the gates, long box buildings were stacked with slender columns supporting arches opening the rooms to the marsh wind. It was a place of faded white, yet once this city must have gleamed. By torchlight, Ives trod the hard, baked pathways, overgrown with marsh grass. He wandered through the factory city, roaming from building to building, marvelling at its emptiness and the dead reeds that gathered against the broken doors. He kept his ear open for predators. He walked amongst the decaying remnants of an unfamiliar culture.

He stared for a long moment at the railway wheelhouse he found. No train was on the turntable, but the wheelhouse had short sections of track leading from the device. Tracks that led nowhere.

How had they planned to build a railway across the marsh? he wondered.

In the dusk, he found a school, a hospital, a power station, a ballroom, and half a dozen factories with machines clogged with rust.

Ives stepped through the open door of a factory where rows of cold metal machines were arranged like soldiers in formation. A round boiler stood in the corner. Once, it would have provided the steam to power the machines.

Ives examined the great cogs of the machines, wondering what they had once produced. As he examined the decaying factory, a feeling of being watched prickled against his neck. He turned. In the shadows he seemed to see melancholy ghosts crowded into the factory room. He took a step closer, expecting the shadows to dissipate. The ghosts remained, only they seemed to shrink against the wall as if they were afraid of him. Poor and thin things, they were of little weight. More pitiable than frightening. Seven and seven and seven multiplied, young and old, their flesh insubstantial, their eyes hollow, bearing mutilations: missing fingers, hands, arms, where the factory machines had bitten. The noncoms were not good masters. Ives sensed he was in the company of ghosts who had died in the factory.

Ives did not fear spirits. Father Trevor, the Company's spiritualist, had made contact with dozens of fallen soldiers in the barracks. Ives had attended a half dozen séances. The soldier ghosts were respectfully honoured by many soldiers. They were not harmful to the living. In fact, there were tales of the ghosts helping their living comrades. But most ghosts stayed in the Dead House, honoured by the memorial friezes and bronze funerary monuments. On festival days, Ives made respectful tributes to the soldiers fallen in battle.

But who honoured the ghosts in an abandoned city?

He was not a very religious man. He was more a man of action than ritual, but Ives's duty was clear. From his belt he took salt and carefully drew a circle on the factory floor. When he sang the words, most of the ghosts dissipated immediately.

One lingered: the spirit of an old man with a fringe of grey hair. Some spirits were always hungry.

"I'll send Father Trevor to you," Ives said with a respectful bow. "Grandfather, you will be given the respect owed to you."

344

The old ghost shook his head. With a frail arm he pointed upwards. Then he moved to the wall and melted into the brickwork to become a shadow.

With a final song of respect, Ives kicked the floor to break the salt circle. An unattended circle was an invitation to malicious spirits from other cities. He climbed the wrought iron spiral staircase to the upper level.

Ives wandered through rooms containing long, low beds where the factory slaves would have slept after their long days of work. In a smaller room, he found the sign of the creator daubed on the wall. He took that as a good omen. He set his chronometer for dawn and settled down, ignoring the beds with their nest of spiders and making himself comfortable in his sleeping sack of sewn blankets. He would make good time tomorrow. He would meet with the so-called smugglers, integrate himself within them, and learn their secrets. It was the beginning of his new life.

The grandfather ghost's shadow stuttered on the wall; Ives bid the ghost a polite goodnight and settled down for the night. Ghosts did not concern him. Outside, the marsh dogs howled. It was annoying, but he felt sleep approaching.

What did concern Ives was the sudden shuddering, cranking noise that reverberated through the factory, like the fast beat of the automatic Steam Rigotti. And the curious green glow that flitted through the cracks in the door.

Armed with his snap matchlock, Ives opened the door. Bathed in green light, he followed the corridor to the source of the automatic gun sound. Within that lit corridor, a feeling of aloneness tried to snatch at his soul. But Ives was not afraid.

He had no fear of ghosts but was he was afraid of the creature he found within the green light, standing against a clattering machine, because it looked at Ives with his own face. A fetch, a double-goer, a ghost in the glass.

And as Ives was reasonably certain that he wasn't dead, it must be a malicious and deceptive spirit. The machine thumped and clattered. It was a rectangular contraption with cranks and levels and many moving columns, number wheels, and sector gears. The clacking noise came from the clatter of its ivory and metal components.

"Oh, hello," said the apparition. The doppelganger spoke with Ives's own voice. It wore Ives's face, although it was dressed like a Londorner foreigner. "I'm Ives," said the doppelgänger.

"No. *I'm* Ives."

"We have the same name? That's confusing, but not unexpected. Call me Colston." That sent a chill along Ives's spine. This doppelgänger knew much about him. Colston was Granny Tonkin's child name for Ives because of Ives's fondness for the sticky buns.

"What are you?" asked Ives. "Why are you here?" His hand was steady on the matchlock. The doppelgänger was more substantial than a ghost, although it still had an unearthly quality. But if it was partly made of flesh, then it could be injured.

"Look, it's difficult to explain. I don't know your level of education. How are you versed in atomic mechanics?"

"I don't know those words," said Ives. He was at a loss as to how to proceed. The apparition appeared amiable, and his instincts told him that it was no threat. But who knew what devious intrigues a doppelgänger used?

"Let me explain," said Colston. "Wait a moment while I disengage the difference engine. I can't hear the thoughts in my own head with the noise." He took a slim tool from his belt and made some adjustments to the machine. Quietness and darkness shrouded the room.

"Here," said Ives, activating his torch. "Now, speak, doppelgänger."

"Doppelgänger? Is that a spirit? Is that what you think I am? There's no such thing as ghosts."

"Of course there is."

Colston gestured in apology. "Oh, you're religious? A spiritualist? Well, of course, I respect that. Religion maketh the man, and all that. But doppelgängers and any other type of ghosts are a matter of faith, and I'm more a man of science. But, of course, I respect your beliefs."

Ives looked at the doppelgänger curiously. What manner of spirit denied its own existence? "Ghosts are a matter of fact. Everyone in the Empire knows that. A ghost moves in the shadows of these very walls."

Colston stared at the wall where, in the torchlight, the grandfather ghost moved. Obligingly, the grandfather materialised for a moment before merging back into the brickwork. "That's a ghost!" whispered Colston. "You have real ghosts in your world."

"What do you mean 'in my world?'"

"I am not from this place."

"No, of course not," said Ives. "You're from the spirit dimension."

"Not quite, old chap." Colston shook his head. "I knew there'd be differences, but this is incredible. But I'm not. A ghost, I mean. Do you have other occult entities here?"

"Yes. All kinds of entities. As you well know."

"There are some in my world who believe in such, but they are not widely accepted."

"That's nonsense." Ives found it strange that the doppelgänger continued to persist in his strange assertions.

"You don't have to be afraid of me, Ives."

"I'm not afraid."

Colston smiled. "Of course you're not. I think you're a soldier of some kind. You have a military bearing. Am I right?"

Ives shook his head, forgetting that he was posing as a son of the Castle trading family. But hadn't Granny said you should never lie to a doppelgänger, least they use the lie to hook into your spirit?

"As a child growing up, I always wanted to be a soldier," said Colston. "But I became interested in science. And science has bought me here." He patted the machine.

"I was always interested in mathematics and science," said Ives. "But the needs of the war showed me my duty."

"Which war?"

"The Quiet War."

"I am not familiar with that one." Colston looked puzzled.

"The unspoken war, between all the cities of England. The war that is not acknowledged?"

"You're telling me that you're a soldier in a civil war? That England is at war with itself?"

"Yes. And has been for these past fifty years," said Ives.

"I never imagined such a thing." Colston looked a little dazed as he sank to the floor. Ives had never known a spirit that could present such a convincing facsimile of human sensations.

Leaving Colston to the distraction of his emotions for a moment, he walked around the clattering machine. "What is this?" he asked. He had never seen such a complicated, extravagant, such a wondrous device.

"This is an N abacus difference engine. And I'm afraid it's got a little bit out of hand."

"You say it bought you here?" The machine looked immensely complicated, with thousands of working parts.

"It did," said Colston. "Let me explain. This is an automatic mechanical calculator inspired by the work of Babbage. Each time the columns rotate, the number wheels turn and make additions. Using Newton's method of divided differences, the machine calculates and tabulates polynomial functions."

"The columns turn and make calculations?" The doppelgänger was spinning an interesting tale. Ives had always been interested in mathematics; as a child, it was considered that he had some talent. His teachers encouraged him to attend the university, but he was always more interested in doing his duty against Bristoll's enemies. But the machine was fascinating. "How accurate is the machine?"

"One hundred percent accurate," said Colston with a smile. "But this machine, which I helped to design, does more than that. Supplementary columns and constructed random wheels were added. This machine calculates the differences between differences and loops the results into the number columns in a pulse shaping feed. I think this machine interfaces with atomic mechanics and by looking defines and constructs multiple different potentialities or realties."

"You talk like a Londorner." Ives didn't understand Colston's words. "Are you trying to devour me, doppelgänger?"

"Please call me, Colston. Doppelgänger is such a pejorative name. And we are brothers, after all."

"Brothers?"

"In a way," said Colston. "According to the inventor, this machine has created sixty-four atomic multiplications of the world."

"Sixty-four?"

Colston nodded. "And with more turns of the machine, the numbers grow bigger, approaching infinity. And each one is different. As the professor often says, the mistakes they do creep in, like rats ferreting about in the arithmetic sewers. I think the machine created you, brother. You live in a ghost world, Ives."

This was dangerous doppelgänger talk. And nonsense. Yet, mathematically, it might be possible. Other worlds such as the spirit world existed. Why not multiple worlds of reality? It was an interesting thought experiment. "So, you're saying my world isn't real?"

"It's real now," said Colston with a grin. "I only know that I am pleased to meet you. But unfortunately, I have to leave you. The power is limited, and we have another sixty-three ghost worlds to visit."

"But how does the machine work?" asked Ives. "How *can* it work?" It seemed as if what Colston was saying could be true. He was no doppelgänger, and Ives felt a kinship towards him, as one does for family or an ancestor ghost.

Colston smiled. "I don't know the exact reasoning of the reckoning of this machine. I admit to you, brother, that I was reckless. When the professor said it was ready, I was keen to go on this adventure. But if I'd waited until I understood this machine, then I might have waited a lifetime. Of course, I wouldn't have made it, if it wasn't for..."

"Hello," said a small figure, walking into the room; a very familiar figure.

Colston grinned. "May I present Professor Wiggins, of Oxford University."

Familiar and not. Of course, Ives had never seen young Wiggins in civvies, but he couldn't fail to recognise him and, most of all, that look of insatiable intelligence.

The professor walked over, holding out his hand in a very confident manner. "Yes. As I imagined," he tapped his head. "But to see it here is jolly gratifying. So, you are the other Colston, are you? This is incredible. Fortunately, we still appear to be intact. That's a relief."

"Intact?" asked Ives faintly, shaking Professor Wiggins's hand.

"I had the fear that if original and the iteration were to meet, then – poof!"

"Poof?"

"The end of the world, my dear fellow. But I am glad to see that hasn't come to pass."

"So, you invented this device, Professor?" asked Ives.

Professor Wiggins nodded. "Indeed. And an extrapolation I made on the simple abacus, if you can believe it."

"I can believe it, sir."

"And Ives, or shall I say your doppelgänger, has been quite some help. I say, did I say something amusing?"

"Ah, just a minor joke sir, between us, nothing to worry about," said Colston.

"Is my doppelgänger not with you?" asked Professor Wiggins. "I would have liked to have met him."

"He is not, sir. But he is very much like you," said Ives.

A whining noise filled the air. In a few quick steps, Professor Wiggins crossed the room. His hands played over the machine's control panel. Steam rose from unseen pipes and the number wheels turned.

Colston ran to join the professor, shouting, "I wish you well, Brother Soldier." The room glowed with bright, green light.

"Wait!" shouted Ives. "Can you take me with you?"

"We can," said the professor. "If that's what you want?"

"I do," shouted Ives. He would very much like to see those different worlds, to meet his ghost brothers, to travel between the realities. Who knew what lay between the different numbers worlds, the ghost worlds? Ives would gather intelligence from these atomic worlds, and he would return with that information to end the Quiet War, to heal the differences between England's cities. Anything could be possible in a universe that approached infinity.

And if he couldn't do that, the very least he could do was to gather all the information he could and give the problem to Private Wiggins.

"Come then, Brother," said Colston above the roaring noise of the cranking difference engine. "Let's visit the worlds together."

And Ives stepped forward, without hesitation, reckless as he always was, and fearless.